# The Little Fox & Tanuki

KORISENMAN

## Mi Tagawa

# Table of Contents

The Little Fox & Tanuki

KORISENMAN

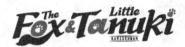

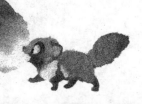

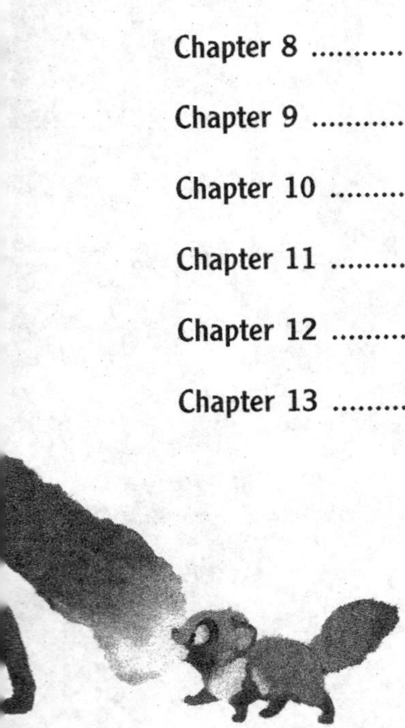

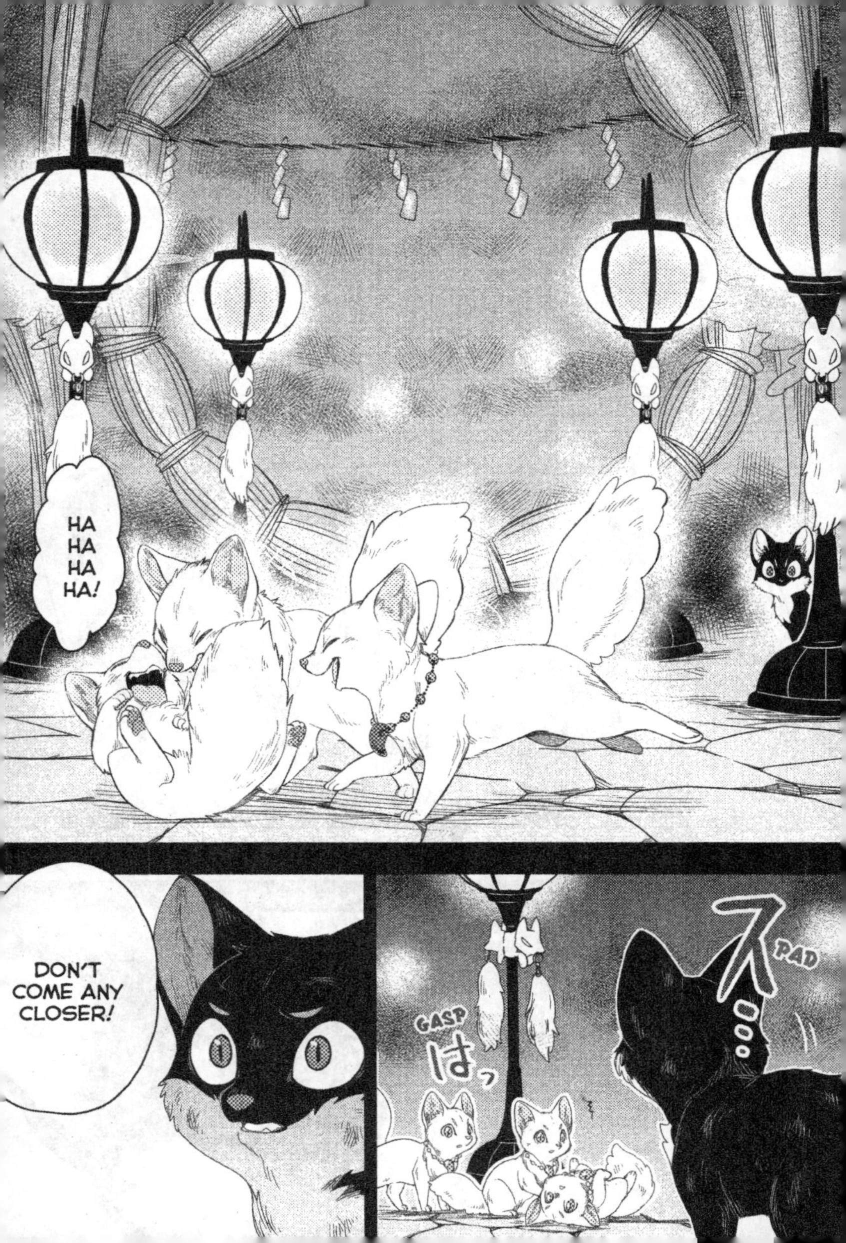
HA HA HA HA!
PAD
GASP
はっ
DON'T COME ANY CLOSER!

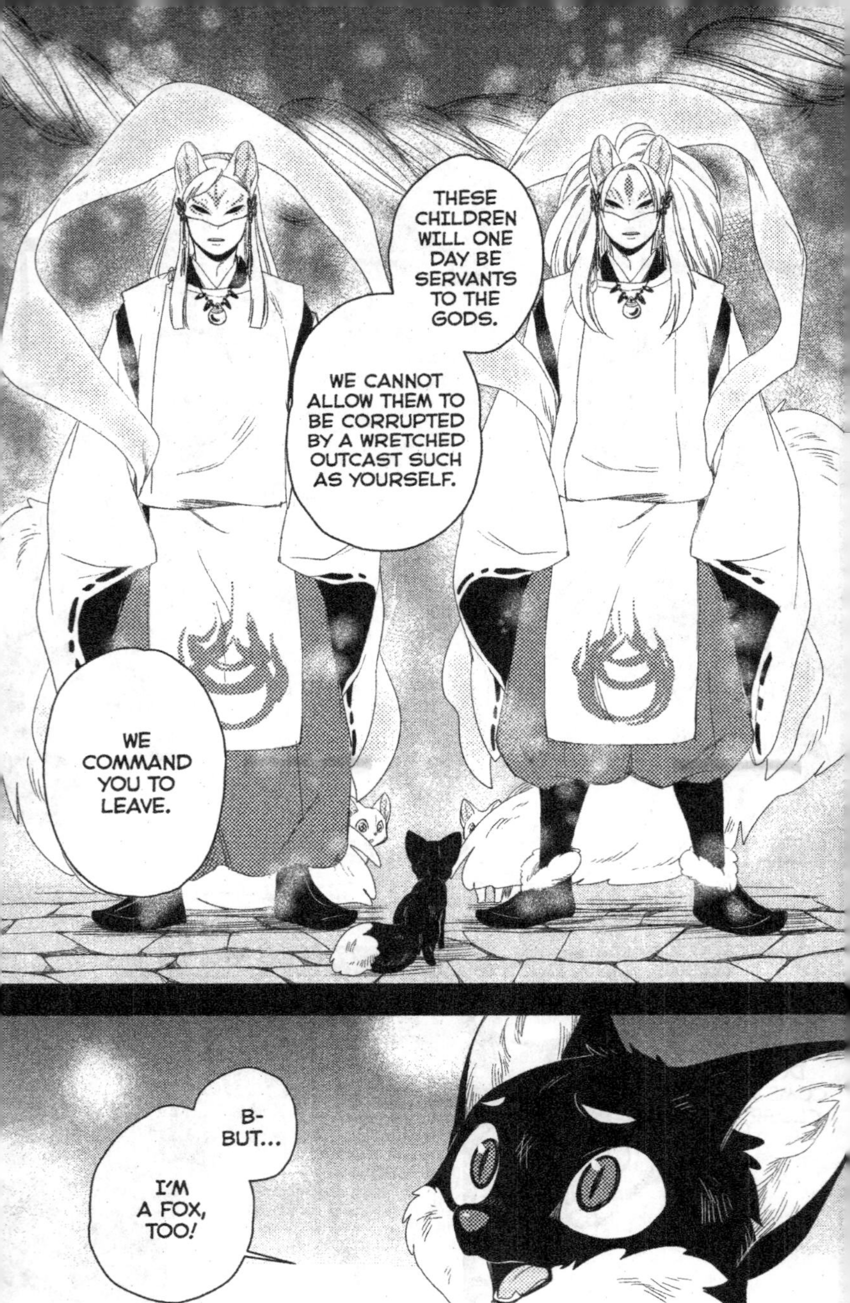
THESE CHILDREN WILL ONE DAY BE SERVANTS TO THE GODS.
WE CANNOT ALLOW THEM TO BE CORRUPTED BY A WRETCHED OUTCAST SUCH AS YOURSELF.
WE COMMAND YOU TO LEAVE.
B-BUT...
I'M A FOX, TOO!

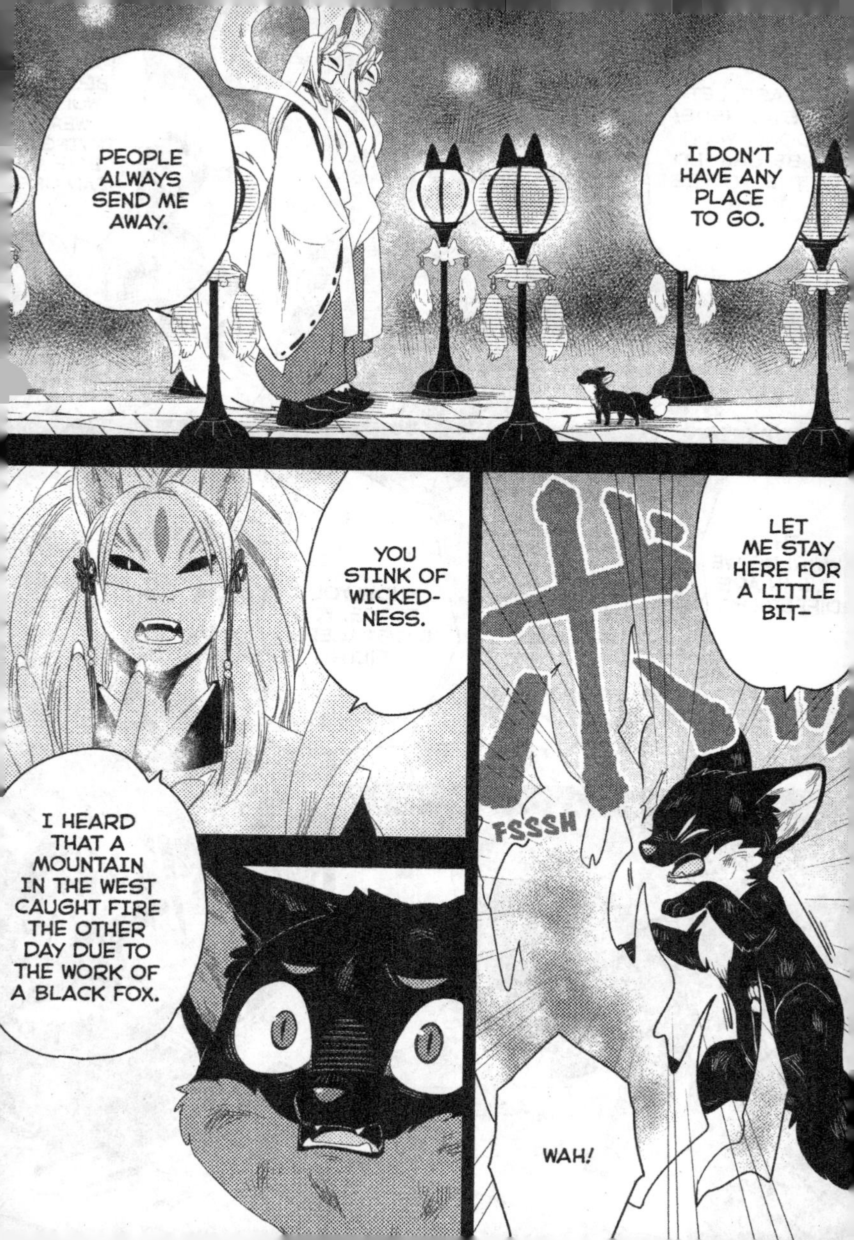
I DON'T HAVE ANY PLACE TO GO.
PEOPLE ALWAYS SEND ME AWAY.
LET ME STAY HERE FOR A LITTLE BIT–
FSSSH
WAH!
YOU STINK OF WICKED-NESS.
I HEARD THAT A MOUNTAIN IN THE WEST CAUGHT FIRE THE OTHER DAY DUE TO THE WORK OF A BLACK FOX.

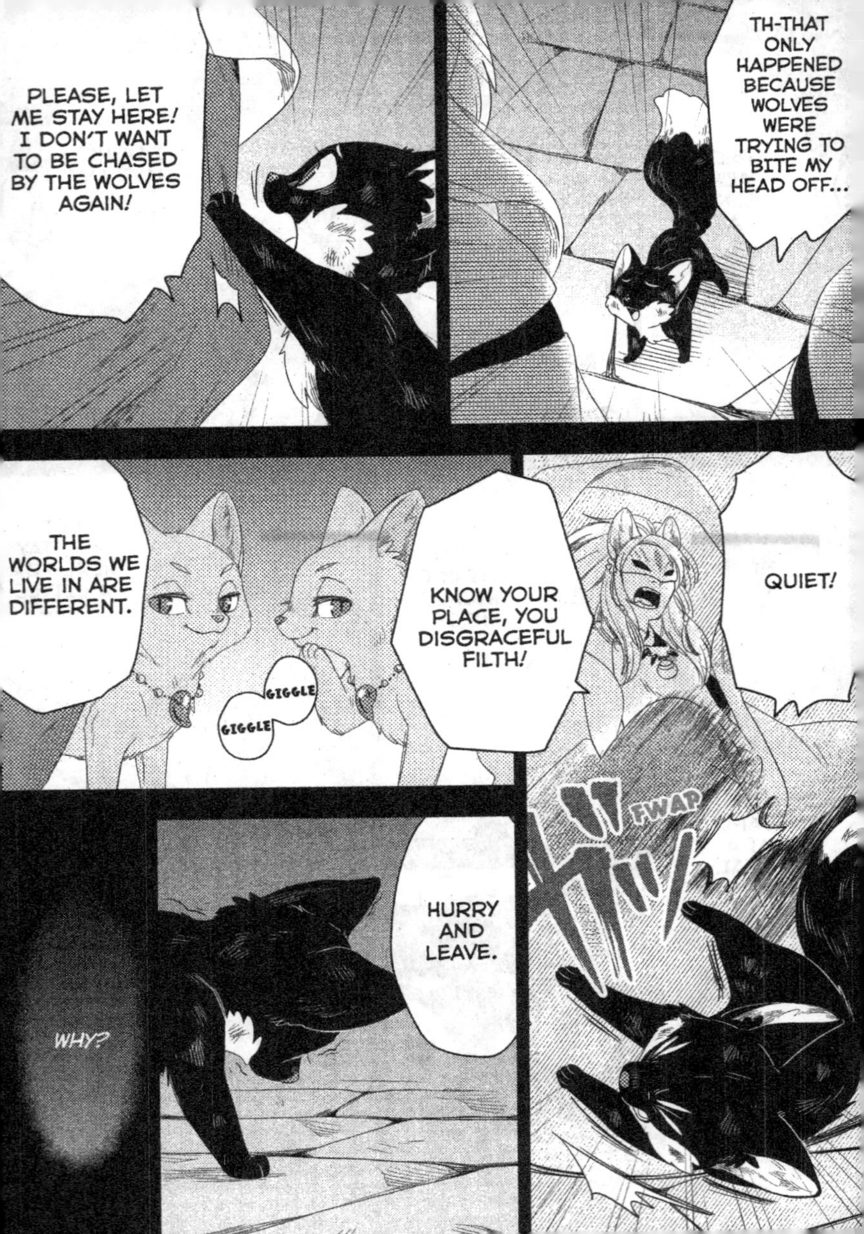
TH-THAT ONLY HAPPENED BECAUSE WOLVES WERE TRYING TO BITE MY HEAD OFF...
PLEASE, LET ME STAY HERE! I DON'T WANT TO BE CHASED BY THE WOLVES AGAIN!
QUIET!
FWAP
KNOW YOUR PLACE, YOU DISGRACEFUL FILTH!
THE WORLDS WE LIVE IN ARE DIFFERENT.
GIGGLE
GIGGLE
HURRY AND LEAVE.
WHY?

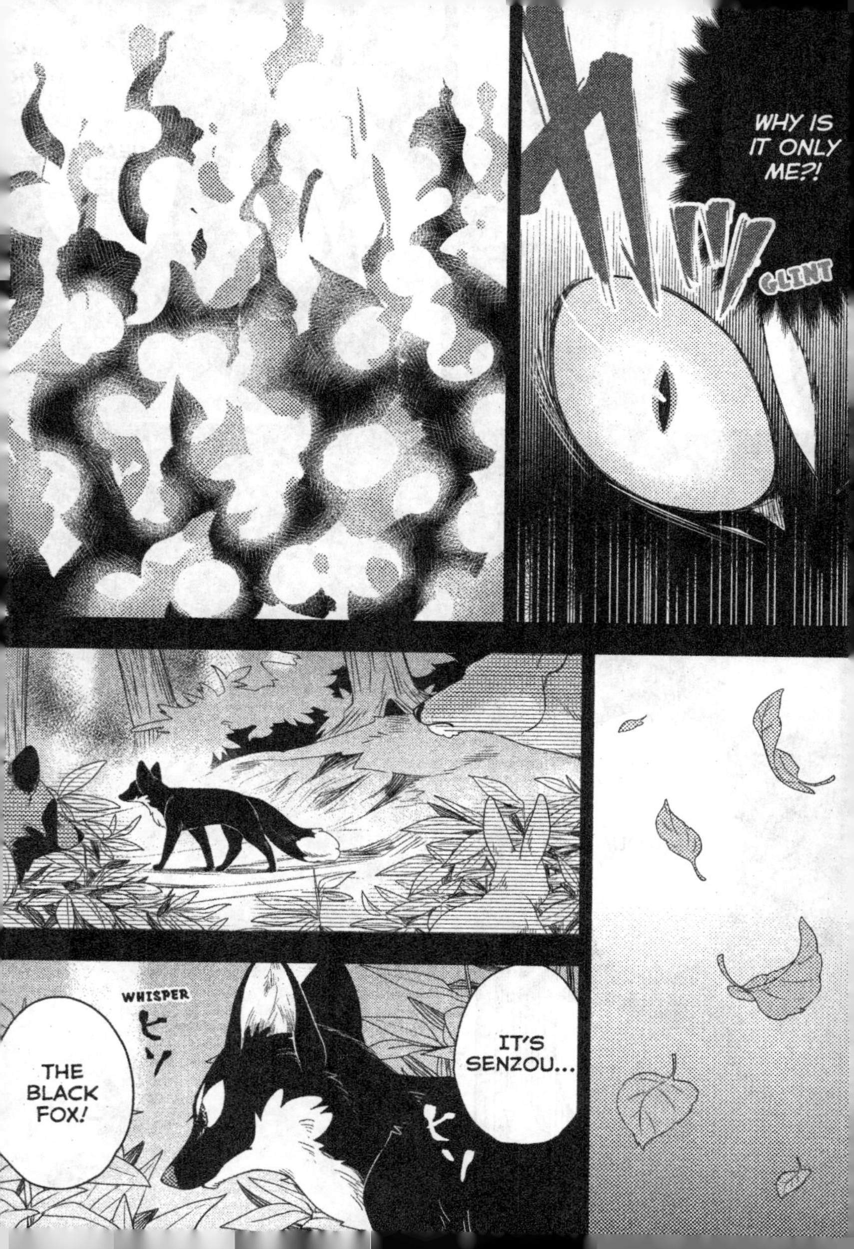
WHY IS IT ONLY ME?!
GLINT
IT'S SENZOU...
ヒソ
WHISPER
ヒソ
THE BLACK FOX!

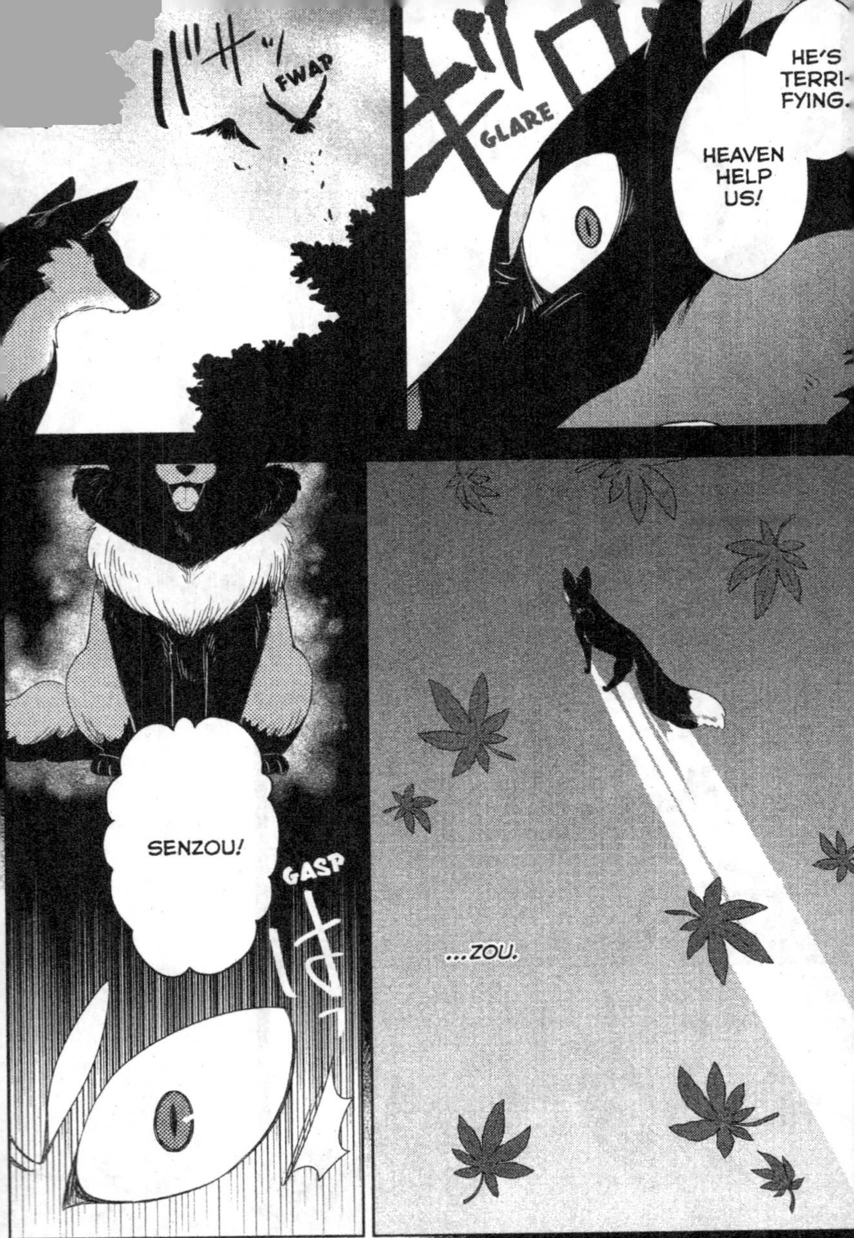
GLARE
HE'S TERRI-FYING.
HEAVEN HELP US!
FWAP
...ZOU.
SENZOU!
GASP

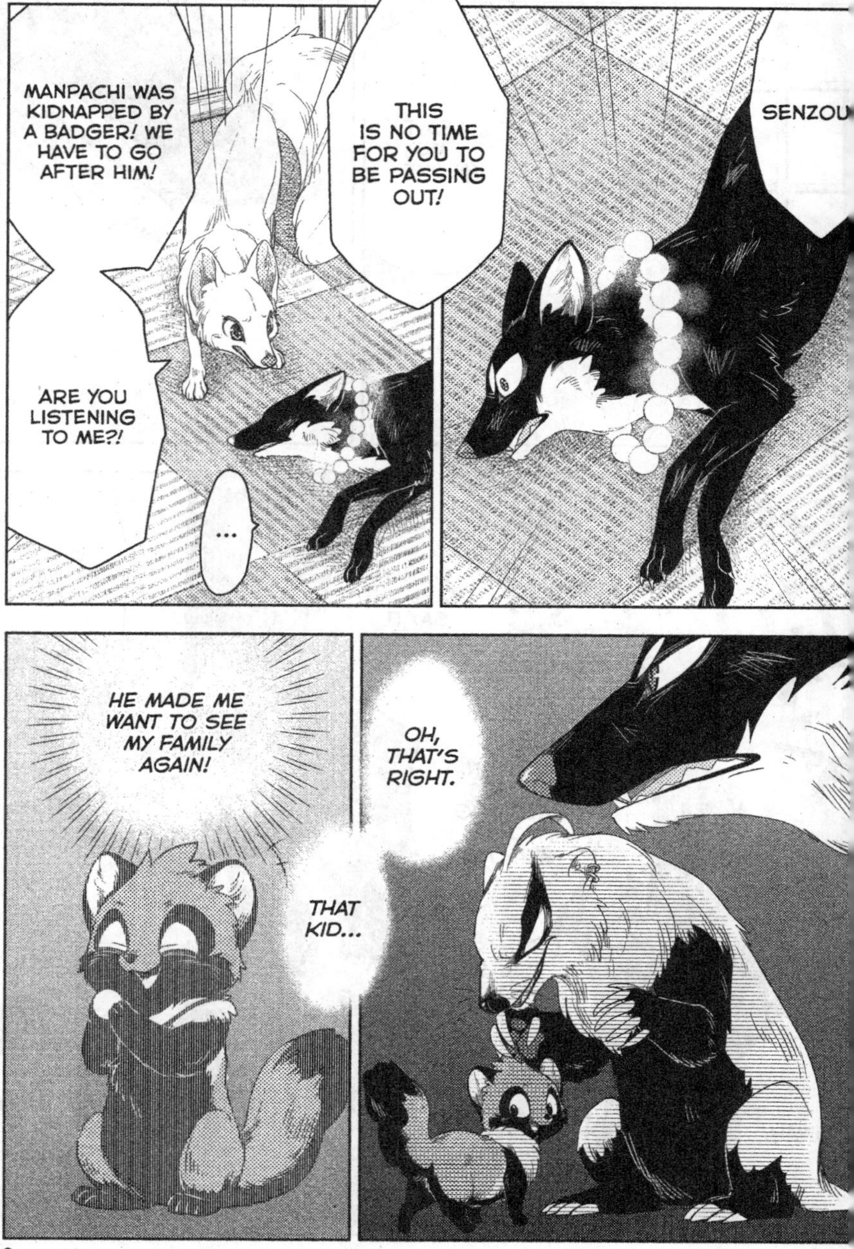
SENZOU
THIS IS NO TIME FOR YOU TO BE PASSING OUT!
MANPACHI WAS KIDNAPPED BY A BADGER! WE HAVE TO GO AFTER HIM!
ARE YOU LISTENING TO ME?!
...
OH, THAT'S RIGHT.
THAT KID...
HE MADE ME WANT TO SEE MY FAMILY AGAIN!

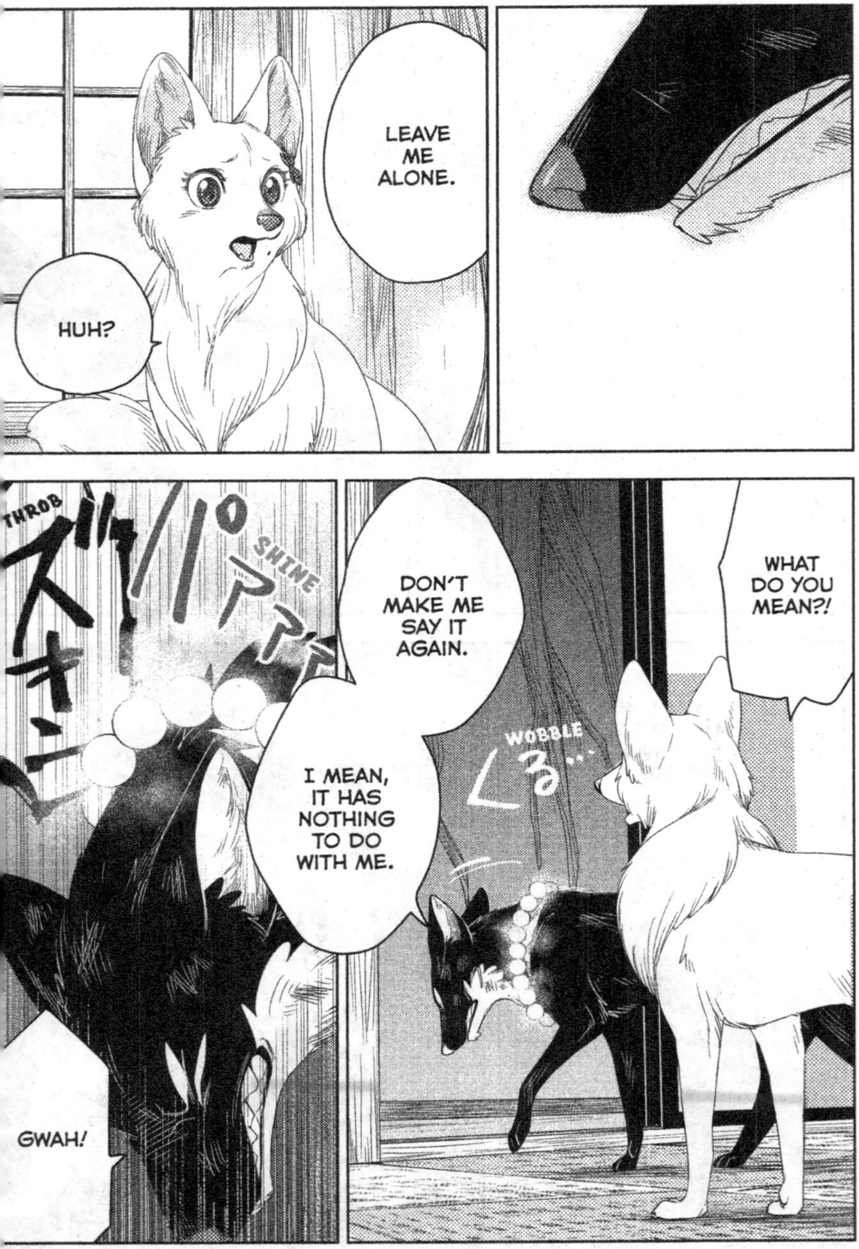
LEAVE ME ALONE.
HUH?
WHAT DO YOU MEAN?!
DON'T MAKE ME SAY IT AGAIN.
WOBBLE
くる‥
I MEAN, IT HAS NOTHING TO DO WITH ME.
THROB
SHINE
GWAH!

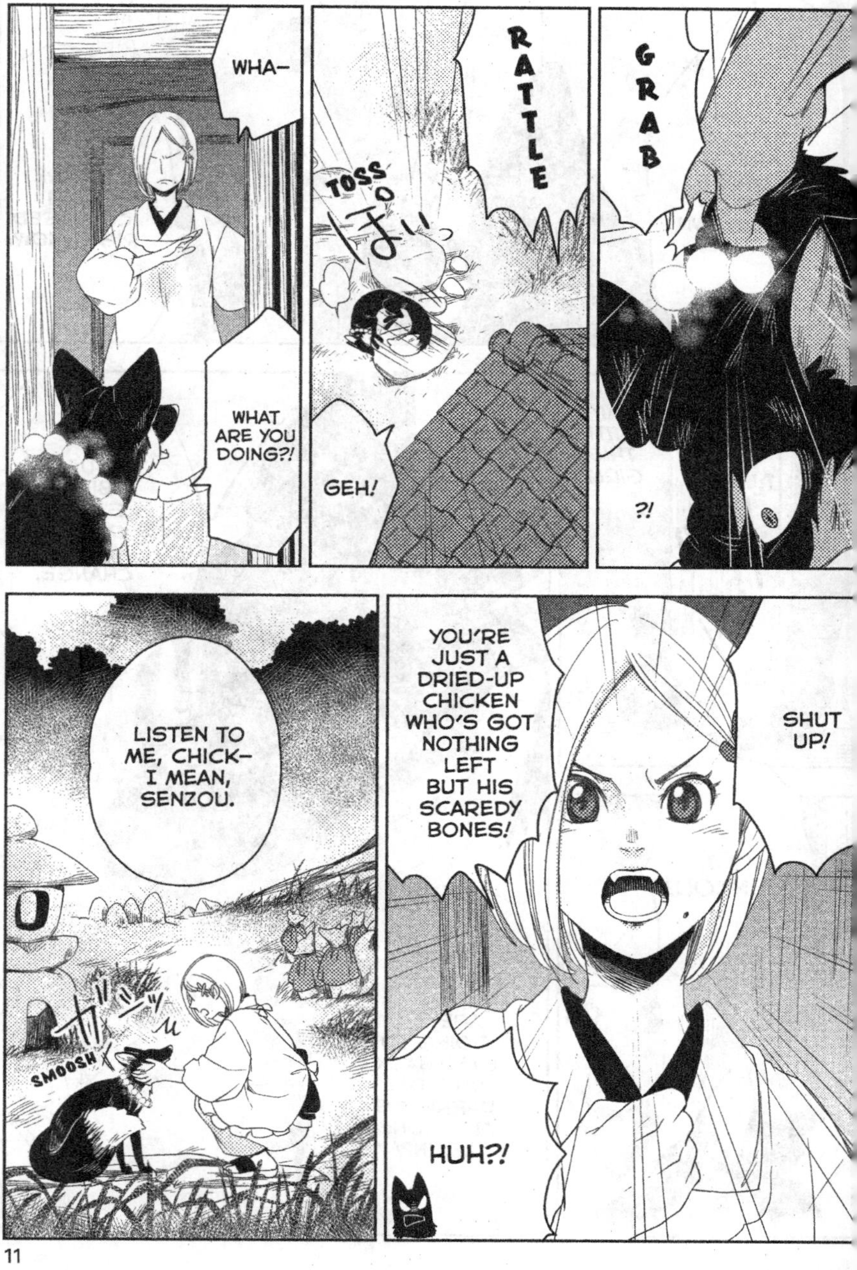
GRAB
?!
RATTLE
TOSS
ぽいっ
GEH!
WHA–
WHAT ARE YOU DOING?!
SHUT UP!
YOU'RE JUST A DRIED-UP CHICKEN WHO'S GOT NOTHING LEFT BUT HIS SCAREDY BONES!
HUH?!
LISTEN TO ME, CHICK– I MEAN, SENZOU.
SMOOSH

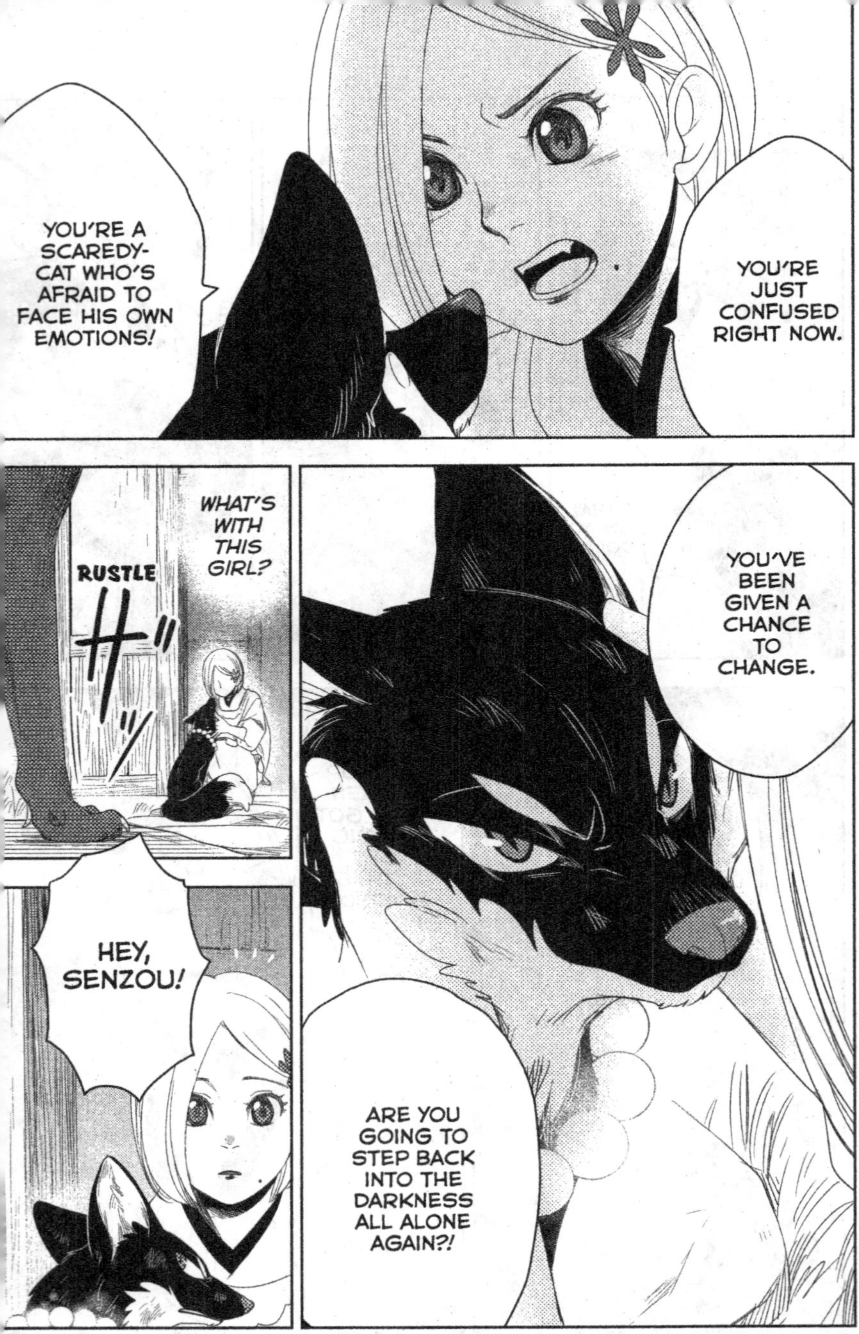
YOU'RE JUST CONFUSED RIGHT NOW.
YOU'RE A SCAREDY-CAT WHO'S AFRAID TO FACE HIS OWN EMOTIONS!
YOU'VE BEEN GIVEN A CHANCE TO CHANGE.
ARE YOU GOING TO STEP BACK INTO THE DARKNESS ALL ALONE AGAIN?!
WHAT'S WITH THIS GIRL?
RUSTLE
HEY, SENZOU!

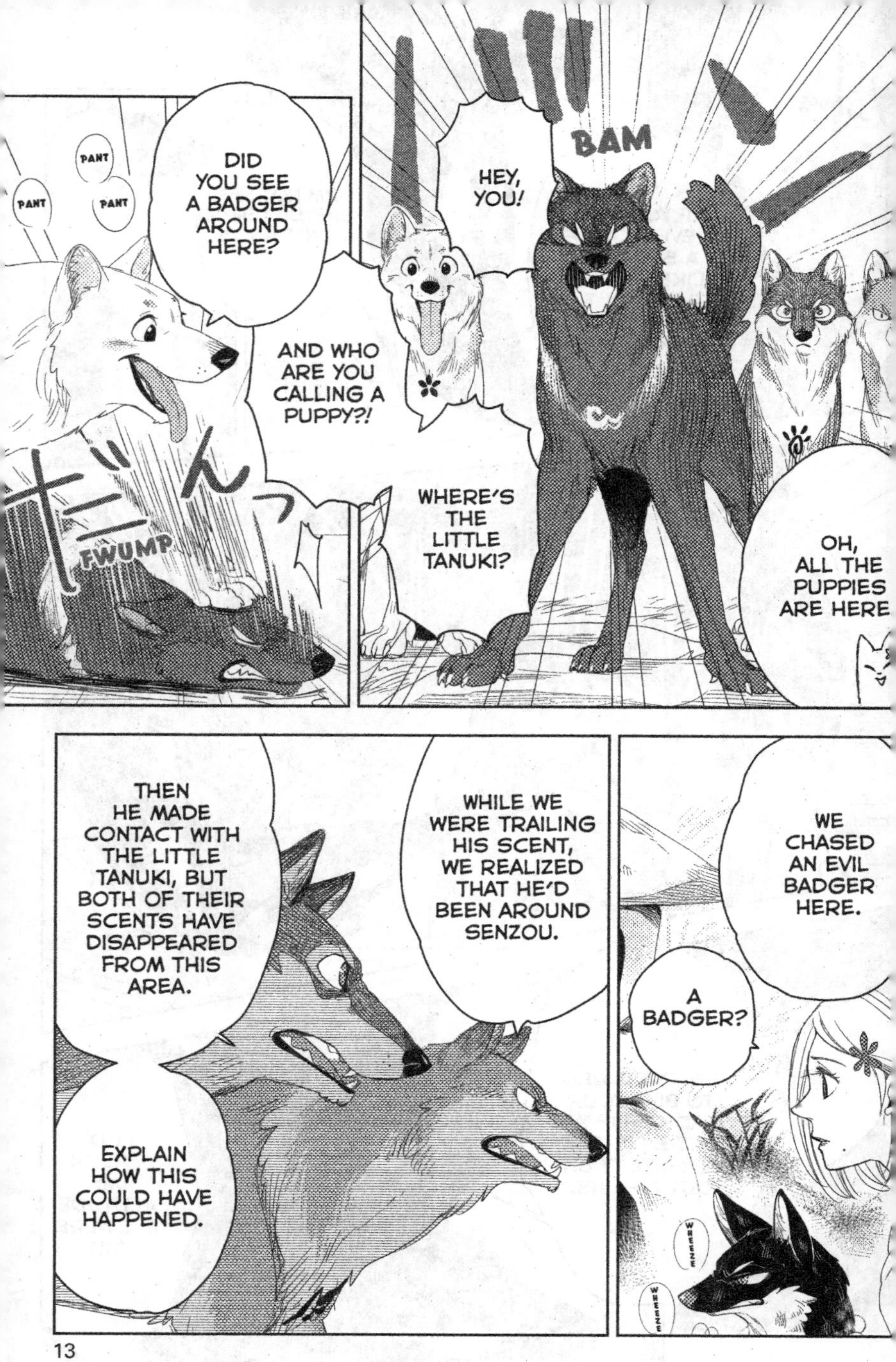
BAM
HEY, YOU!
OH, ALL THE PUPPIES ARE HERE
AND WHO ARE YOU CALLING A PUPPY?!
WHERE'S THE LITTLE TANUKI?
DID YOU SEE A BADGER AROUND HERE?
PANT
PANT
PANT
FWUMP
WE CHASED AN EVIL BADGER HERE.
A BADGER?
WHEEZE
WHEEZE
WHILE WE WERE TRAILING HIS SCENT, WE REALIZED THAT HE'D BEEN AROUND SENZOU.
THEN HE MADE CONTACT WITH THE LITTLE TANUKI, BUT BOTH OF THEIR SCENTS HAVE DISAPPEARED FROM THIS AREA.
EXPLAIN HOW THIS COULD HAVE HAPPENED.

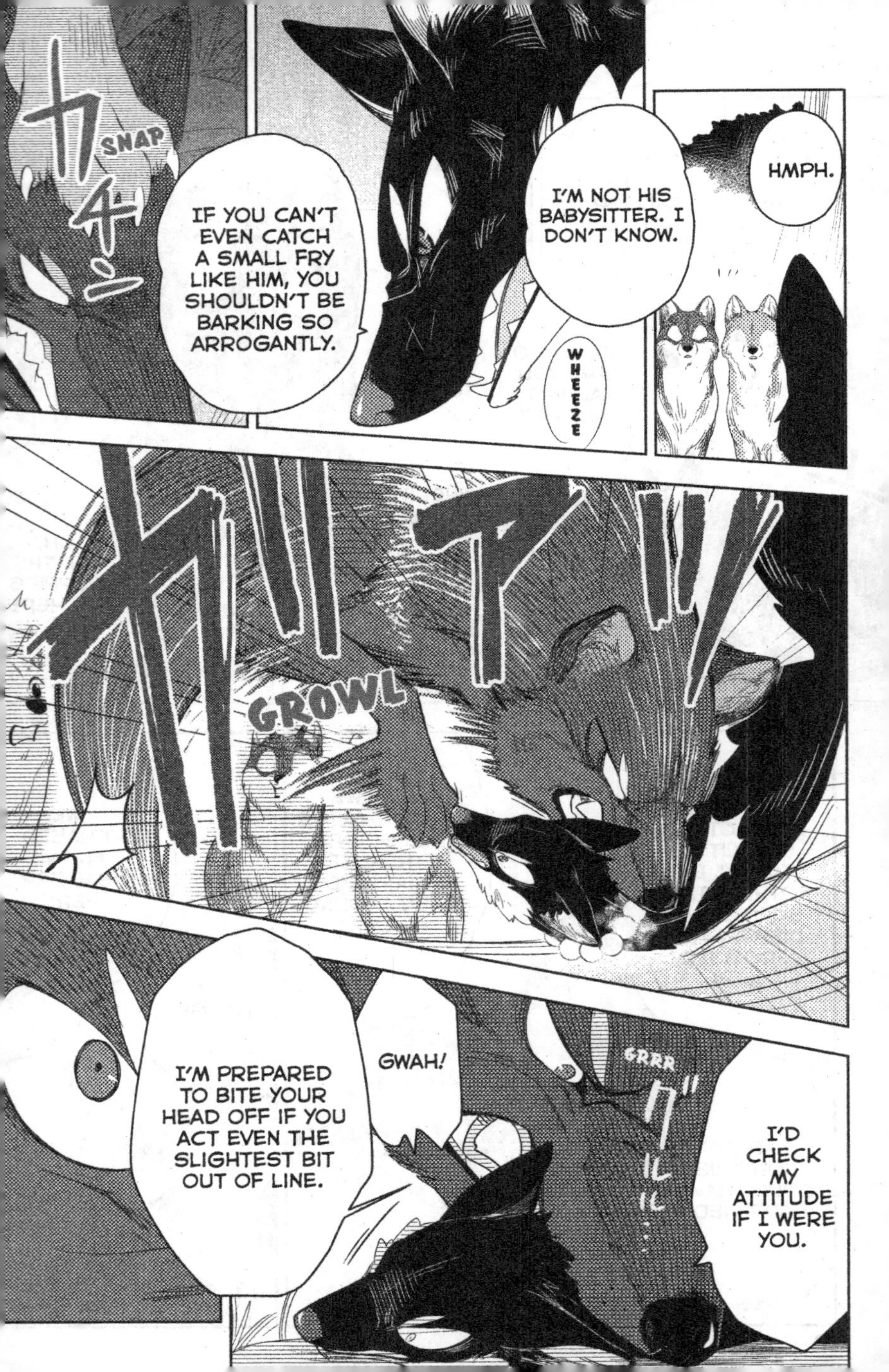
HMPH.
I'M NOT HIS BABYSITTER. I DON'T KNOW.
WHEEZE
SNAP
IF YOU CAN'T EVEN CATCH A SMALL FRY LIKE HIM, YOU SHOULDN'T BE BARKING SO ARROGANTLY.
GROWL
GRRR
I'D CHECK MY ATTITUDE IF I WERE YOU.
GWAH!
I'M PREPARED TO BITE YOUR HEAD OFF IF YOU ACT EVEN THE SLIGHTEST BIT OUT OF LINE.

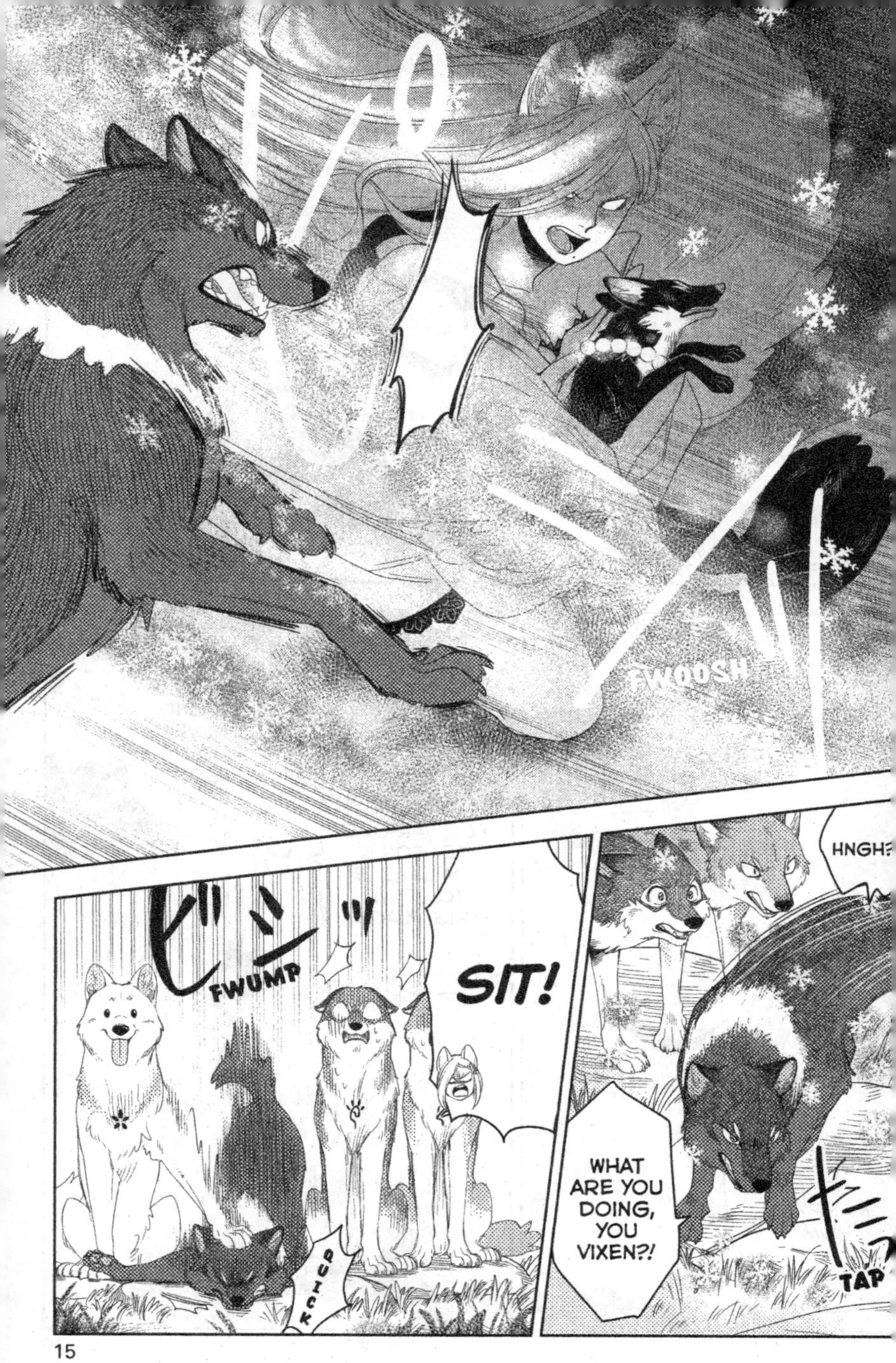
FWOOSH
HNGH?
WHAT ARE YOU DOING, YOU VIXEN?!
TAP
SIT!
FWUMP
QUICK

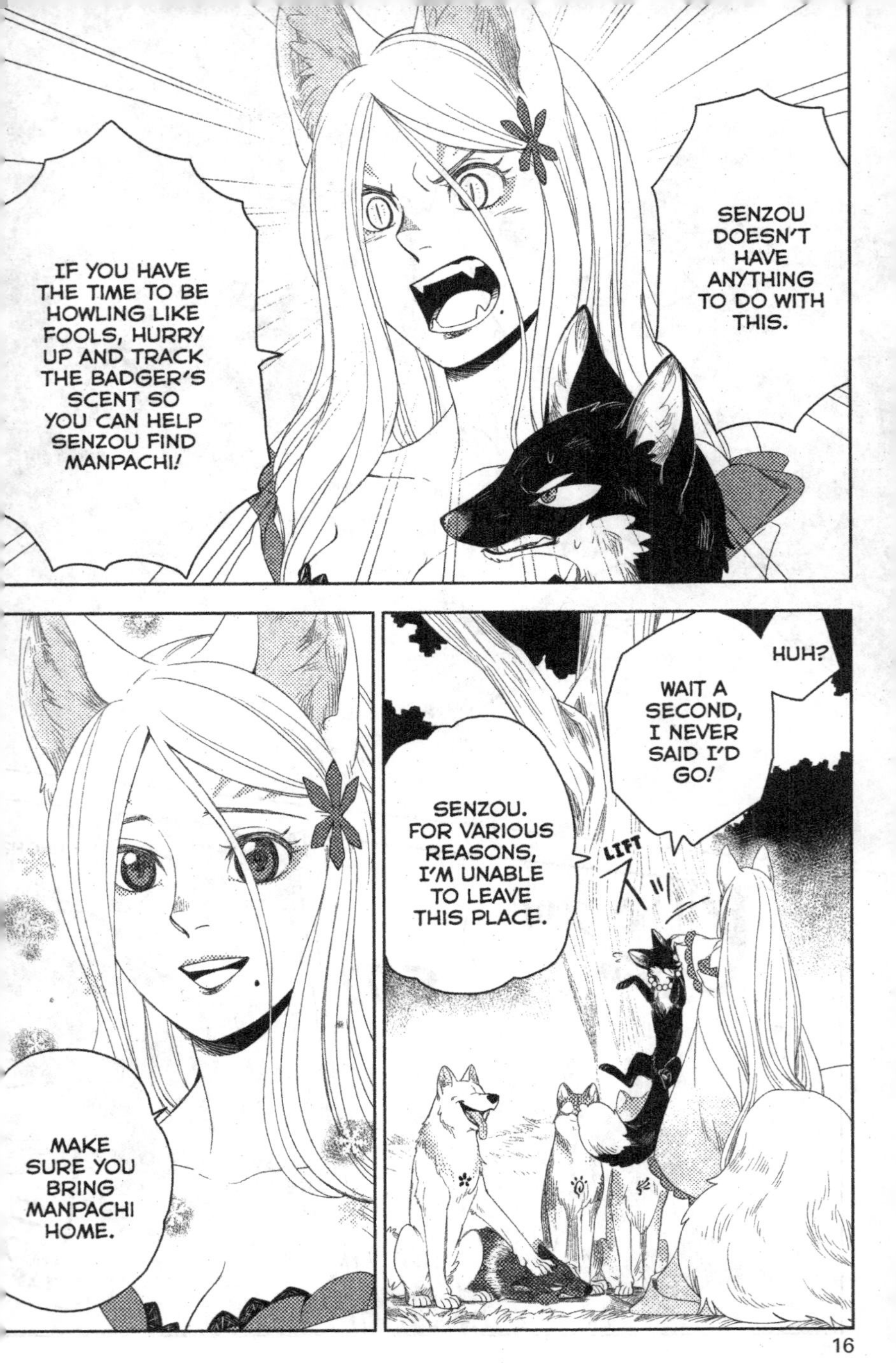
SENZOU DOESN'T HAVE ANYTHING TO DO WITH THIS.
IF YOU HAVE THE TIME TO BE HOWLING LIKE FOOLS, HURRY UP AND TRACK THE BADGER'S SCENT SO YOU CAN HELP SENZOU FIND MANPACHI!
HUH?
WAIT A SECOND, I NEVER SAID I'D GO!
SENZOU. FOR VARIOUS REASONS, I'M UNABLE TO LEAVE THIS PLACE.
LIFT
スッ
MAKE SURE YOU BRING MANPACHI HOME.

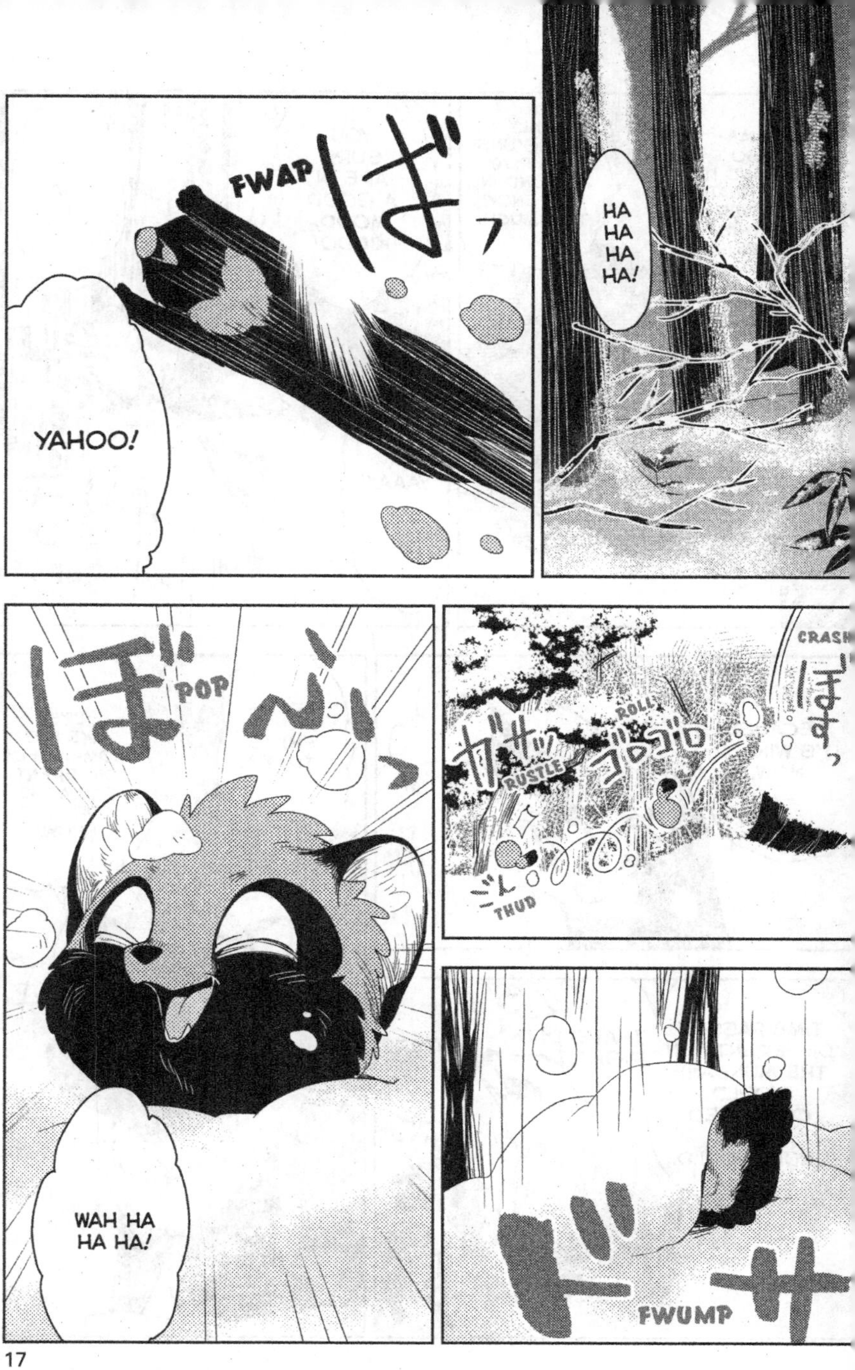
HA HA HA HA!
FWAP
ばっ
YAHOO!
CRASH
ぼすっ
ゴロゴロ
ROLL
ガサッ
RUSTLE
THUD
ドサ
FWUMP
ぼふっ
POP
WAH HA HA HA!

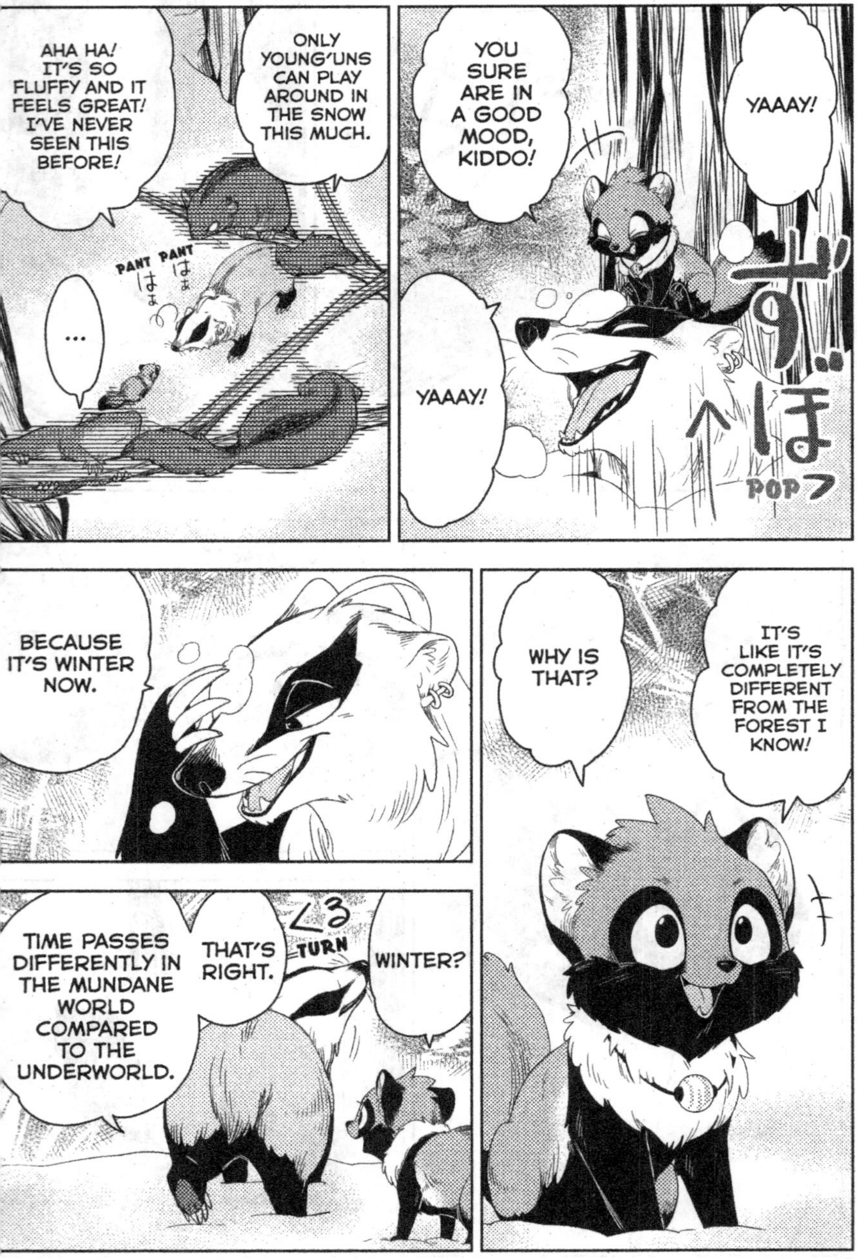
YAAAY!
YOU SURE ARE IN A GOOD MOOD, KIDDO!
YAAAY!
ずぼ
POP
ONLY YOUNG'UNS CAN PLAY AROUND IN THE SNOW THIS MUCH.
AHA HA! IT'S SO FLUFFY AND IT FEELS GREAT! I'VE NEVER SEEN THIS BEFORE!
PANT PANT
はぁはぁ
...
IT'S LIKE IT'S COMPLETELY DIFFERENT FROM THE FOREST I KNOW!
WHY IS THAT?
BECAUSE IT'S WINTER NOW.
WINTER?
くる
TURN
THAT'S RIGHT.
TIME PASSES DIFFERENTLY IN THE MUNDANE WORLD COMPARED TO THE UNDERWORLD.

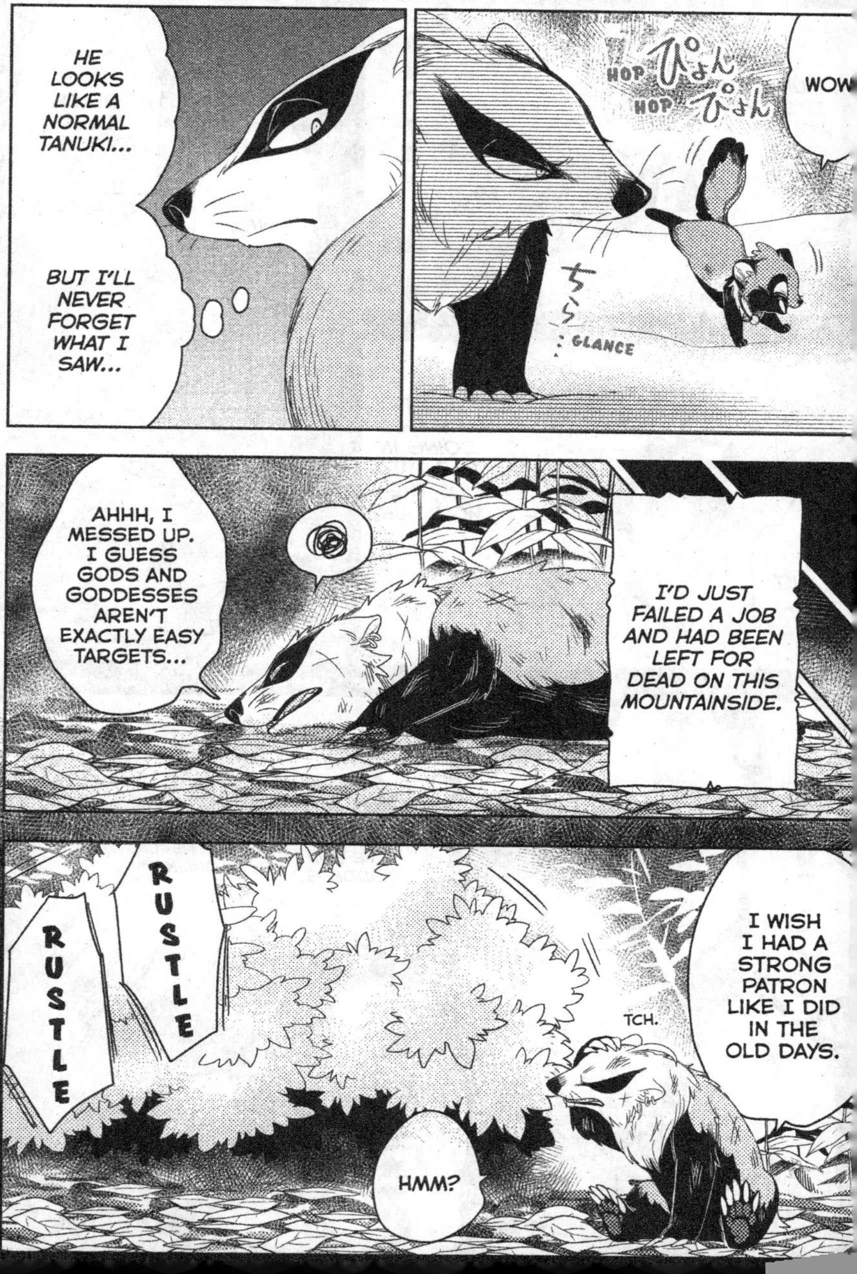
WOW
HOP HOP ぴょんぴょん
ちら GLANCE
HE LOOKS LIKE A NORMAL TANUKI...
BUT I'LL NEVER FORGET WHAT I SAW...
I'D JUST FAILED A JOB AND HAD BEEN LEFT FOR DEAD ON THIS MOUNTAINSIDE.
AHHH, I MESSED UP. I GUESS GODS AND GODDESSES AREN'T EXACTLY EASY TARGETS...
I WISH I HAD A STRONG PATRON LIKE I DID IN THE OLD DAYS.
TCH.
RUSTLE
RUSTLE
HMM?

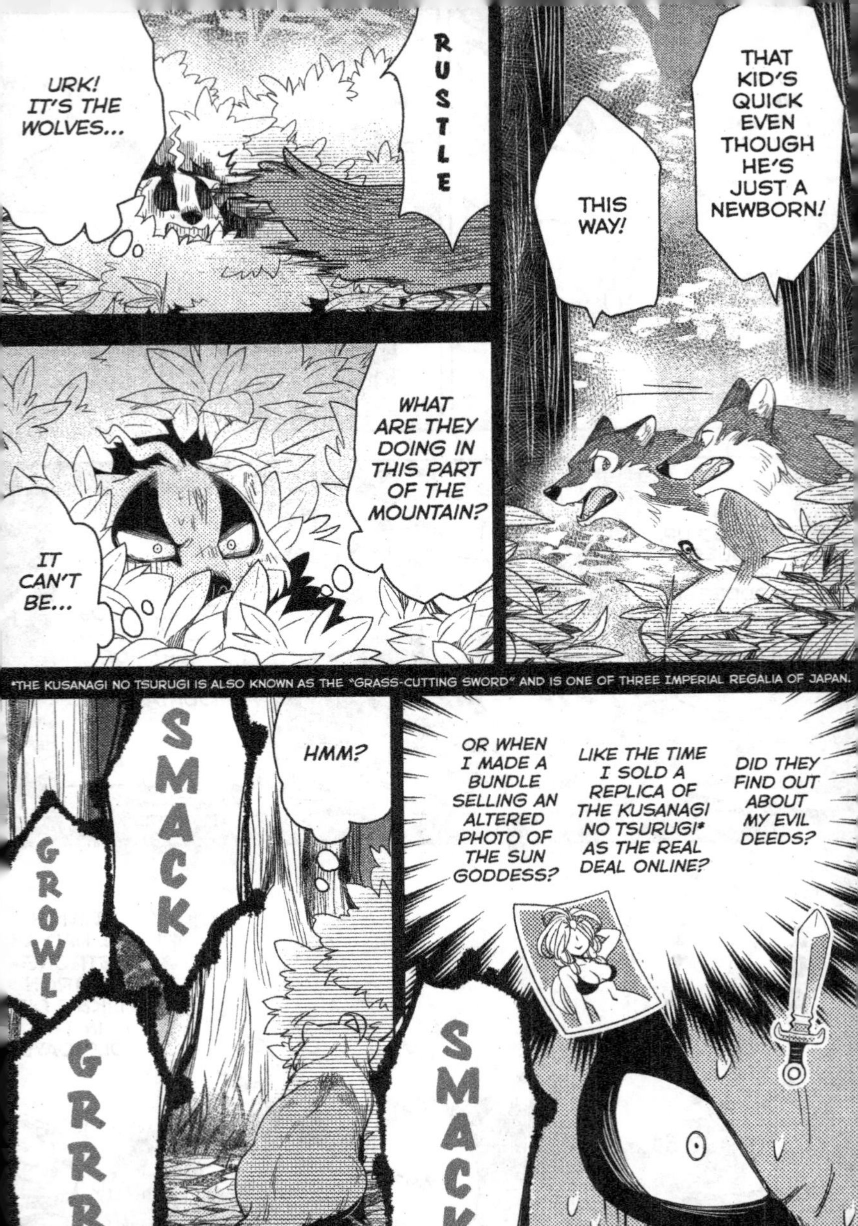
THAT KID'S QUICK EVEN THOUGH HE'S JUST A NEWBORN!
THIS WAY!
RUSTLE
URK! IT'S THE WOLVES...
WHAT ARE THEY DOING IN THIS PART OF THE MOUNTAIN?
IT CAN'T BE...
DID THEY FIND OUT ABOUT MY EVIL DEEDS?
LIKE THE TIME I SOLD A REPLICA OF THE KUSANAGI NO TSURUGI* AS THE REAL DEAL ONLINE?
OR WHEN I MADE A BUNDLE SELLING AN ALTERED PHOTO OF THE SUN GODDESS?
SMACK
HMM?
SMACK
GROWL
GRRR

*THE KUSANAGI NO TSURUGI IS ALSO KNOWN AS THE "GRASS-CUTTING SWORD" AND IS ONE OF THREE IMPERIAL REGALIA OF JAPAN.

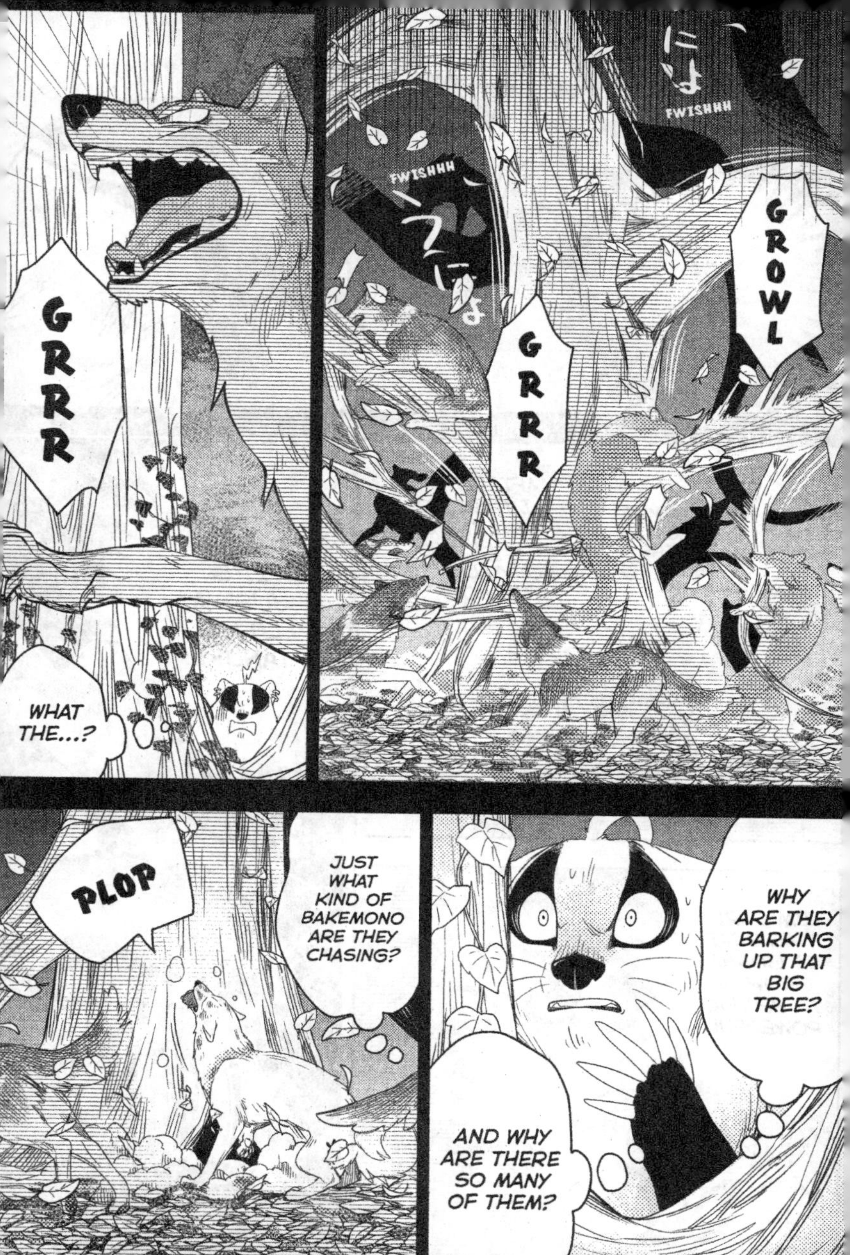
にょ
FWISHHH
GROWL
FWISHHH
GRRR
GRRR
WHAT THE...?
WHY ARE THEY BARKING UP THAT BIG TREE?
AND WHY ARE THERE SO MANY OF THEM?
JUST WHAT KIND OF BAKEMONO ARE THEY CHASING?
PLOP

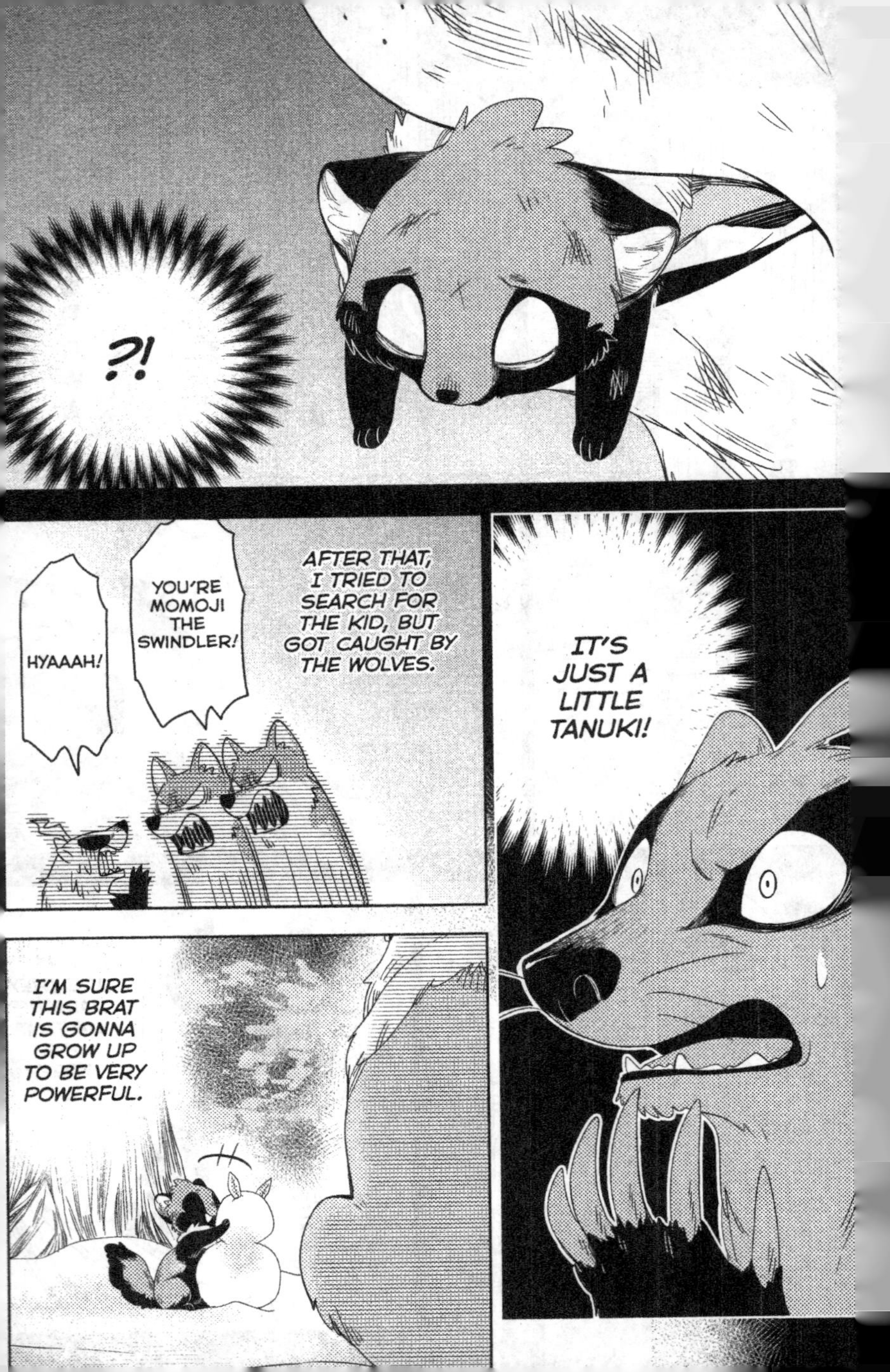
?!
IT'S JUST A LITTLE TANUKI!
AFTER THAT, I TRIED TO SEARCH FOR THE KID, BUT GOT CAUGHT BY THE WOLVES.
YOU'RE MOMOJI THE SWINDLER!
HYAAAH!
I'M SURE THIS BRAT IS GONNA GROW UP TO BE VERY POWERFUL.

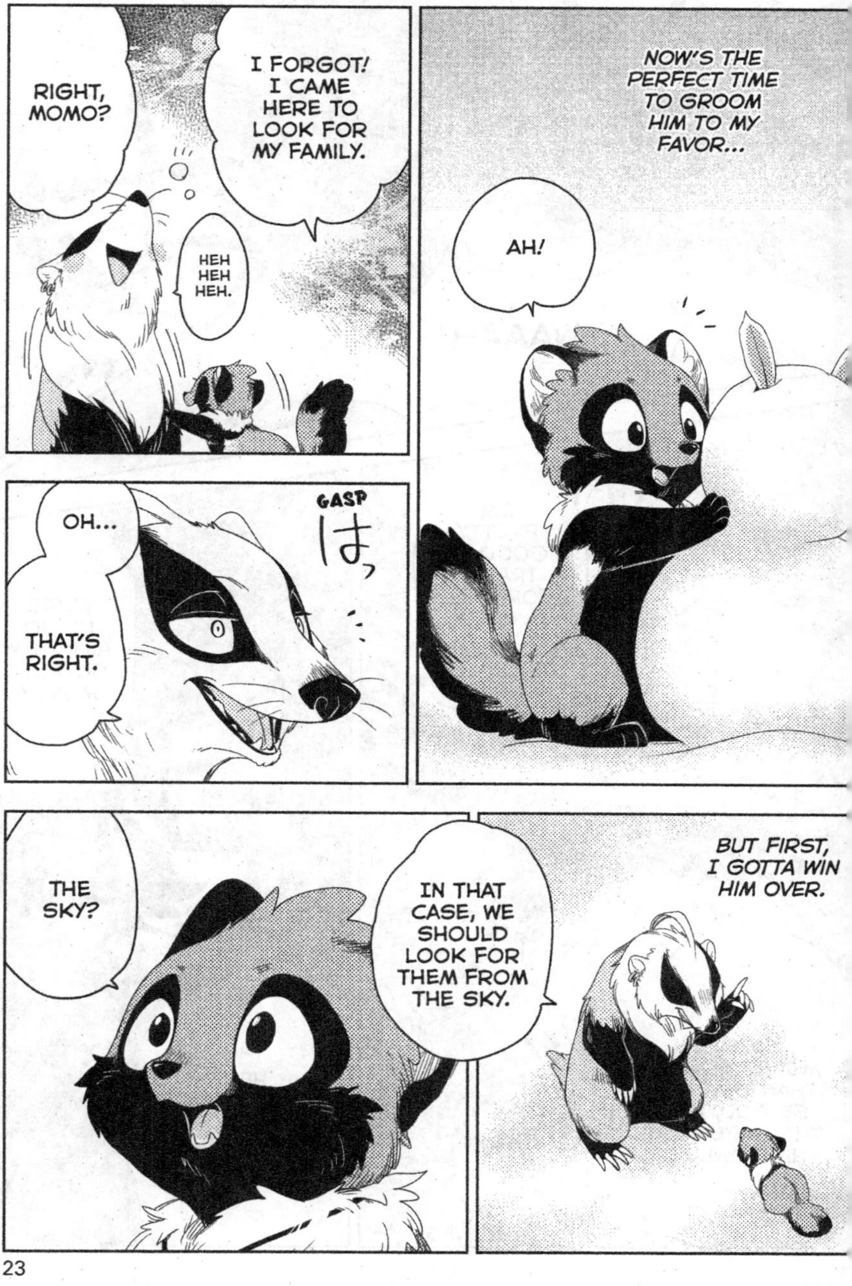
NOW'S THE PERFECT TIME TO GROOM HIM TO MY FAVOR...
AH!
I FORGOT! I CAME HERE TO LOOK FOR MY FAMILY.
RIGHT, MOMO?
HEH HEH HEH.
GASP
はっ
OH...
THAT'S RIGHT.
BUT FIRST, I GOTTA WIN HIM OVER.
IN THAT CASE, WE SHOULD LOOK FOR THEM FROM THE SKY.
THE SKY?

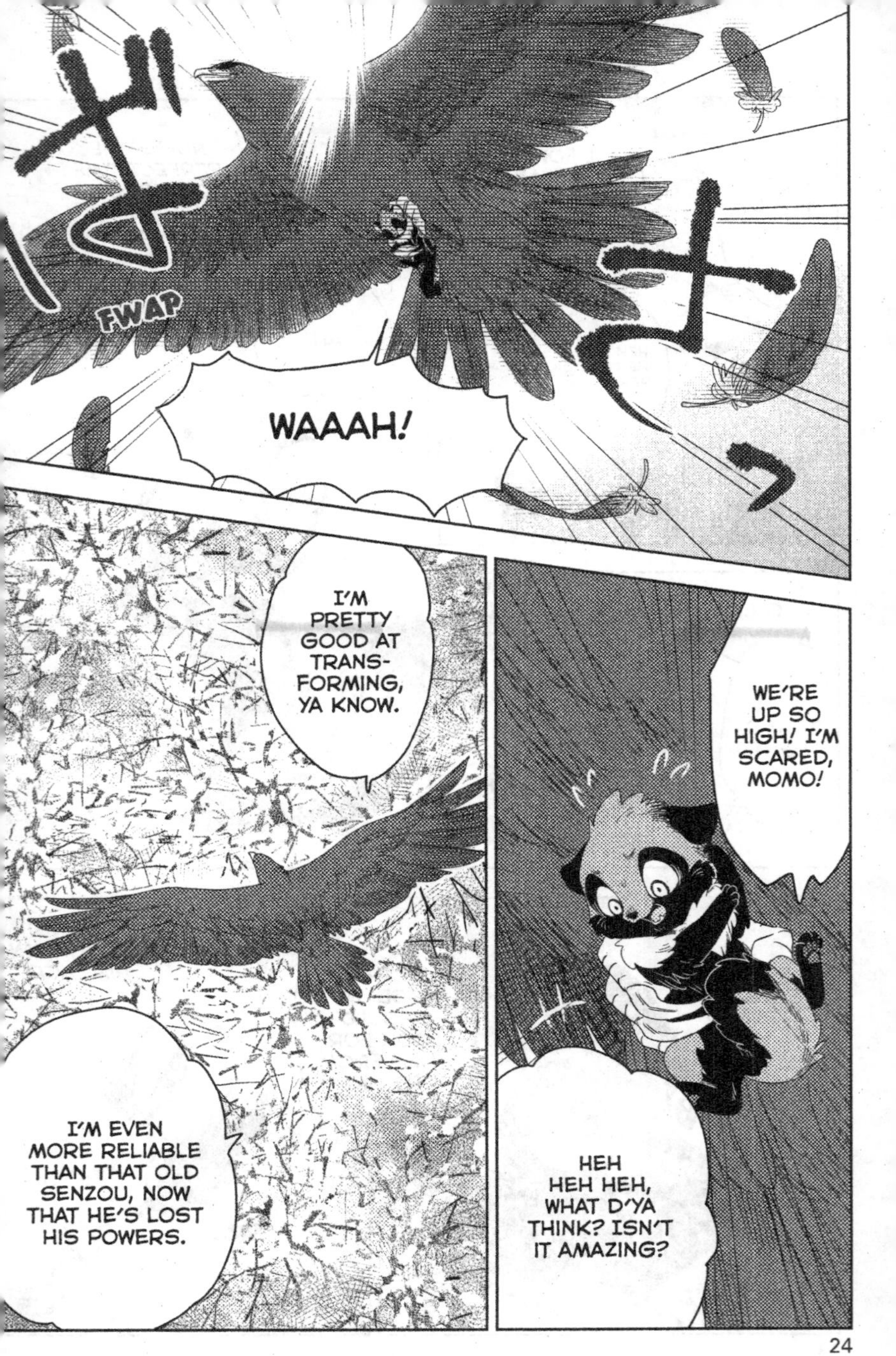
ばさっ
FWAP
WAAAH!
WE'RE UP SO HIGH! I'M SCARED, MOMO!
HEH HEH HEH, WHAT D'YA THINK? ISN'T IT AMAZING?
I'M PRETTY GOOD AT TRANS-FORMING, YA KNOW.
I'M EVEN MORE RELIABLE THAN THAT OLD SENZOU, NOW THAT HE'S LOST HIS POWERS.

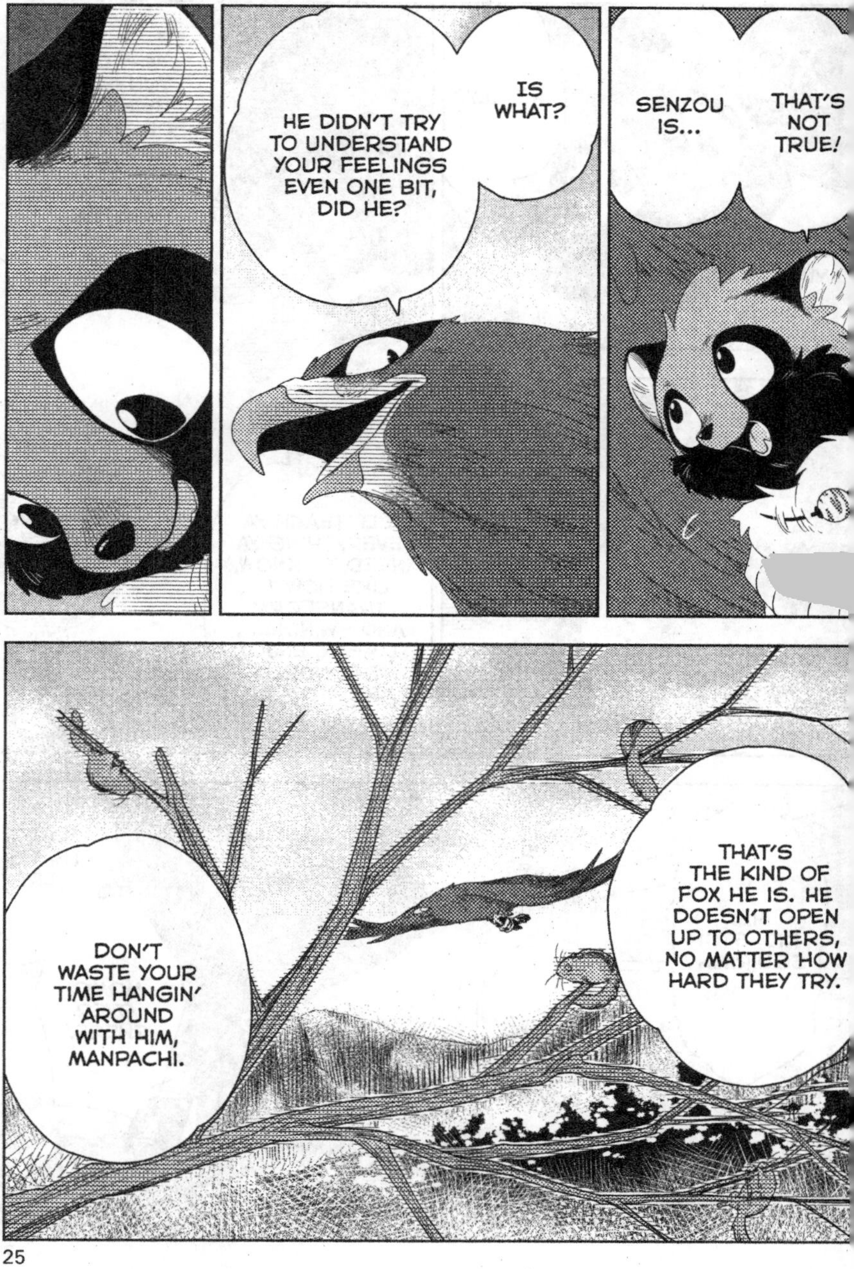
THAT'S NOT TRUE!
SENZOU IS...
IS WHAT?
HE DIDN'T TRY TO UNDERSTAND YOUR FEELINGS EVEN ONE BIT, DID HE?
THAT'S THE KIND OF FOX HE IS. HE DOESN'T OPEN UP TO OTHERS, NO MATTER HOW HARD THEY TRY.
DON'T WASTE YOUR TIME HANGIN' AROUND WITH HIM, MANPACHI.

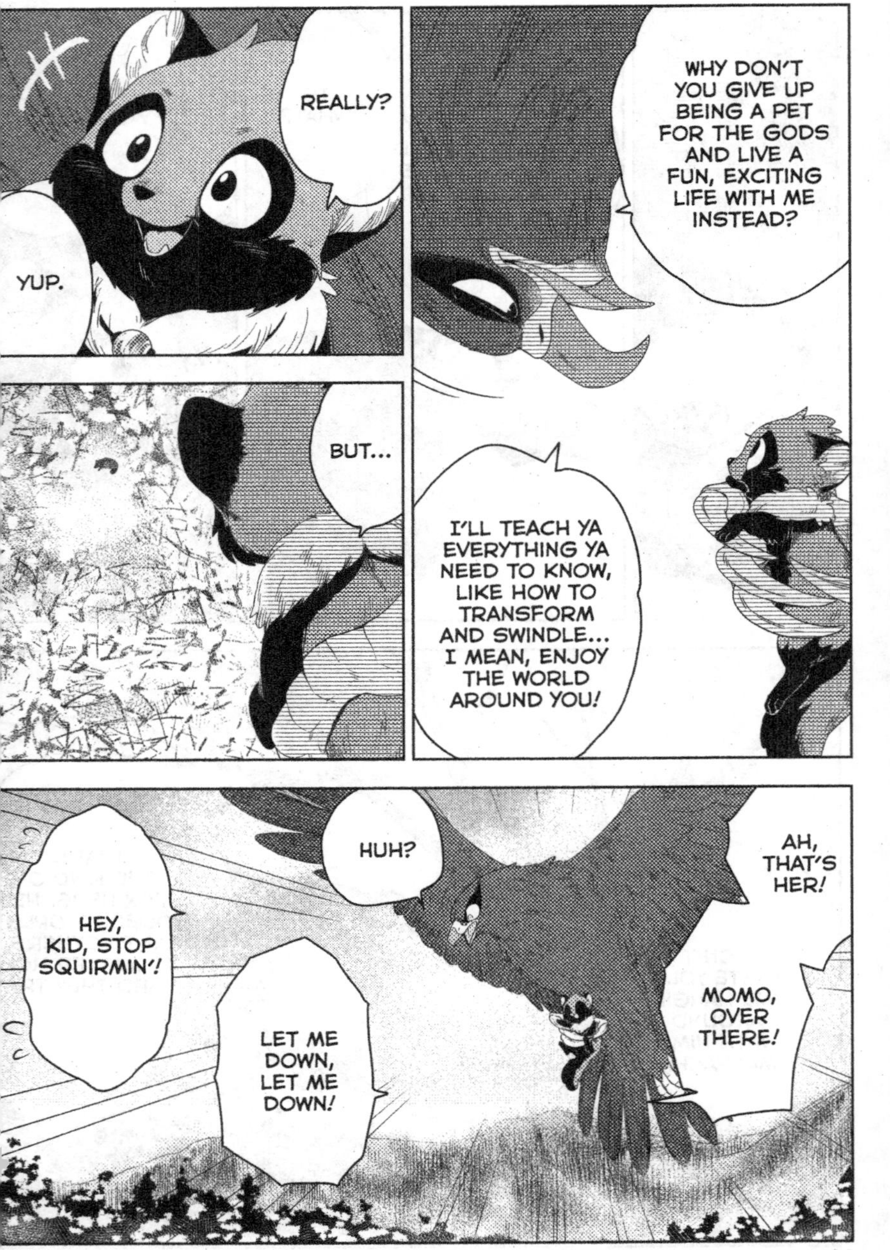
WHY DON'T YOU GIVE UP BEING A PET FOR THE GODS AND LIVE A FUN, EXCITING LIFE WITH ME INSTEAD?
I'LL TEACH YA EVERYTHING YA NEED TO KNOW, LIKE HOW TO TRANSFORM AND SWINDLE... I MEAN, ENJOY THE WORLD AROUND YOU!
REALLY?
YUP.
BUT...
AH, THAT'S HER!
MOMO, OVER THERE!
HUH?
LET ME DOWN, LET ME DOWN!
HEY, KID, STOP SQUIRMIN'!

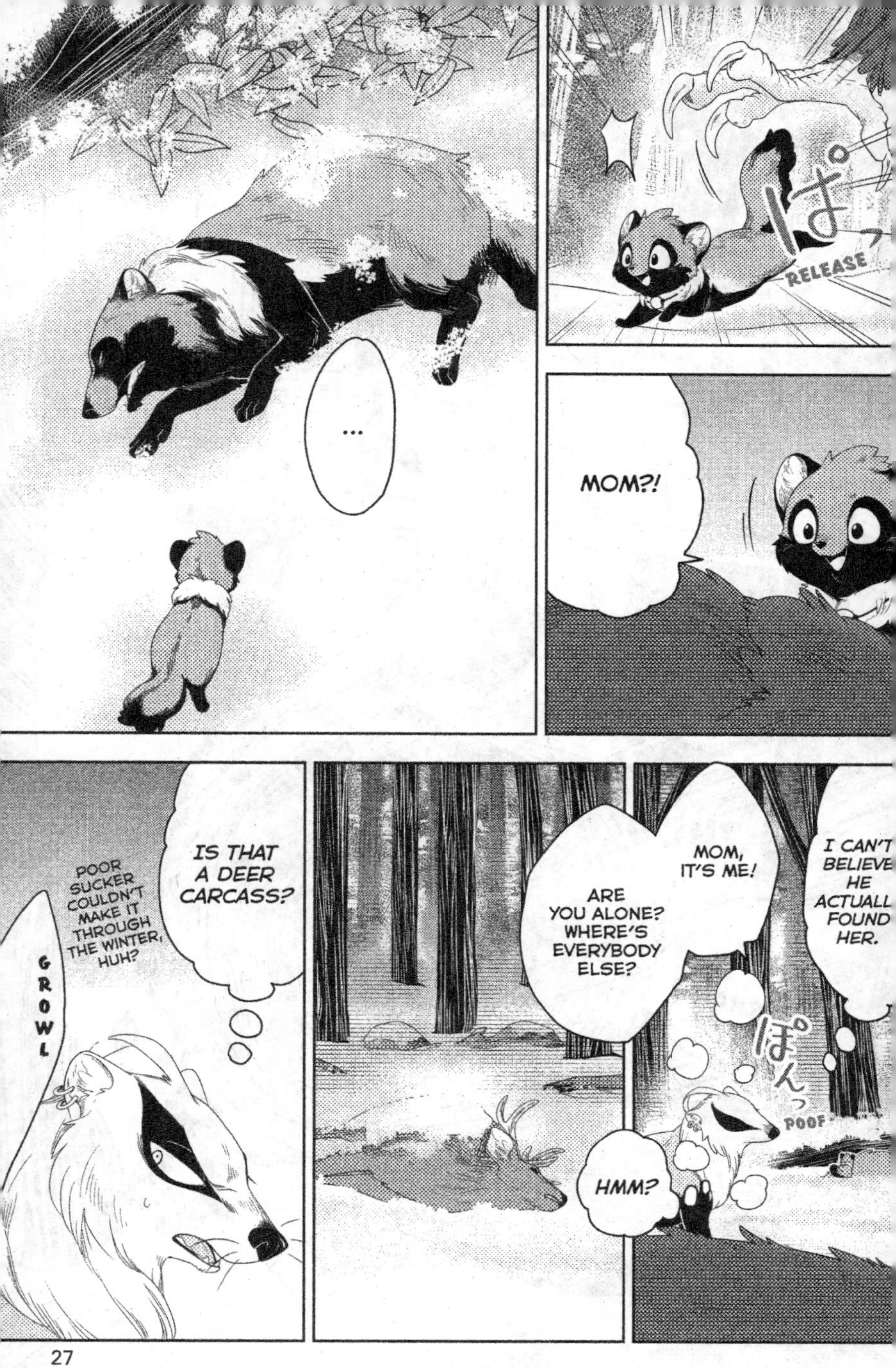
ぱっ
RELEASE
MOM?!
...
I CAN'T BELIEVE HE ACTUALL FOUND HER.
MOM, IT'S ME!
ARE YOU ALONE? WHERE'S EVERYBODY ELSE?
ぽんっ
POOF
HMM?
IS THAT A DEER CARCASS?
POOR SUCKER COULDN'T MAKE IT THROUGH THE WINTER, HUH?
GROWL

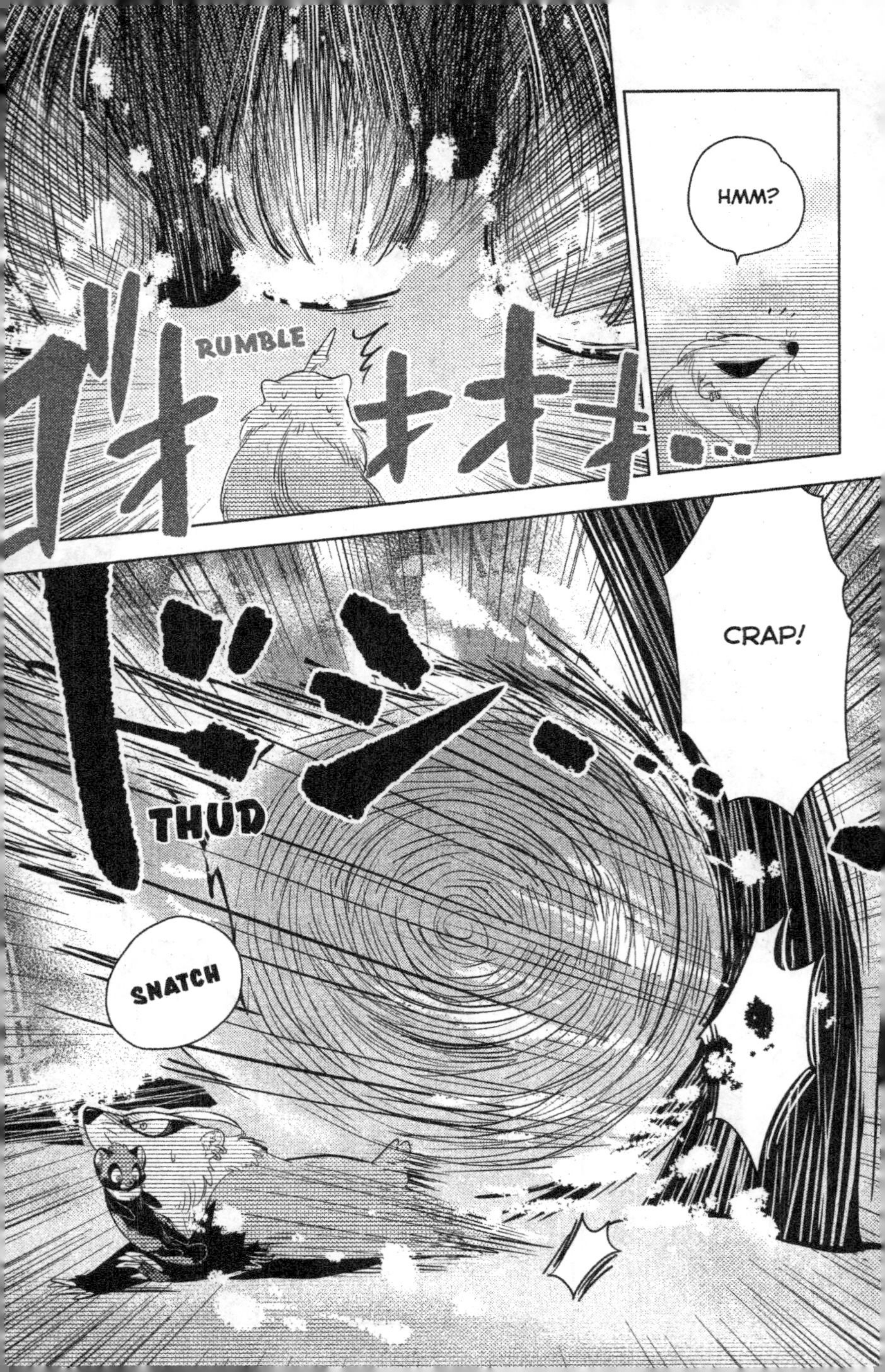
HMM?
RUMBLE
CRAP!
THUD
SNATCH

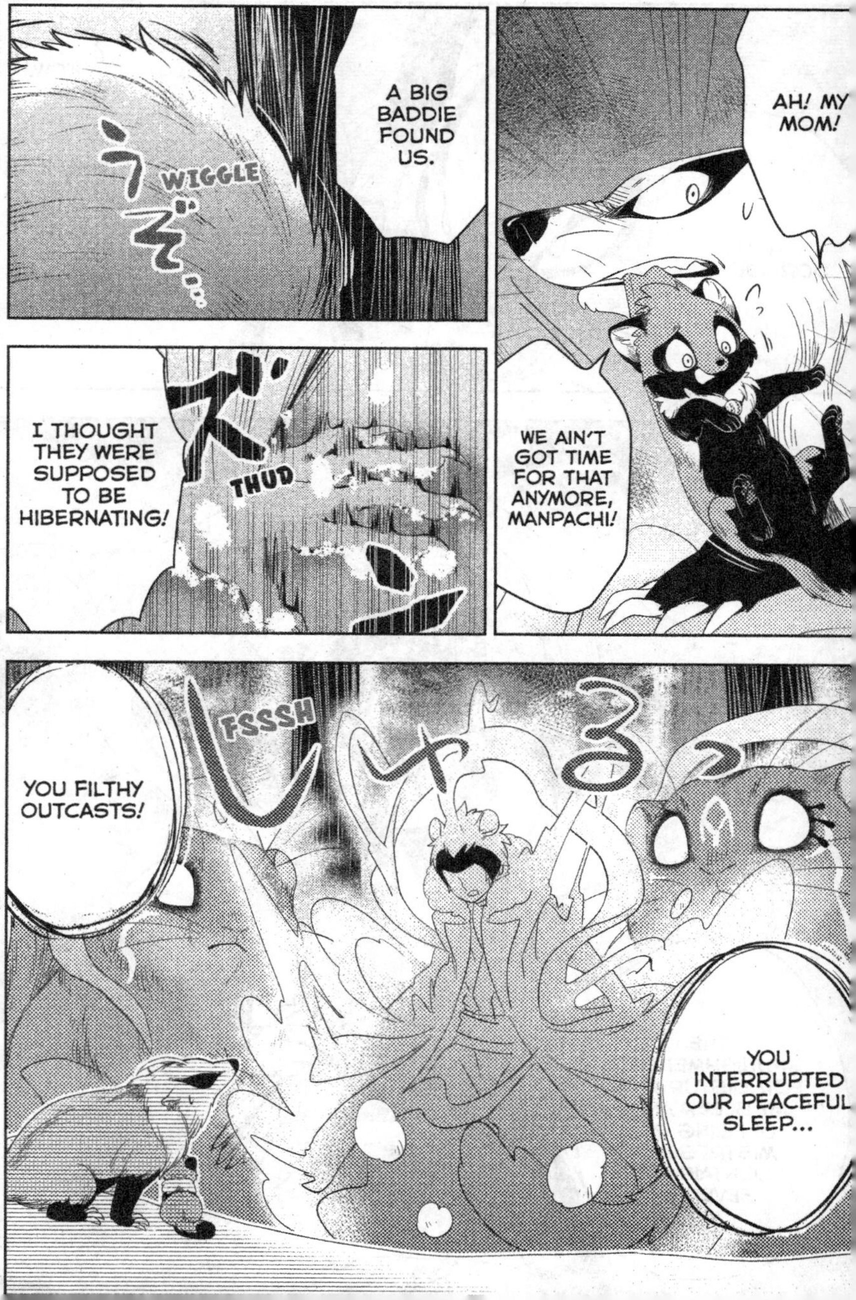
AH! MY MOM!
WE AIN'T GOT TIME FOR THAT ANYMORE, MANPACHI!
A BIG BADDIE FOUND US.
WIGGLE
THUD
I THOUGHT THEY WERE SUPPOSED TO BE HIBERNATING!
FSSSH
YOU INTERRUPTED OUR PEACEFUL SLEEP...
YOU FILTHY OUTCASTS!

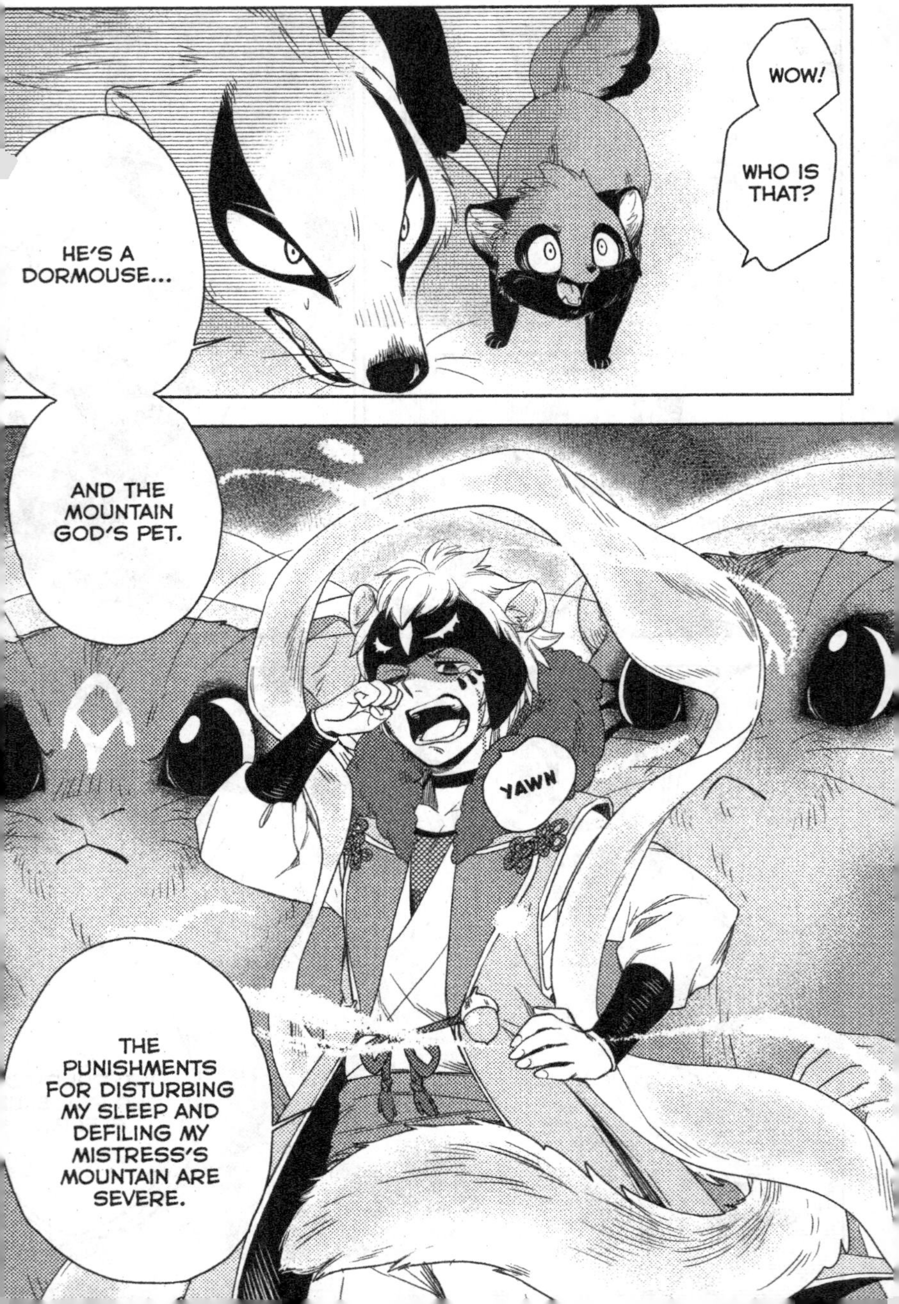
WOW!
WHO IS THAT?
HE'S A DORMOUSE...
AND THE MOUNTAIN GOD'S PET.
YAWN
THE PUNISHMENTS FOR DISTURBING MY SLEEP AND DEFILING MY MISTRESS'S MOUNTAIN ARE SEVERE.

# Chapter 8

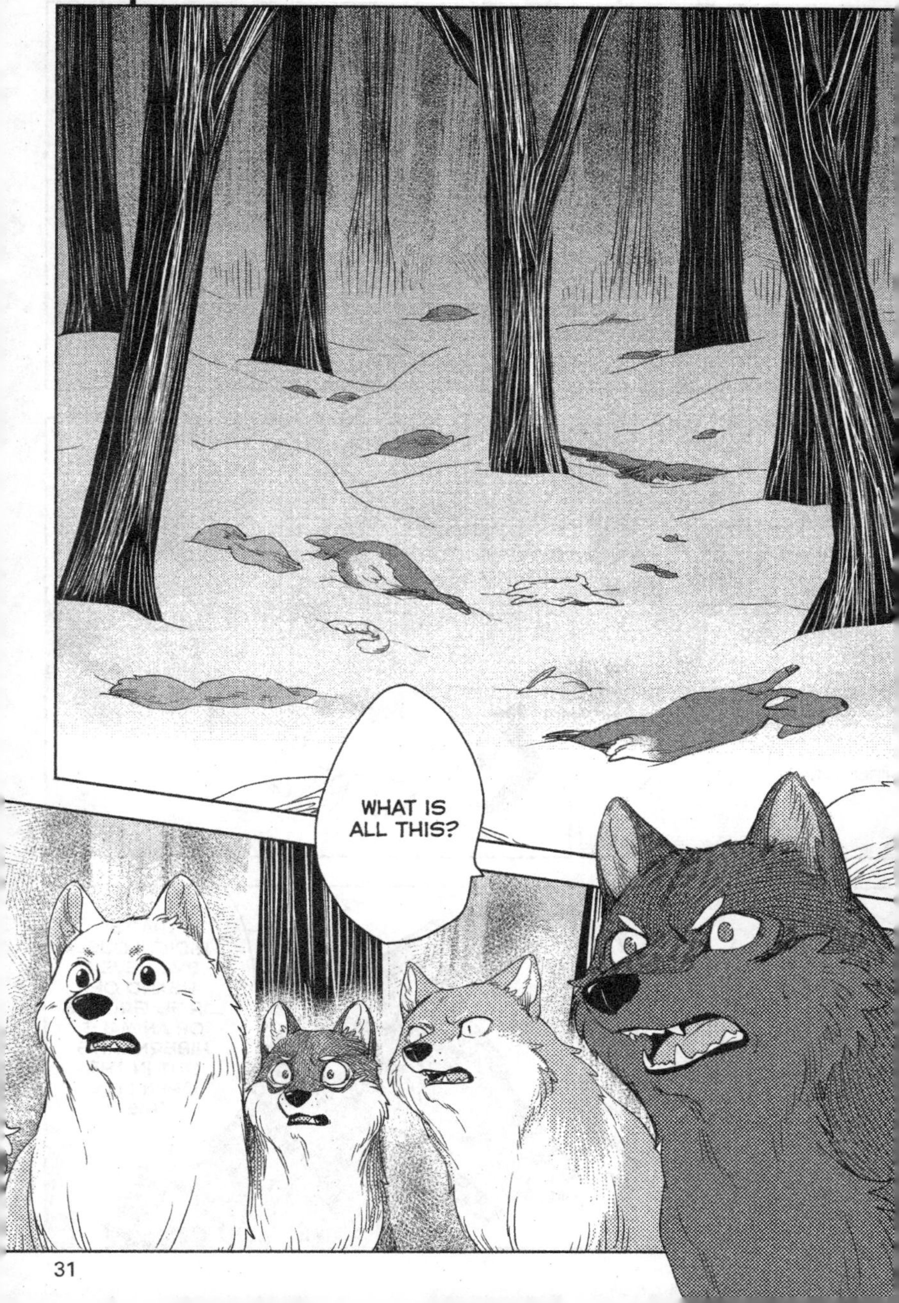
WHAT IS ALL THIS?

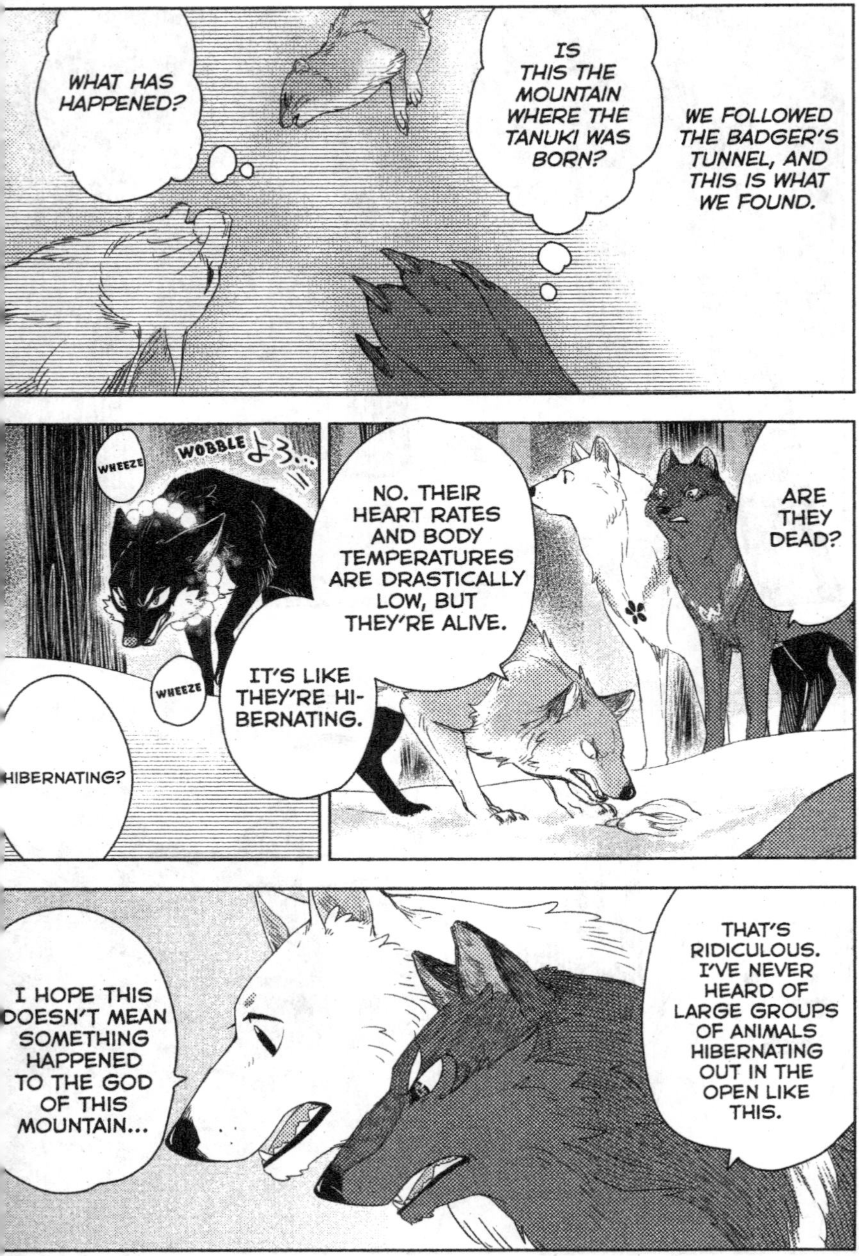
WE FOLLOWED THE BADGER'S TUNNEL, AND THIS IS WHAT WE FOUND.
IS THIS THE MOUNTAIN WHERE THE TANUKI WAS BORN?
WHAT HAS HAPPENED?
ARE THEY DEAD?
NO. THEIR HEART RATES AND BODY TEMPERATURES ARE DRASTICALLY LOW, BUT THEY'RE ALIVE.
IT'S LIKE THEY'RE HI-BERNATING.
WOBBLE よろ…
WHEEZE
WHEEZE
HIBERNATING?
THAT'S RIDICULOUS. I'VE NEVER HEARD OF LARGE GROUPS OF ANIMALS HIBERNATING OUT IN THE OPEN LIKE THIS.
I HOPE THIS DOESN'T MEAN SOMETHING HAPPENED TO THE GOD OF THIS MOUNTAIN...

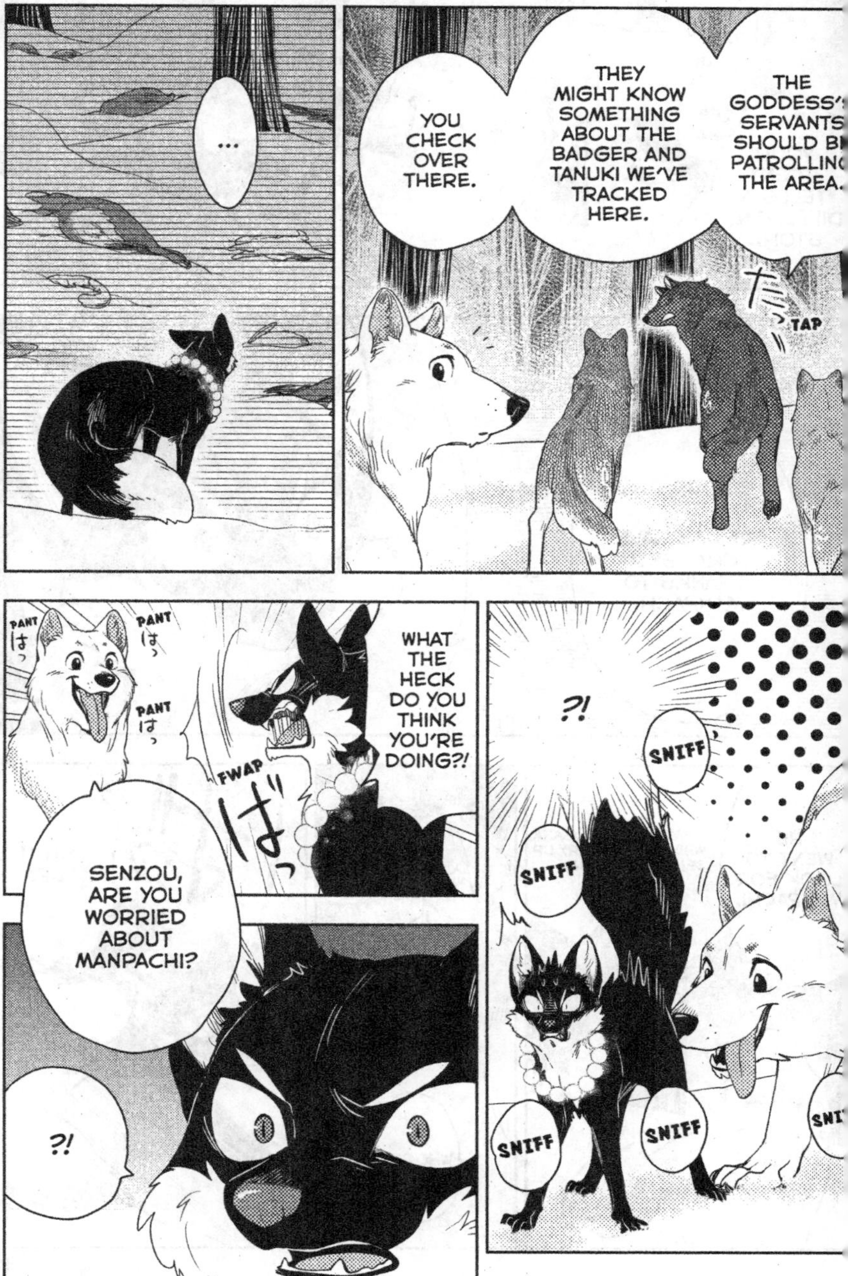
THE GODDESS'S SERVANTS SHOULD B PATROLLIN THE AREA.
THEY MIGHT KNOW SOMETHING ABOUT THE BADGER AND TANUKI WE'VE TRACKED HERE.
YOU CHECK OVER THERE.
TAP
...
?!
SNIFF
SNIFF
SNIFF
SNIFF
SNI
WHAT THE HECK DO YOU THINK YOU'RE DOING?!
PANT
PANT
PANT
FWAP
SENZOU, ARE YOU WORRIED ABOUT MANPACHI?
?!

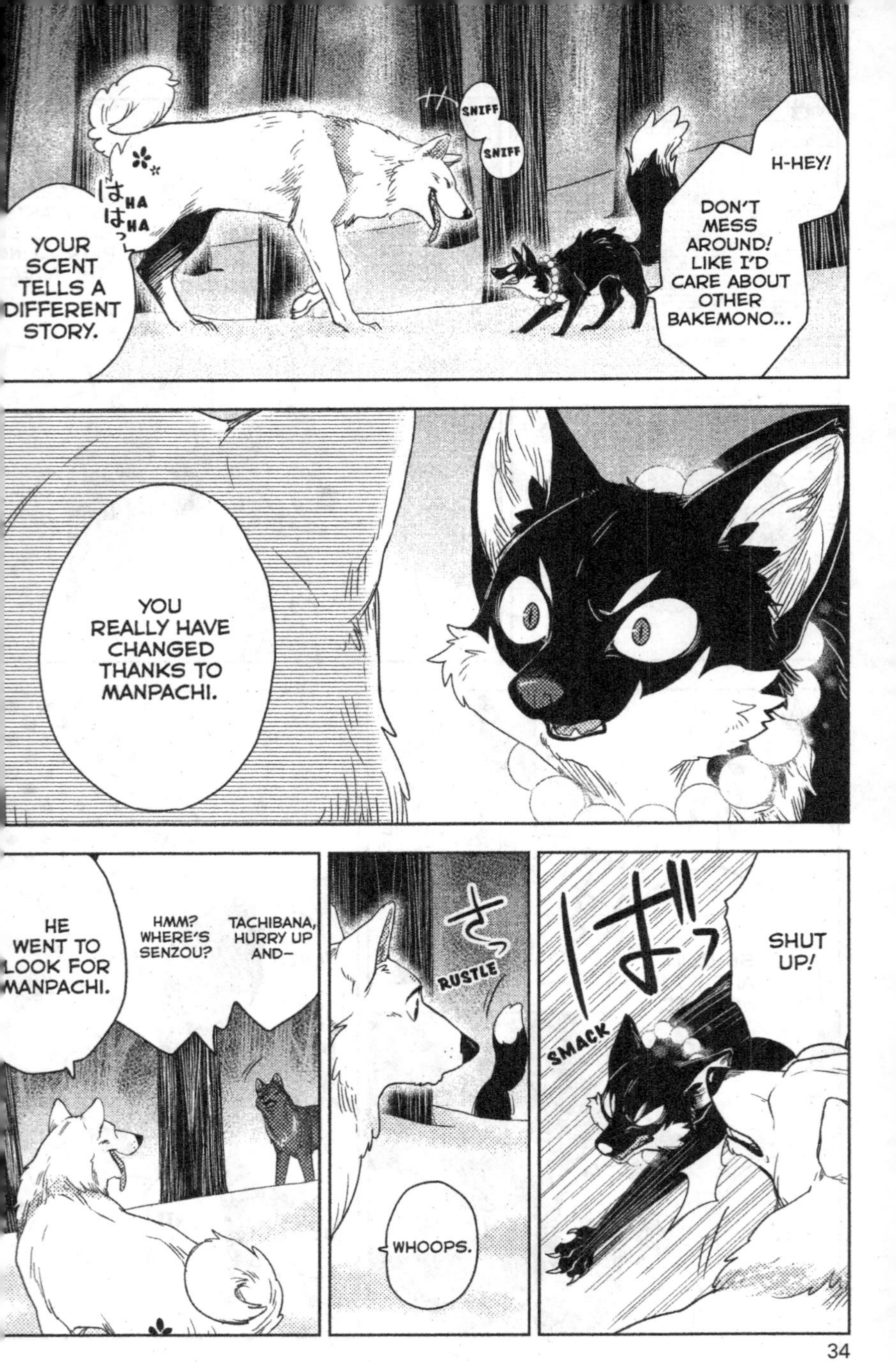
H-HEY!
DON'T MESS AROUND! LIKE I'D CARE ABOUT OTHER BAKEMONO...
SNIFF
SNIFF
はは HA HA
YOUR SCENT TELLS A DIFFERENT STORY.
YOU REALLY HAVE CHANGED THANKS TO MANPACHI.
SHUT UP!
ばっ SMACK
さっ RUSTLE
WHOOPS.
TACHIBANA, HURRY UP AND–
HMM? WHERE'S SENZOU?
HE WENT TO LOOK FOR MANPACHI.

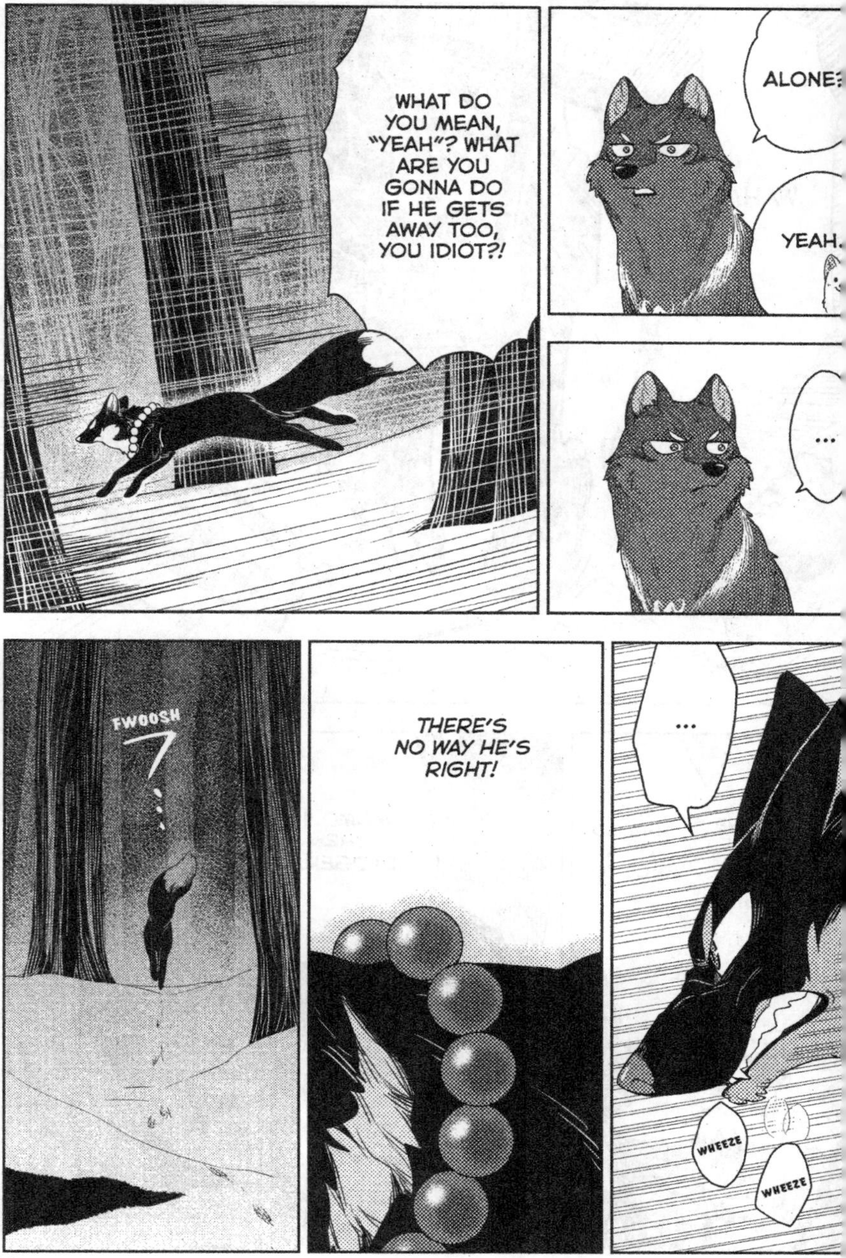
ALONE
YEAH.
...
WHAT DO YOU MEAN, "YEAH"? WHAT ARE YOU GONNA DO IF HE GETS AWAY TOO, YOU IDIOT?!
...
WHEEZE
WHEEZE
THERE'S NO WAY HE'S RIGHT!
FWOOSH

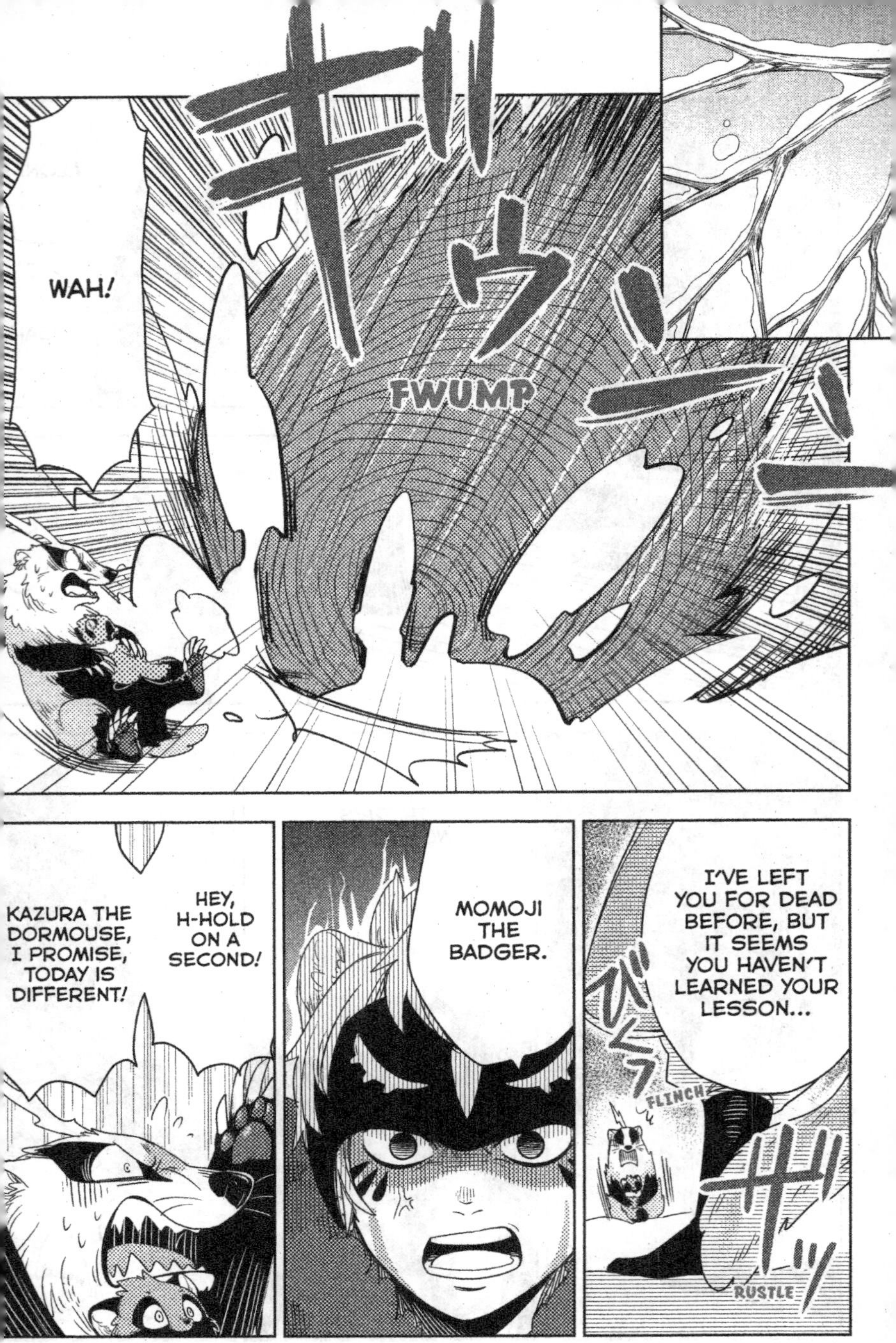
FWUMP
WAH!
I'VE LEFT YOU FOR DEAD BEFORE, BUT IT SEEMS YOU HAVEN'T LEARNED YOUR LESSON...
FLINCH
RUSTLE
MOMOJI THE BADGER.
HEY, H-HOLD ON A SECOND!
KAZURA THE DORMOUSE, I PROMISE, TODAY IS DIFFERENT!

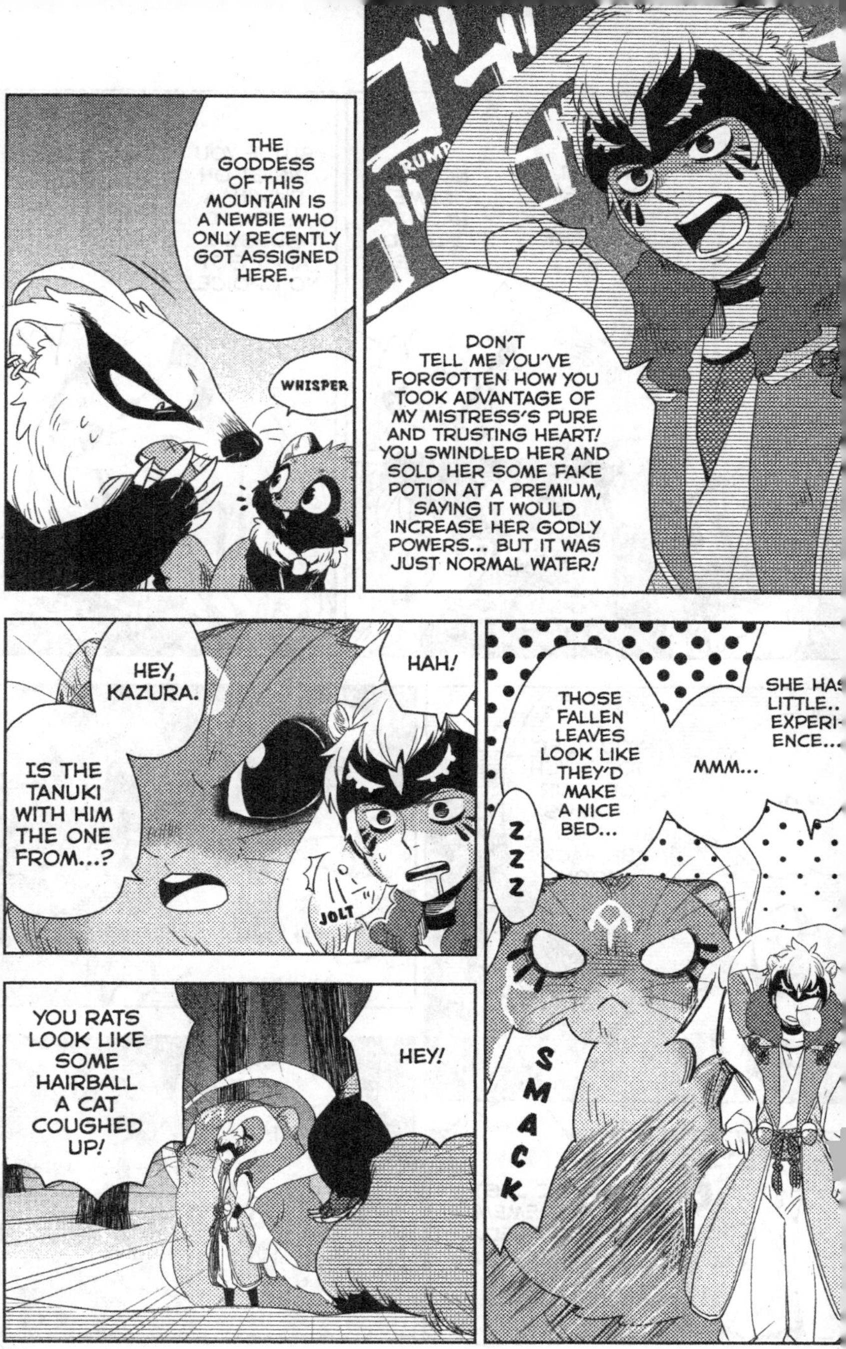
DON'T TELL ME YOU'VE FORGOTTEN HOW YOU TOOK ADVANTAGE OF MY MISTRESS'S PURE AND TRUSTING HEART! YOU SWINDLED HER AND SOLD HER SOME FAKE POTION AT A PREMIUM, SAYING IT WOULD INCREASE HER GODLY POWERS... BUT IT WAS JUST NORMAL WATER!
THE GODDESS OF THIS MOUNTAIN IS A NEWBIE WHO ONLY RECENTLY GOT ASSIGNED HERE.
WHISPER
SHE HAS LITTLE... EXPERIENCE...
MMM...
THOSE FALLEN LEAVES LOOK LIKE THEY'D MAKE A NICE BED...
ZZZ
SMACK
HAH!
HEY, KAZURA.
IS THE TANUKI WITH HIM THE ONE FROM...?
JOLT
HEY!
YOU RATS LOOK LIKE SOME HAIRBALL A CAT COUGHED UP!

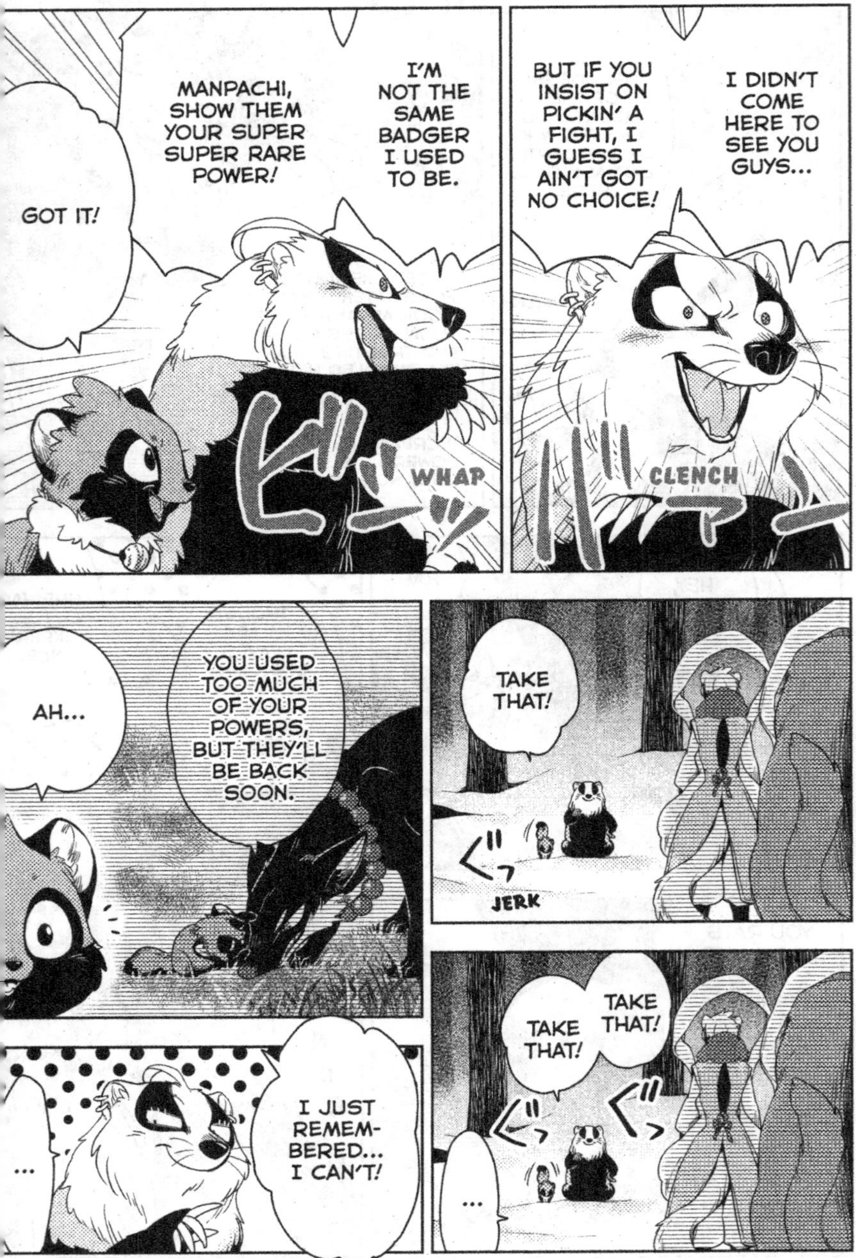
I DIDN'T COME HERE TO SEE YOU GUYS...
BUT IF YOU INSIST ON PICKIN' A FIGHT, I GUESS I AIN'T GOT NO CHOICE!
CLENCH
I'M NOT THE SAME BADGER I USED TO BE.
MANPACHI, SHOW THEM YOUR SUPER SUPER RARE POWER!
GOT IT!
WHAP
TAKE THAT!
JERK
YOU USED TOO MUCH OF YOUR POWERS, BUT THEY'LL BE BACK SOON.
AH...
TAKE THAT!
TAKE THAT!
...
I JUST REMEMBERED... I CAN'T!
...

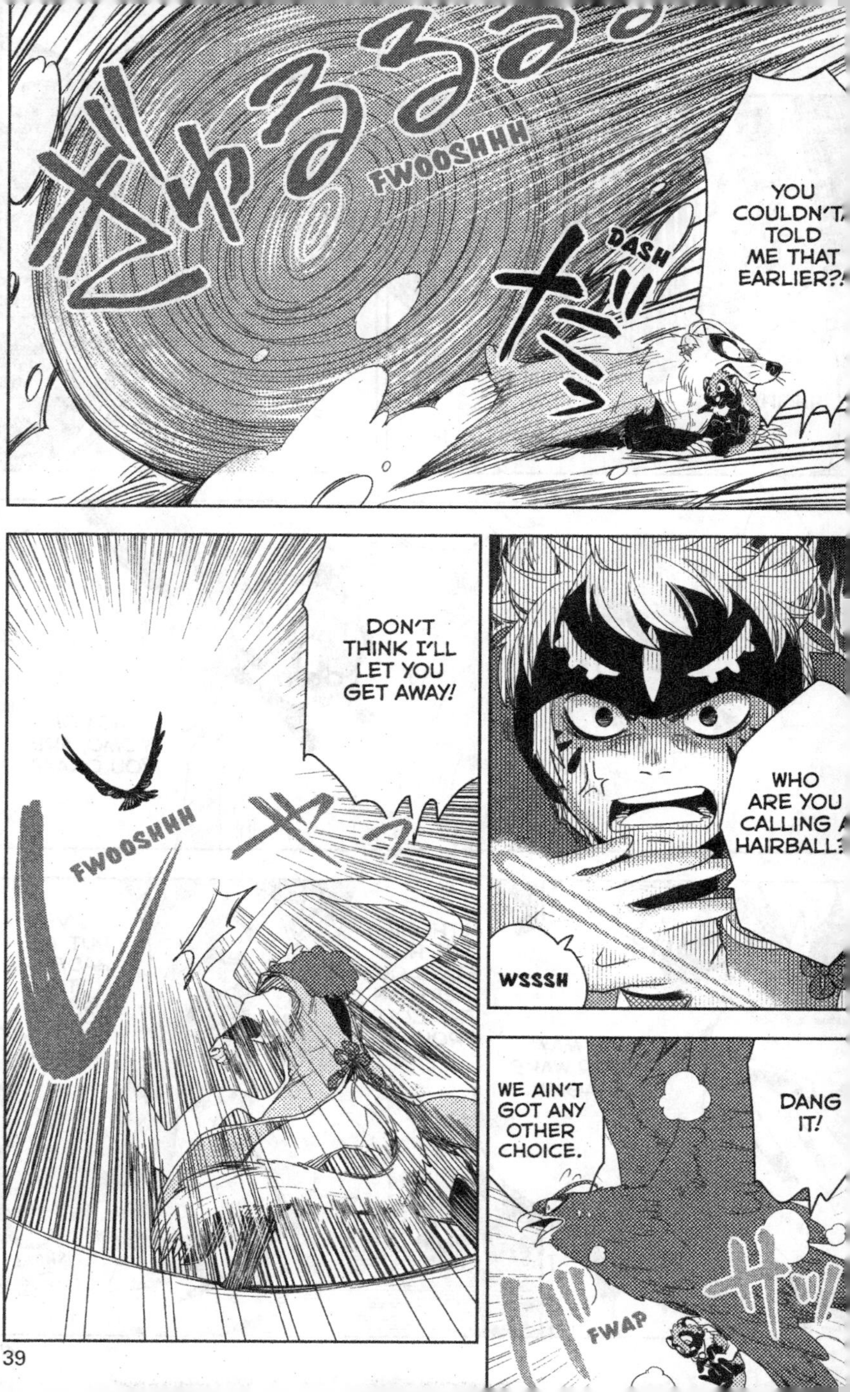
FWOOSHHH
DASH
YOU COULDN'T TOLD ME THAT EARLIER?!
WHO ARE YOU CALLING A HAIRBALL?!
WSSSH
DANG IT!
WE AIN'T GOT ANY OTHER CHOICE.
FWAP
DON'T THINK I'LL LET YOU GET AWAY!
FWOOSHHH

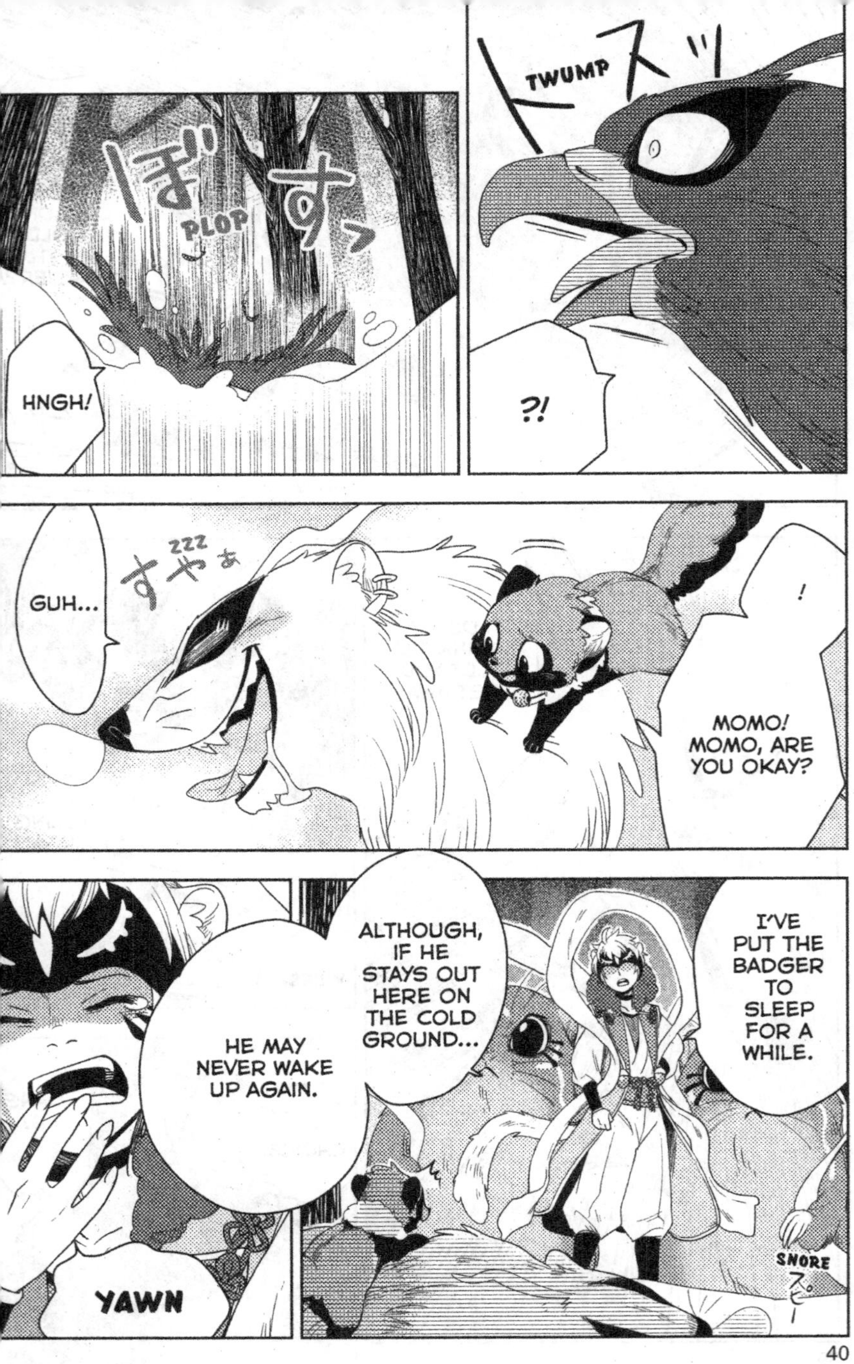
TWUMP
トスッ
?!
ぼすっ
PLOP
HNGH!
!
MOMO! MOMO, ARE YOU OKAY?
ZZZ
すやぁ
GUH...
I'VE PUT THE BADGER TO SLEEP FOR A WHILE.
SNORE
スピー
ALTHOUGH, IF HE STAYS OUT HERE ON THE COLD GROUND...
HE MAY NEVER WAKE UP AGAIN.
YAWN

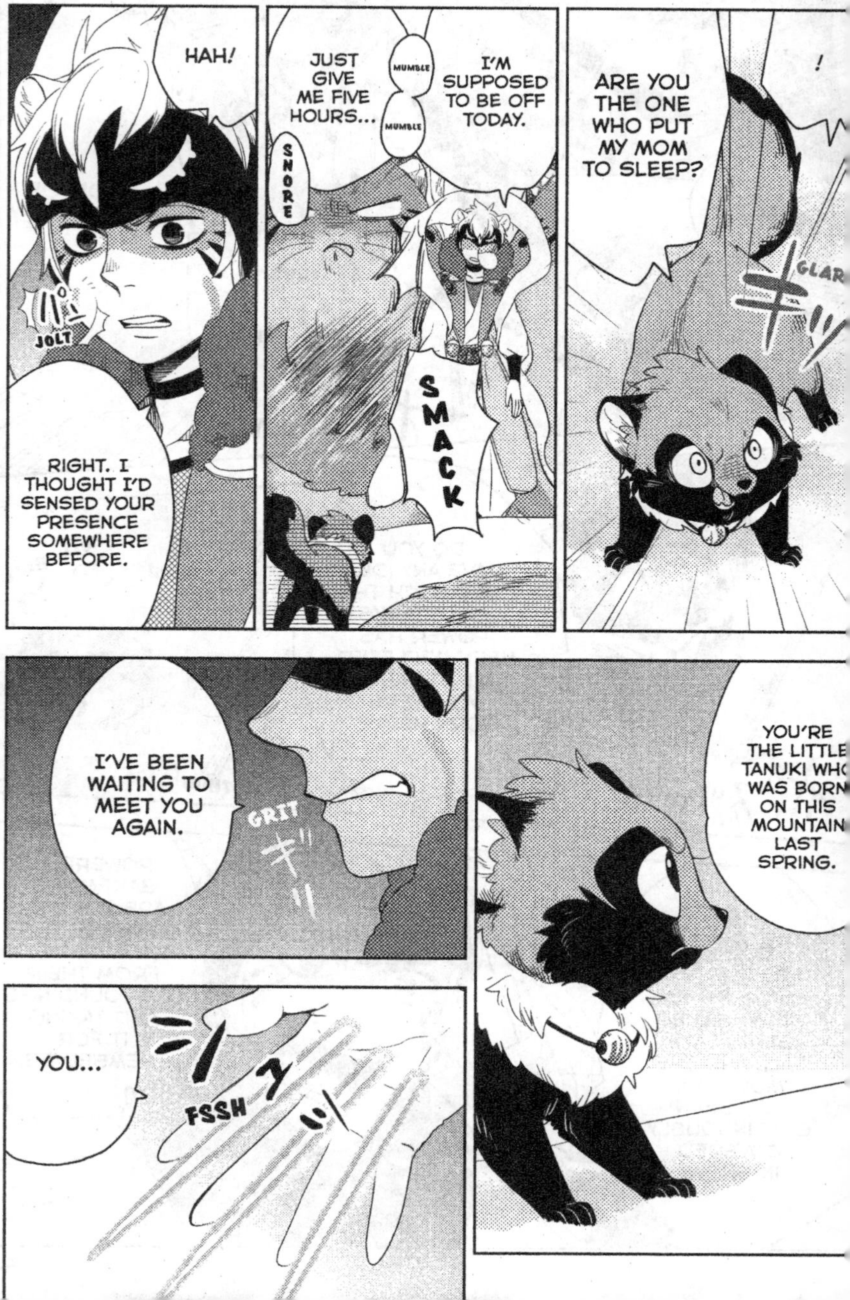
ARE YOU THE ONE WHO PUT MY MOM TO SLEEP?
!
GLAR
I'M SUPPOSED TO BE OFF TODAY.
MUMBLE
MUMBLE
JUST GIVE ME FIVE HOURS...
SNORE
SMACK
HAH!
JOLT
RIGHT. I THOUGHT I'D SENSED YOUR PRESENCE SOMEWHERE BEFORE.
YOU'RE THE LITTLE TANUKI WHO WAS BORN ON THIS MOUNTAIN LAST SPRING.
I'VE BEEN WAITING TO MEET YOU AGAIN.
GRIT
YOU...
FSSH

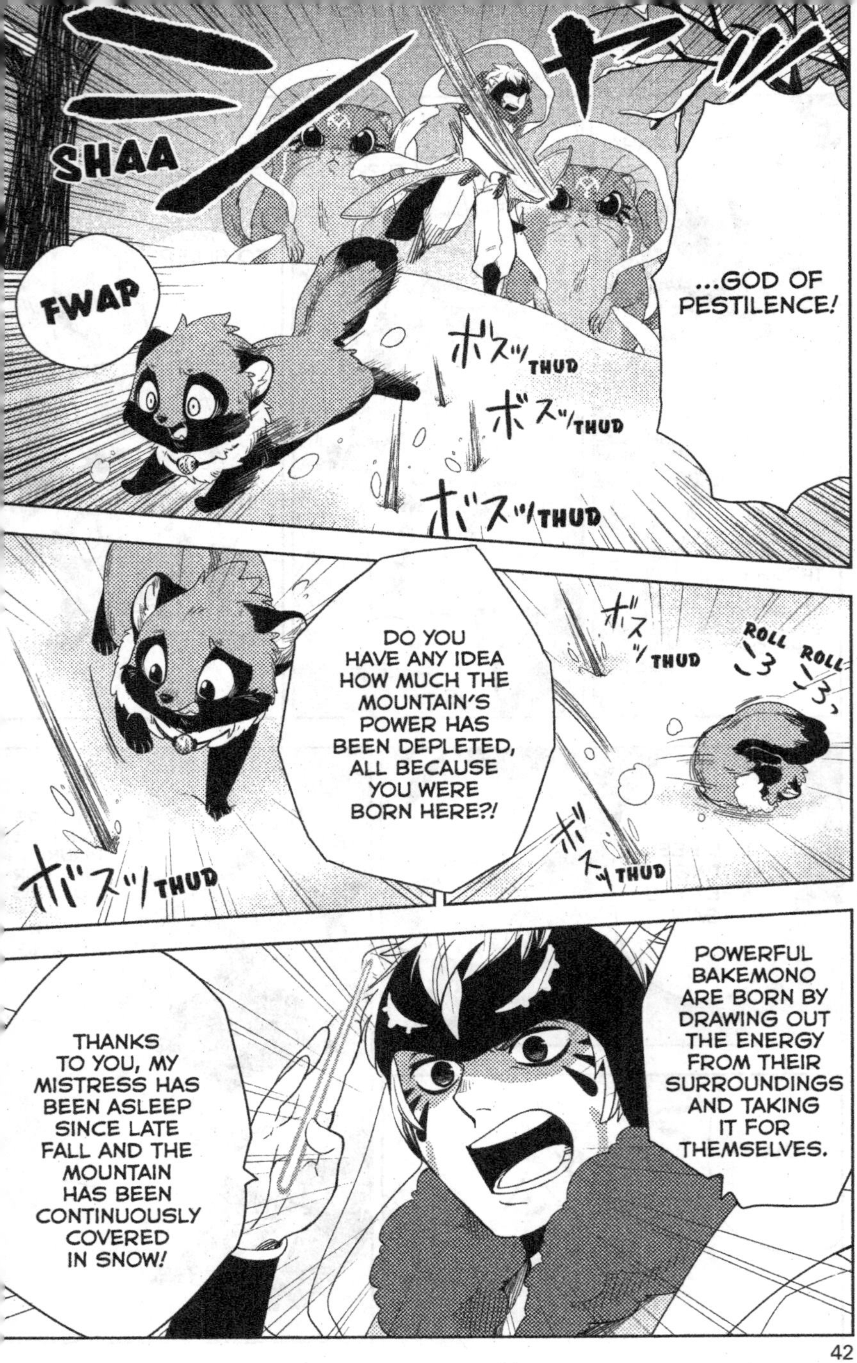
...GOD OF PESTILENCE!
SHAA
FWAP
ボスッ THUD
ボスッ THUD
ボスッ THUD
ROLL ROLL
ころ ころ
ボスッ THUD
DO YOU HAVE ANY IDEA HOW MUCH THE MOUNTAIN'S POWER HAS BEEN DEPLETED, ALL BECAUSE YOU WERE BORN HERE?!
ボスッ THUD
ボスッ THUD
POWERFUL BAKEMONO ARE BORN BY DRAWING OUT THE ENERGY FROM THEIR SURROUNDINGS AND TAKING IT FOR THEMSELVES.
THANKS TO YOU, MY MISTRESS HAS BEEN ASLEEP SINCE LATE FALL AND THE MOUNTAIN HAS BEEN CONTINUOUSLY COVERED IN SNOW!

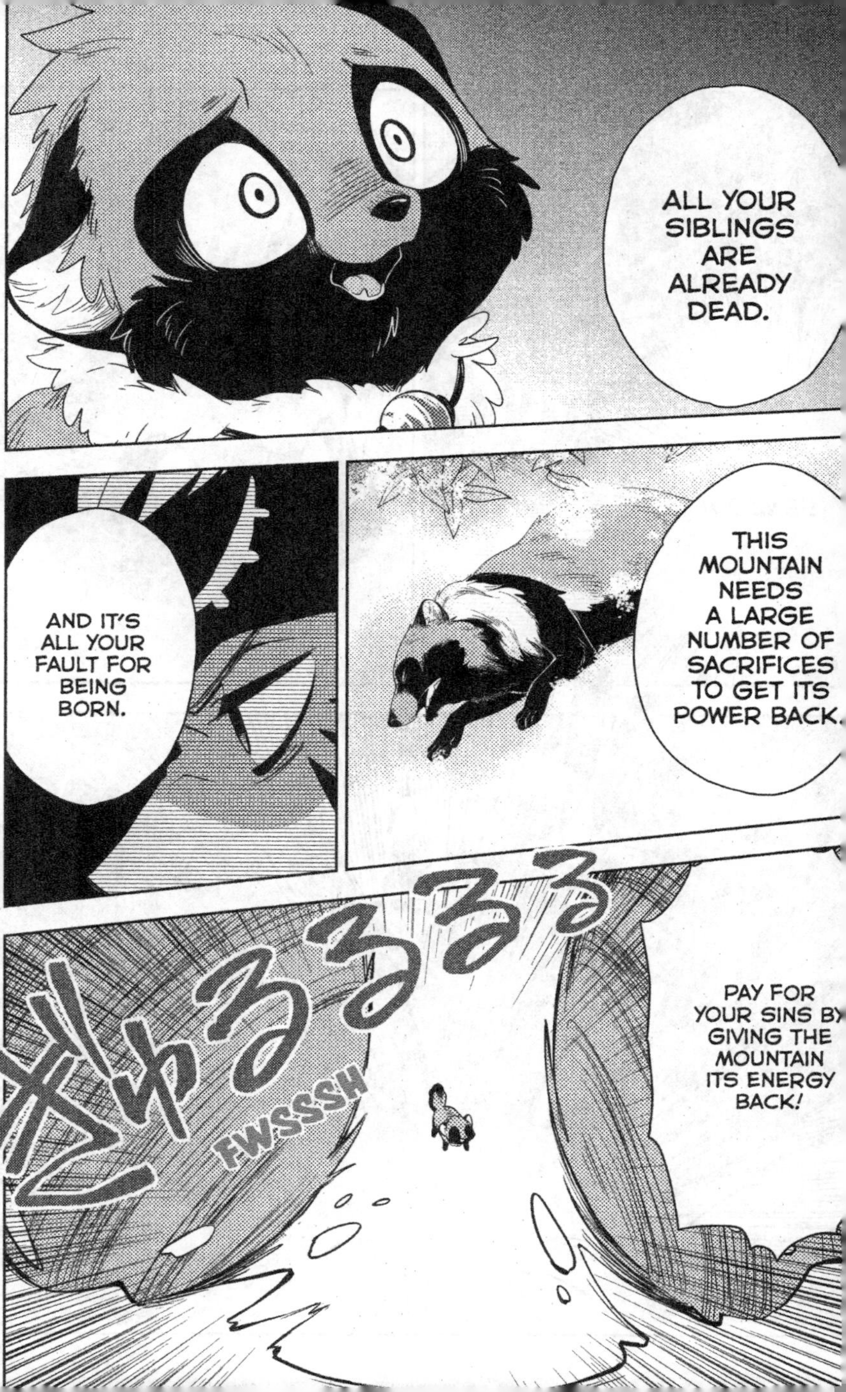
ALL YOUR SIBLINGS ARE ALREADY DEAD.
THIS MOUNTAIN NEEDS A LARGE NUMBER OF SACRIFICES TO GET ITS POWER BACK.
AND IT'S ALL YOUR FAULT FOR BEING BORN.
PAY FOR YOUR SINS BY GIVING THE MOUNTAIN ITS ENERGY BACK!
FWSSSH

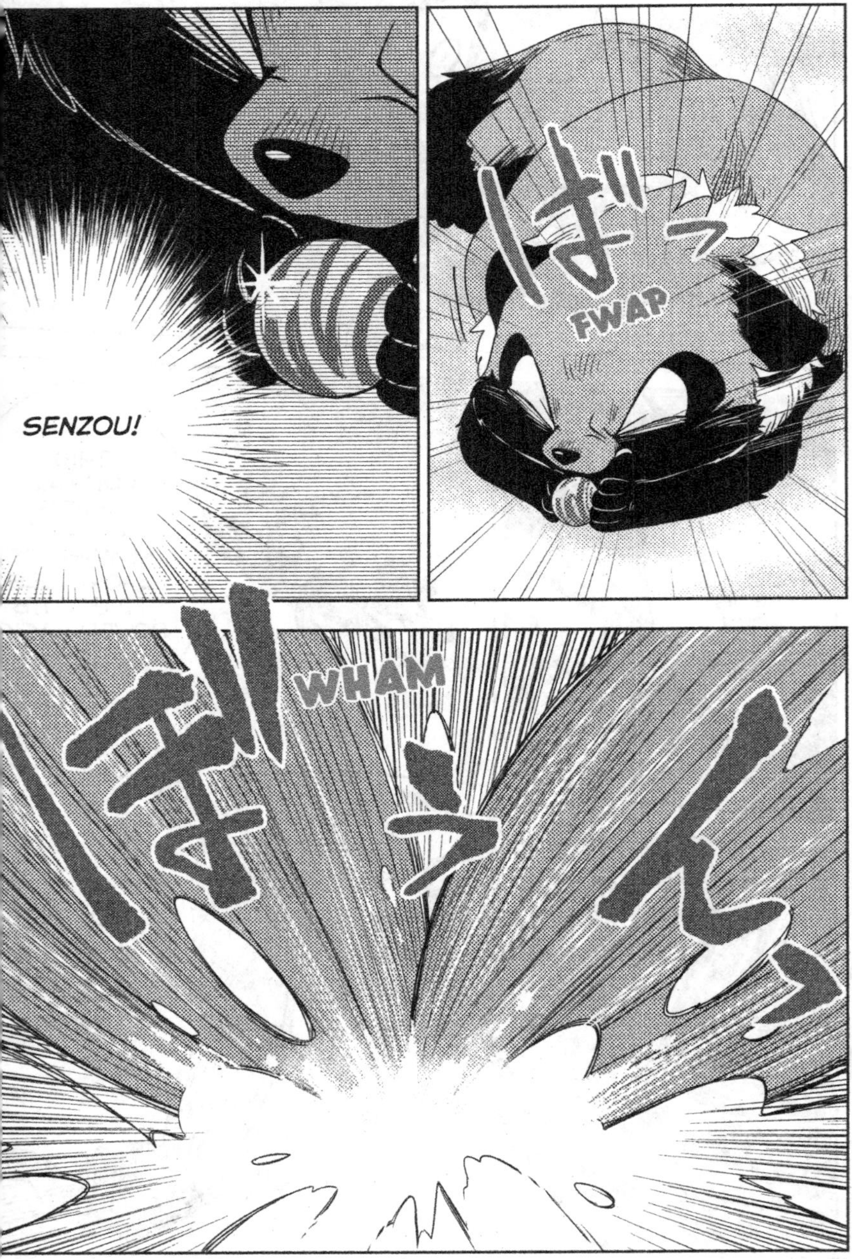
FWAP
SENZOU!
WHAM

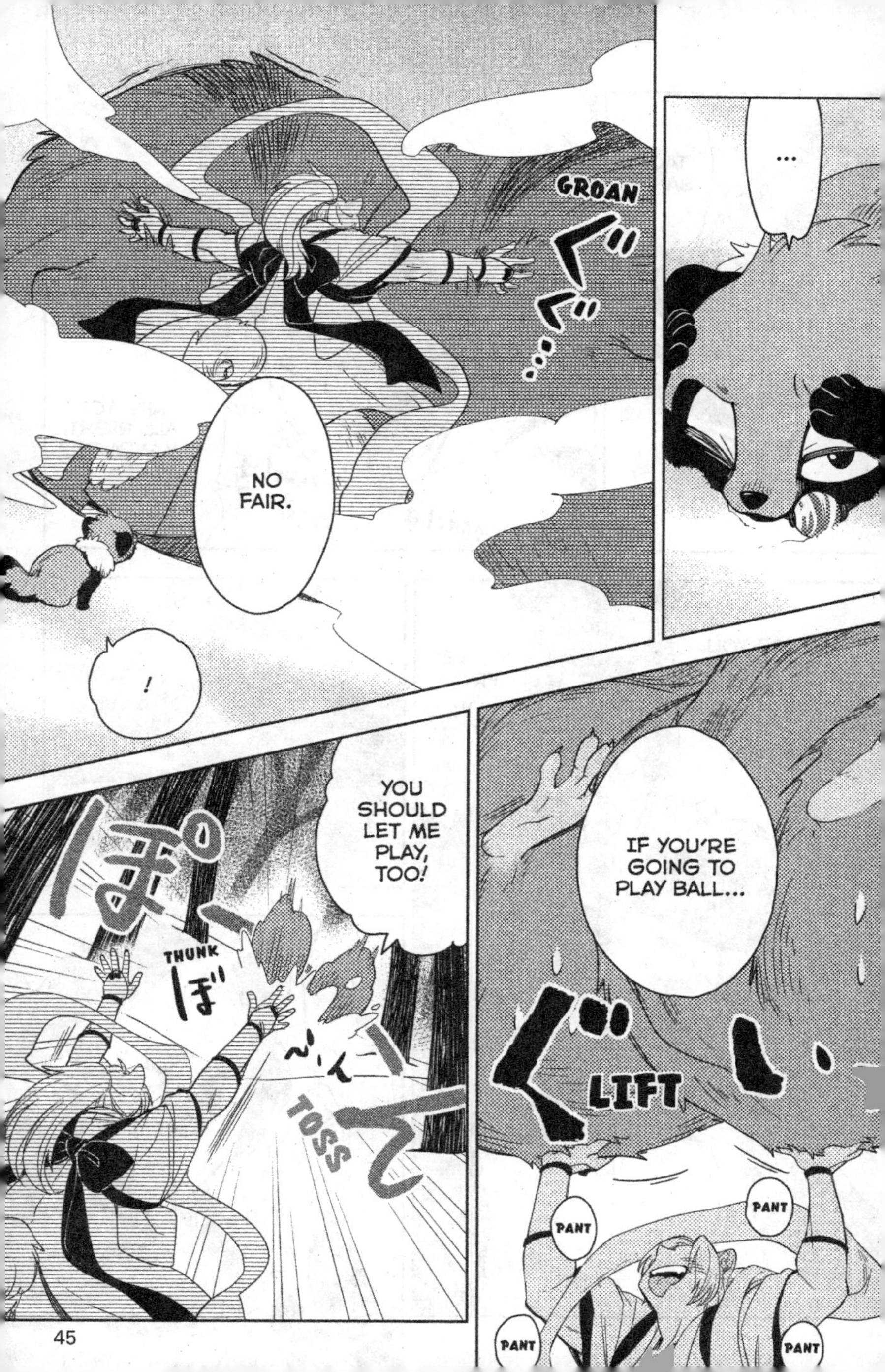
...
GROAN
NO FAIR.
!
IF YOU'RE GOING TO PLAY BALL...
LIFT
PANT
PANT
PANT
PANT
YOU SHOULD LET ME PLAY, TOO!
THUNK
TOSS

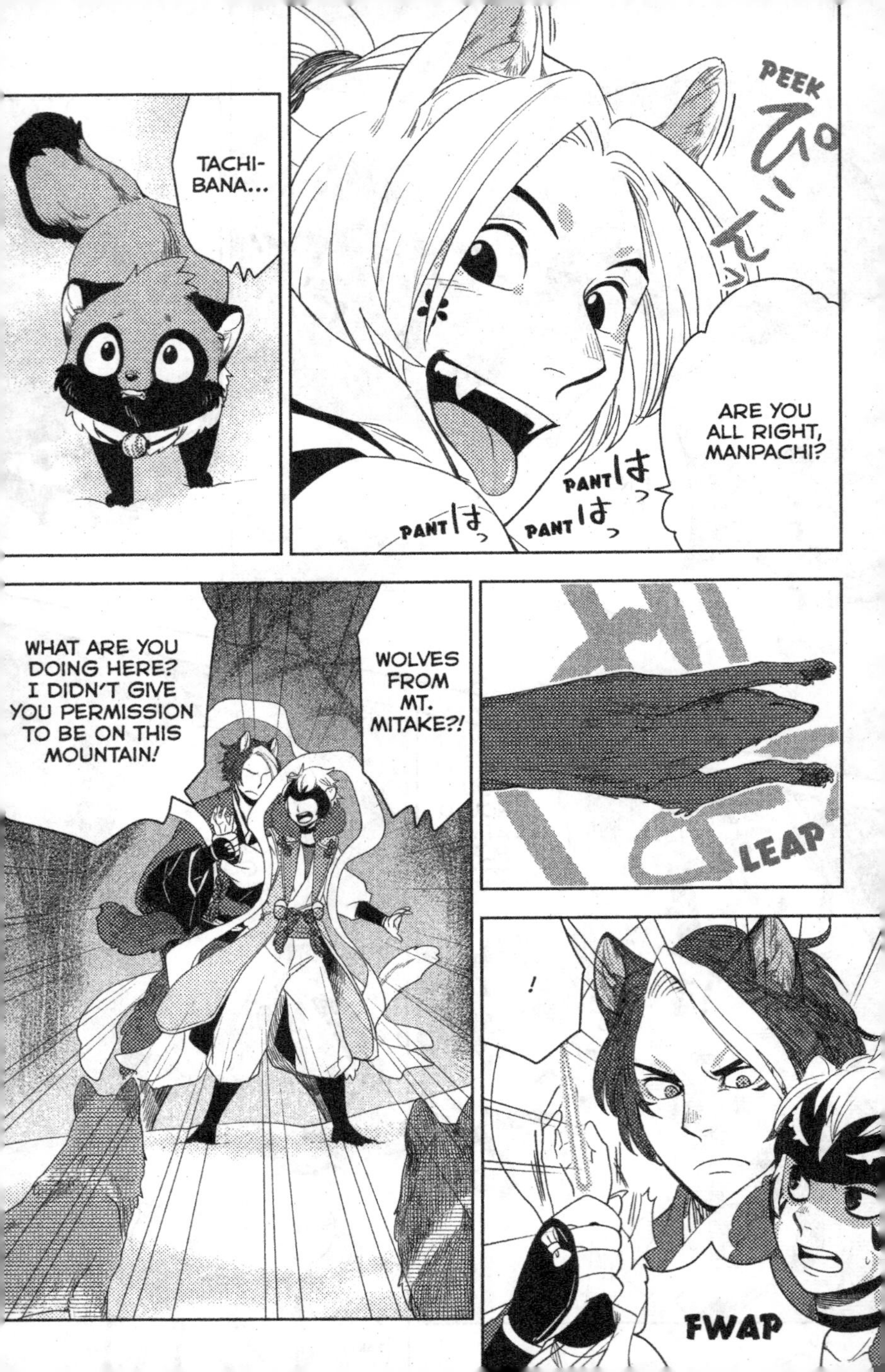
PEEK
ぴこん
ARE YOU ALL RIGHT, MANPACHI?
PANT はっ
PANT はっ
PANT はっ
TACHI-BANA...
LEAP
!
FWAP
WOLVES FROM MT. MITAKE?!
WHAT ARE YOU DOING HERE? I DIDN'T GIVE YOU PERMISSION TO BE ON THIS MOUNTAIN!

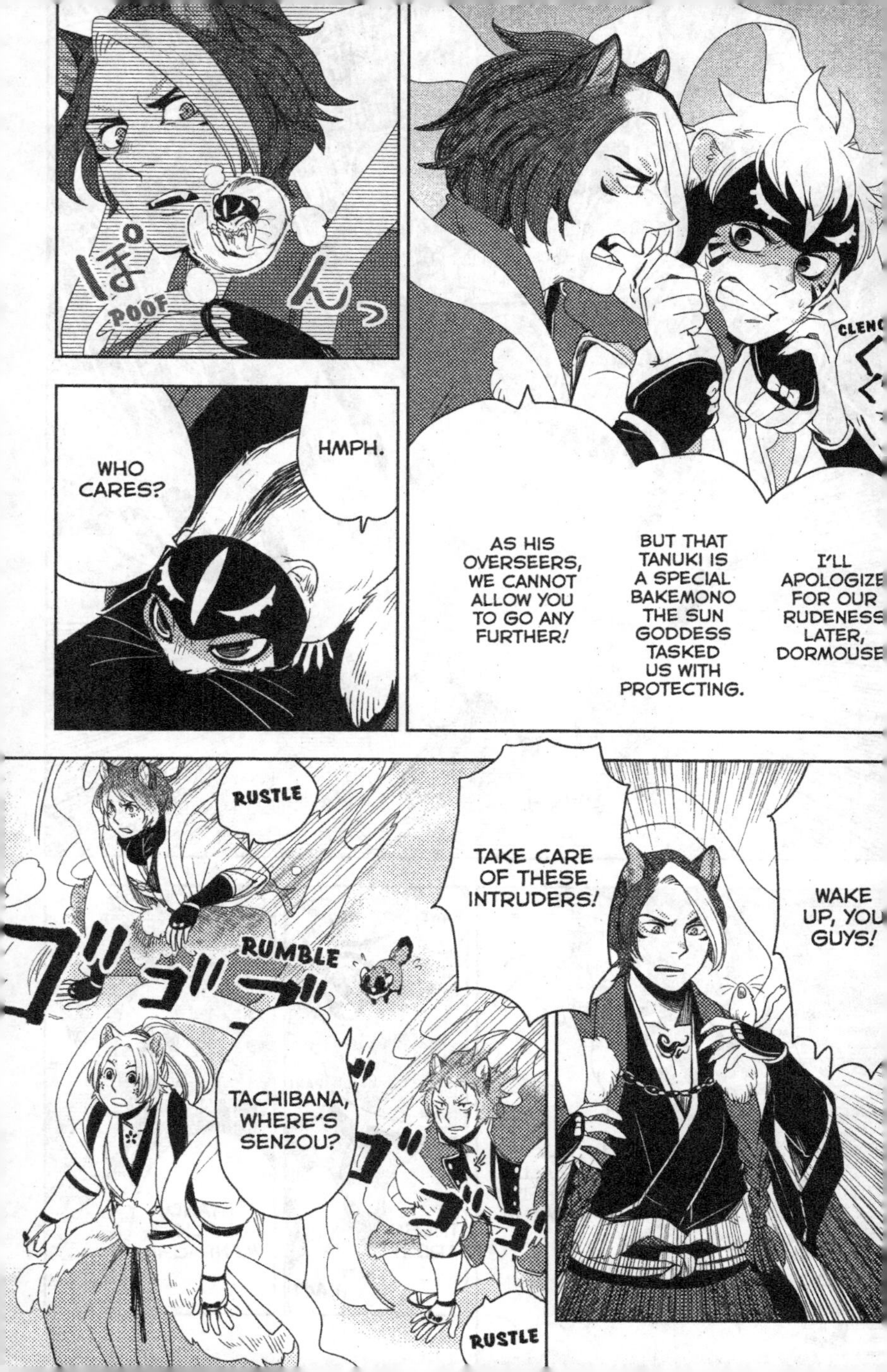
CLENC
I'LL APOLOGIZE FOR OUR RUDENESS LATER, DORMOUSE
BUT THAT TANUKI IS A SPECIAL BAKEMONO THE SUN GODDESS TASKED US WITH PROTECTING.
AS HIS OVERSEERS, WE CANNOT ALLOW YOU TO GO ANY FURTHER!
ぽんっ
POOF
HMPH.
WHO CARES?
WAKE UP, YOU GUYS!
TAKE CARE OF THESE INTRUDERS!
RUSTLE
RUMBLE
TACHIBANA, WHERE'S SENZOU?
RUSTLE

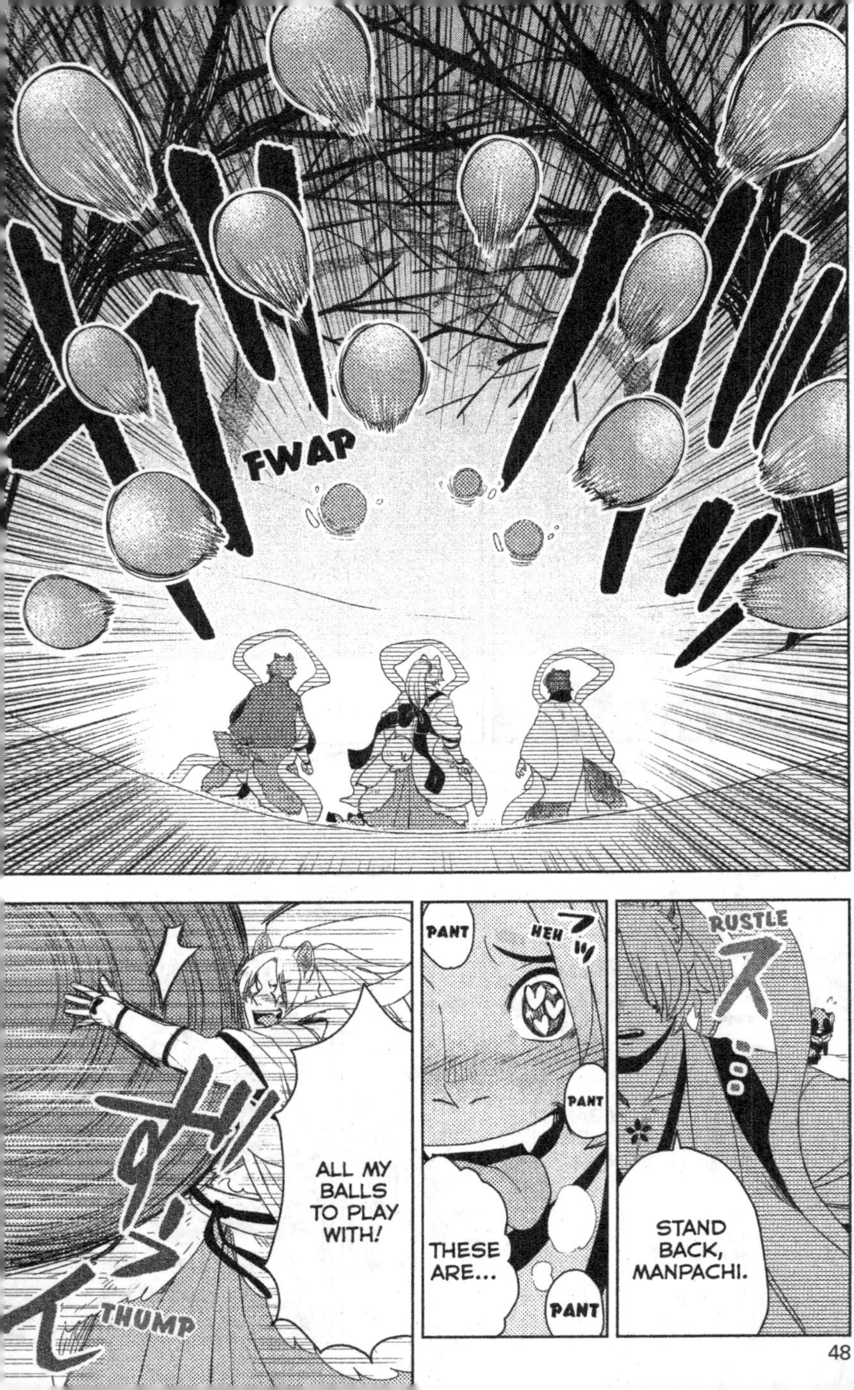
FWAP
RUSTLE
STAND BACK, MANPACHI.
HEH
PANT
PANT
PANT
THESE ARE...
ALL MY BALLS TO PLAY WITH!
THUMP

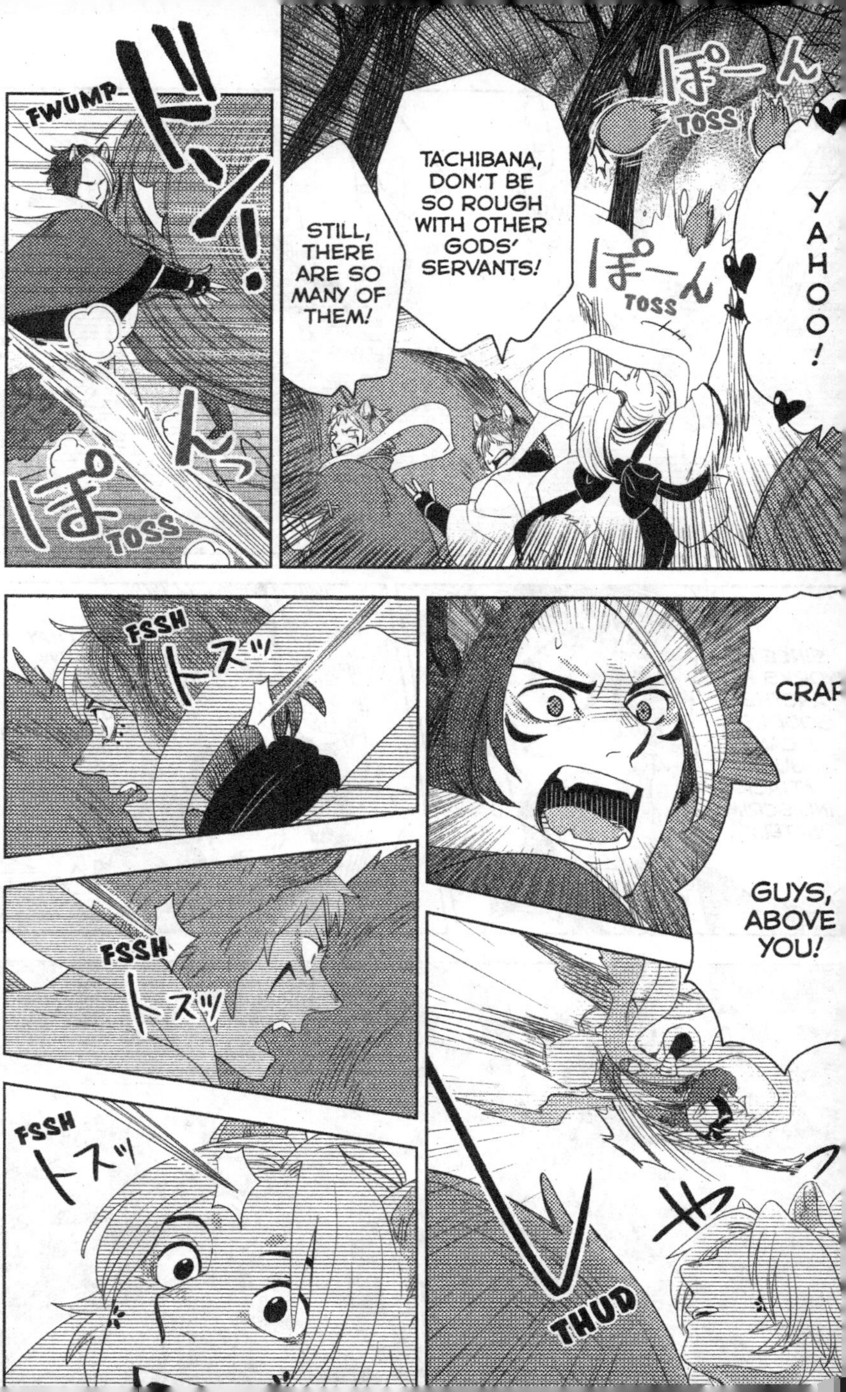
ぽーん
TOSS
YAHOO!
ぽーん
TOSS
TACHIBANA, DON'T BE SO ROUGH WITH OTHER GODS' SERVANTS!
STILL, THERE ARE SO MANY OF THEM!
FWUMP
ドン!
ぽんっ
TOSS
CRAP
GUYS, ABOVE YOU!
やっ
THUD
FSSH
トスッ
FSSH
トスッ
FSSH
トスッ

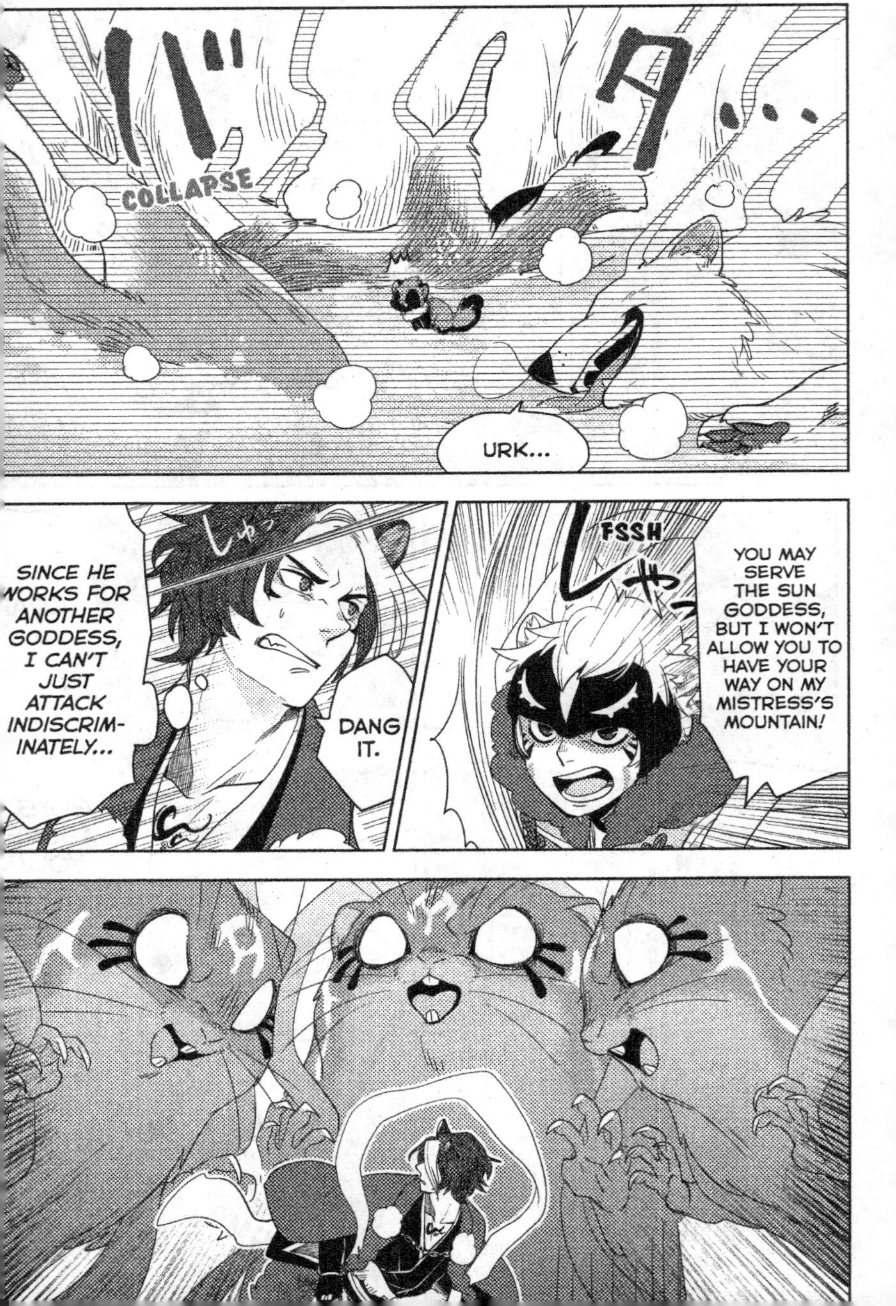
バ
タ...
COLLAPSE
URK...
FSSH
YOU MAY SERVE THE SUN GODDESS, BUT I WON'T ALLOW YOU TO HAVE YOUR WAY ON MY MISTRESS'S MOUNTAIN!
DANG IT.
SINCE HE WORKS FOR ANOTHER GODDESS, I CAN'T JUST ATTACK INDISCRIMINATELY...

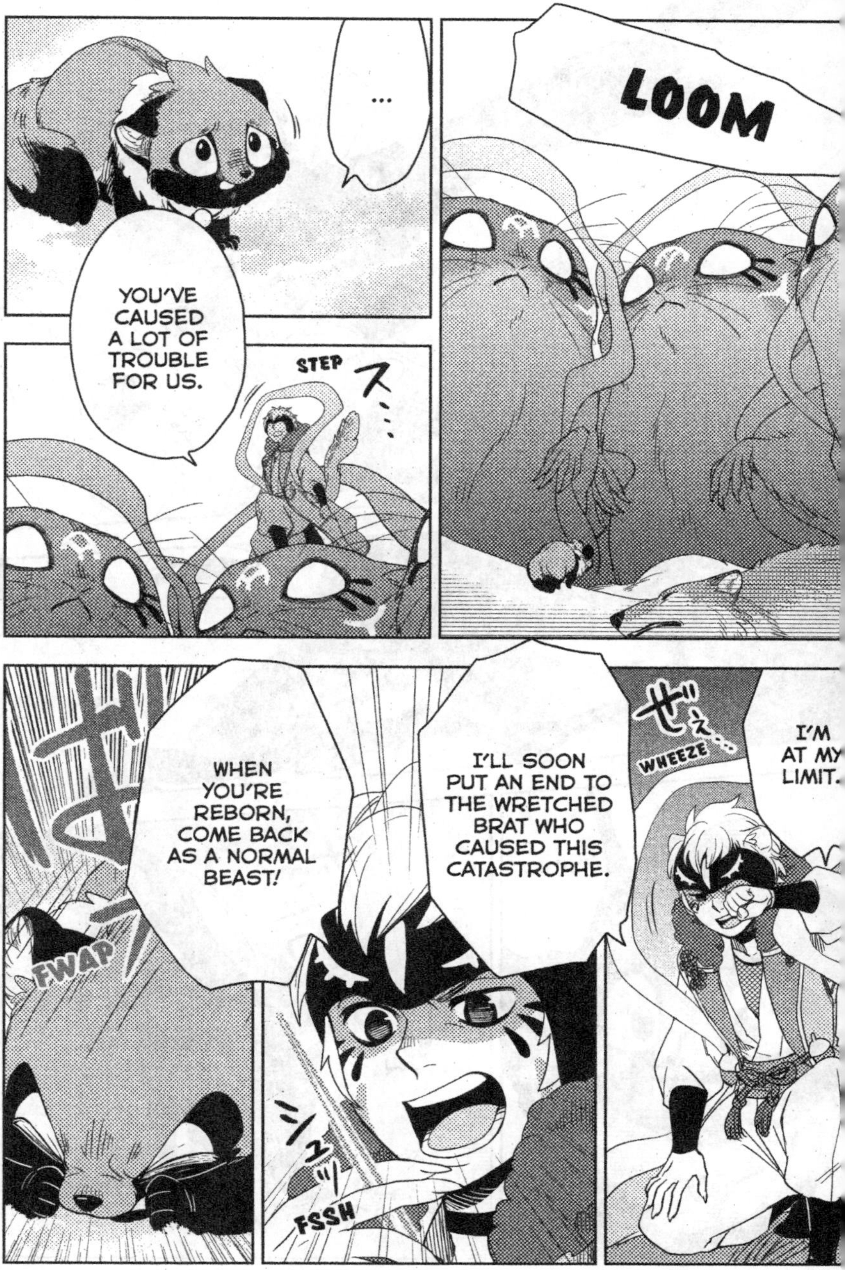
LOOM
...
YOU'VE CAUSED A LOT OF TROUBLE FOR US.
STEP
ス…
ぜぇ…
WHEEZE
I'M AT MY LIMIT.
I'LL SOON PUT AN END TO THE WRETCHED BRAT WHO CAUSED THIS CATASTROPHE.
シュッ
FSSH
WHEN YOU'RE REBORN, COME BACK AS A NORMAL BEAST!
FWAP

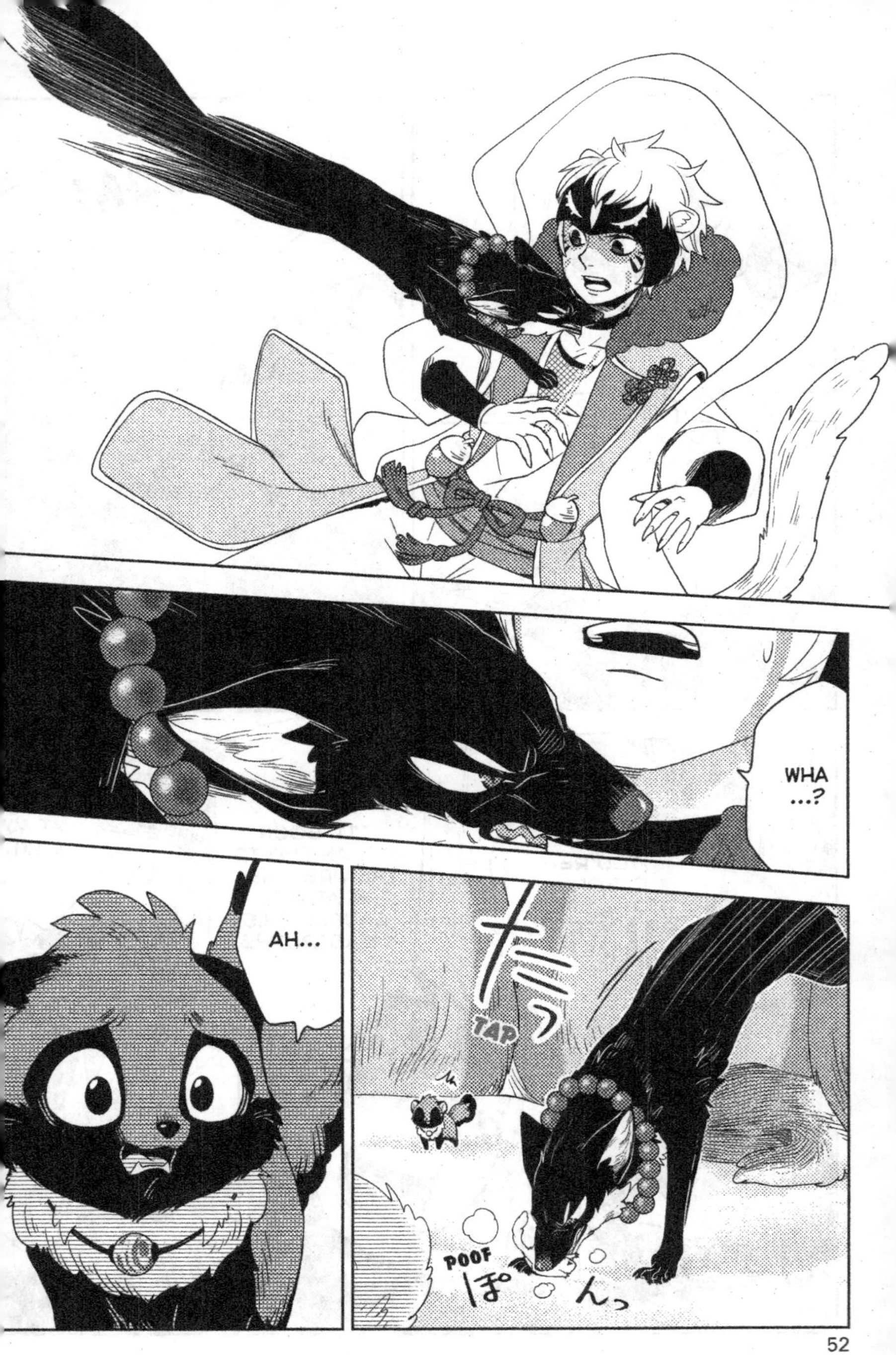
WHA ...?
TAP
POOF
ぽんっ
AH...

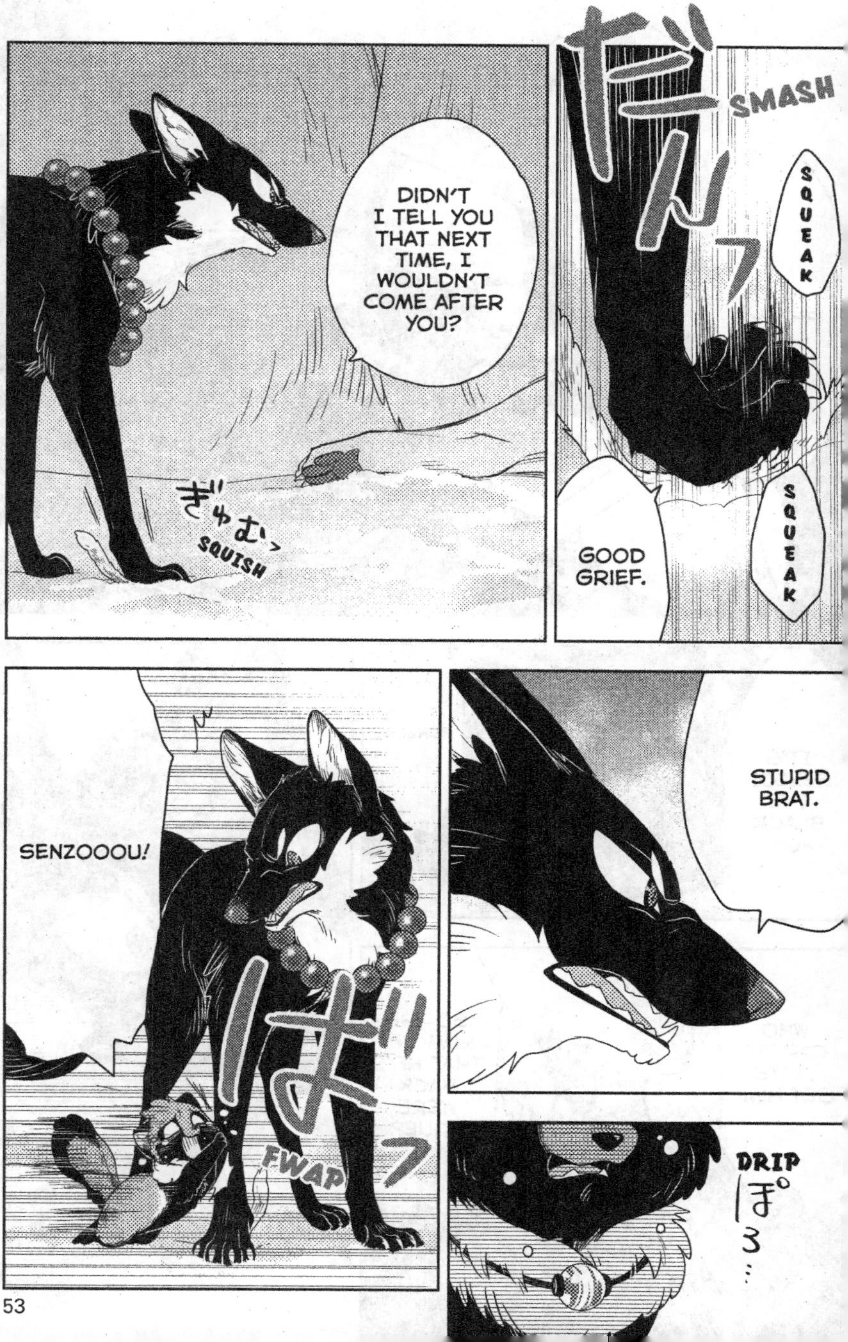
だんっ
SMASH
SQUEAK
SQUEAK
GOOD GRIEF.
DIDN'T I TELL YOU THAT NEXT TIME, I WOULDN'T COME AFTER YOU?
ぎゅむっ
SQUISH
STUPID BRAT.
DRIP
ぽろ…
SENZOOOU!
ぼっ
FWAP

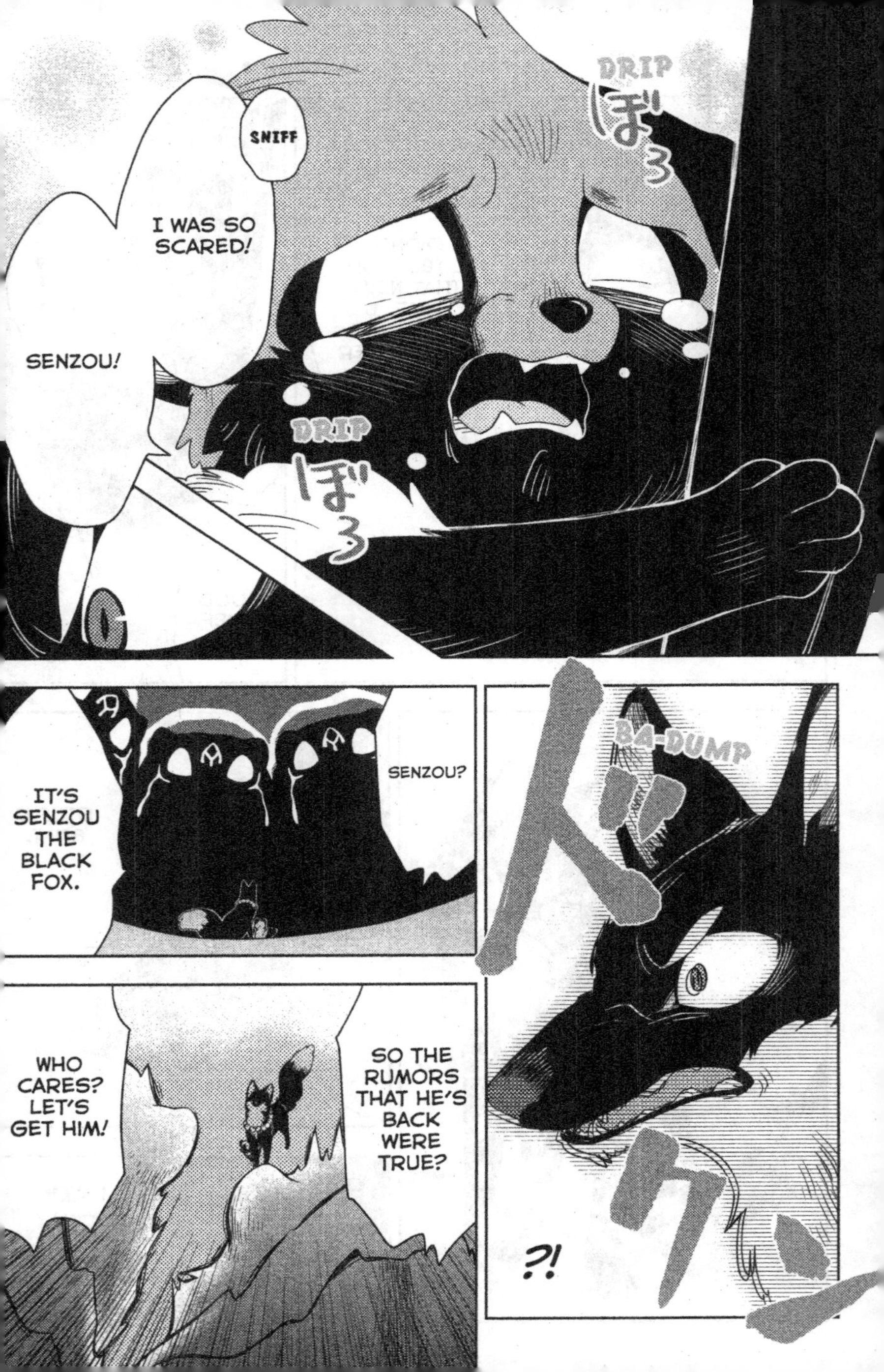
DRIP
ぼろ
SNIFF
I WAS SO SCARED!
DRIP
ぼろ
SENZOU!
BA-DUMP
ドクン
?!
SENZOU?
IT'S SENZOU THE BLACK FOX.
SO THE RUMORS THAT HE'S BACK WERE TRUE?
WHO CARES? LET'S GET HIM!

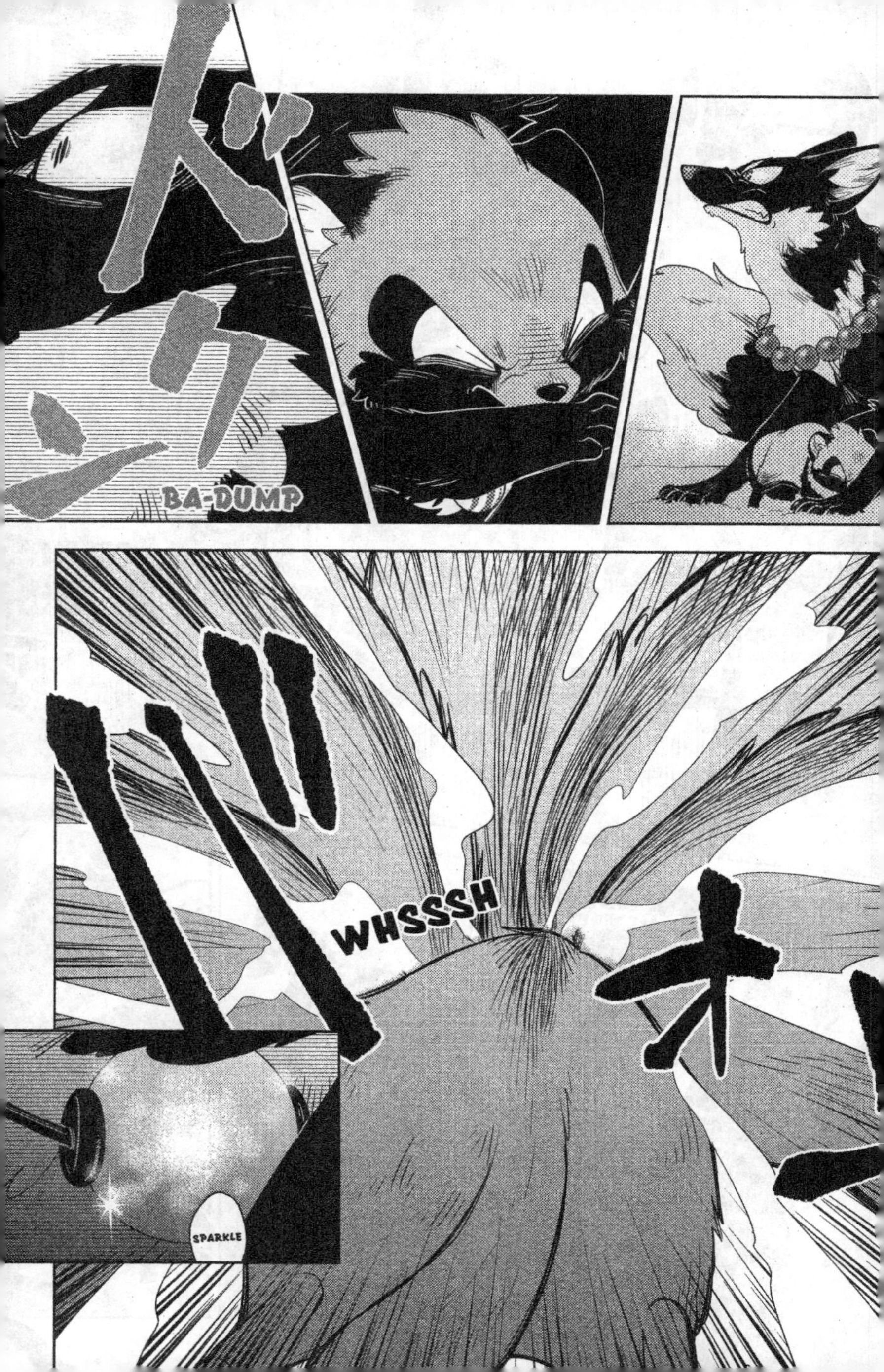
ドクン
BA-DUMP
WHSSSH
SPARKLE

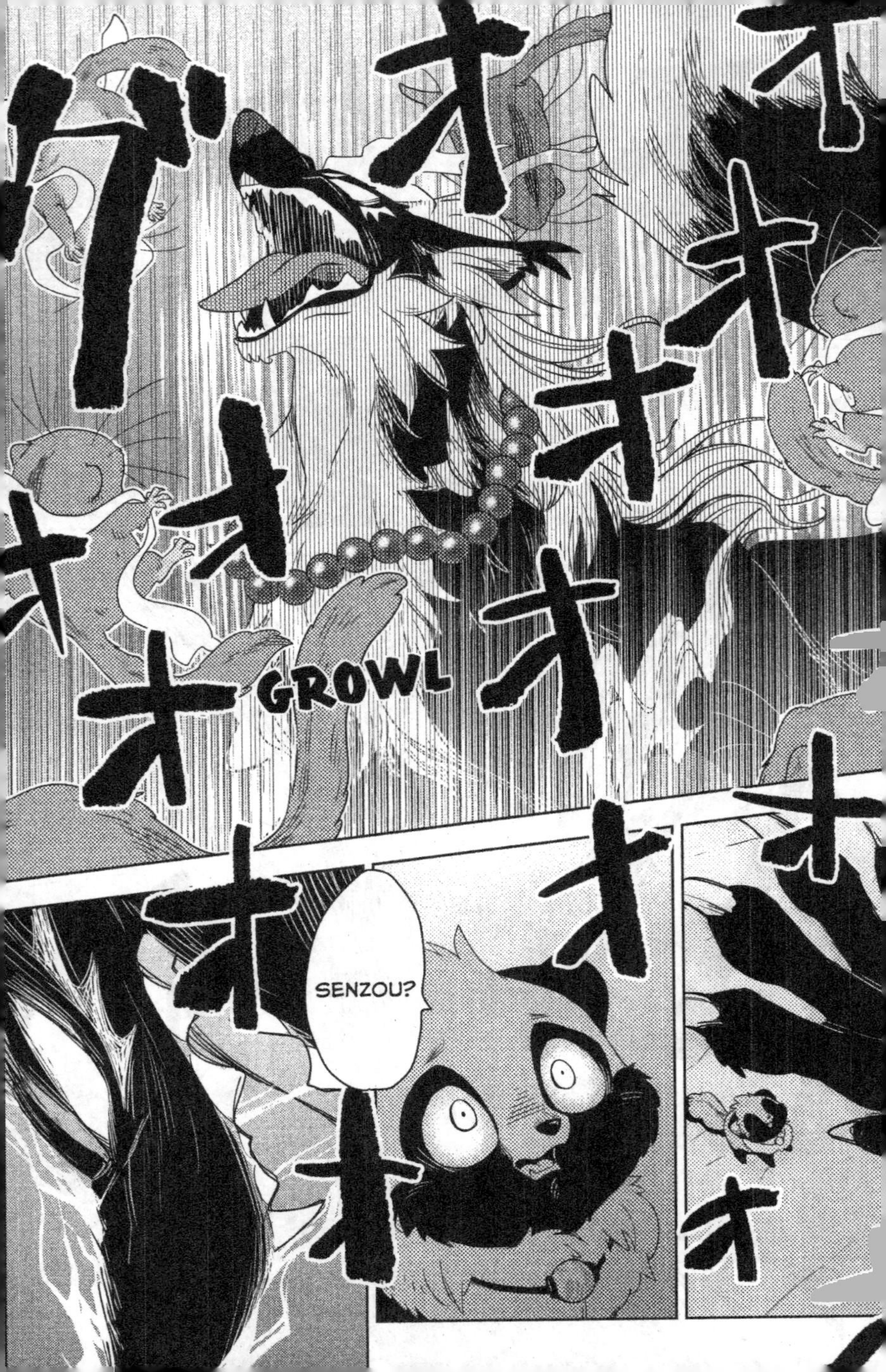
GROWL
SENZOU?

# Chapter 9

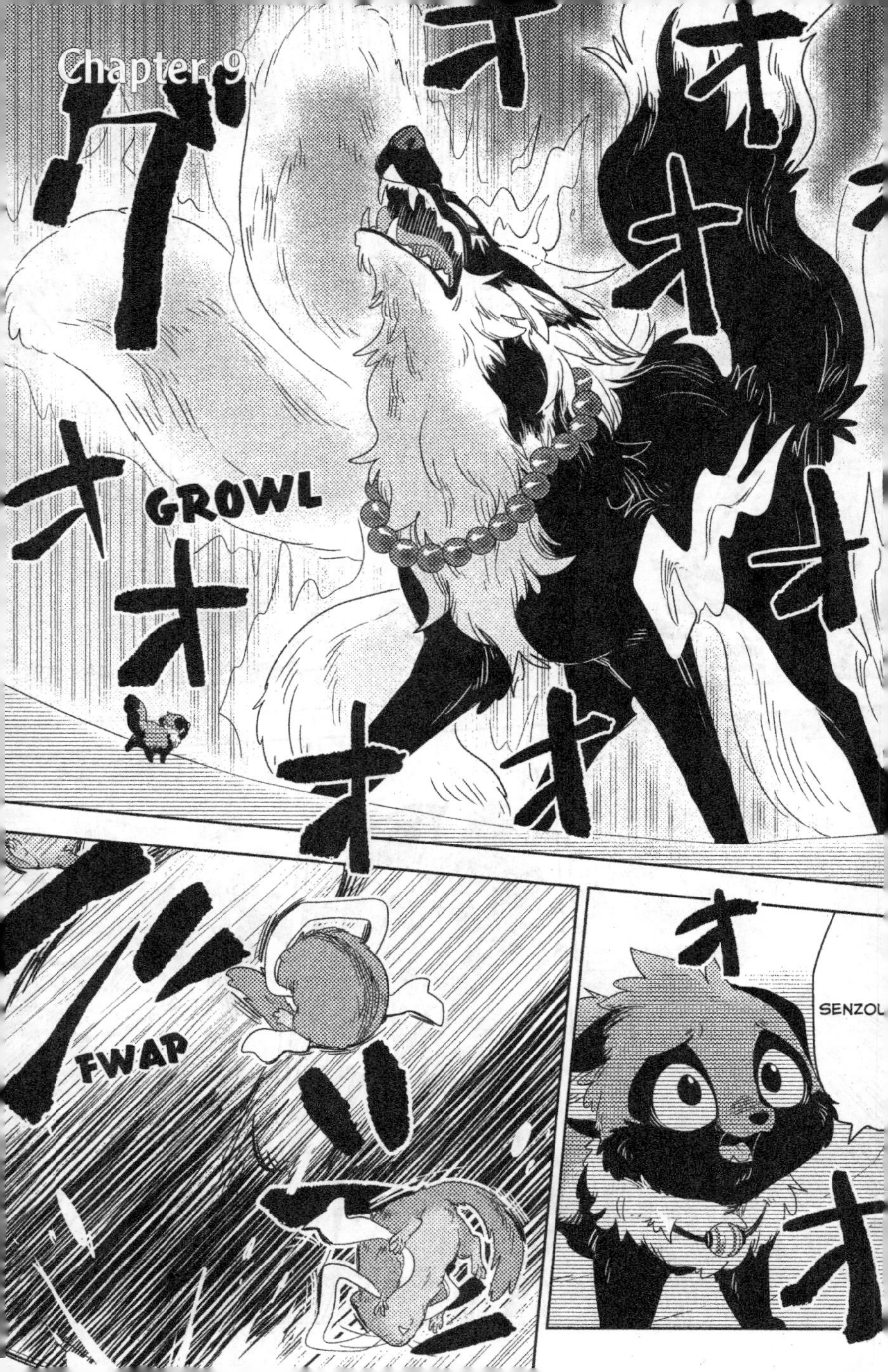
GROWL
SENZOU
FWAP

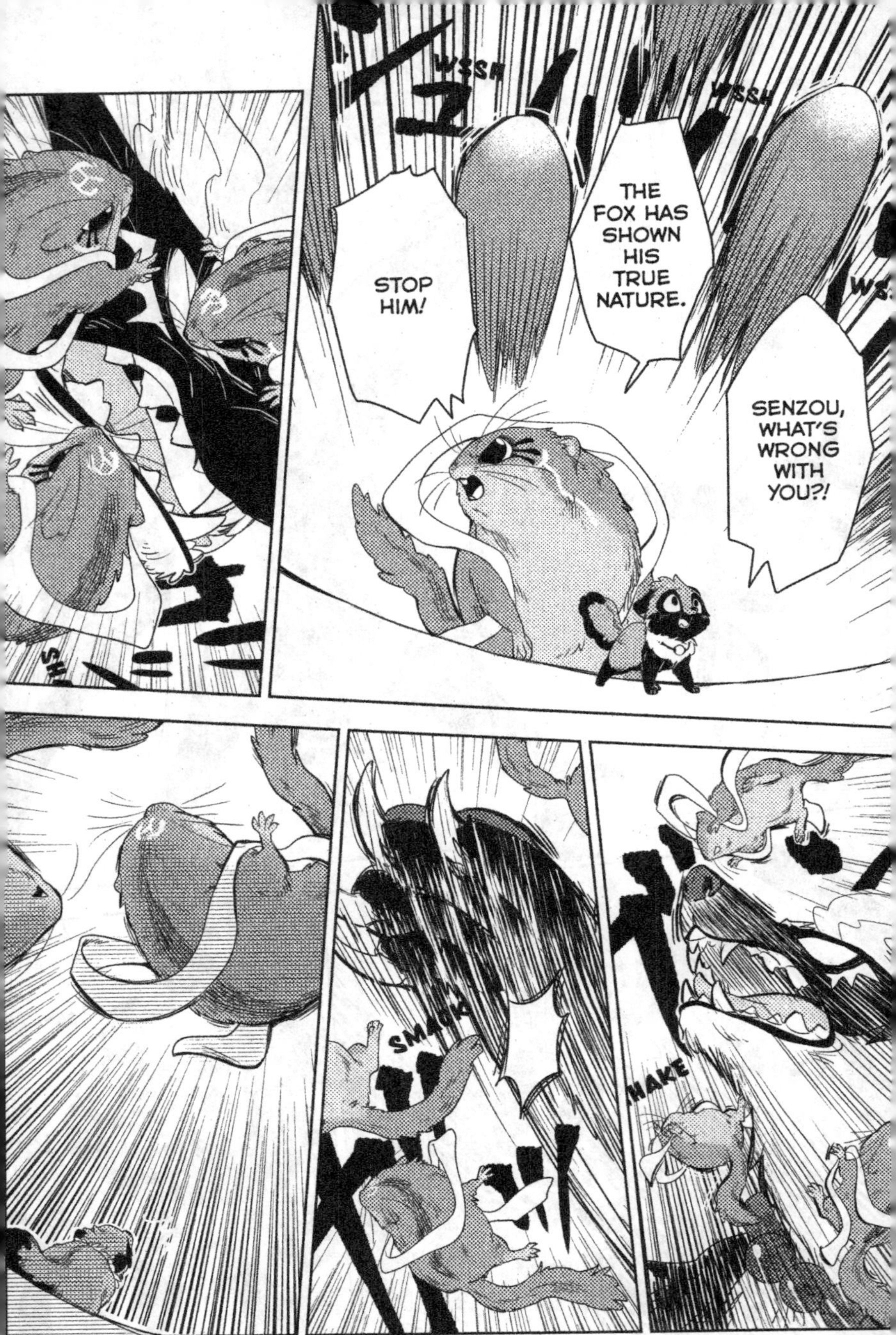
WSSH
WSSH
SENZOU, WHAT'S WRONG WITH YOU?!
THE FOX HAS SHOWN HIS TRUE NATURE.
STOP HIM!
SMACK

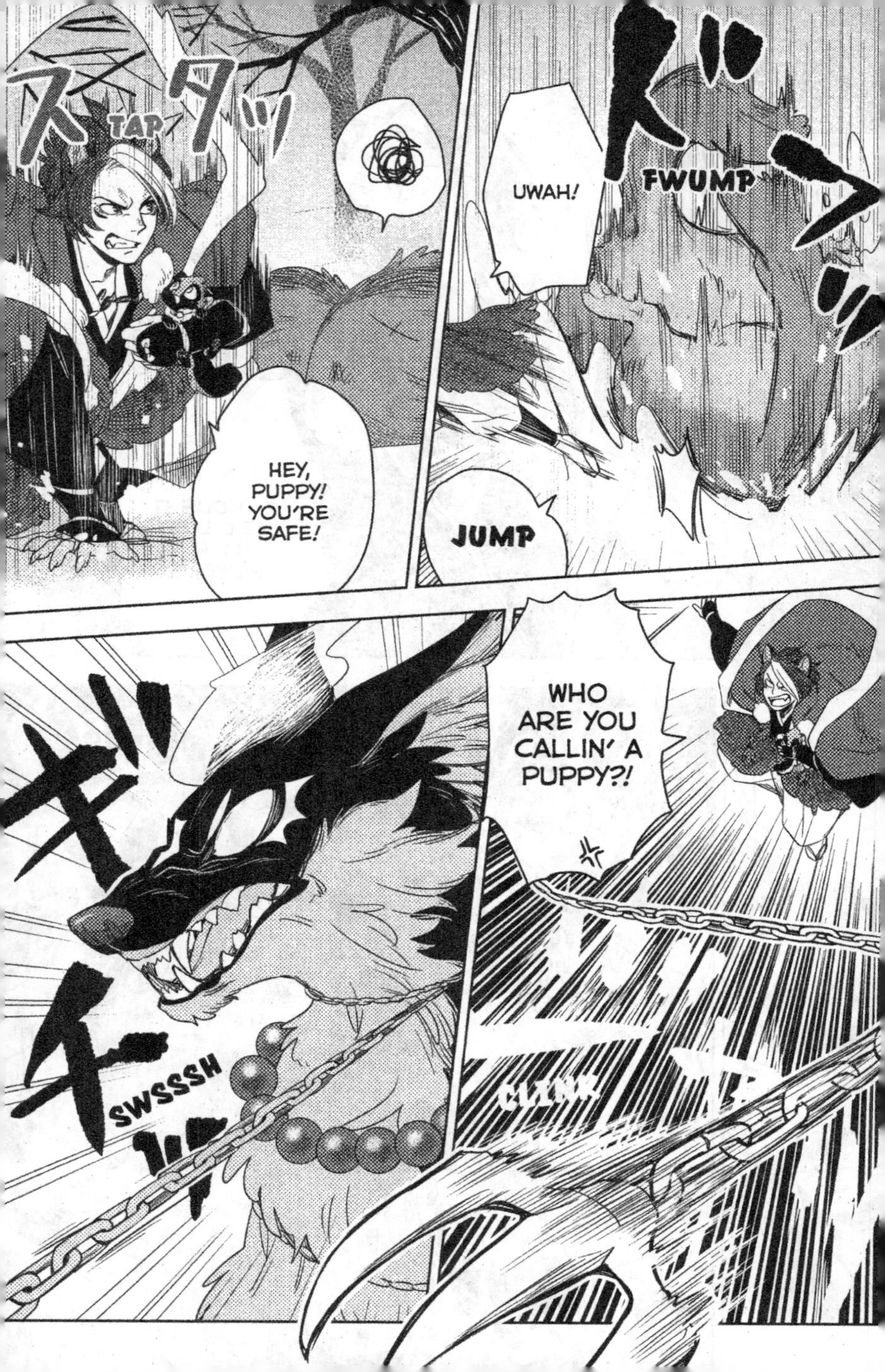
FWUMP
UWAH!
JUMP
TAP
HEY, PUPPY! YOU'RE SAFE!
WHO ARE YOU CALLIN' A PUPPY?!
CLINK
SWSSSH

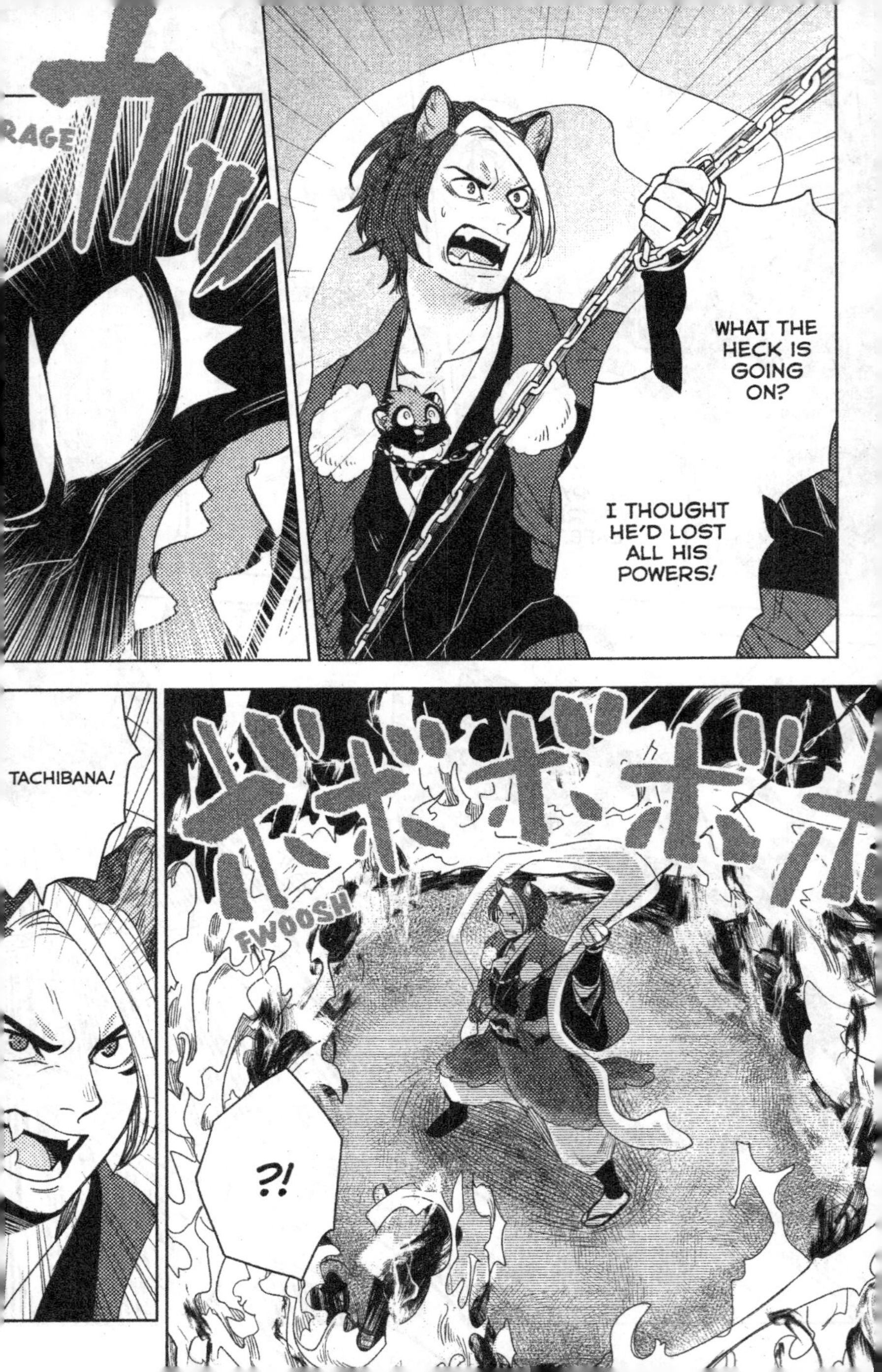
WHAT THE HECK IS GOING ON?
I THOUGHT HE'D LOST ALL HIS POWERS!
RAGE
FWOOSH
?!
TACHIBANA!

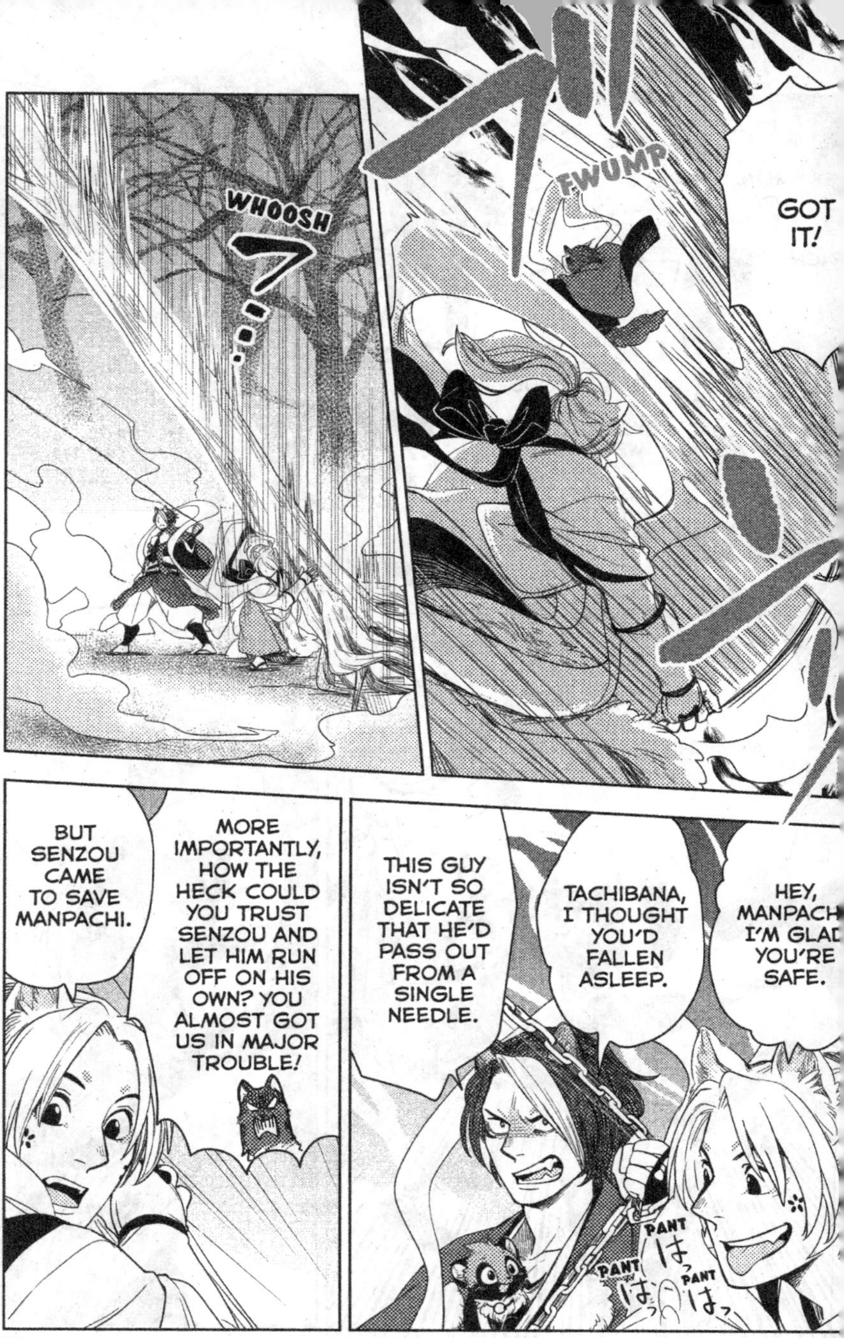
GOT IT!
FWUMP
WHOOSH
HEY, MANPACH I'M GLAD YOU'RE SAFE.
TACHIBANA, I THOUGHT YOU'D FALLEN ASLEEP.
THIS GUY ISN'T SO DELICATE THAT HE'D PASS OUT FROM A SINGLE NEEDLE.
PANT
PANT
PANT
MORE IMPORTANTLY, HOW THE HECK COULD YOU TRUST SENZOU AND LET HIM RUN OFF ON HIS OWN? YOU ALMOST GOT US IN MAJOR TROUBLE!
BUT SENZOU CAME TO SAVE MANPACHI.

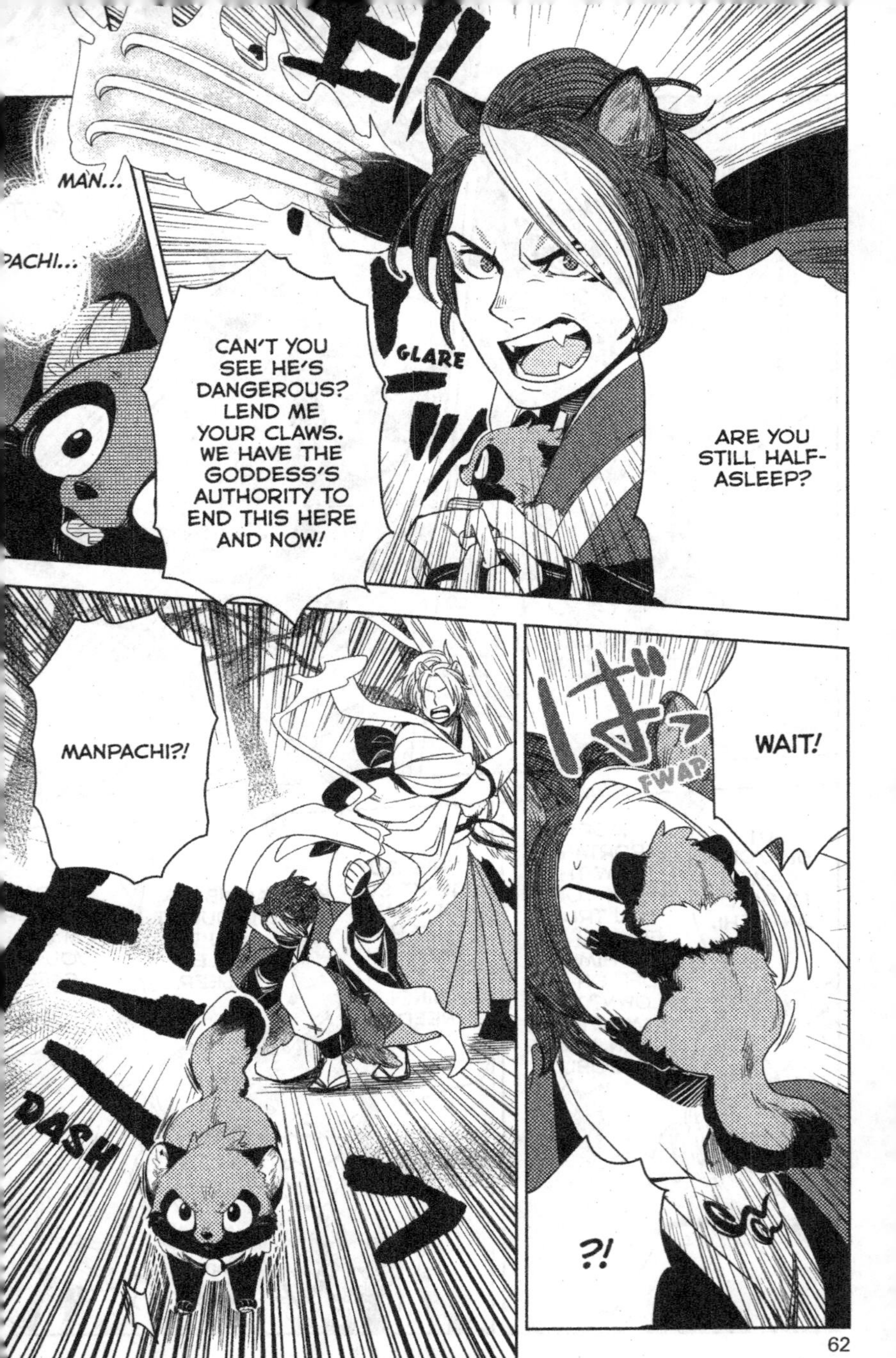
ARE YOU STILL HALF-ASLEEP?
CAN'T YOU SEE HE'S DANGEROUS? LEND ME YOUR CLAWS. WE HAVE THE GODDESS'S AUTHORITY TO END THIS HERE AND NOW!
GLARE
MAN...
PACHI...
WAIT!
FWAP
?!
MANPACHI?!
DASH

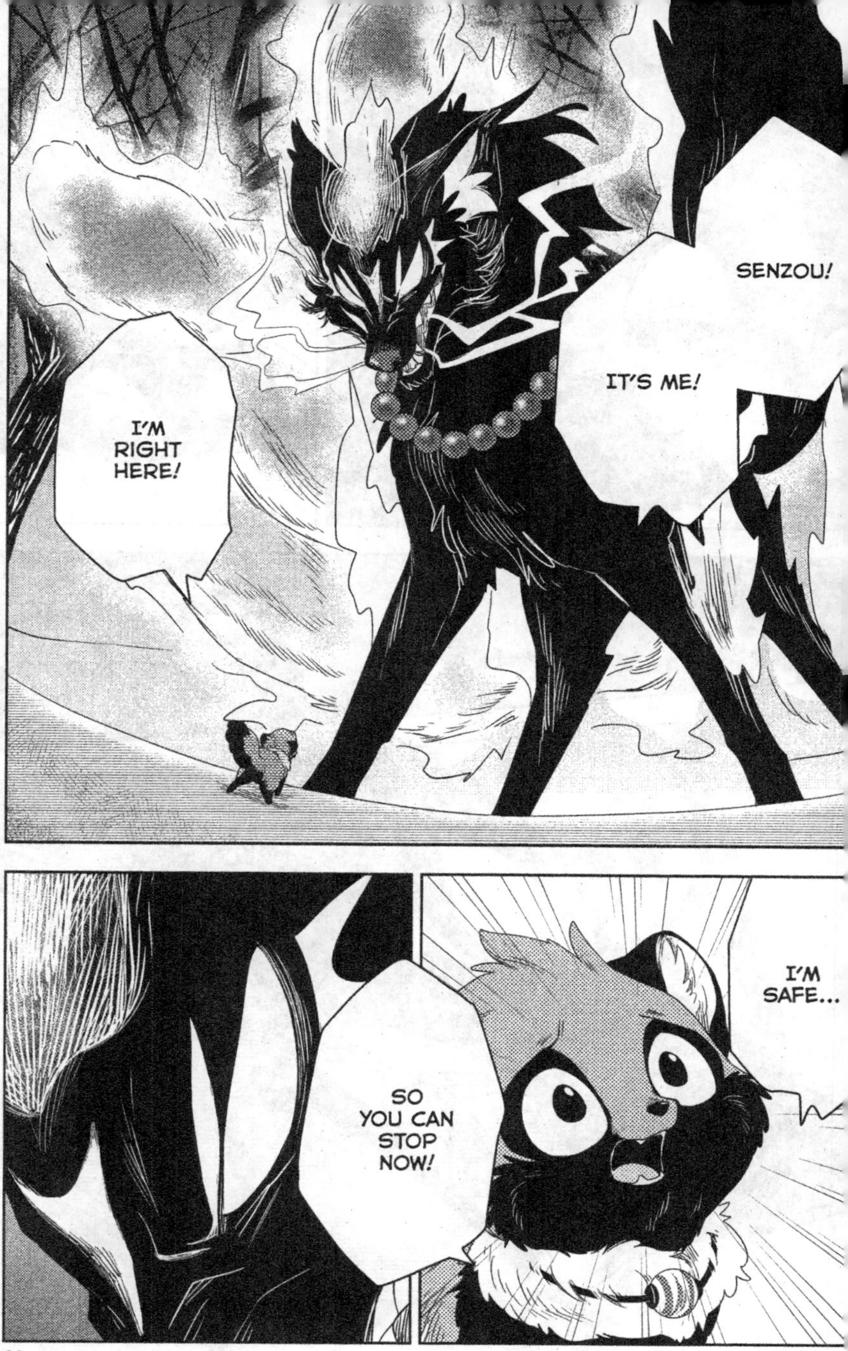
SENZOU!
IT'S ME!
I'M RIGHT HERE!
I'M SAFE...
SO YOU CAN STOP NOW!

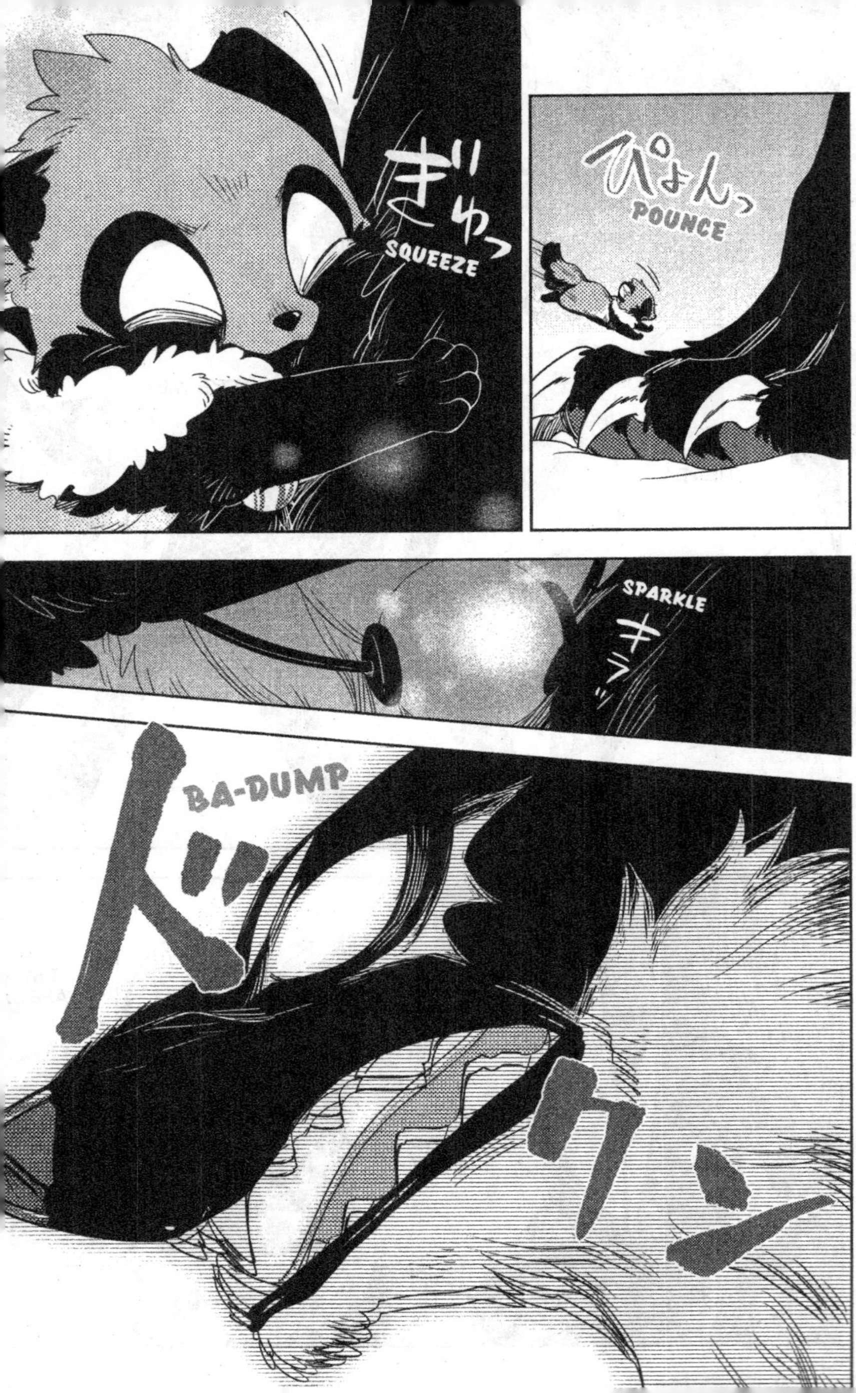
ぴょんっ
POUNCE
ぎゅっ
SQUEEZE
SPARKLE
キラッ
BA-DUMP
ドクン

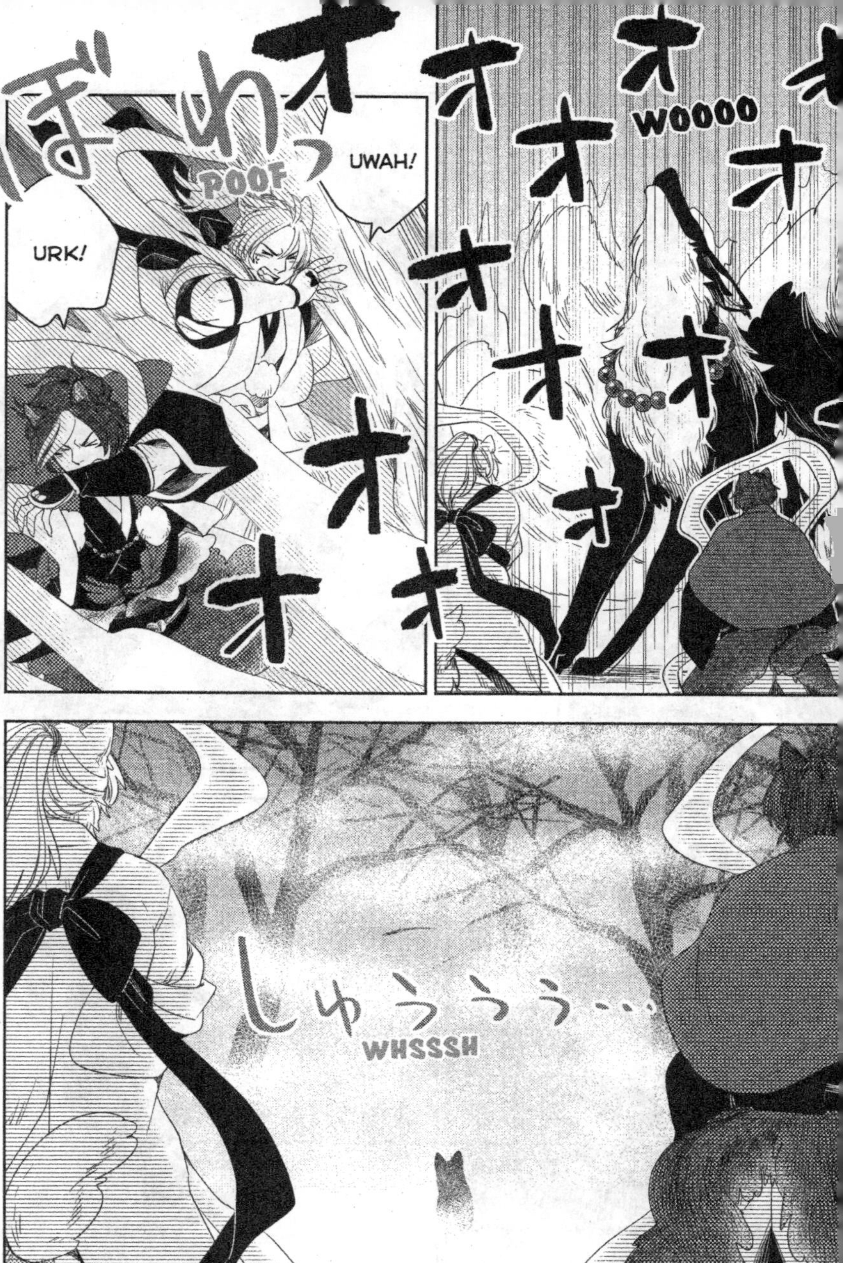
WOOOO
ぼわっ
POOF
UWAH!
URK!
しゅうううう…
WHSSSH

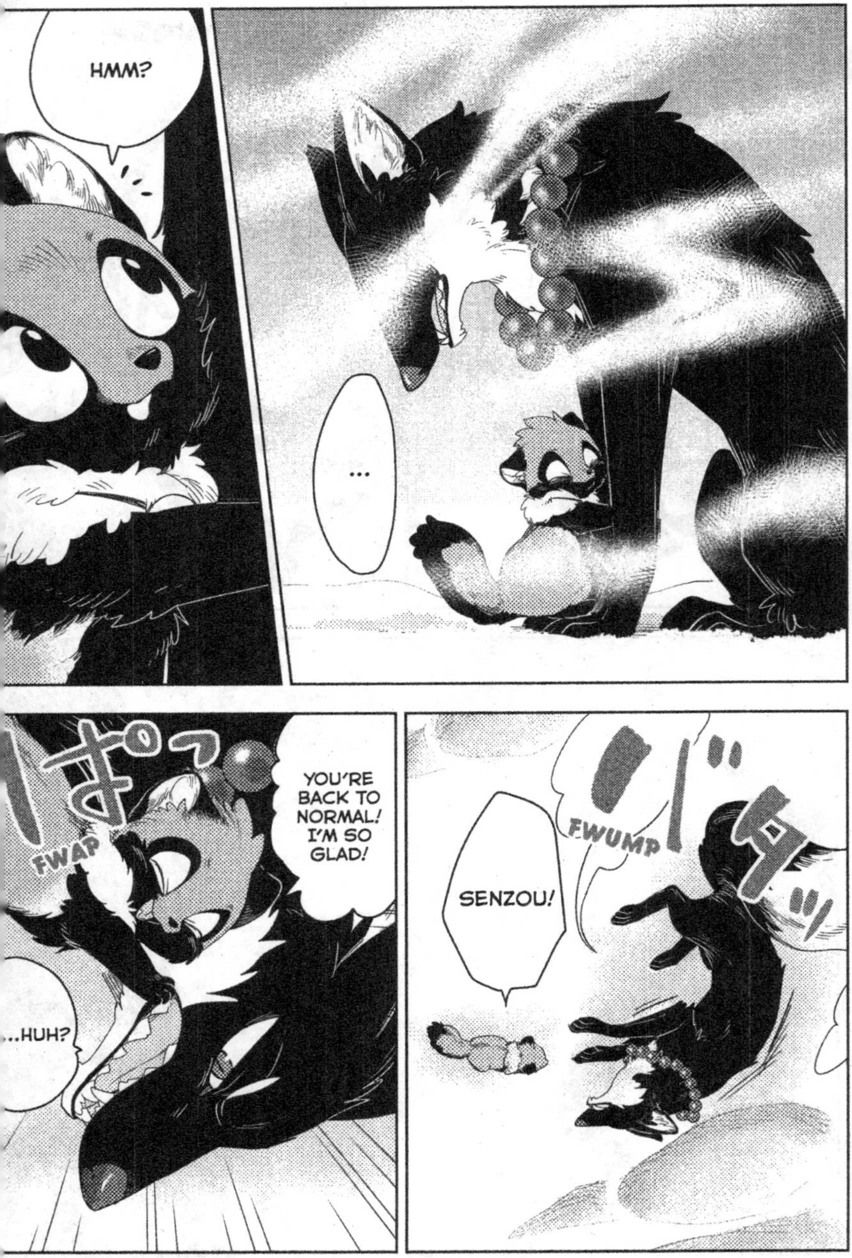
...
HMM?
バタッ
FWUMP
SENZOU!
YOU'RE BACK TO NORMAL! I'M SO GLAD!
ぱっ
FWAP
...HUH?

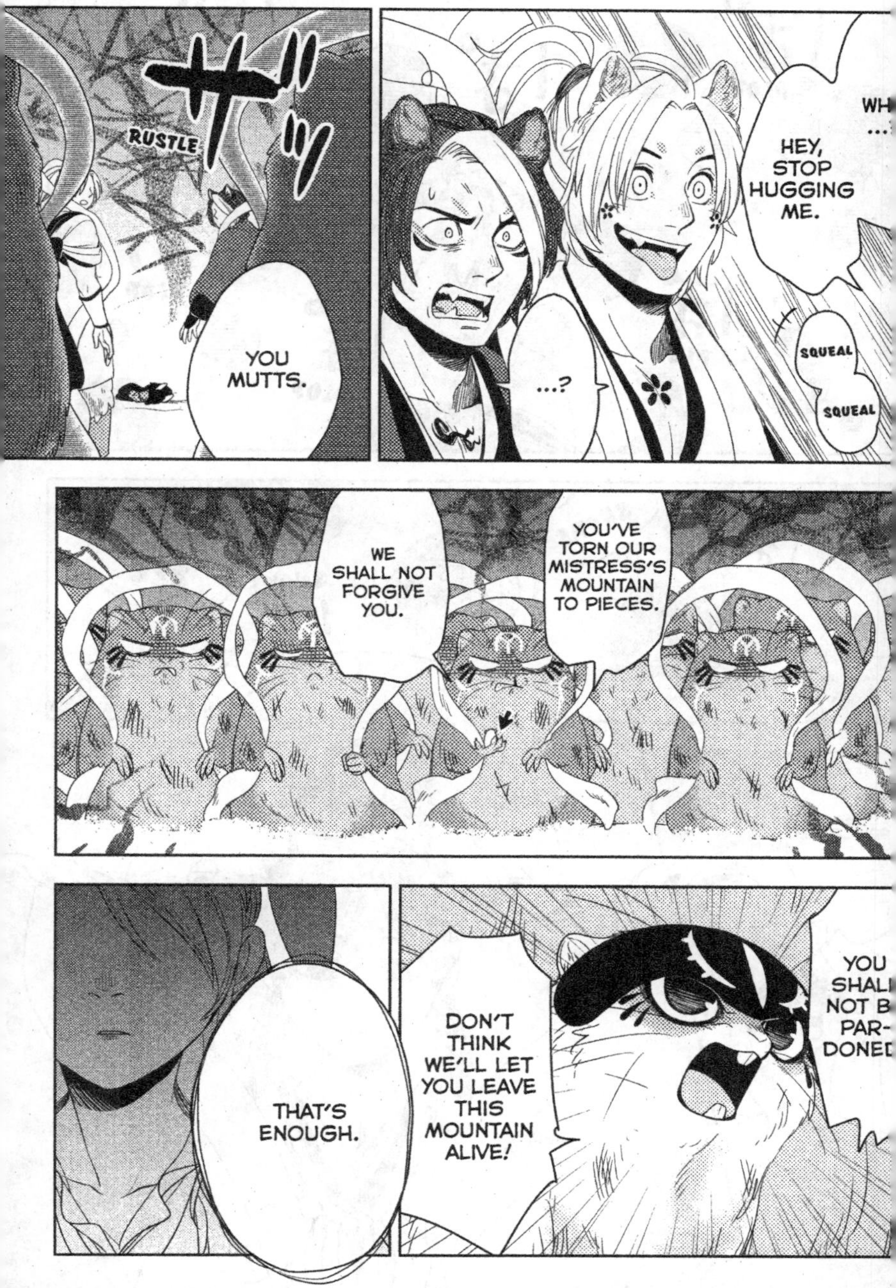
WH...
HEY, STOP HUGGING ME.
SQUEAL
SQUEAL
...?
RUSTLE
YOU MUTTS.
YOU'VE TORN OUR MISTRESS'S MOUNTAIN TO PIECES.
WE SHALL NOT FORGIVE YOU.
YOU SHAL NOT B PAR- DONED
DON'T THINK WE'LL LET YOU LEAVE THIS MOUNTAIN ALIVE!
THAT'S ENOUGH.

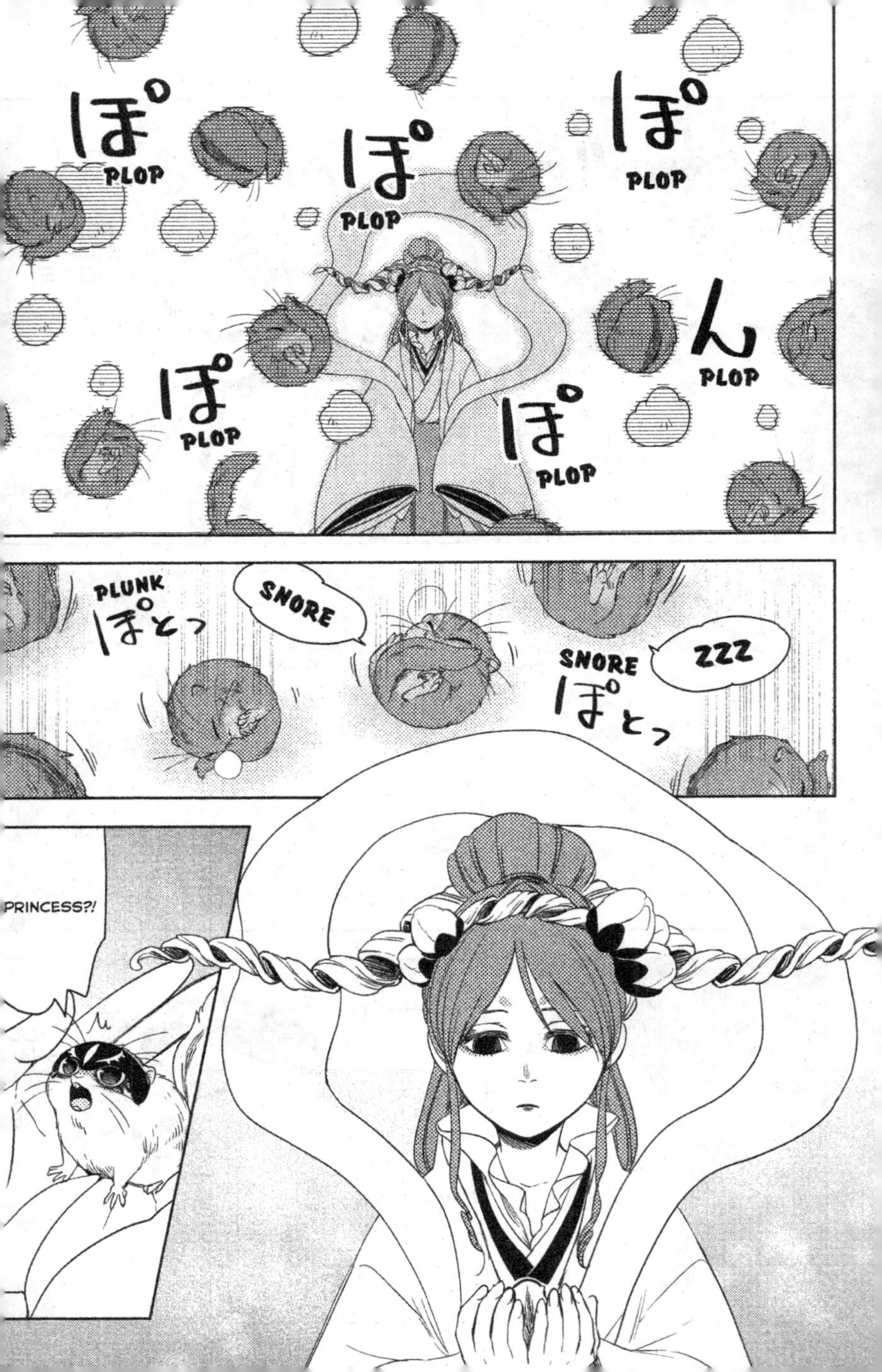
ぽ PLOP
ぽ PLOP
ん PLOP
ぽ PLOP
ぽ PLOP
ぽ PLOP
ZZZ
SNORE ぽとっ
SNORE
PLUNK ぽとっ
PRINCESS?!

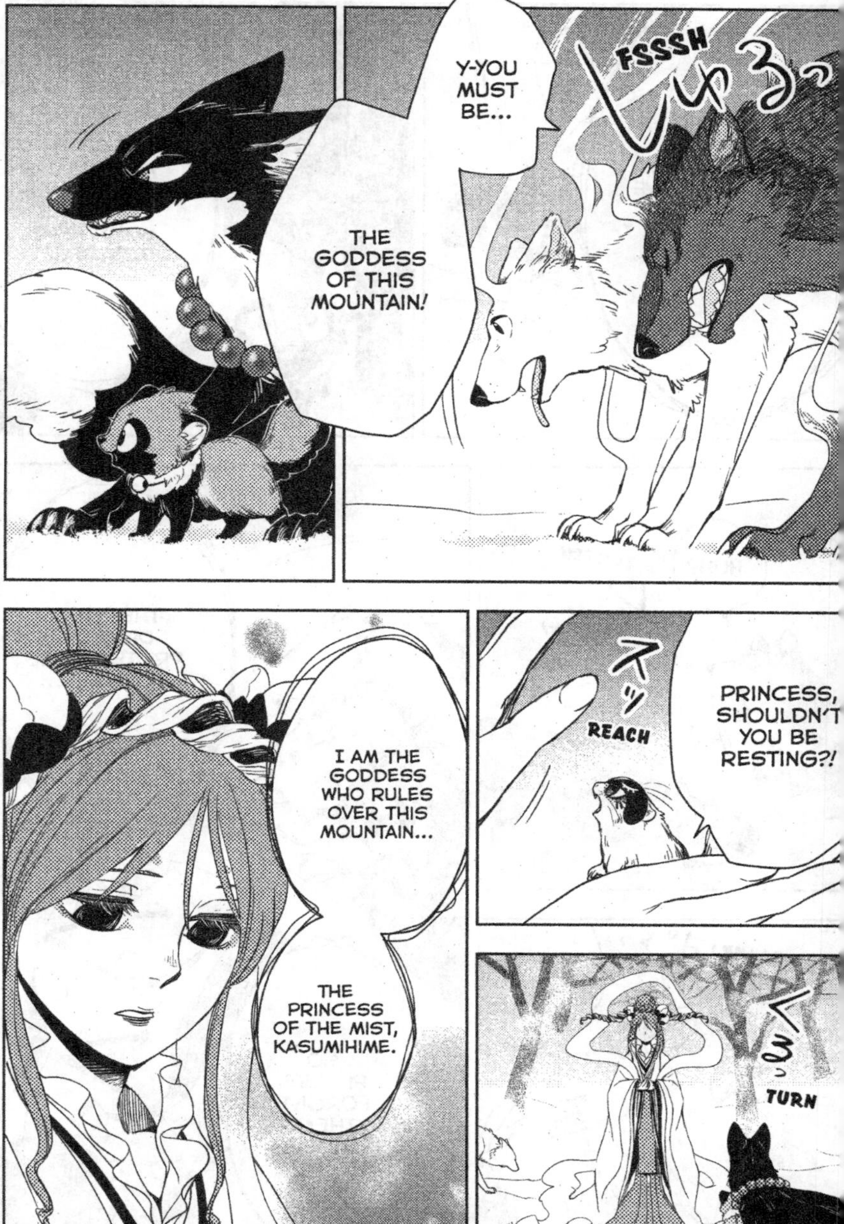
しゅるっ
FSSSH
Y-YOU MUST BE...
THE GODDESS OF THIS MOUNTAIN!
スッ
REACH
PRINCESS, SHOULDN'T YOU BE RESTING?!
くるっ
TURN
I AM THE GODDESS WHO RULES OVER THIS MOUNTAIN...
THE PRINCESS OF THE MIST, KASUMIHIME.

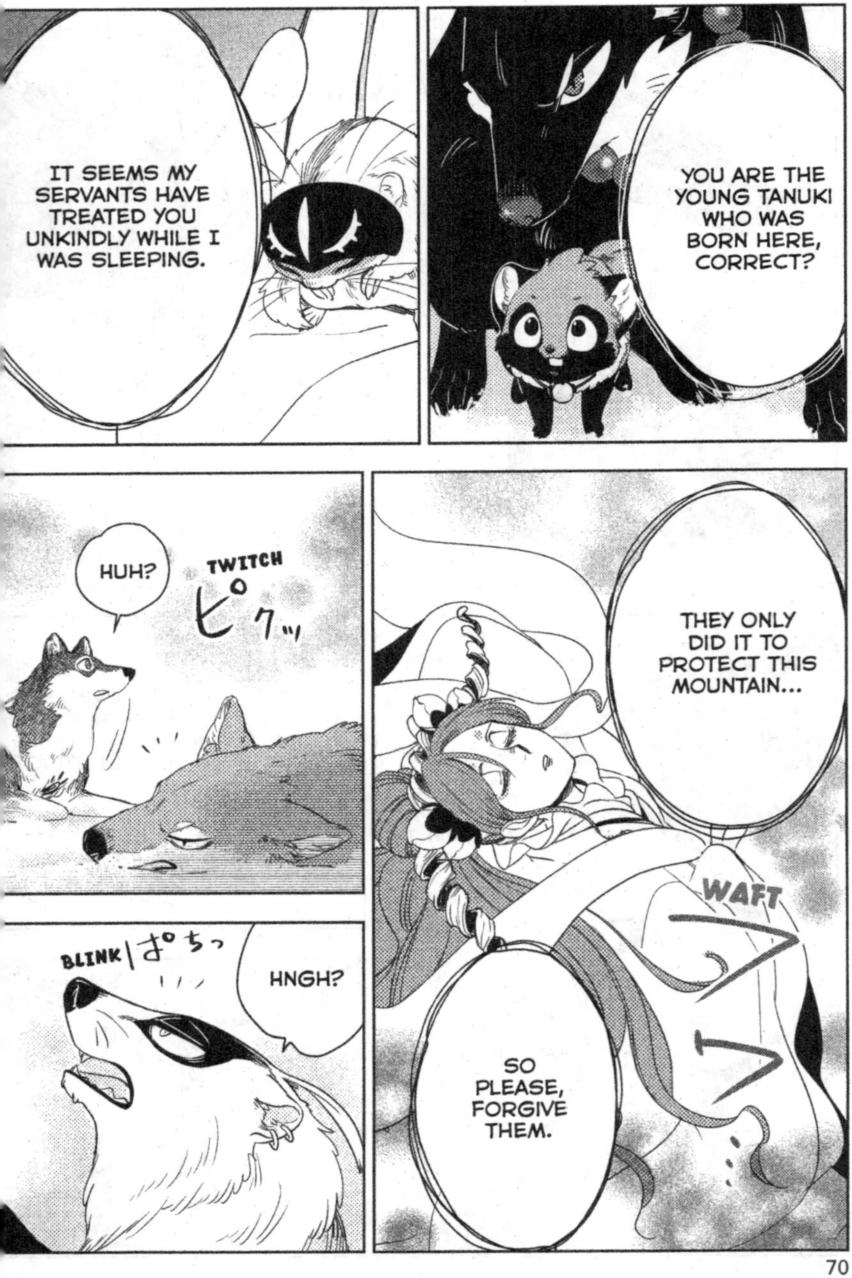
YOU ARE THE YOUNG TANUKI WHO WAS BORN HERE, CORRECT?
IT SEEMS MY SERVANTS HAVE TREATED YOU UNKINDLY WHILE I WAS SLEEPING.
THEY ONLY DID IT TO PROTECT THIS MOUNTAIN...
WAFT
SO PLEASE, FORGIVE THEM.
TWITCH
ピクッ
HUH?
HNGH?
BLINK
ぱちっ

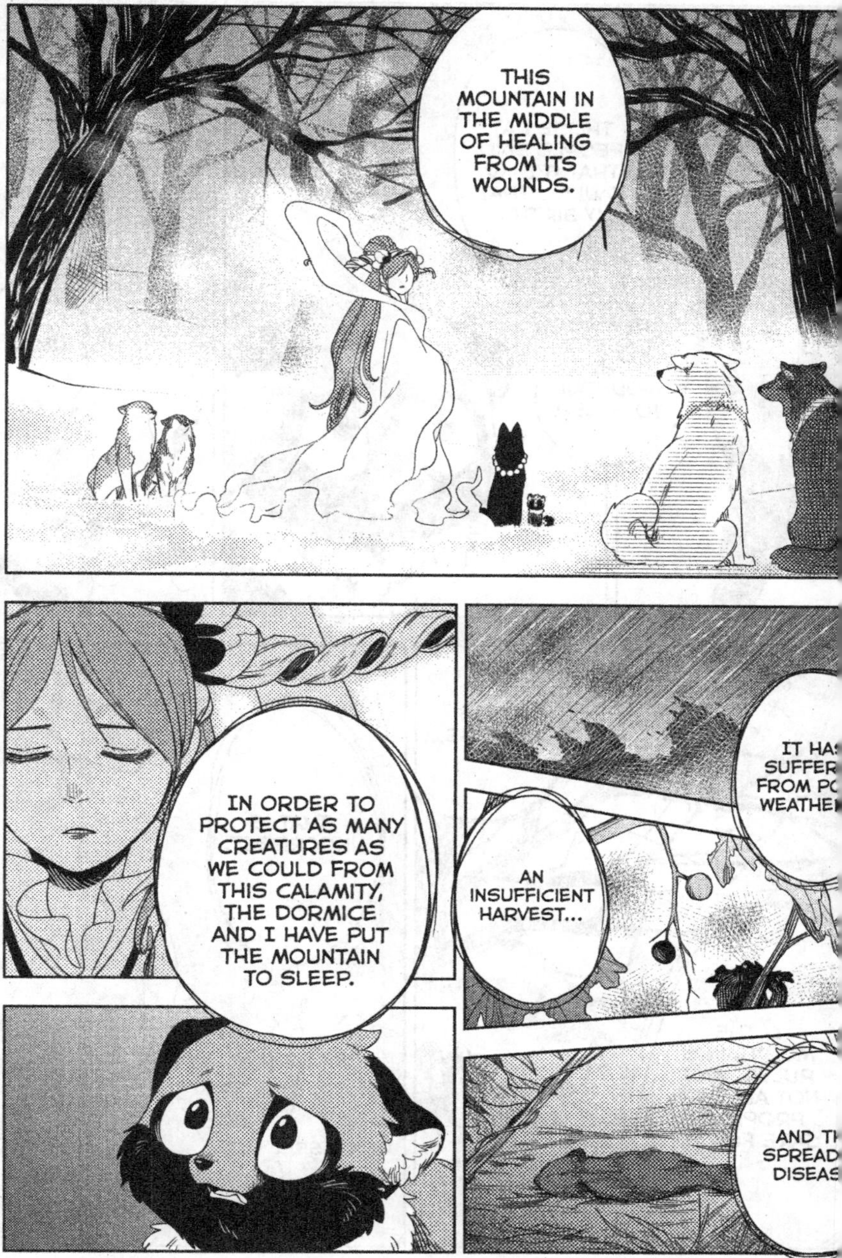
THIS MOUNTAIN IN THE MIDDLE OF HEALING FROM ITS WOUNDS.
IT HA SUFFER FROM PO WEATHE
AN INSUFFICIENT HARVEST...
AND T SPREAD DISEAS
IN ORDER TO PROTECT AS MANY CREATURES AS WE COULD FROM THIS CALAMITY, THE DORMICE AND I HAVE PUT THE MOUNTAIN TO SLEEP.

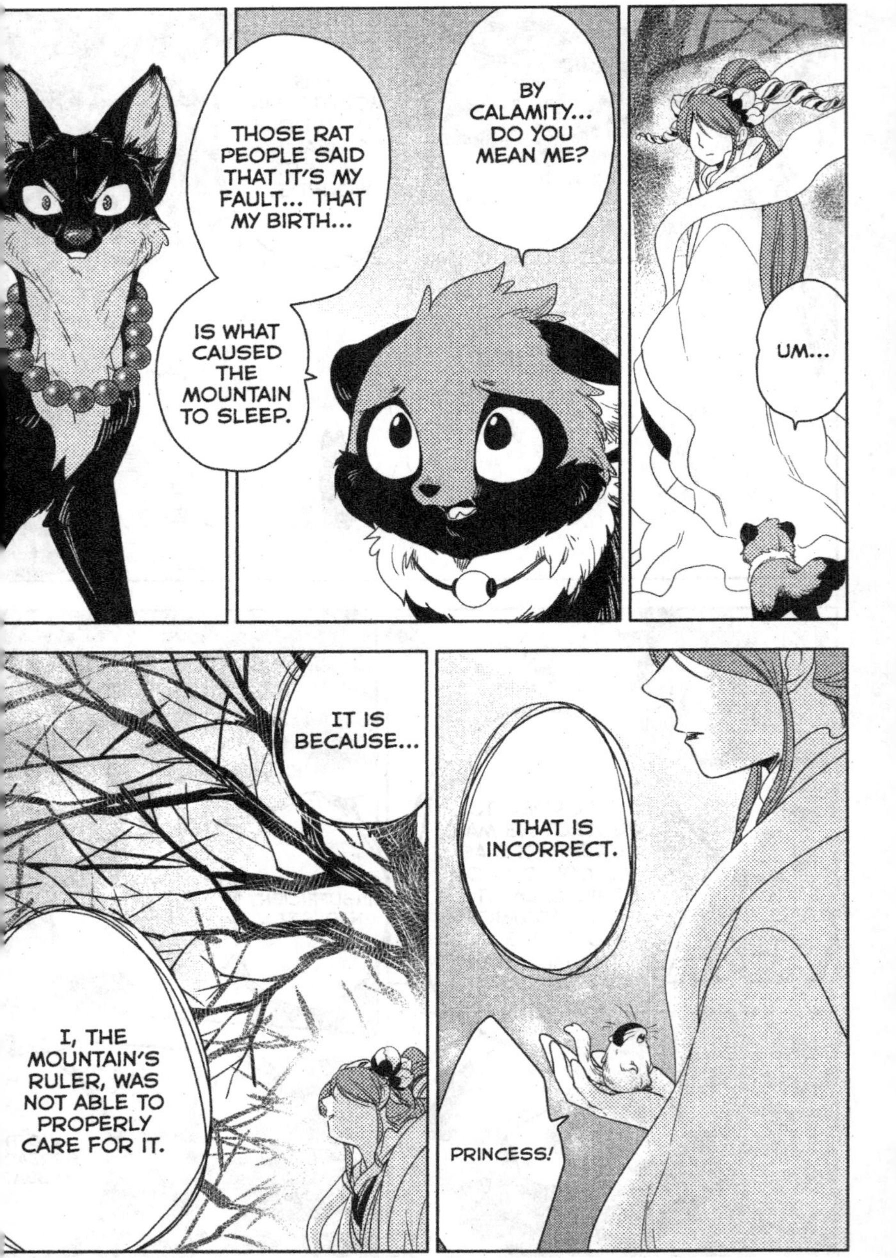
UM...
BY CALAMITY... DO YOU MEAN ME?
THOSE RAT PEOPLE SAID THAT IT'S MY FAULT... THAT MY BIRTH...
IS WHAT CAUSED THE MOUNTAIN TO SLEEP.
THAT IS INCORRECT.
PRINCESS!
IT IS BECAUSE...
I, THE MOUNTAIN'S RULER, WAS NOT ABLE TO PROPERLY CARE FOR IT.

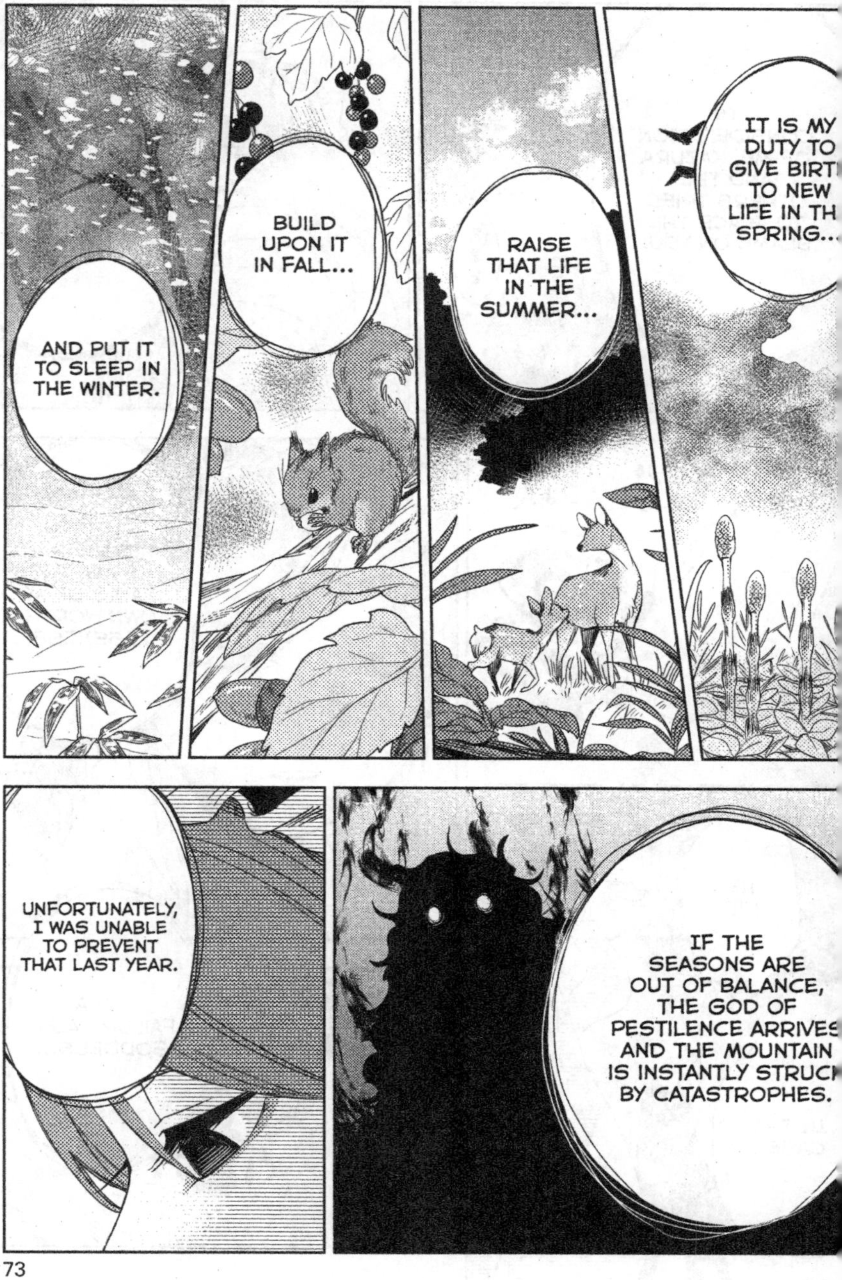

IT IS MY DUTY TO GIVE BIRT TO NEW LIFE IN TH SPRING...
RAISE THAT LIFE IN THE SUMMER...
BUILD UPON IT IN FALL...
AND PUT IT TO SLEEP IN THE WINTER.
IF THE SEASONS ARE OUT OF BALANCE, THE GOD OF PESTILENCE ARRIVES AND THE MOUNTAIN IS INSTANTLY STRUC BY CATASTROPHES.
UNFORTUNATELY, I WAS UNABLE TO PREVENT THAT LAST YEAR.

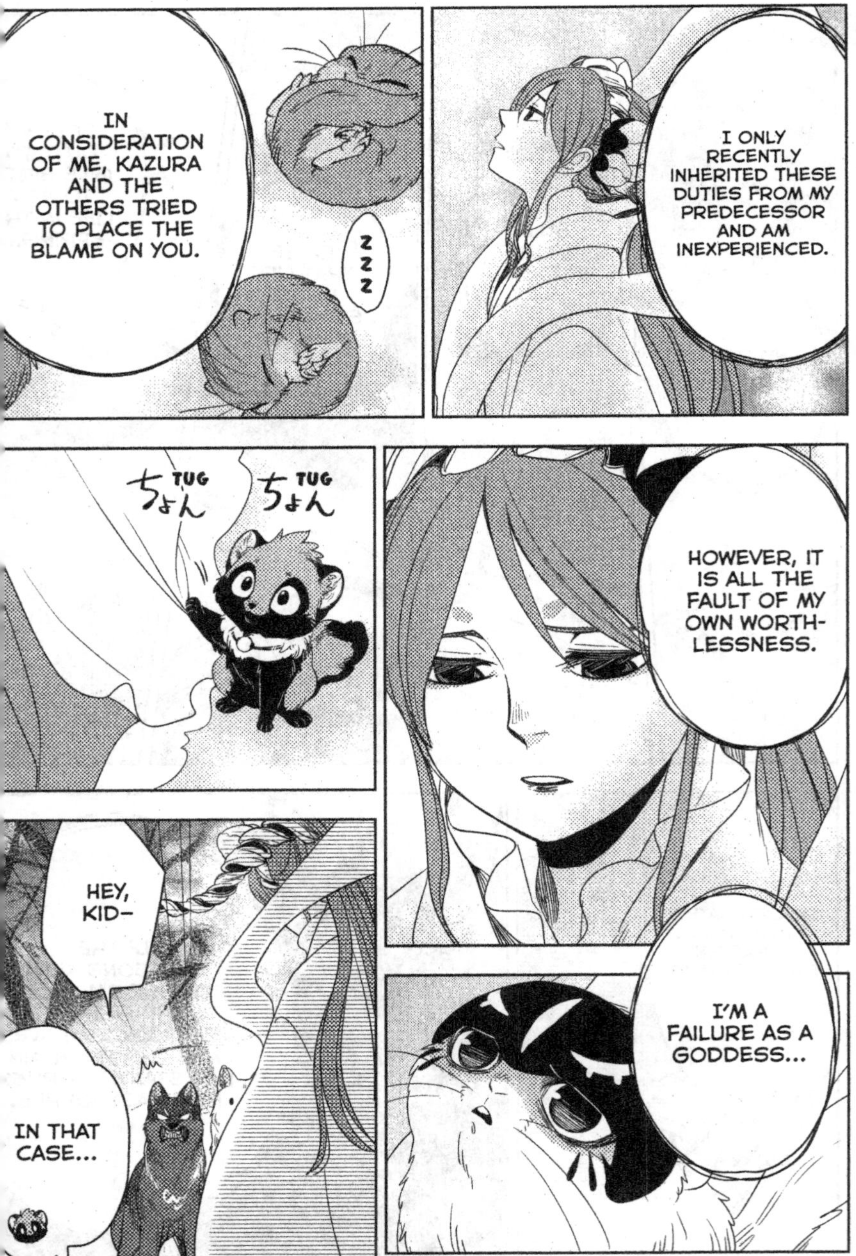
I ONLY RECENTLY INHERITED THESE DUTIES FROM MY PREDECESSOR AND AM INEXPERIENCED.
IN CONSIDERATION OF ME, KAZURA AND THE OTHERS TRIED TO PLACE THE BLAME ON YOU.
ZZZ
HOWEVER, IT IS ALL THE FAULT OF MY OWN WORTH-LESSNESS.
I'M A FAILURE AS A GODDESS...
ちょん TUG
ちょん TUG
HEY, KID-
IN THAT CASE...

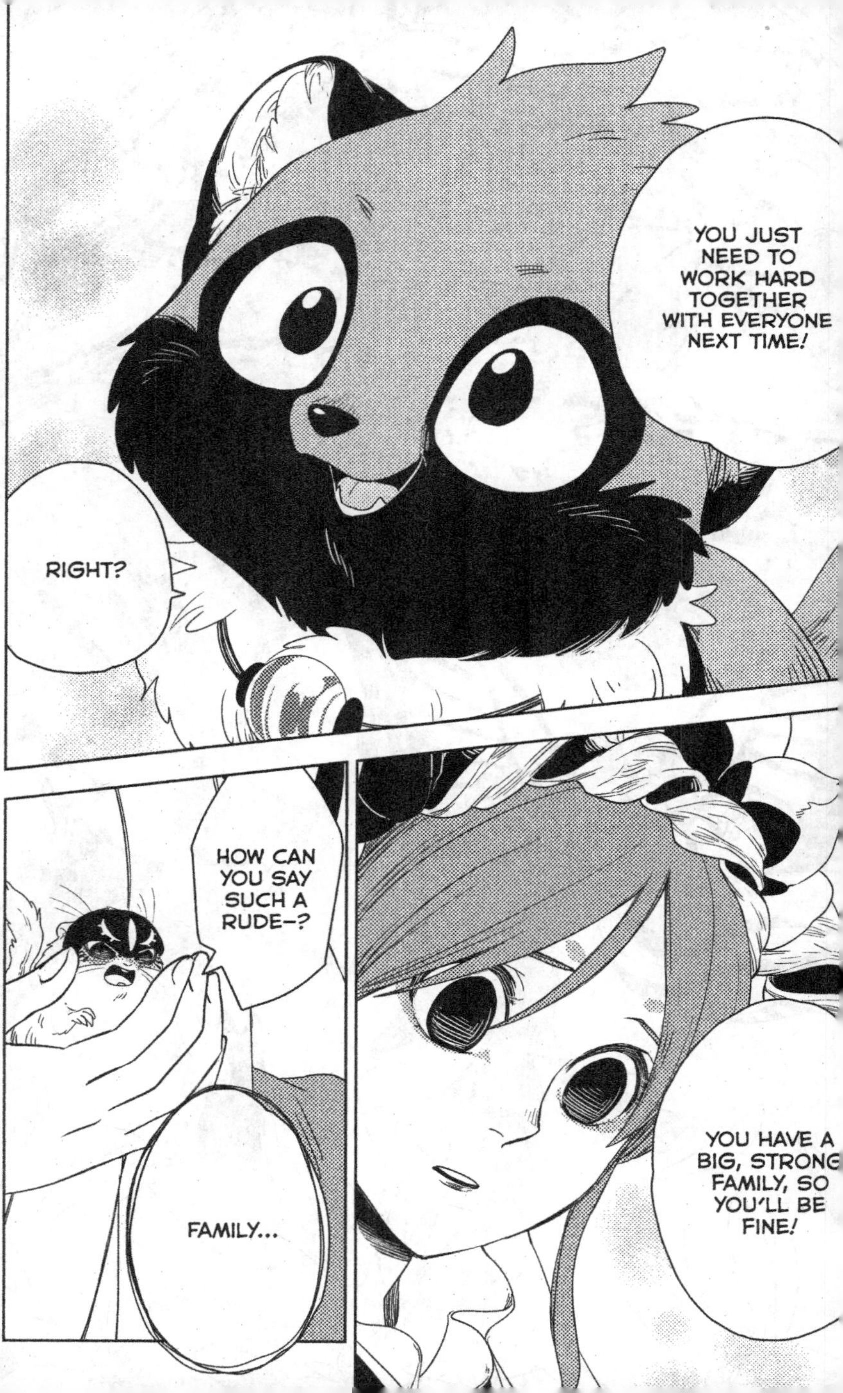
YOU JUST NEED TO WORK HARD TOGETHER WITH EVERYONE NEXT TIME!
RIGHT?
YOU HAVE A BIG, STRONG FAMILY, SO YOU'LL BE FINE!
HOW CAN YOU SAY SUCH A RUDE–?
FAMILY...

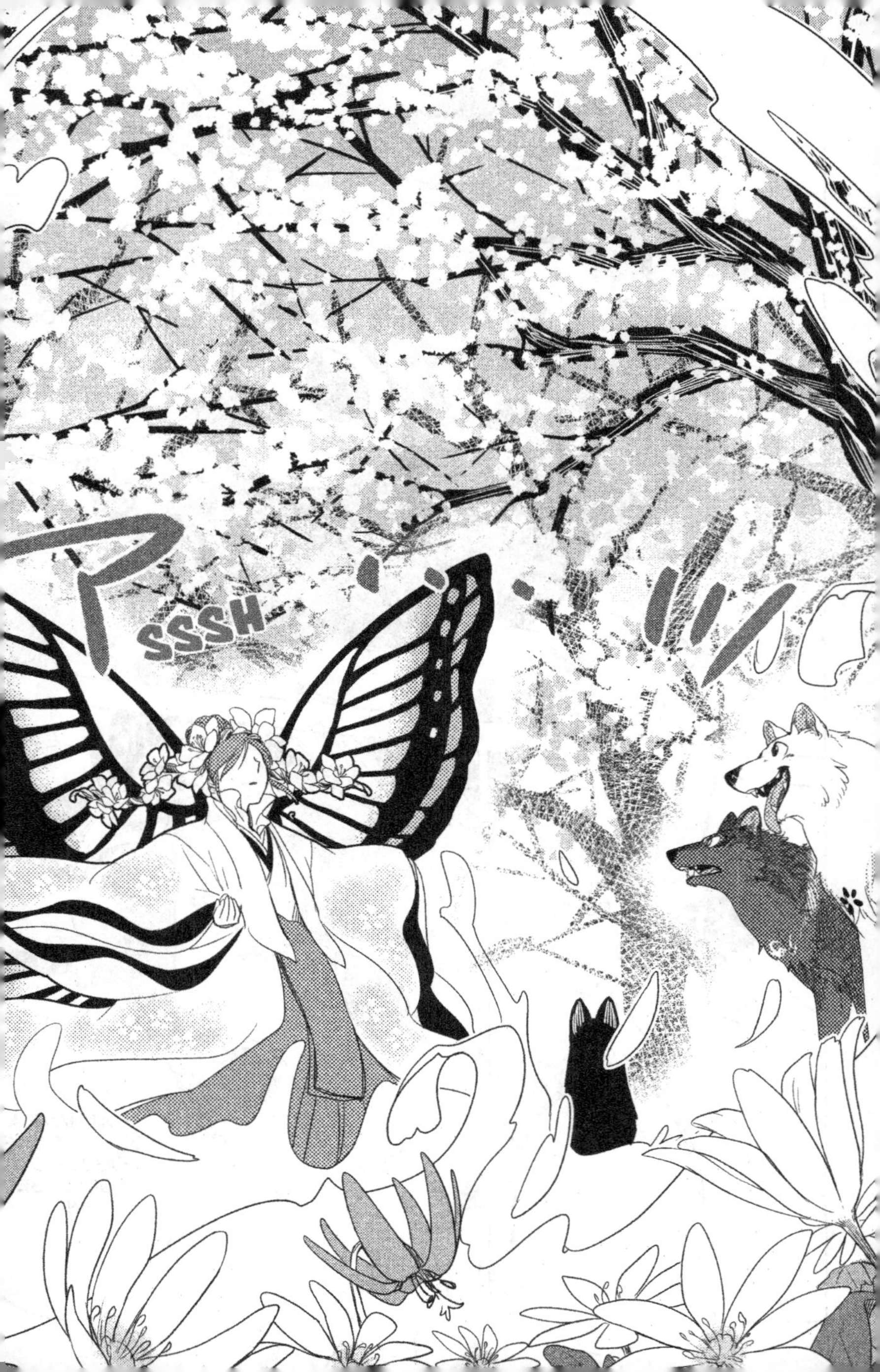
SSSH

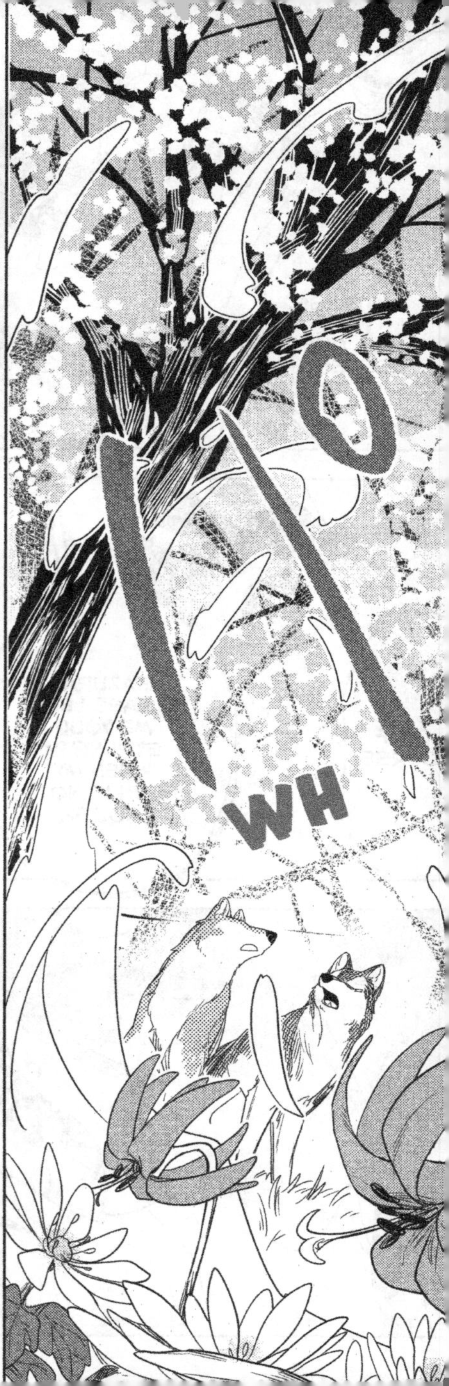
O
WH
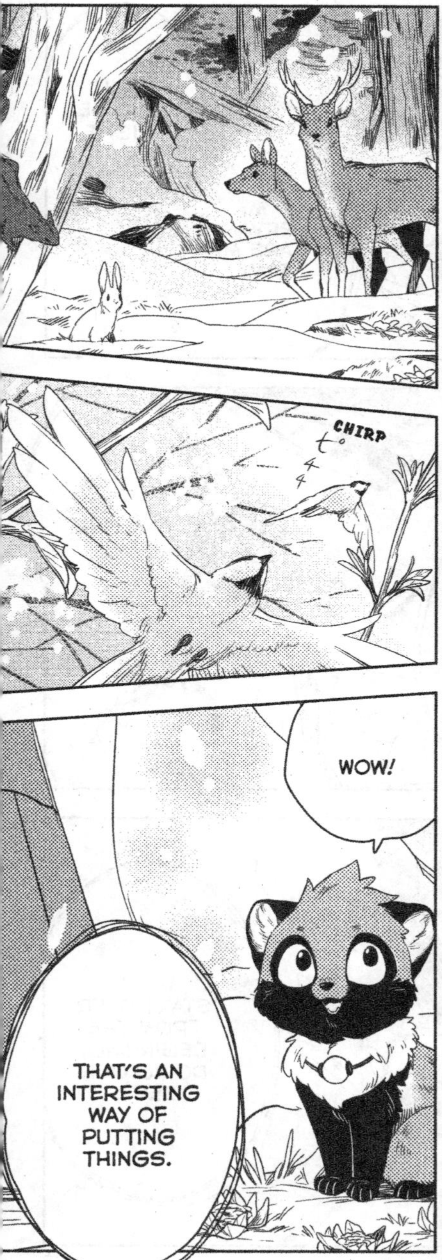
CHIRP
WOW!
THAT'S AN INTERESTING WAY OF PUTTING THINGS.

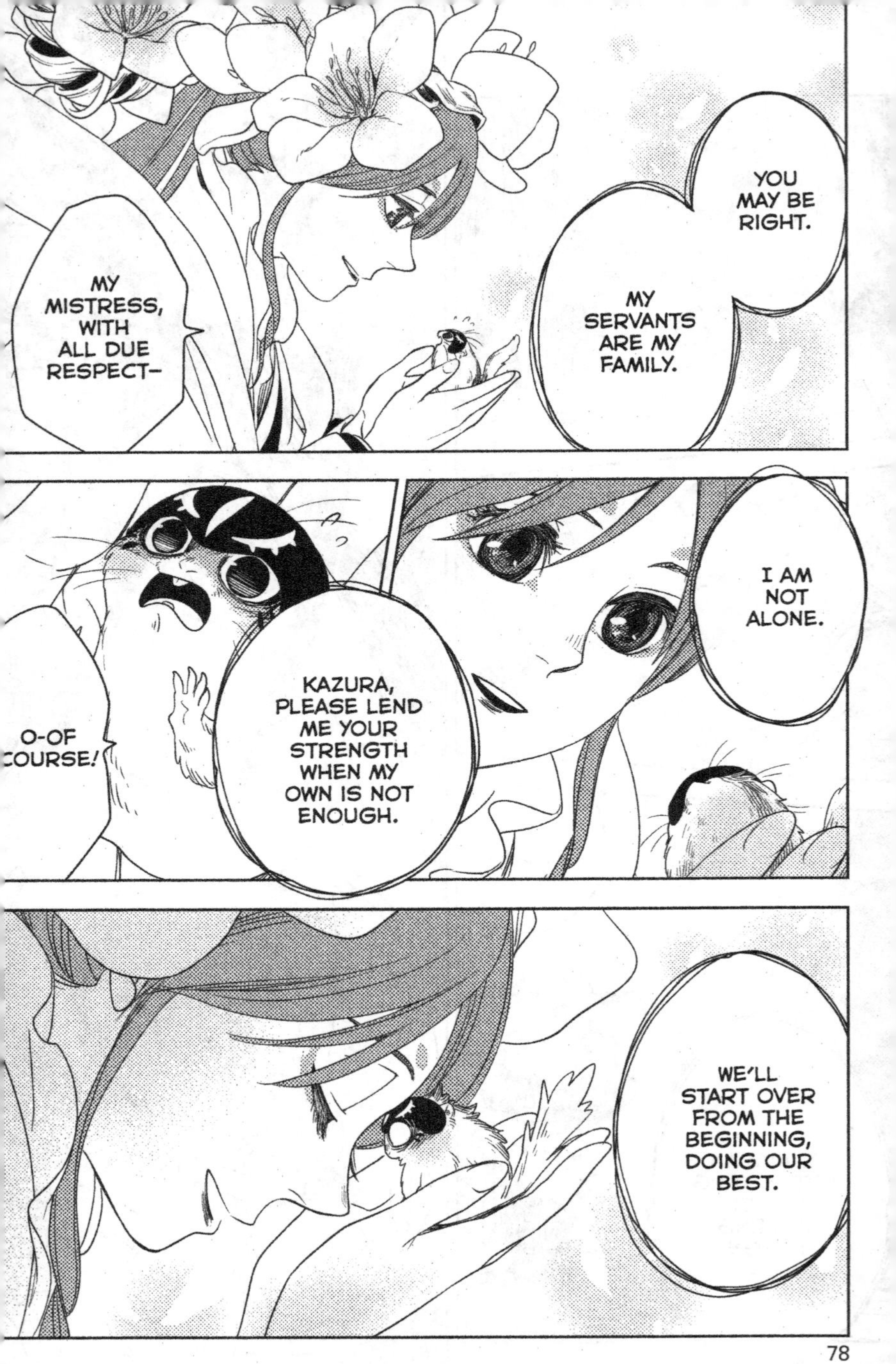
YOU MAY BE RIGHT.
MY SERVANTS ARE MY FAMILY.
MY MISTRESS, WITH ALL DUE RESPECT–
I AM NOT ALONE.
KAZURA, PLEASE LEND ME YOUR STRENGTH WHEN MY OWN IS NOT ENOUGH.
O-OF COURSE!
WE'LL START OVER FROM THE BEGINNING, DOING OUR BEST.

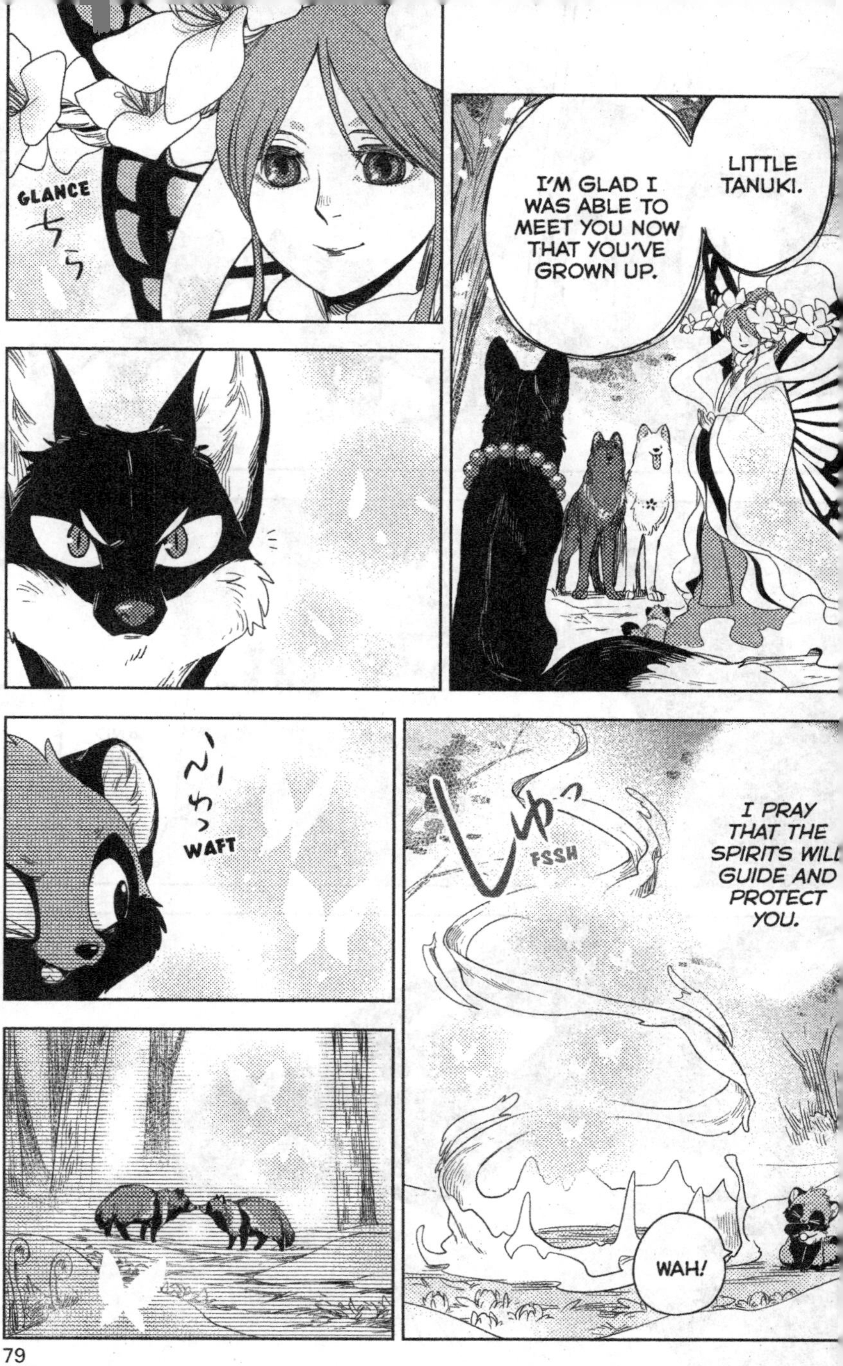
LITTLE TANUKI.
I'M GLAD I WAS ABLE TO MEET YOU NOW THAT YOU'VE GROWN UP.
GLANCE
FSSH
I PRAY THAT THE SPIRITS WILL GUIDE AND PROTECT YOU.
WAH!
WAFT

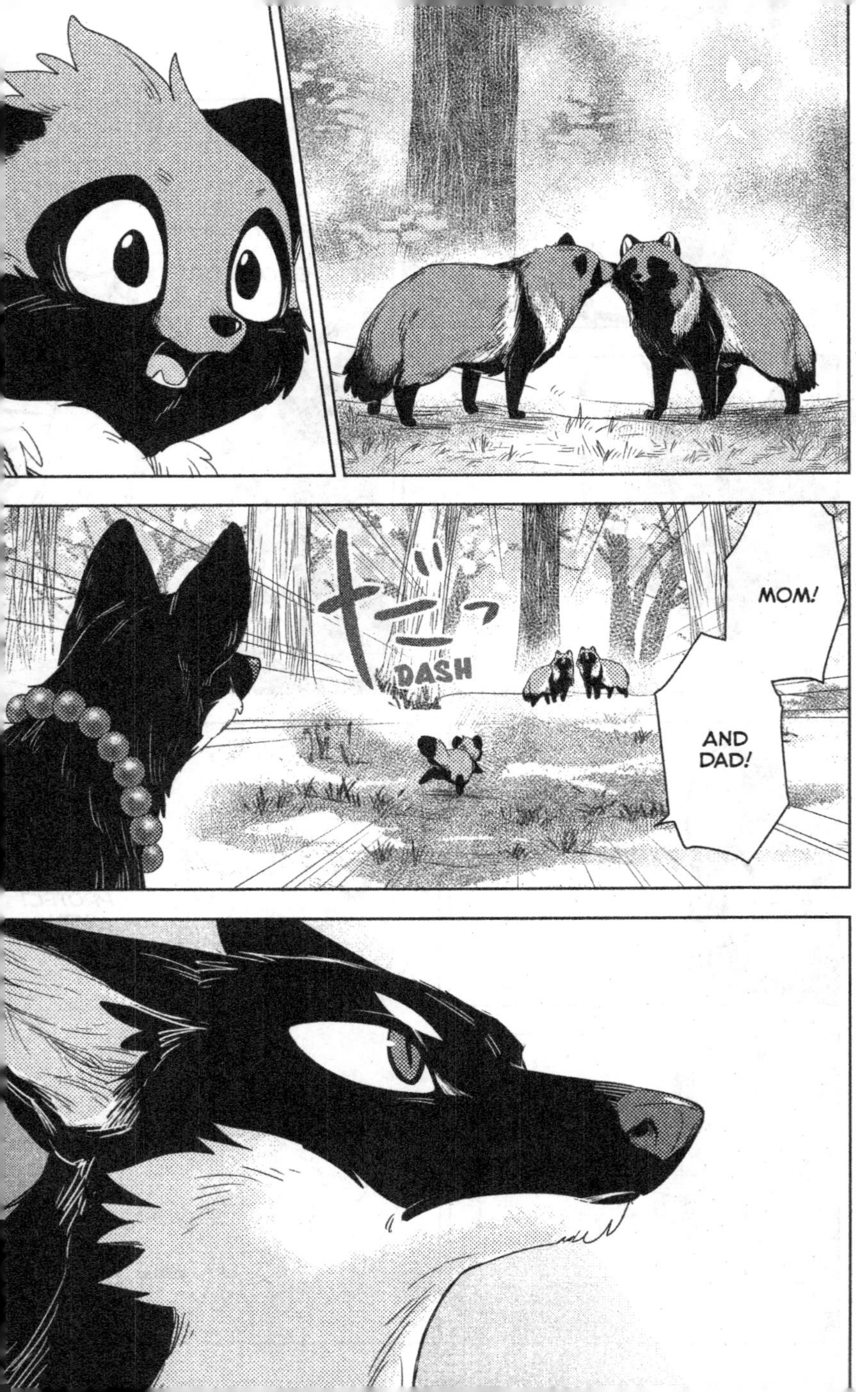
MOM!
AND DAD!
DASH

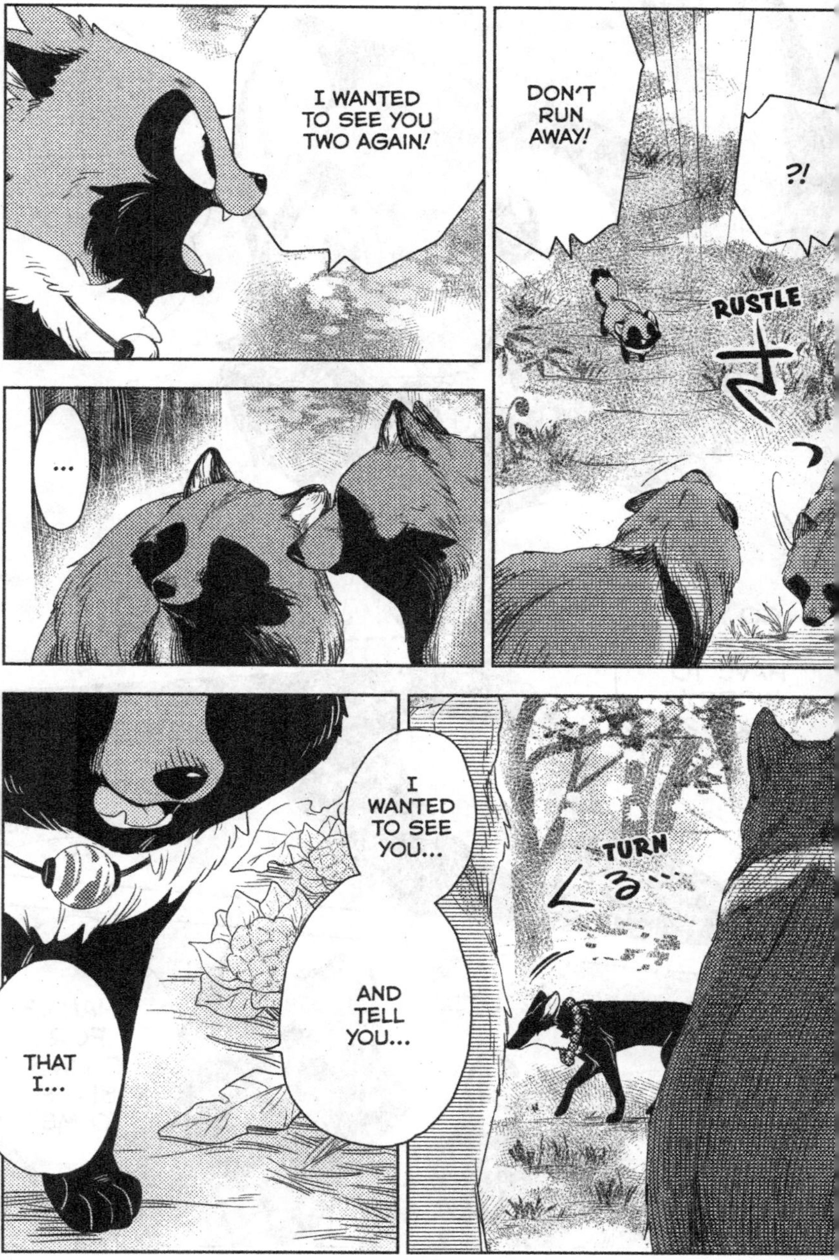
?!
DON'T RUN AWAY!
RUSTLE
I WANTED TO SEE YOU TWO AGAIN!
...
TURN
I WANTED TO SEE YOU...
AND TELL YOU...
THAT I...

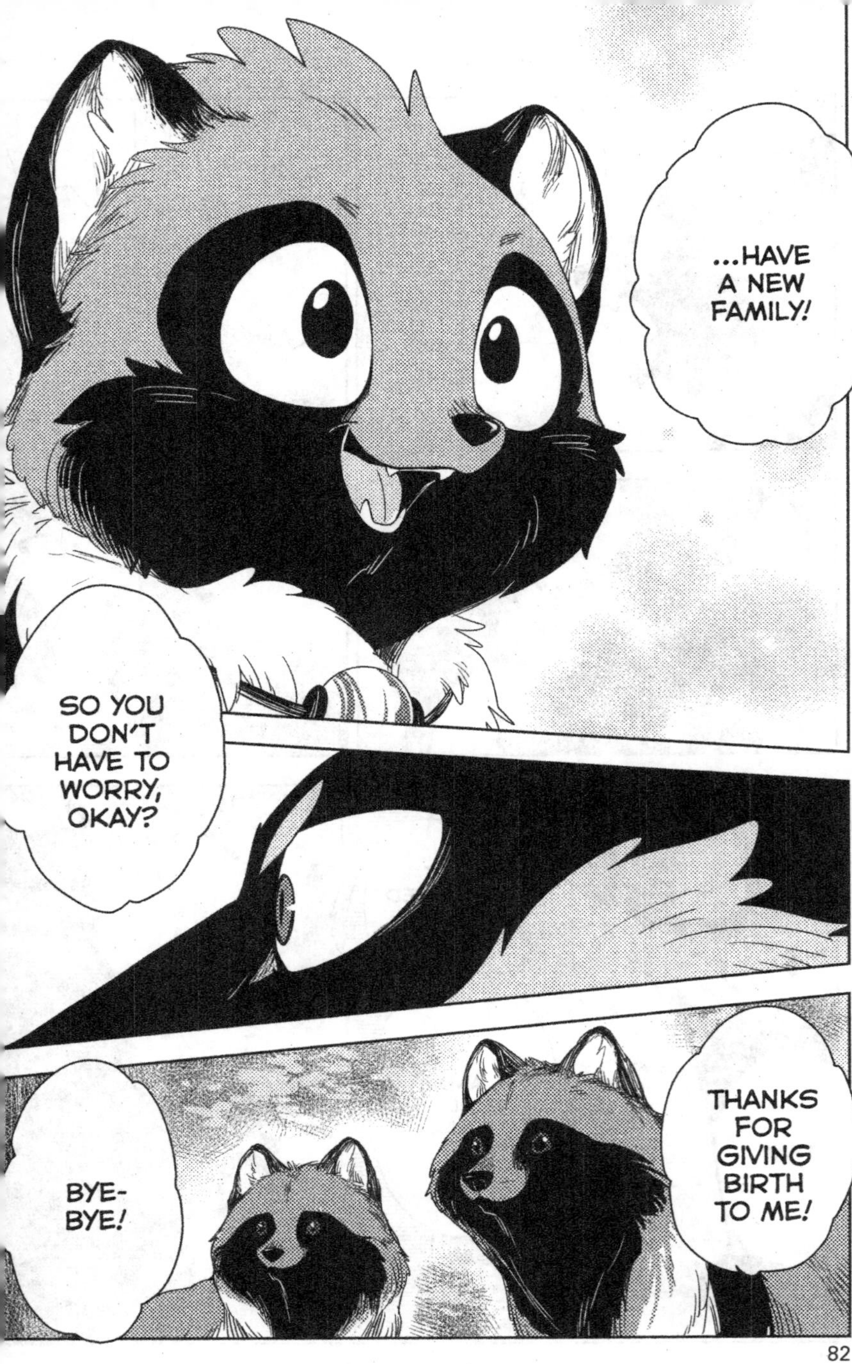
...HAVE A NEW FAMILY!
SO YOU DON'T HAVE TO WORRY, OKAY?
THANKS FOR GIVING BIRTH TO ME!
BYE-BYE!

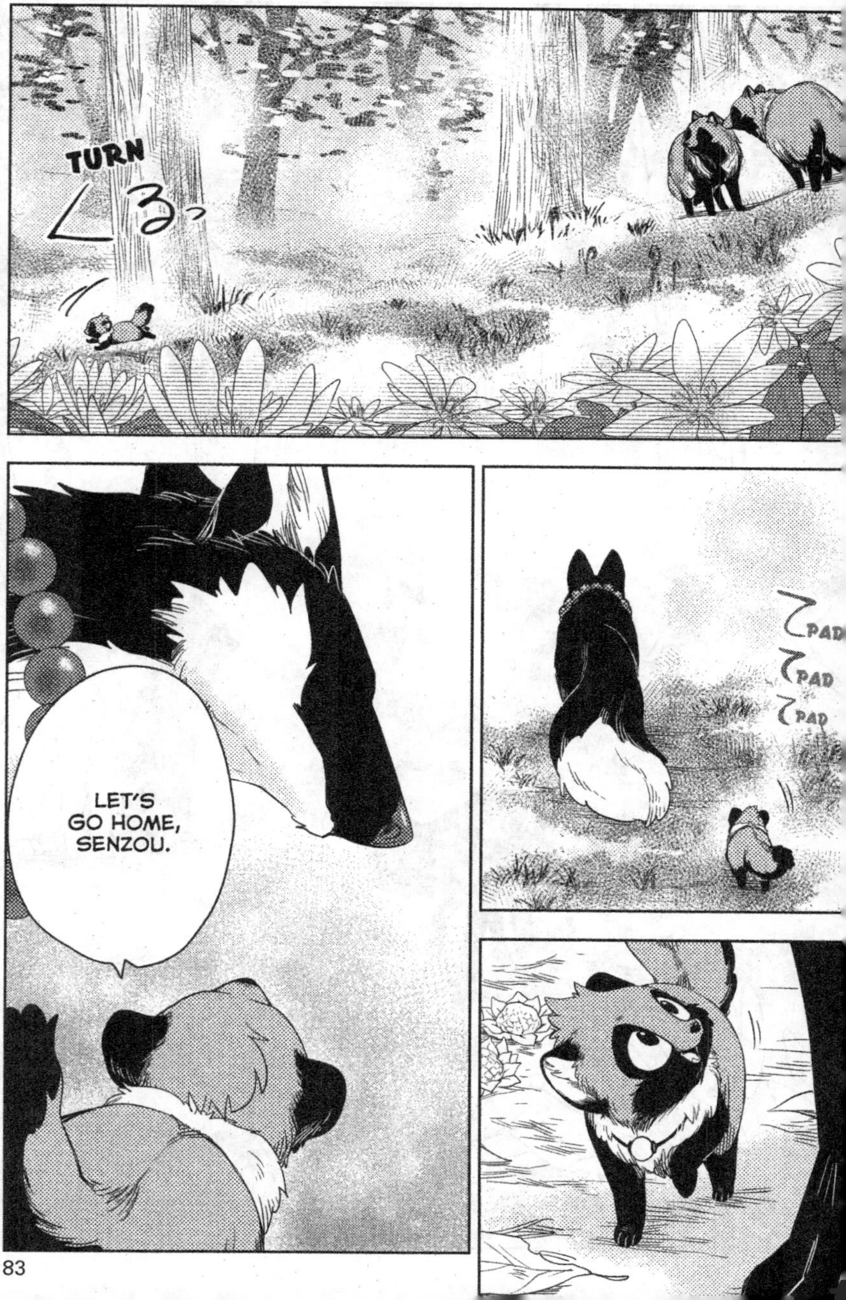
TURN
くるっ
PAD
PAD
PAD
LET'S GO HOME, SENZOU.

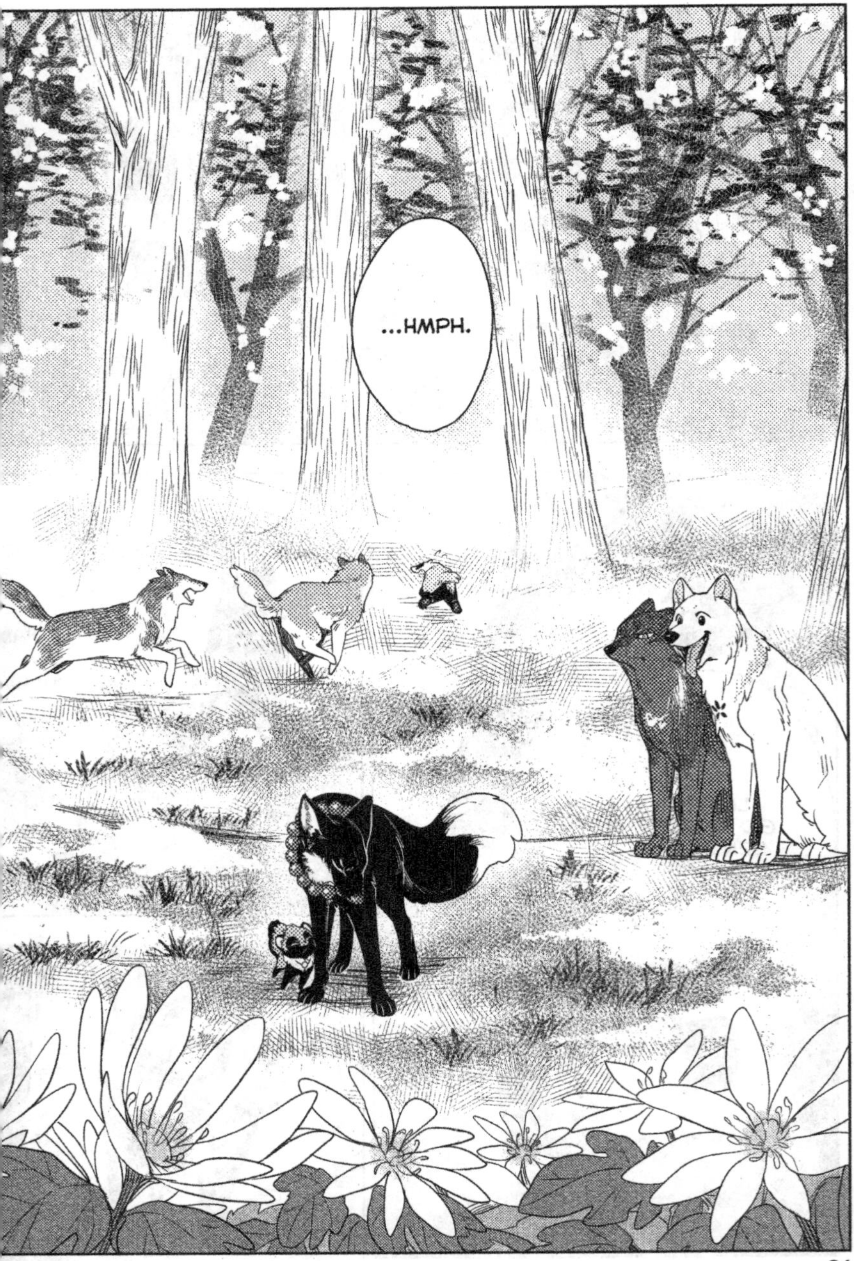
...HMPH.

# Chapter 10

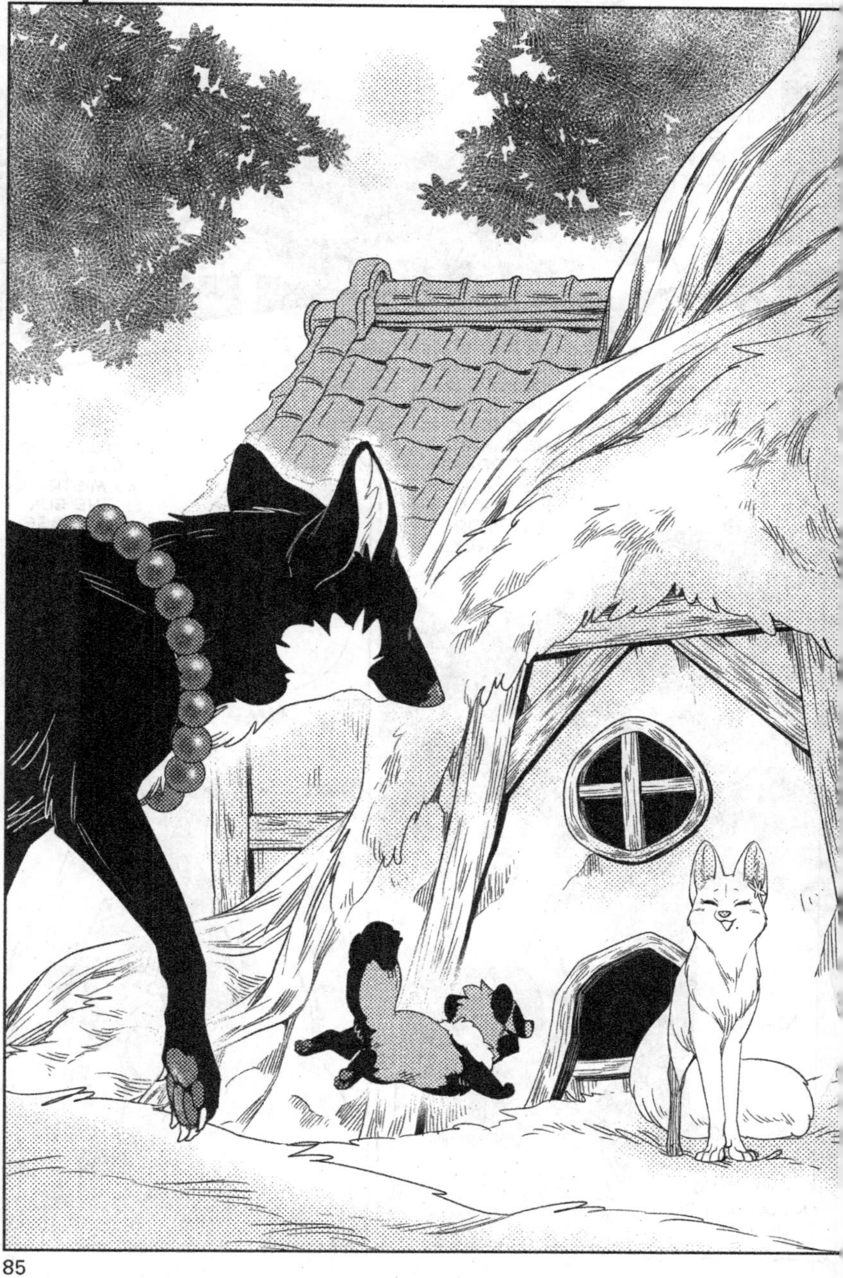

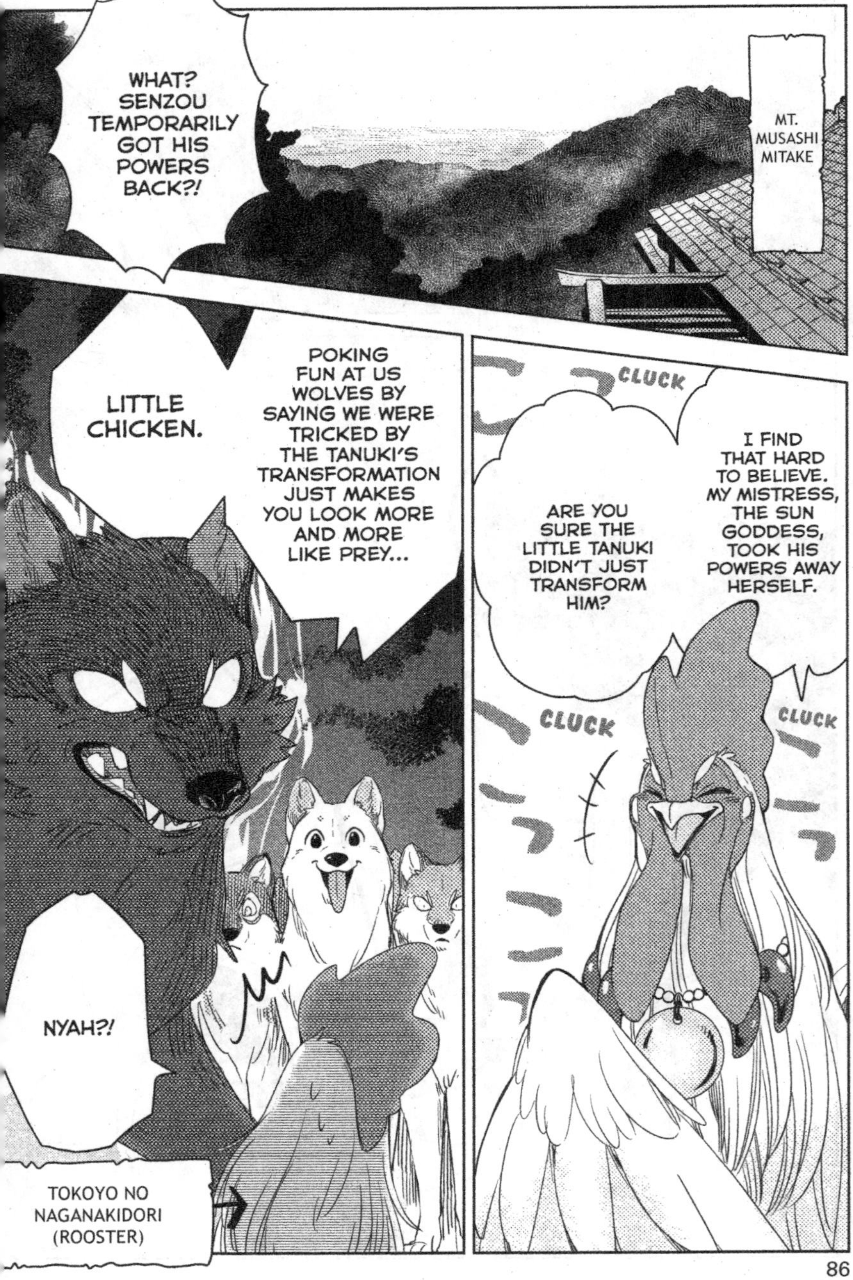
MT. MUSASHI MITAKE
WHAT? SENZOU TEMPORARILY GOT HIS POWERS BACK?!
CLUCK
I FIND THAT HARD TO BELIEVE. MY MISTRESS, THE SUN GODDESS, TOOK HIS POWERS AWAY HERSELF.
ARE YOU SURE THE LITTLE TANUKI DIDN'T JUST TRANSFORM HIM?
CLUCK
CLUCK
POKING FUN AT US WOLVES BY SAYING WE WERE TRICKED BY THE TANUKI'S TRANSFORMATION JUST MAKES YOU LOOK MORE AND MORE LIKE PREY...
LITTLE CHICKEN.
NYAH?!
TOKOYO NO NAGANAKIDORI (ROOSTER)

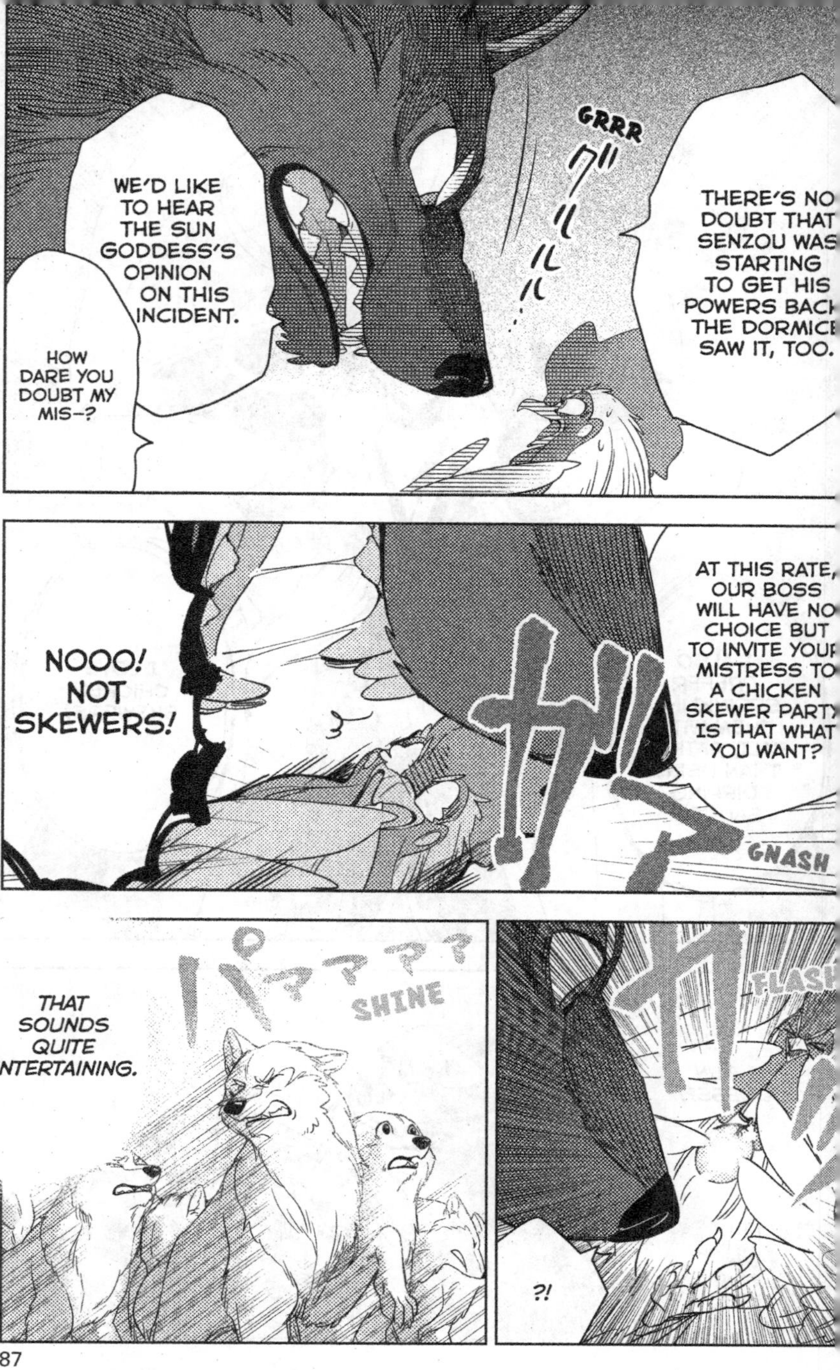
THERE'S NO DOUBT THAT SENZOU WAS STARTING TO GET HIS POWERS BACK THE DORMICE SAW IT, TOO.
GRRR
グルルル
WE'D LIKE TO HEAR THE SUN GODDESS'S OPINION ON THIS INCIDENT.
HOW DARE YOU DOUBT MY MIS--?
AT THIS RATE, OUR BOSS WILL HAVE NO CHOICE BUT TO INVITE YOUR MISTRESS TO A CHICKEN SKEWER PARTY IS THAT WHAT YOU WANT?
GNASH
NOOO! NOT SKEWERS!
FLAS
?!
パァァァ
SHINE
THAT SOUNDS QUITE ENTERTAINING.

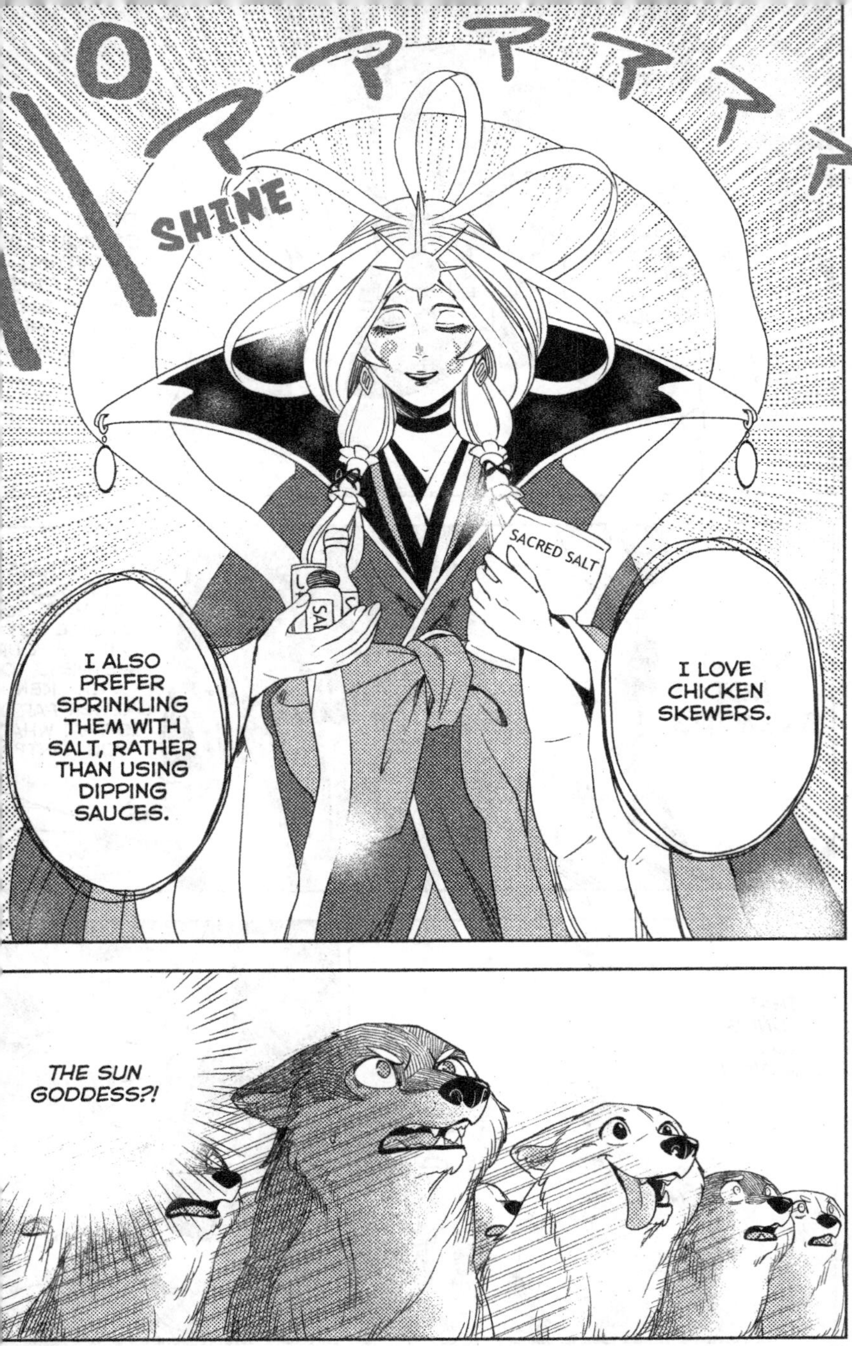
SHINE
SACRED SALT
I LOVE CHICKEN SKEWERS.
I ALSO PREFER SPRINKLING THEM WITH SALT, RATHER THAN USING DIPPING SAUCES.
THE SUN GODDESS?!

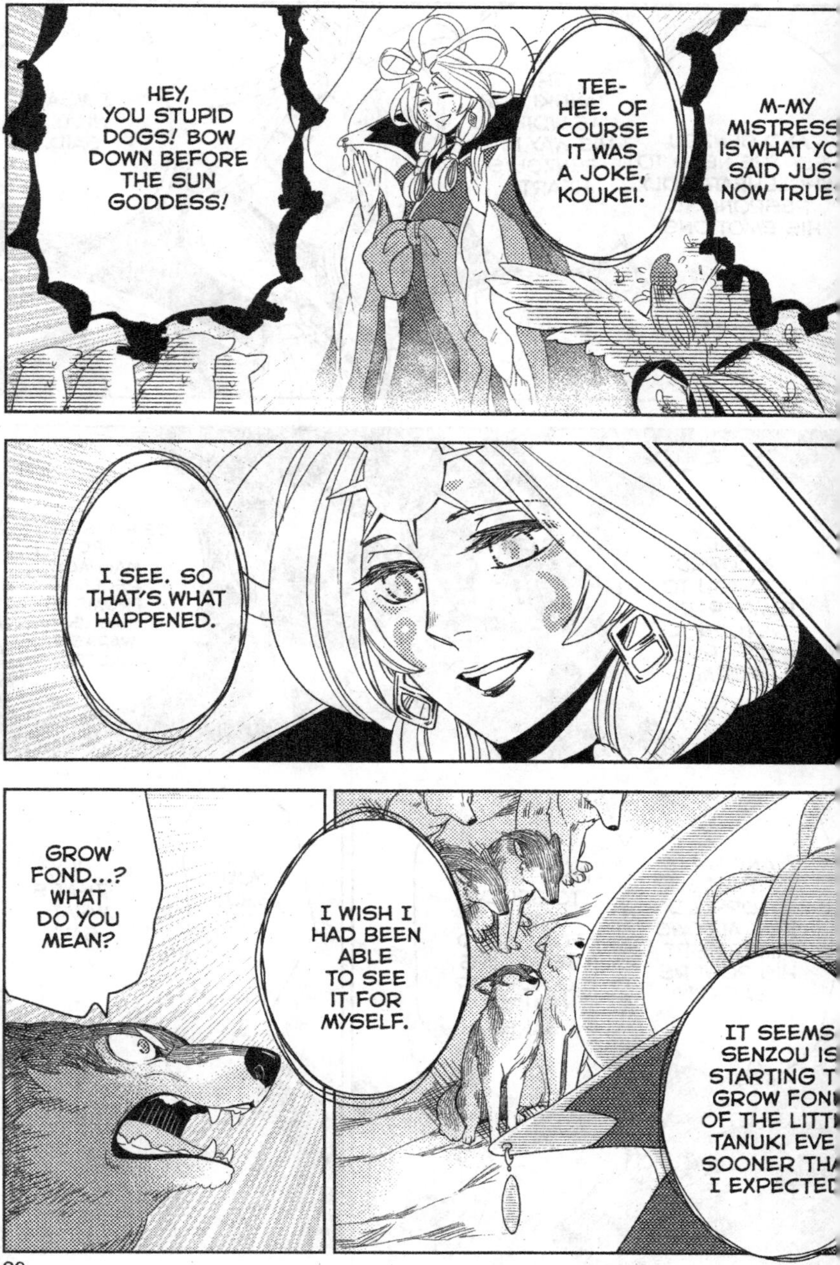
M-MY MISTRESS IS WHAT YO SAID JUS NOW TRUE
TEE-HEE. OF COURSE IT WAS A JOKE, KOUKEI.
HEY, YOU STUPID DOGS! BOW DOWN BEFORE THE SUN GODDESS!
I SEE. SO THAT'S WHAT HAPPENED.
IT SEEMS SENZOU IS STARTING T GROW FON OF THE LITT TANUKI EVE SOONER THA I EXPECTED
I WISH I HAD BEEN ABLE TO SEE IT FOR MYSELF.
GROW FOND...? WHAT DO YOU MEAN?

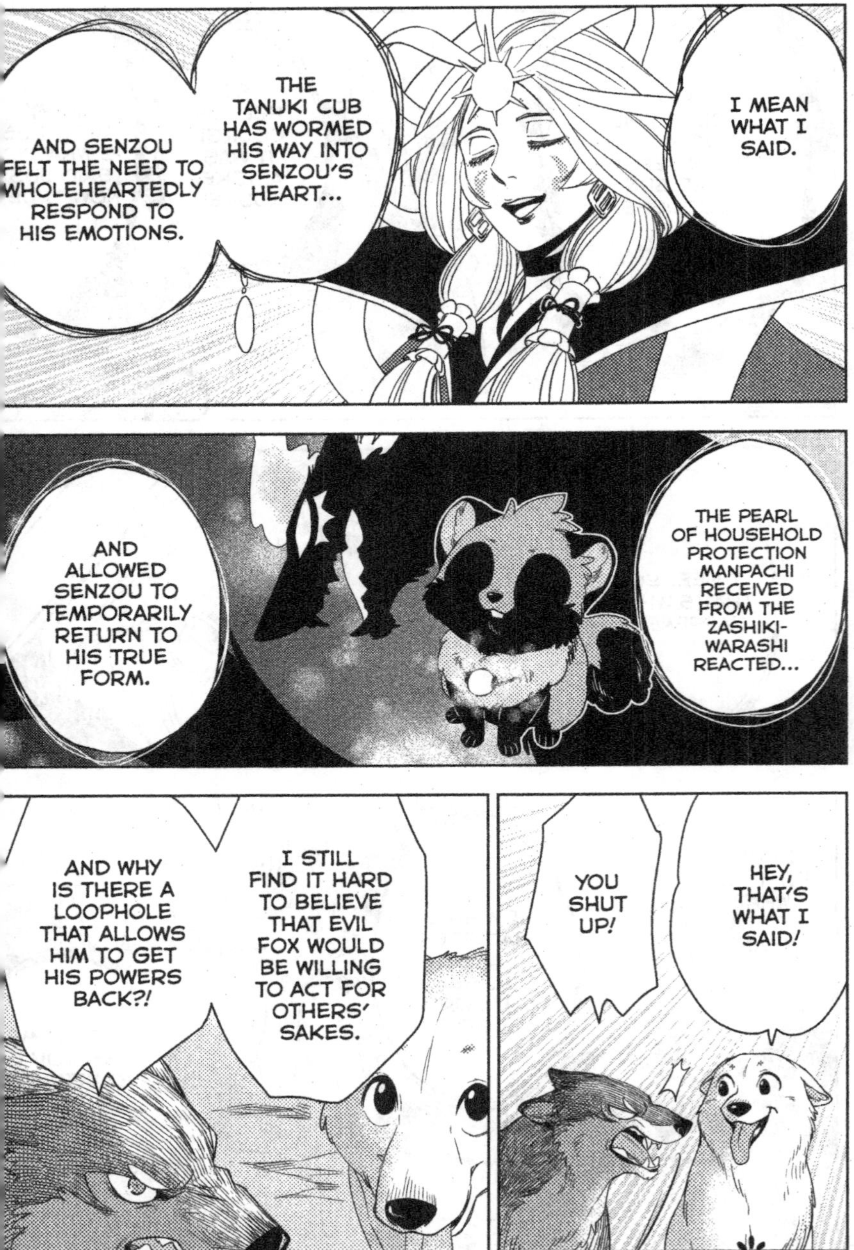
I MEAN WHAT I SAID.
THE TANUKI CUB HAS WORMED HIS WAY INTO SENZOU'S HEART...
AND SENZOU FELT THE NEED TO WHOLEHEARTEDLY RESPOND TO HIS EMOTIONS.
THE PEARL OF HOUSEHOLD PROTECTION MANPACHI RECEIVED FROM THE ZASHIKI-WARASHI REACTED...
AND ALLOWED SENZOU TO TEMPORARILY RETURN TO HIS TRUE FORM.
HEY, THAT'S WHAT I SAID!
YOU SHUT UP!
I STILL FIND IT HARD TO BELIEVE THAT EVIL FOX WOULD BE WILLING TO ACT FOR OTHERS' SAKES.
AND WHY IS THERE A LOOPHOLE THAT ALLOWS HIM TO GET HIS POWERS BACK?!

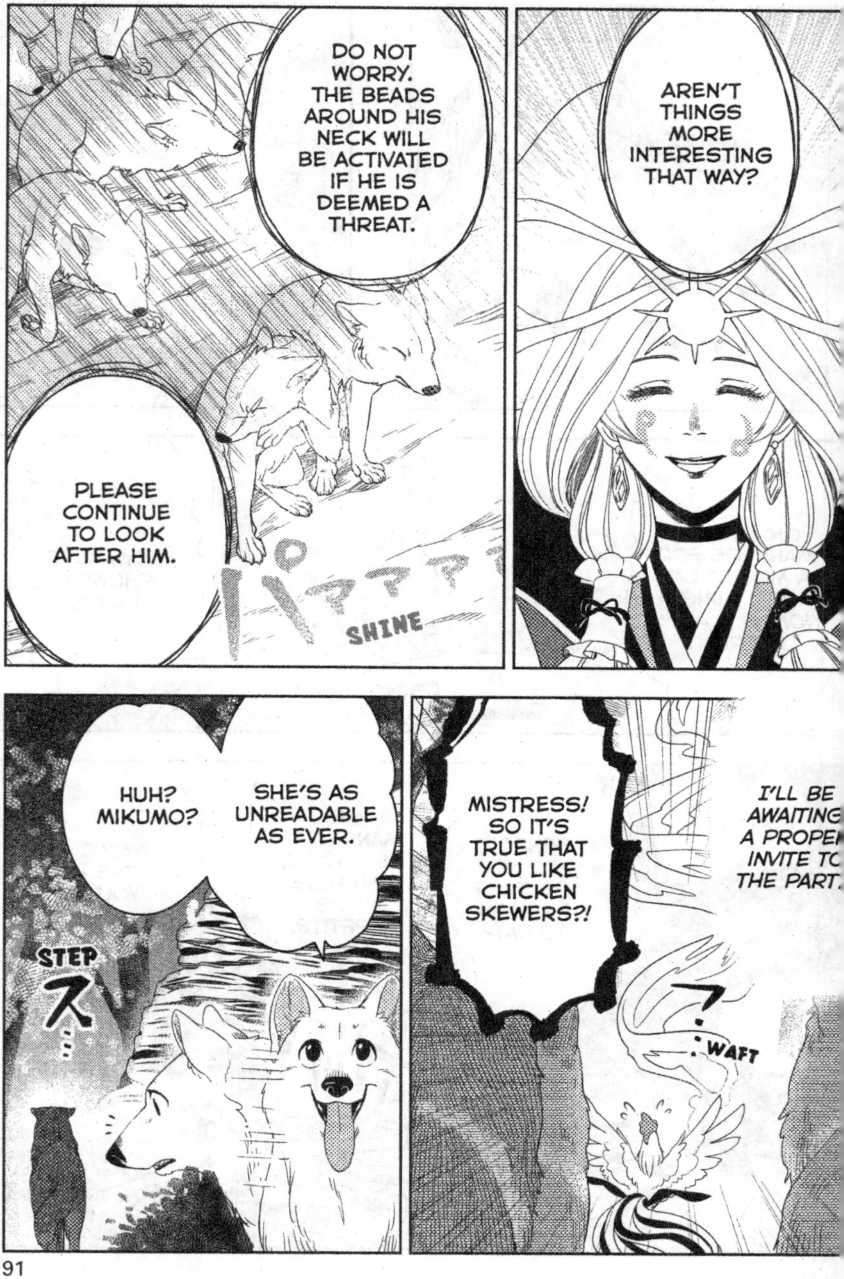

AREN'T THINGS MORE INTERESTING THAT WAY?
DO NOT WORRY. THE BEADS AROUND HIS NECK WILL BE ACTIVATED IF HE IS DEEMED A THREAT.
PLEASE CONTINUE TO LOOK AFTER HIM.
SHINE
I'LL BE AWAITING A PROPE INVITE TO THE PART.
MISTRESS! SO IT'S TRUE THAT YOU LIKE CHICKEN SKEWERS?!
WAFT
SHE'S AS UNREADABLE AS EVER.
HUH? MIKUMO?
STEP

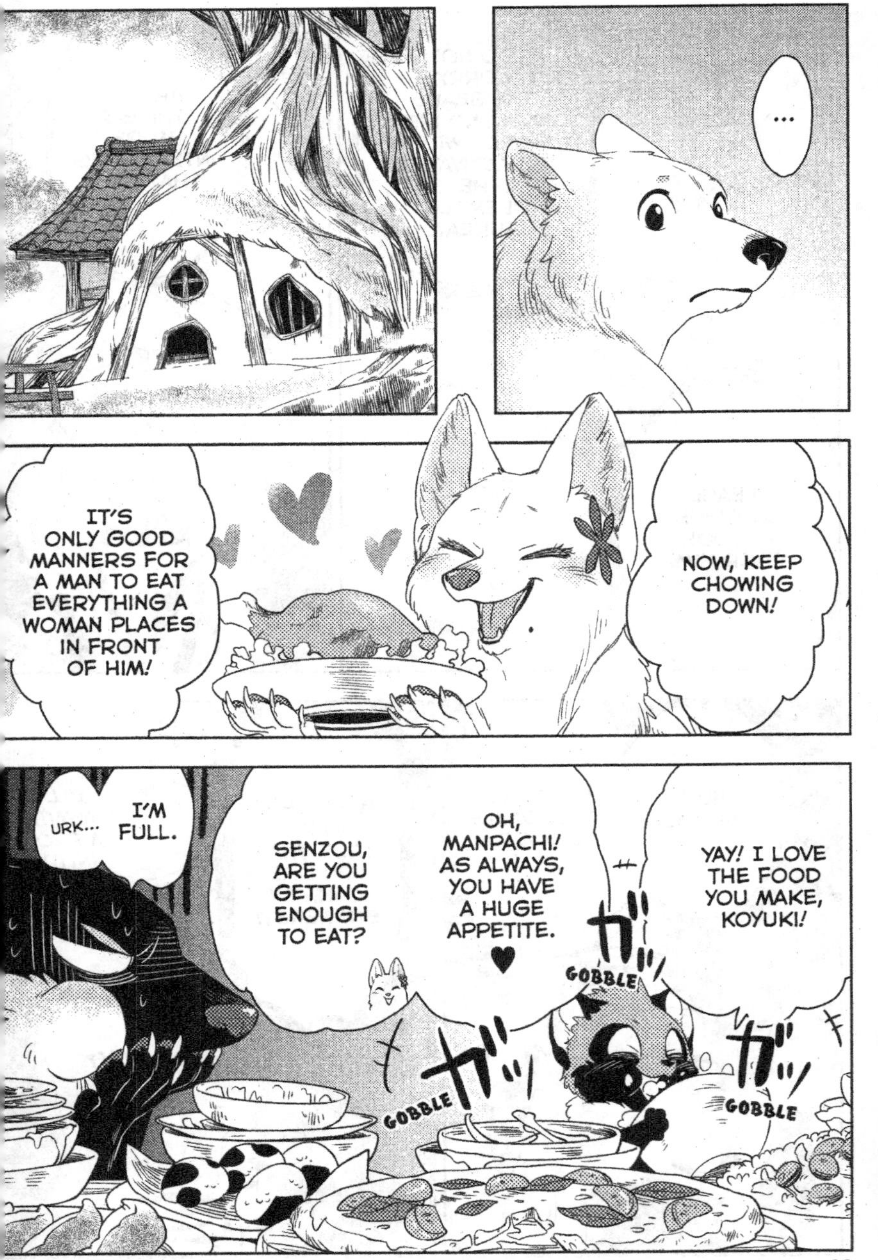
...
NOW, KEEP CHOWING DOWN!
IT'S ONLY GOOD MANNERS FOR A MAN TO EAT EVERYTHING A WOMAN PLACES IN FRONT OF HIM!
YAY! I LOVE THE FOOD YOU MAKE, KOYUKI!
ガッ
GOBBLE
ガッ
GOBBLE
OH, MANPACHI! AS ALWAYS, YOU HAVE A HUGE APPETITE. ♥
ガッ
GOBBLE
SENZOU, ARE YOU GETTING ENOUGH TO EAT?
URK... I'M FULL.

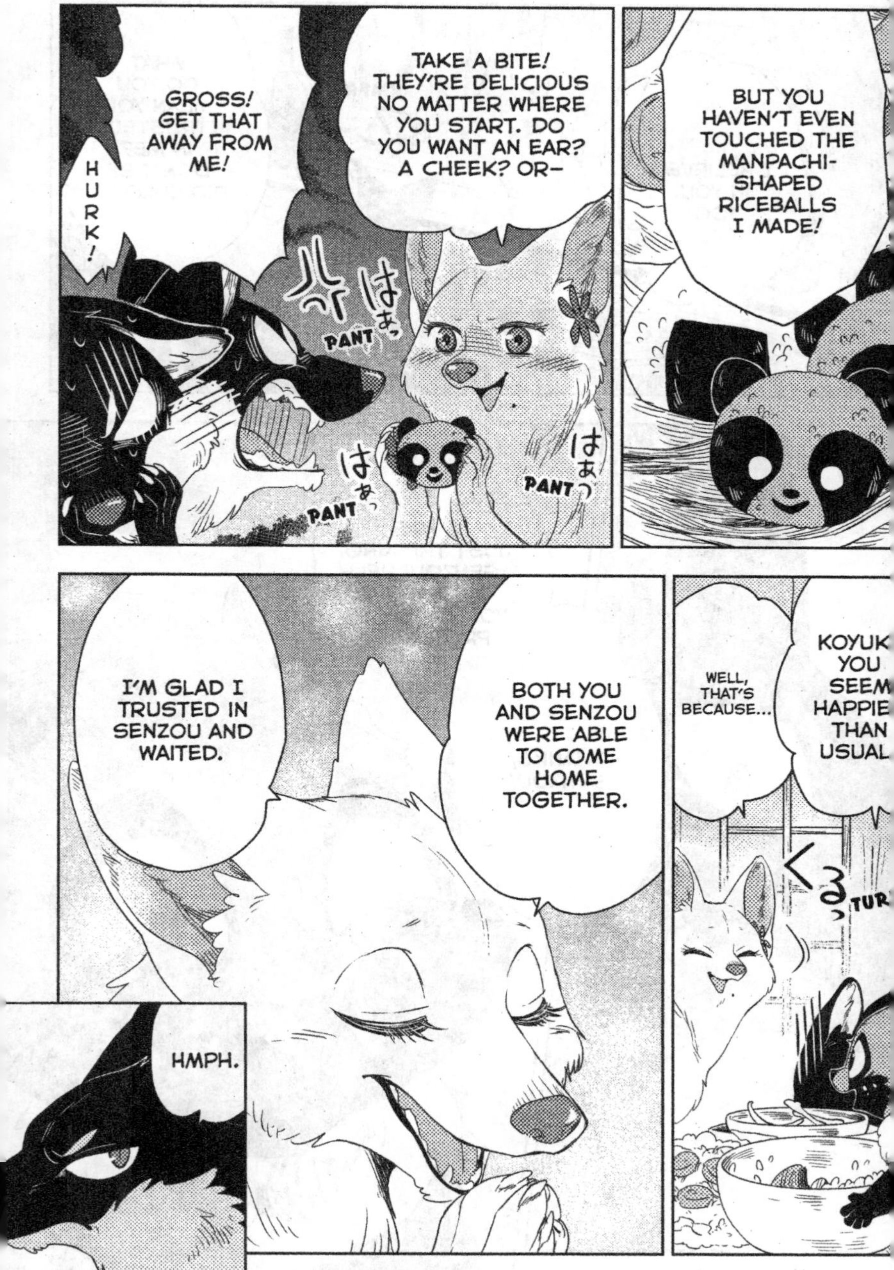
BUT YOU HAVEN'T EVEN TOUCHED THE MANPACHI-SHAPED RICEBALLS I MADE!
TAKE A BITE! THEY'RE DELICIOUS NO MATTER WHERE YOU START. DO YOU WANT AN EAR? A CHEEK? OR–
GROSS! GET THAT AWAY FROM ME!
HURK!
はあっ
PANT
はあっ
PANT
はぁっ
PANT
KOYUK
YOU SEEM HAPPIE THAN USUAL
WELL, THAT'S BECAUSE...
くるっ
TUR
BOTH YOU AND SENZOU WERE ABLE TO COME HOME TOGETHER.
I'M GLAD I TRUSTED IN SENZOU AND WAITED.
HMPH.

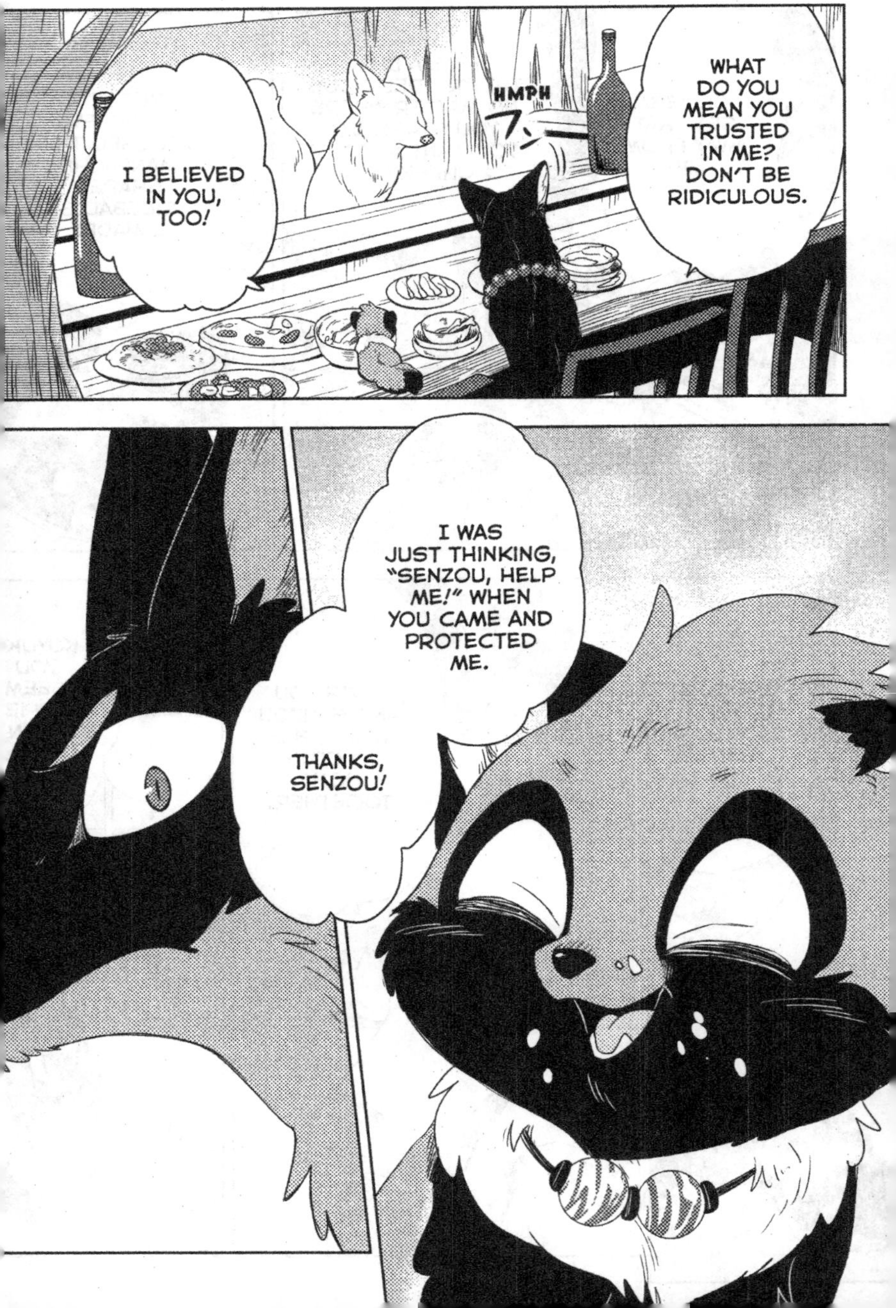
WHAT DO YOU MEAN YOU TRUSTED IN ME? DON'T BE RIDICULOUS.
HMPH
I BELIEVED IN YOU, TOO!
I WAS JUST THINKING, "SENZOU, HELP ME!" WHEN YOU CAME AND PROTECTED ME.
THANKS, SENZOU!

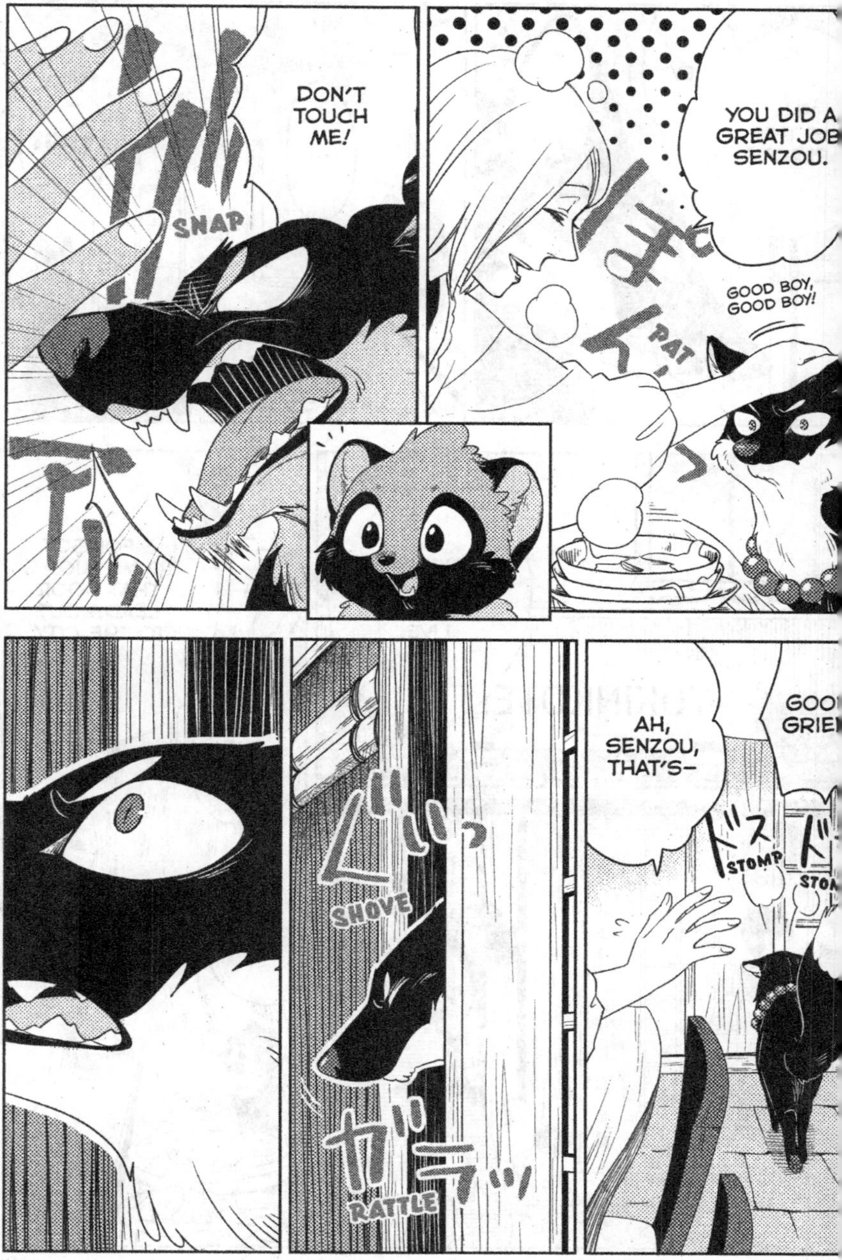
YOU DID A GREAT JOB SENZOU.
GOOD BOY, GOOD BOY!
PAT
DON'T TOUCH ME!
SNAP
GOO GRIE
AH, SENZOU, THAT'S–
STOMP
STOM
SHOVE
RATTLE

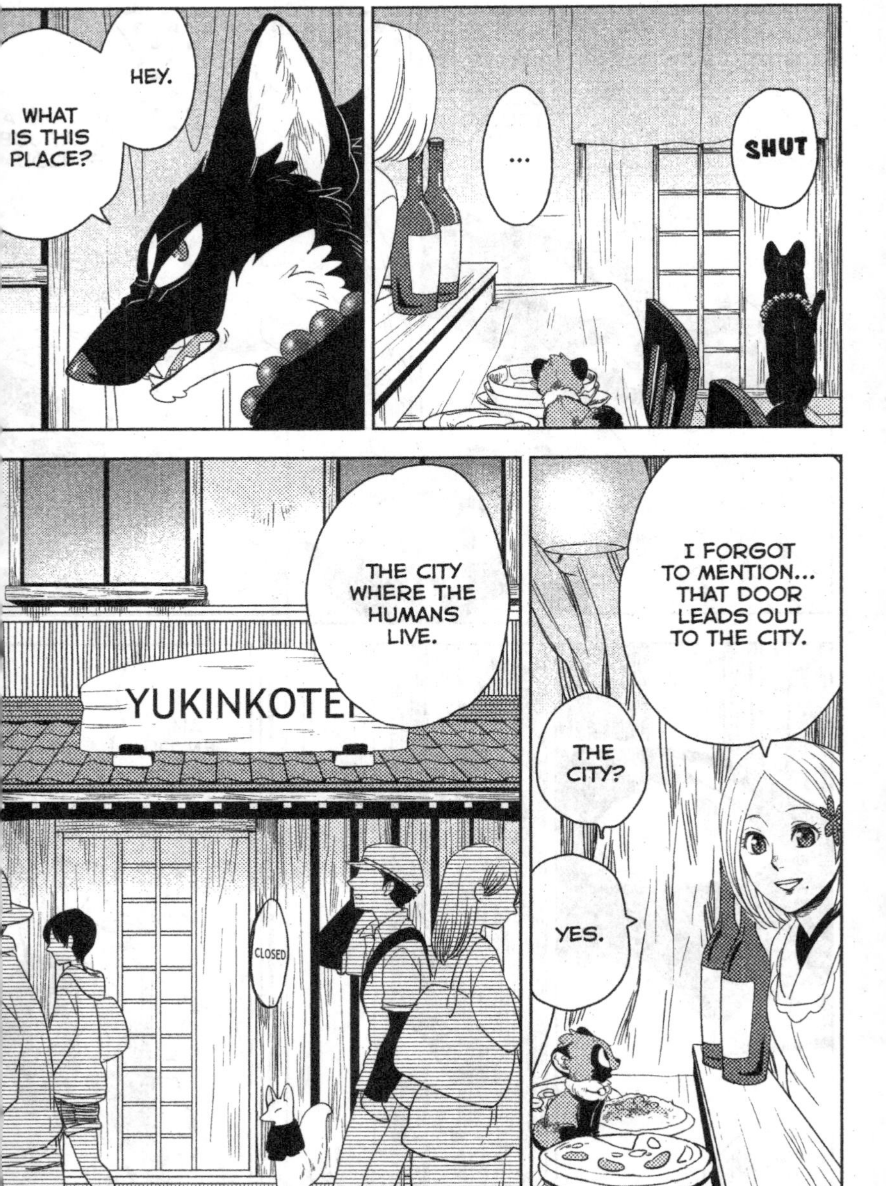
SHUT
...
HEY.
WHAT IS THIS PLACE?
I FORGOT TO MENTION... THAT DOOR LEADS OUT TO THE CITY.
THE CITY?
YES.
THE CITY WHERE THE HUMANS LIVE.
YUKINKOTE
CLOSED

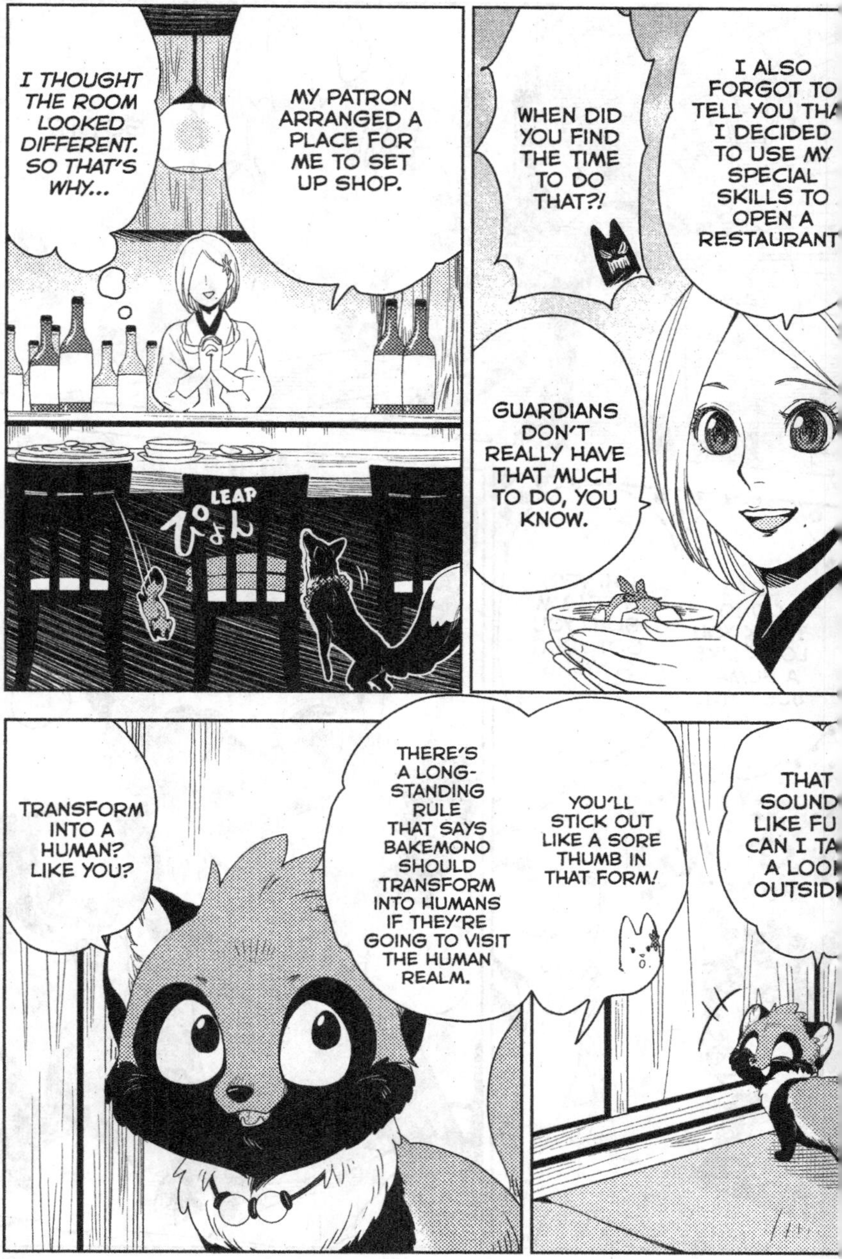
I ALSO FORGOT TO TELL YOU THA I DECIDED TO USE MY SPECIAL SKILLS TO OPEN A RESTAURANT
WHEN DID YOU FIND THE TIME TO DO THAT?!
GUARDIANS DON'T REALLY HAVE THAT MUCH TO DO, YOU KNOW.
MY PATRON ARRANGED A PLACE FOR ME TO SET UP SHOP.
I THOUGHT THE ROOM LOOKED DIFFERENT. SO THAT'S WHY...
LEAP
ぴょん
THAT SOUND LIKE FU CAN I TA A LOO OUTSID
YOU'LL STICK OUT LIKE A SORE THUMB IN THAT FORM!
THERE'S A LONG-STANDING RULE THAT SAYS BAKEMONO SHOULD TRANSFORM INTO HUMANS IF THEY'RE GOING TO VISIT THE HUMAN REALM.
TRANSFORM INTO A HUMAN? LIKE YOU?

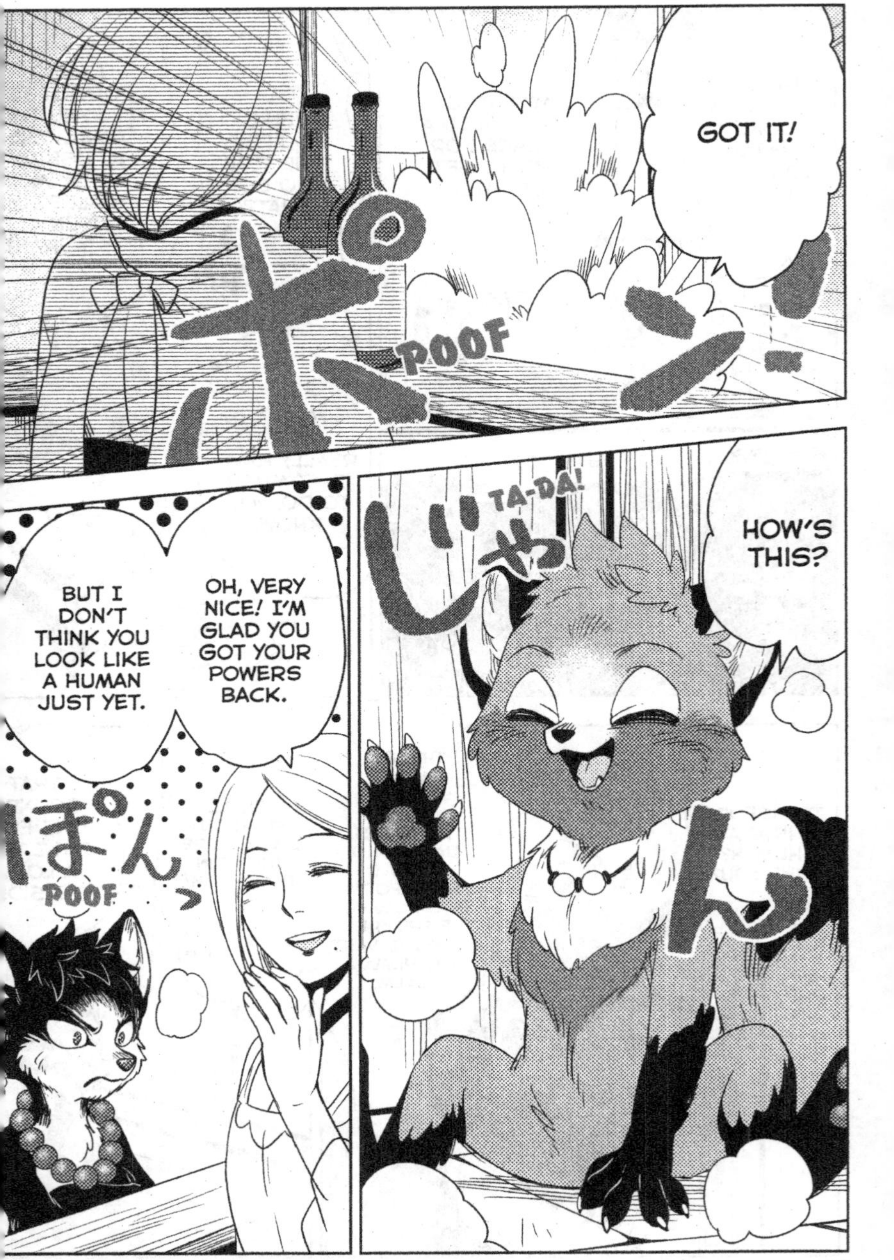
GOT IT!
POOF
HOW'S THIS?
TA-DA!
OH, VERY NICE! I'M GLAD YOU GOT YOUR POWERS BACK.
BUT I DON'T THINK YOU LOOK LIKE A HUMAN JUST YET.
POOF

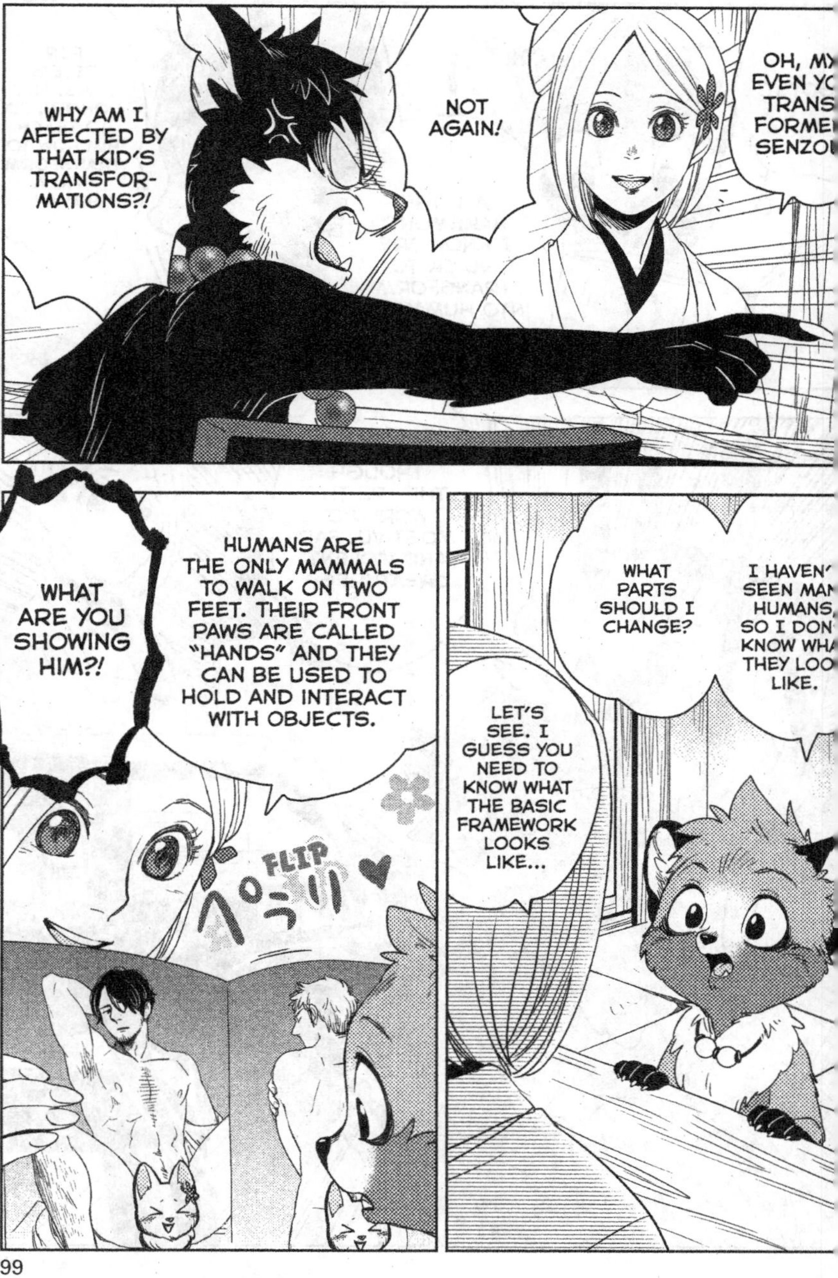
OH, MY EVEN YO TRANS FORME SENZO
NOT AGAIN!
WHY AM I AFFECTED BY THAT KID'S TRANSFOR-MATIONS?!
I HAVEN' SEEN MAN HUMANS, SO I DON KNOW WHA THEY LOO LIKE.
WHAT PARTS SHOULD I CHANGE?
LET'S SEE. I GUESS YOU NEED TO KNOW WHAT THE BASIC FRAMEWORK LOOKS LIKE...
HUMANS ARE THE ONLY MAMMALS TO WALK ON TWO FEET. THEIR FRONT PAWS ARE CALLED "HANDS" AND THEY CAN BE USED TO HOLD AND INTERACT WITH OBJECTS.
WHAT ARE YOU SHOWING HIM?!
FLIP

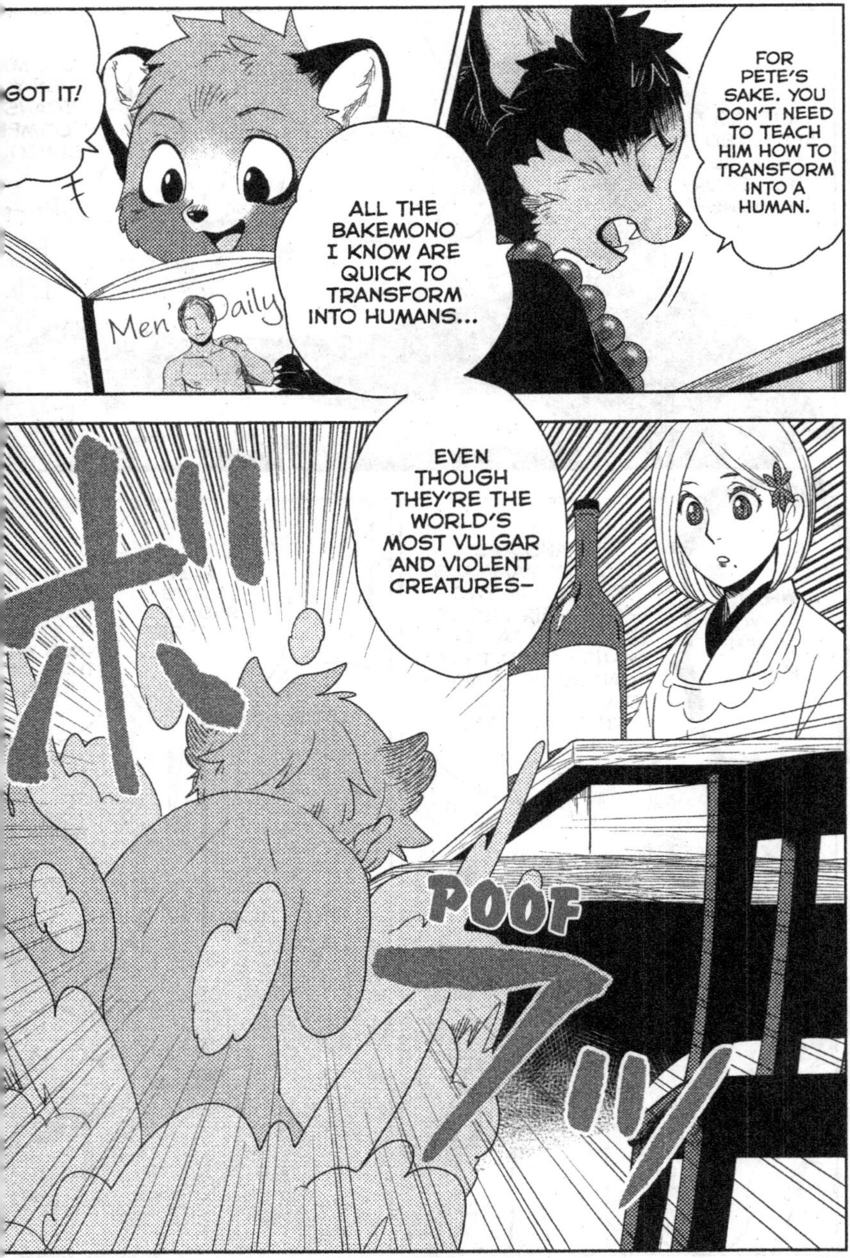
FOR PETE'S SAKE. YOU DON'T NEED TO TEACH HIM HOW TO TRANSFORM INTO A HUMAN.
GOT IT!
Men's Daily
ALL THE BAKEMONO I KNOW ARE QUICK TO TRANSFORM INTO HUMANS...
EVEN THOUGH THEY'RE THE WORLD'S MOST VULGAR AND VIOLENT CREATURES—
POOF

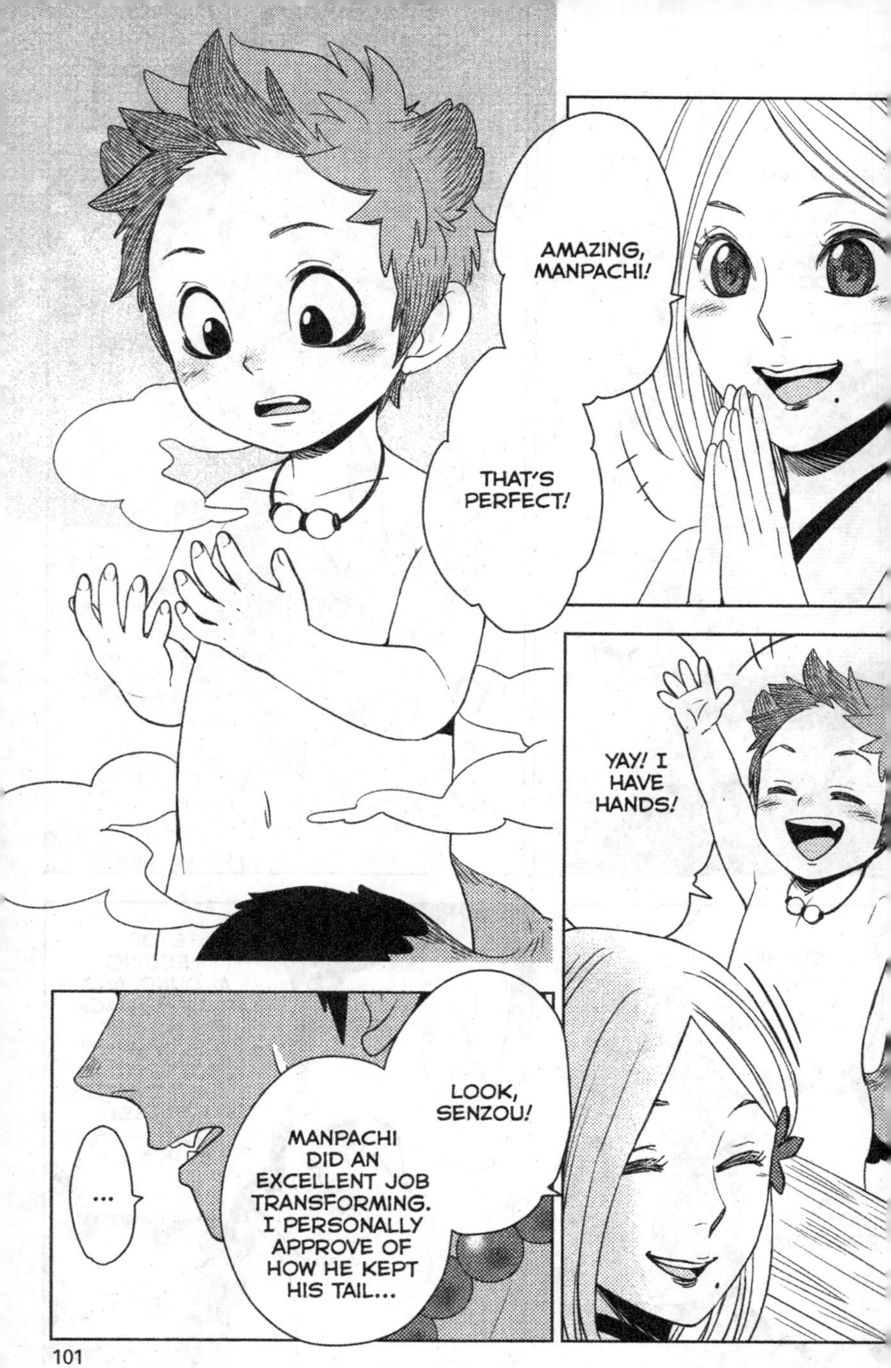
AMAZING, MANPACHI!
THAT'S PERFECT!
YAY! I HAVE HANDS!
LOOK, SENZOU!
MANPACHI DID AN EXCELLENT JOB TRANSFORMING. I PERSONALLY APPROVE OF HOW HE KEPT HIS TAIL...
...

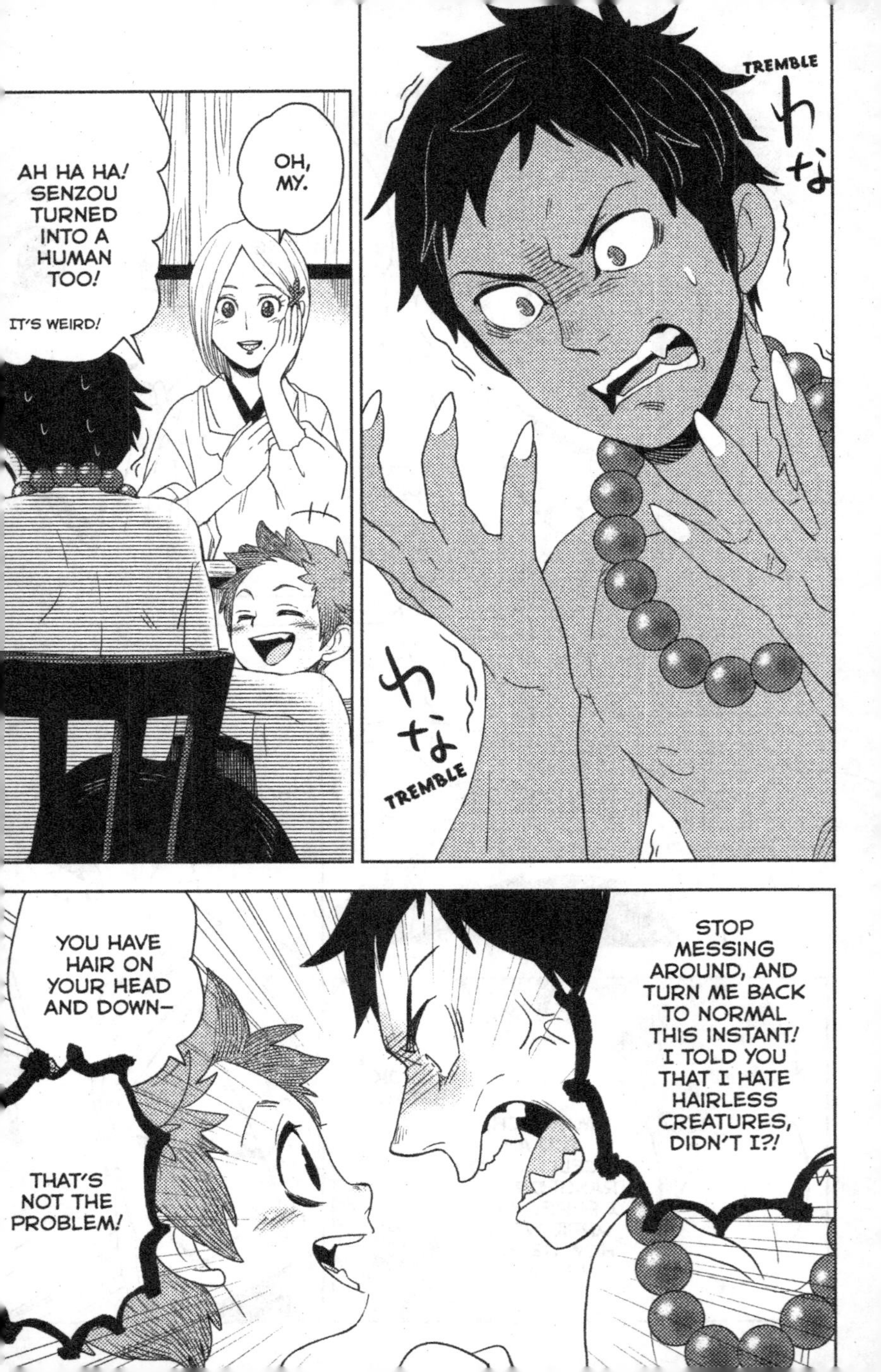
TREMBLE
わな
わな
TREMBLE
OH, MY.
AH HA HA! SENZOU TURNED INTO A HUMAN TOO!
IT'S WEIRD!
STOP MESSING AROUND, AND TURN ME BACK TO NORMAL THIS INSTANT! I TOLD YOU THAT I HATE HAIRLESS CREATURES, DIDN'T I?!
YOU HAVE HAIR ON YOUR HEAD AND DOWN–
THAT'S NOT THE PROBLEM!

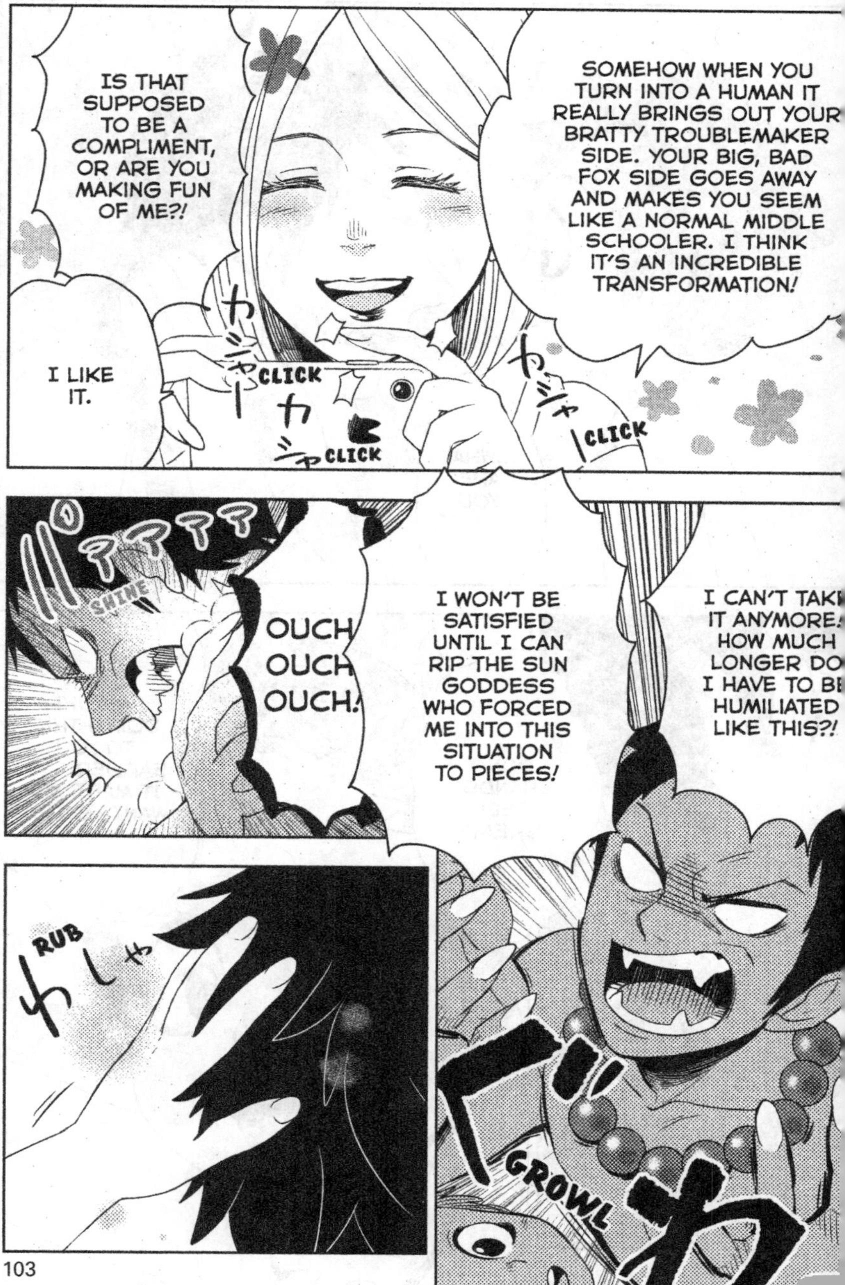
SOMEHOW WHEN YOU TURN INTO A HUMAN IT REALLY BRINGS OUT YOUR BRATTY TROUBLEMAKER SIDE. YOUR BIG, BAD FOX SIDE GOES AWAY AND MAKES YOU SEEM LIKE A NORMAL MIDDLE SCHOOLER. I THINK IT'S AN INCREDIBLE TRANSFORMATION!
IS THAT SUPPOSED TO BE A COMPLIMENT, OR ARE YOU MAKING FUN OF ME?!
CLICK
CLICK
CLICK
I LIKE IT.
I CAN'T TAKE IT ANYMORE! HOW MUCH LONGER DO I HAVE TO BE HUMILIATED LIKE THIS?!
I WON'T BE SATISFIED UNTIL I CAN RIP THE SUN GODDESS WHO FORCED ME INTO THIS SITUATION TO PIECES!
GROWL
SHINE
OUCH OUCH OUCH!
RUB

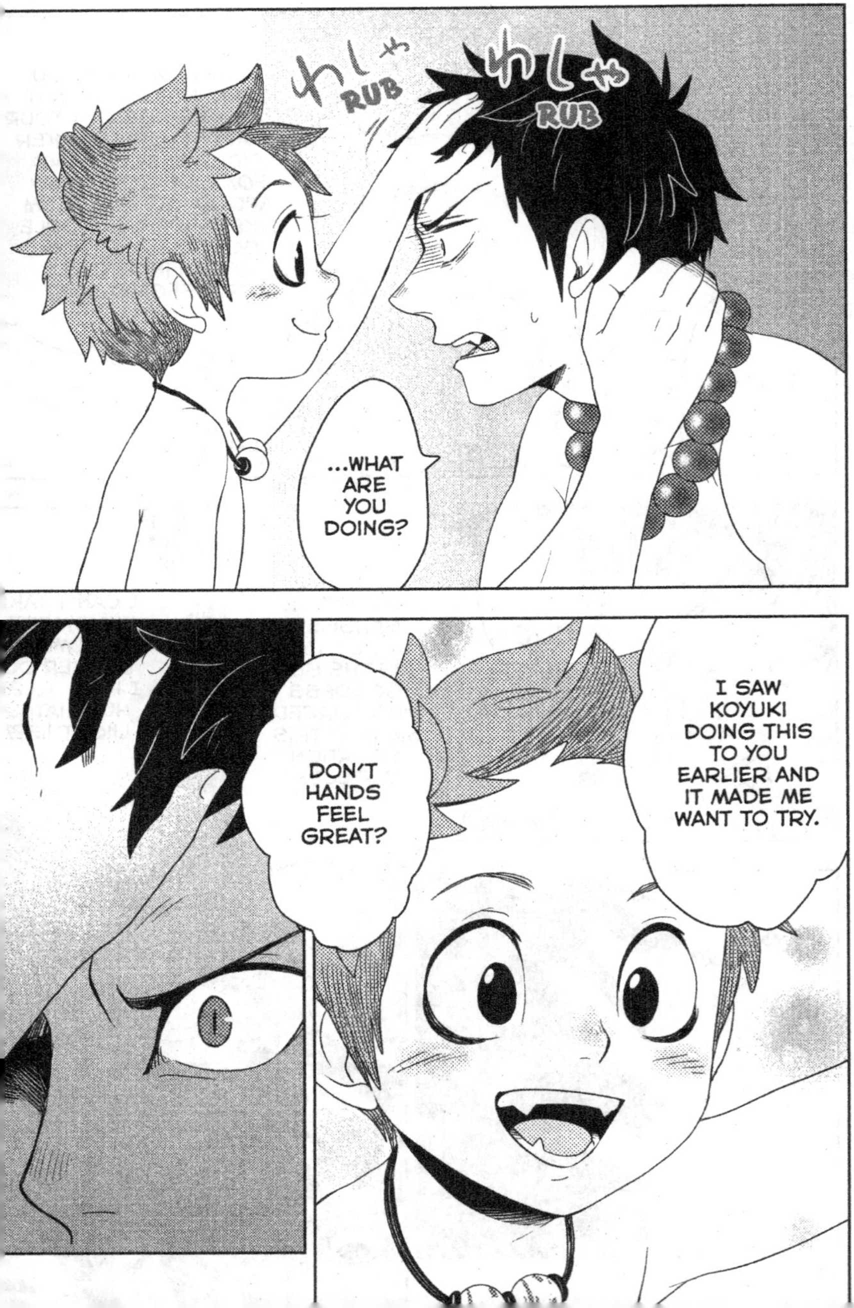
わしゃ RUB
わしゃ RUB
...WHAT ARE YOU DOING?
I SAW KOYUKI DOING THIS TO YOU EARLIER AND IT MADE ME WANT TO TRY.
DON'T HANDS FEEL GREAT?

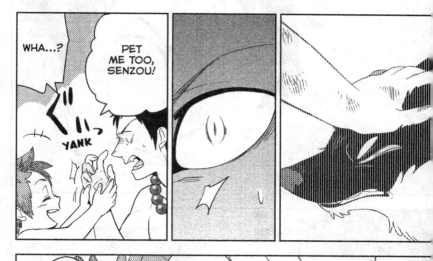

WHA...?

PET ME TOO, SENZOU!

YANK

HA HA!

STOP IT–

RUB

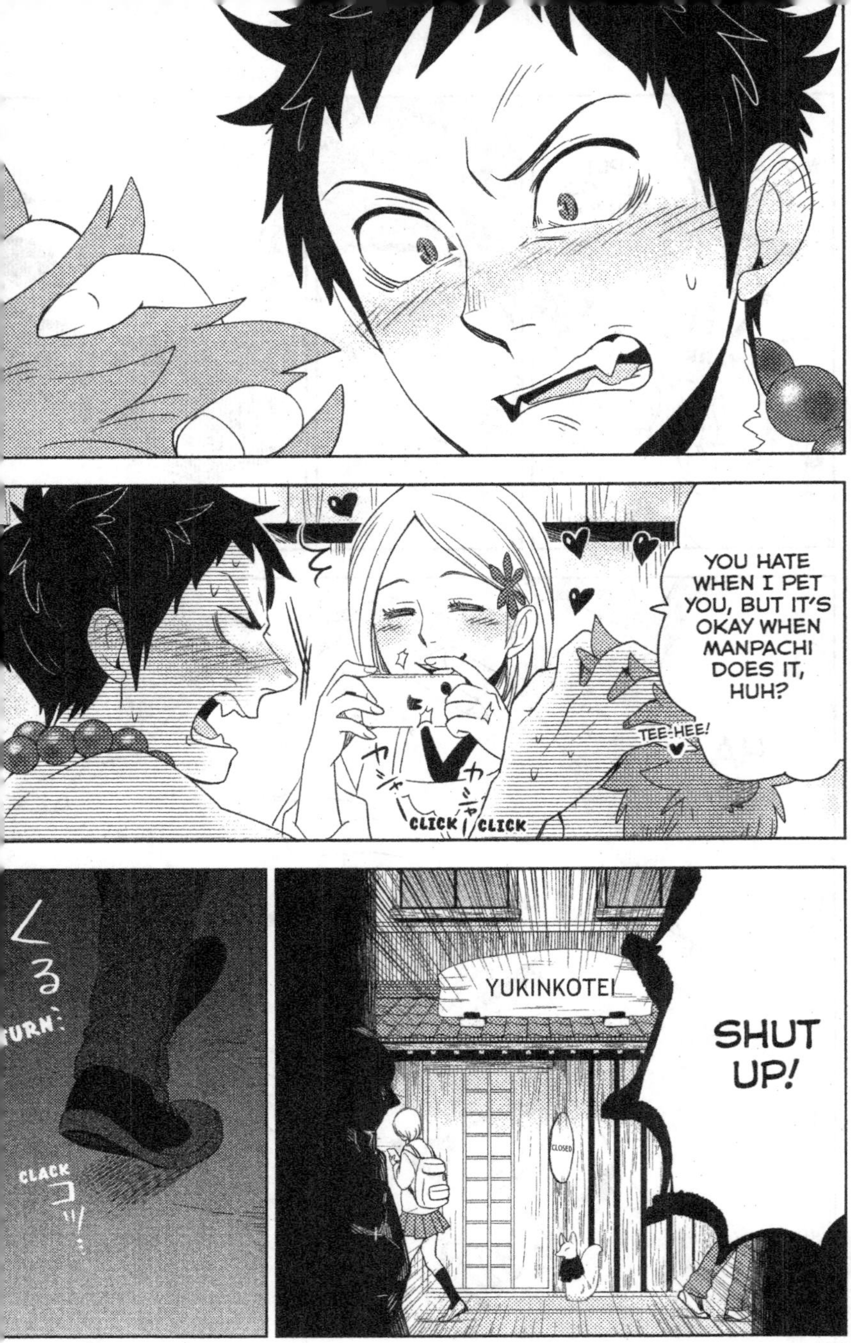
YOU HATE WHEN I PET YOU, BUT IT'S OKAY WHEN MANPACHI DOES IT, HUH?
TEE-HEE!
CLICK
CLICK
YUKINKOTEI
CLOSED
SHUT UP!
くる
TURN
CLACK

# Chapter 11

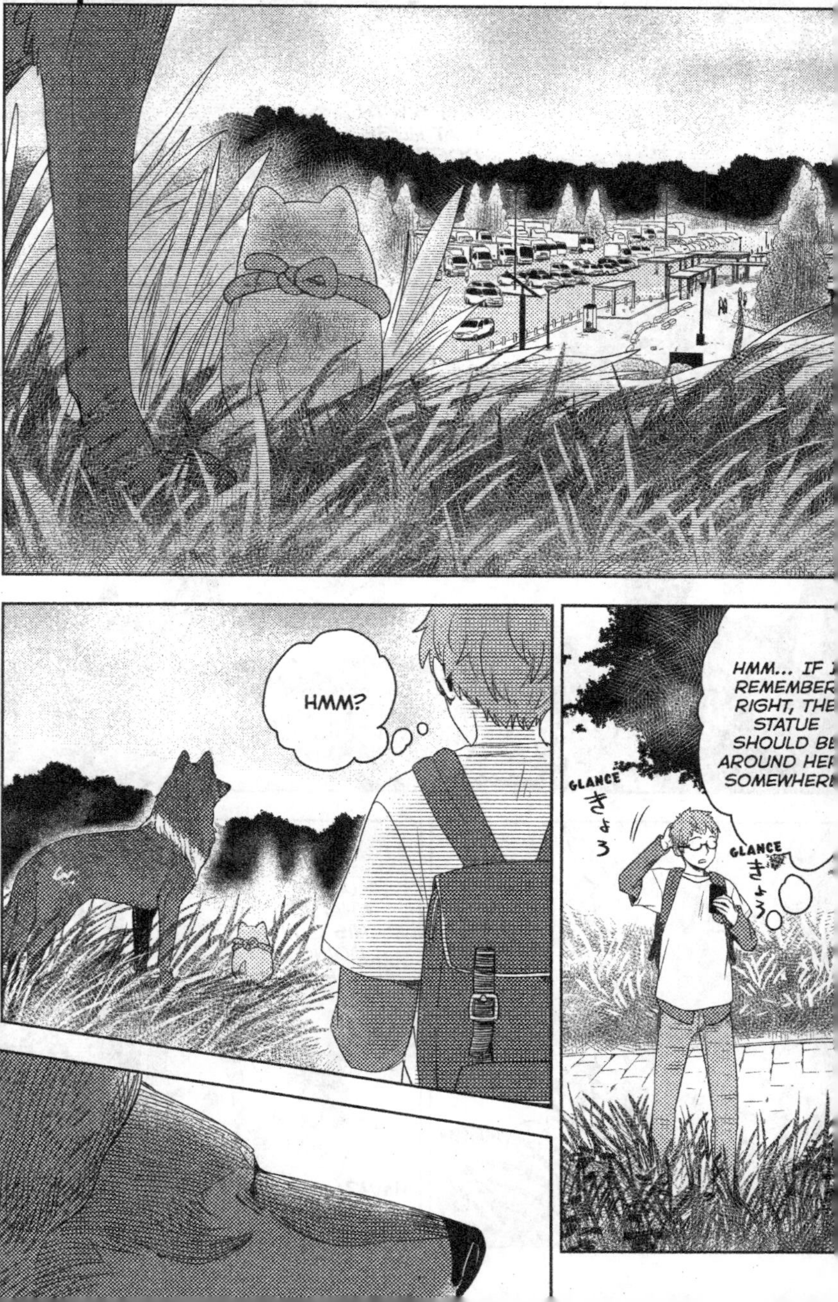
HMM... IF REMEMBER RIGHT, THE STATUE SHOULD BE AROUND HER SOMEWHER
GLANCE
きょろ
GLANCE
きょろ
HMM?

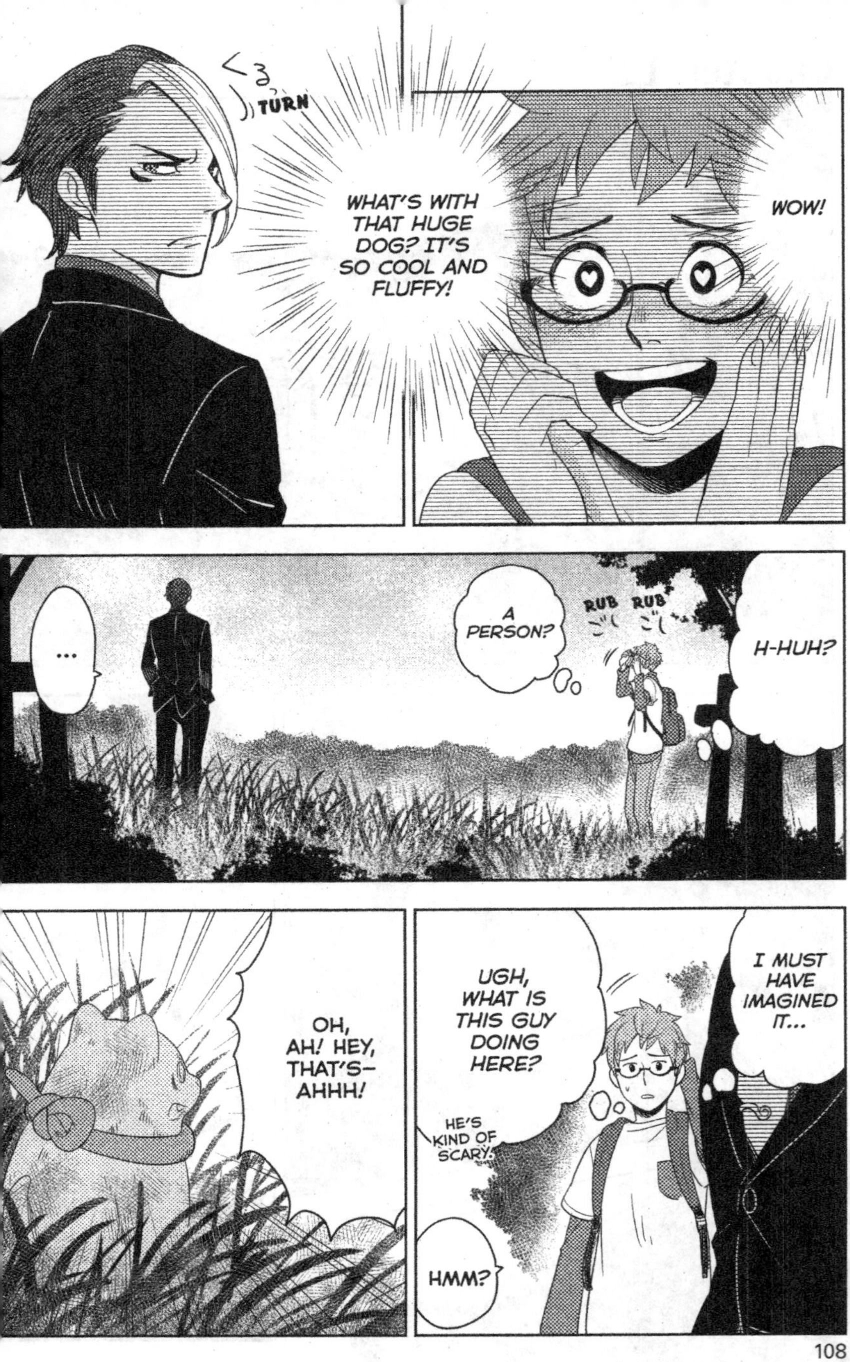
WOW!
WHAT'S WITH THAT HUGE DOG? IT'S SO COOL AND FLUFFY!
TURN
H-HUH?
RUB RUB
A PERSON?
...
I MUST HAVE IMAGINED IT...
UGH, WHAT IS THIS GUY DOING HERE?
HE'S KIND OF SCARY.
HMM?
OH, AH! HEY, THAT'S—AHHH!

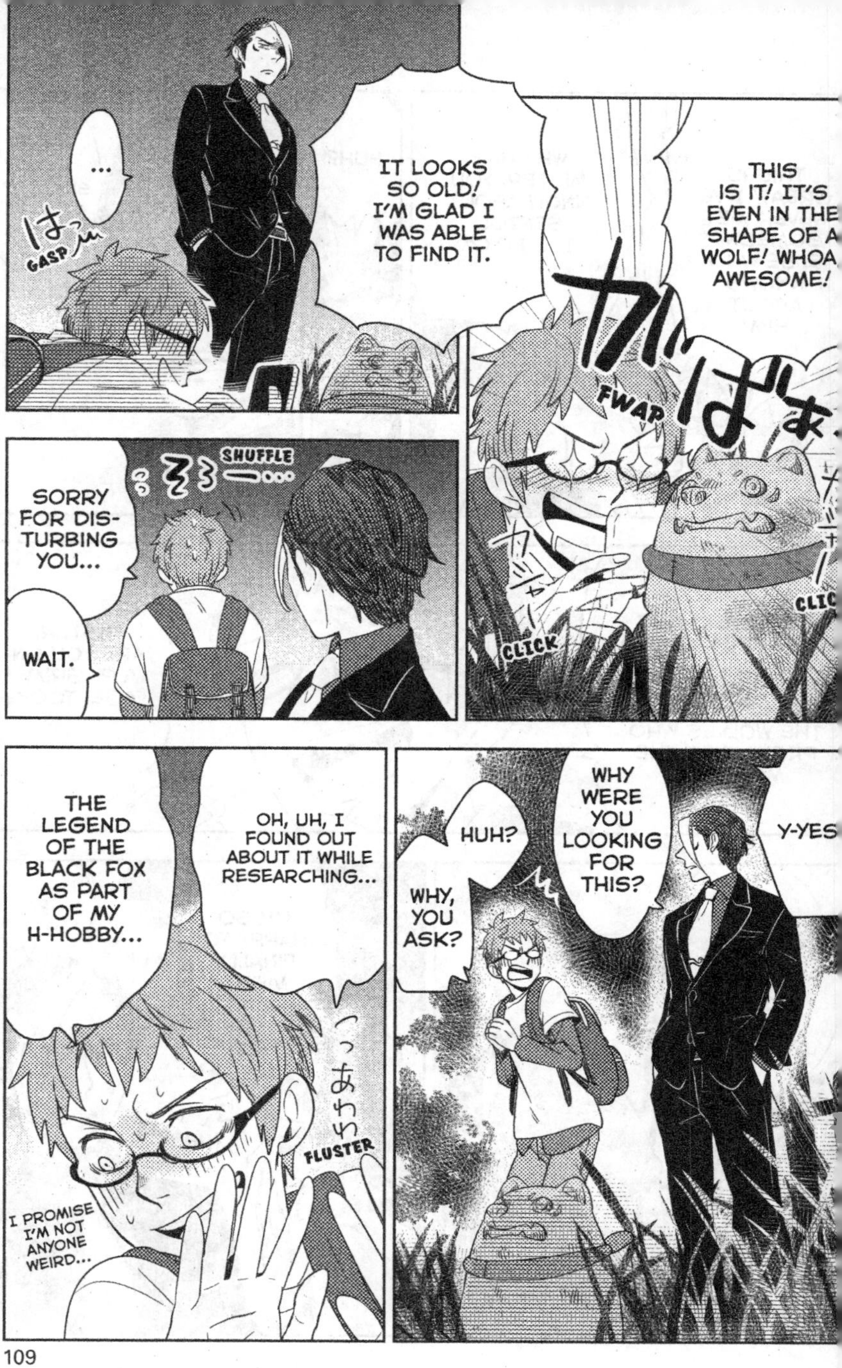
THIS IS IT! IT'S EVEN IN THE SHAPE OF A WOLF! WHOA AWESOME!
FWAP
CLICK
CLICK
IT LOOKS SO OLD! I'M GLAD I WAS ABLE TO FIND IT.
...
GASP
SHUFFLE
SORRY FOR DIS-TURBING YOU...
WAIT.
Y-YES
WHY WERE YOU LOOKING FOR THIS?
HUH?
WHY, YOU ASK?
THE LEGEND OF THE BLACK FOX AS PART OF MY H-HOBBY...
OH, UH, I FOUND OUT ABOUT IT WHILE RESEARCHING...
FLUSTER
I PROMISE I'M NOT ANYONE WEIRD...

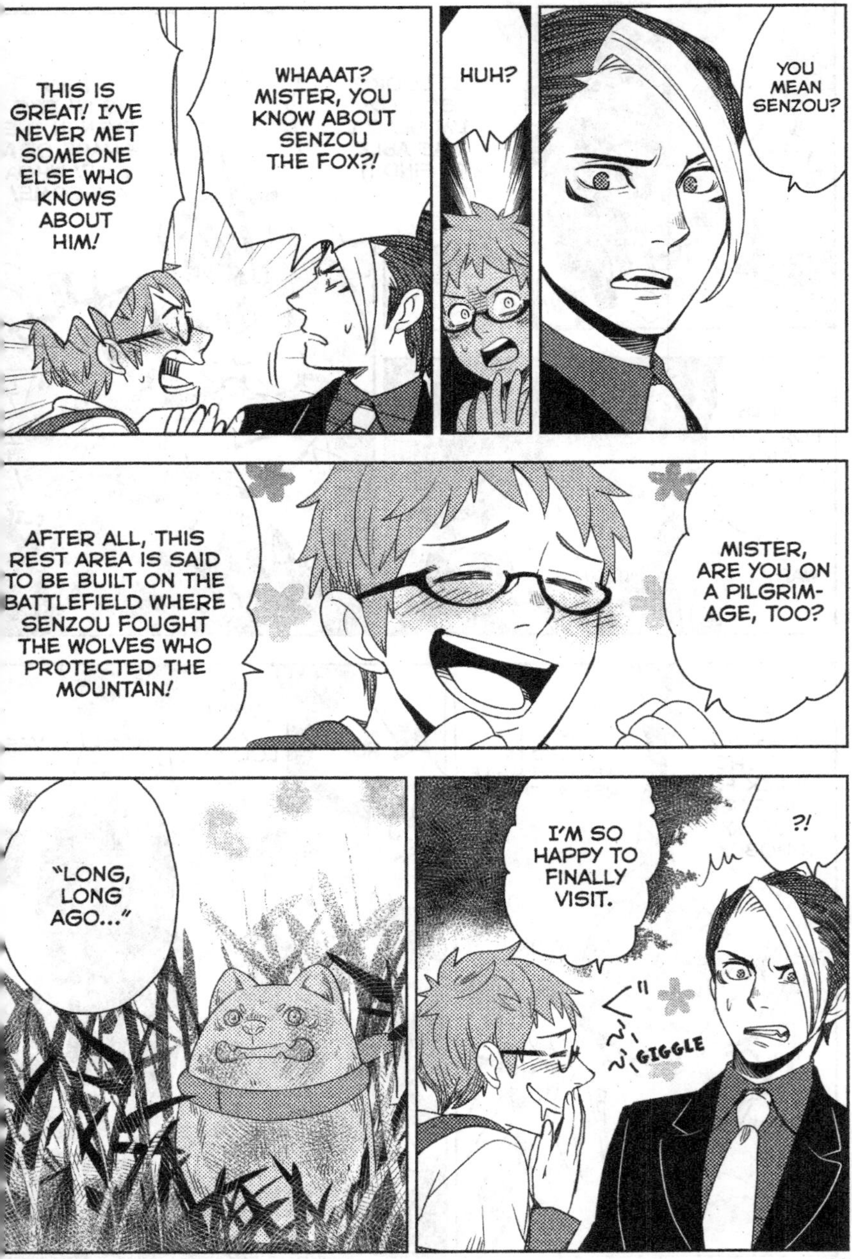
YOU MEAN SENZOU?
HUH?
WHAAAT? MISTER, YOU KNOW ABOUT SENZOU THE FOX?!
THIS IS GREAT! I'VE NEVER MET SOMEONE ELSE WHO KNOWS ABOUT HIM!
MISTER, ARE YOU ON A PILGRIM-AGE, TOO?
AFTER ALL, THIS REST AREA IS SAID TO BE BUILT ON THE BATTLEFIELD WHERE SENZOU FOUGHT THE WOLVES WHO PROTECTED THE MOUNTAIN!
?!
I'M SO HAPPY TO FINALLY VISIT.
GIGGLE
"LONG, LONG AGO..."

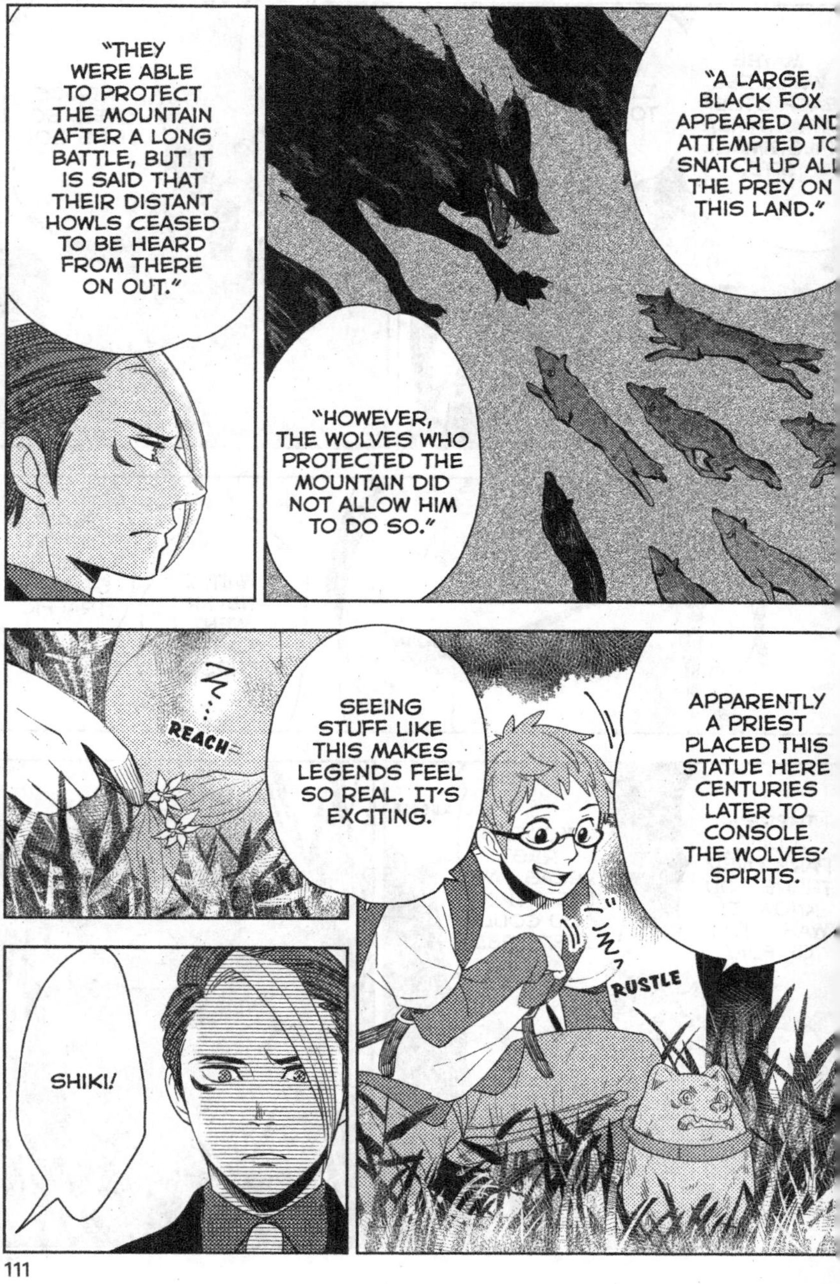
"A LARGE, BLACK FOX APPEARED AND ATTEMPTED TO SNATCH UP ALL THE PREY ON THIS LAND."
"HOWEVER, THE WOLVES WHO PROTECTED THE MOUNTAIN DID NOT ALLOW HIM TO DO SO."
"THEY WERE ABLE TO PROTECT THE MOUNTAIN AFTER A LONG BATTLE, BUT IT IS SAID THAT THEIR DISTANT HOWLS CEASED TO BE HEARD FROM THERE ON OUT."
APPARENTLY A PRIEST PLACED THIS STATUE HERE CENTURIES LATER TO CONSOLE THE WOLVES' SPIRITS.
SEEING STUFF LIKE THIS MAKES LEGENDS FEEL SO REAL. IT'S EXCITING.
RUSTLE
REACH
SHIKI!

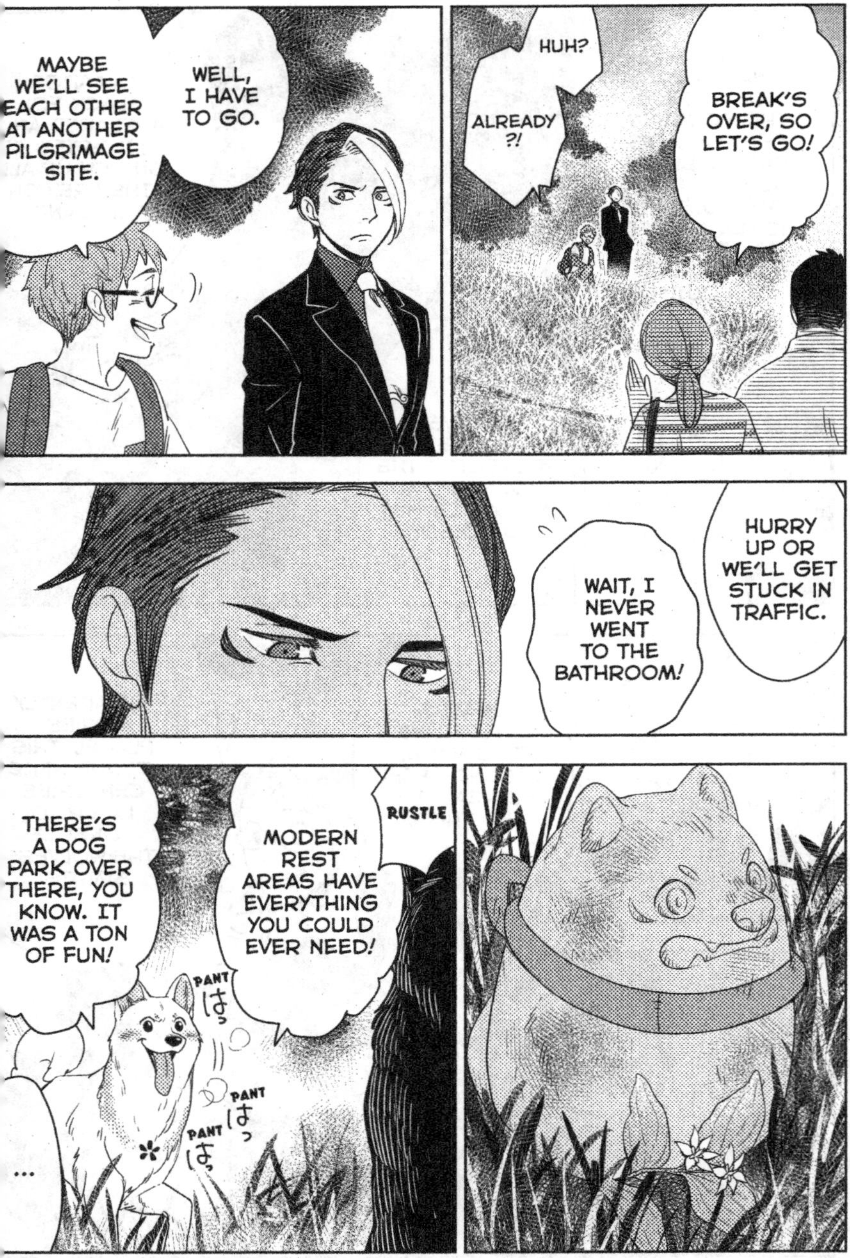
BREAK'S OVER, SO LET'S GO!
HUH?
ALREADY ?!
WELL, I HAVE TO GO.
MAYBE WE'LL SEE EACH OTHER AT ANOTHER PILGRIMAGE SITE.
HURRY UP OR WE'LL GET STUCK IN TRAFFIC.
WAIT, I NEVER WENT TO THE BATHROOM!
RUSTLE
MODERN REST AREAS HAVE EVERYTHING YOU COULD EVER NEED!
THERE'S A DOG PARK OVER THERE, YOU KNOW. IT WAS A TON OF FUN!
PANT はっ
PANT はっ
PANT はっ
...

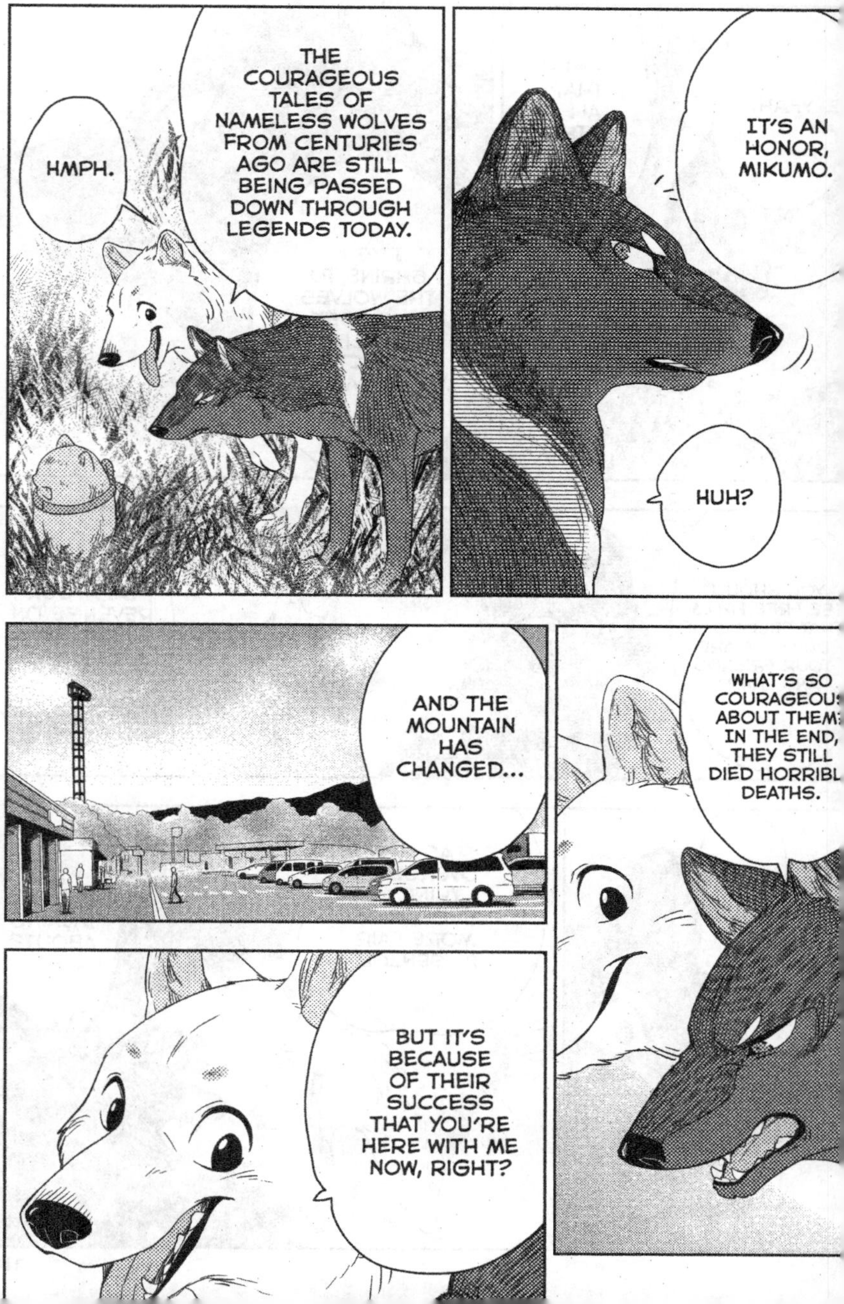
IT'S AN HONOR, MIKUMO.
HUH?
THE COURAGEOUS TALES OF NAMELESS WOLVES FROM CENTURIES AGO ARE STILL BEING PASSED DOWN THROUGH LEGENDS TODAY.
HMPH.
WHAT'S SO COURAGEOU ABOUT THEM IN THE END, THEY STILL DIED HORRIBL DEATHS.
AND THE MOUNTAIN HAS CHANGED...
BUT IT'S BECAUSE OF THEIR SUCCESS THAT YOU'RE HERE WITH ME NOW, RIGHT?

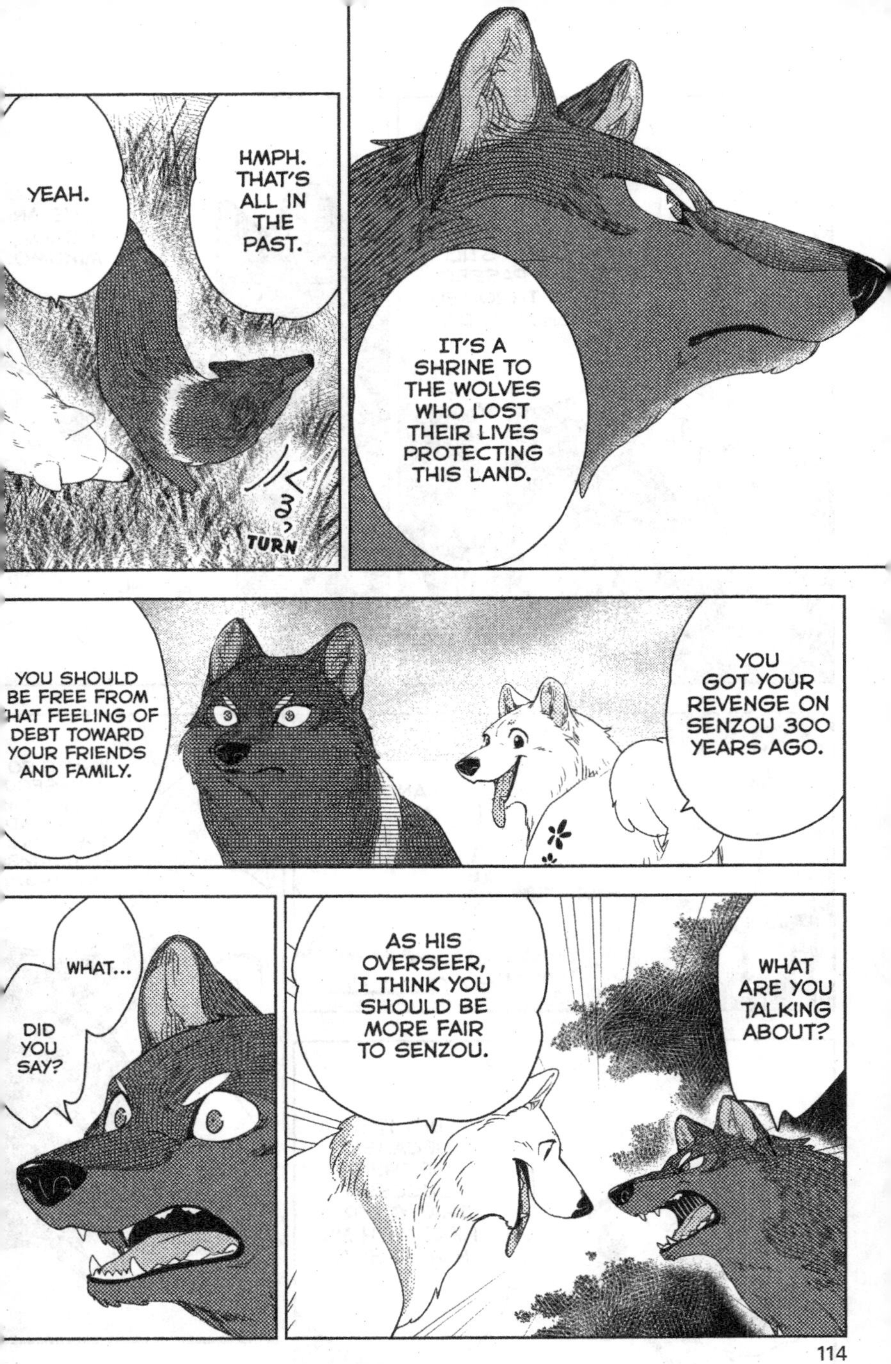
IT'S A SHRINE TO THE WOLVES WHO LOST THEIR LIVES PROTECTING THIS LAND.
HMPH. THAT'S ALL IN THE PAST.
YEAH.
TURN
YOU GOT YOUR REVENGE ON SENZOU 300 YEARS AGO.
YOU SHOULD BE FREE FROM HAT FEELING OF DEBT TOWARD YOUR FRIENDS AND FAMILY.
WHAT ARE YOU TALKING ABOUT?
AS HIS OVERSEER, I THINK YOU SHOULD BE MORE FAIR TO SENZOU.
WHAT...
DID YOU SAY?

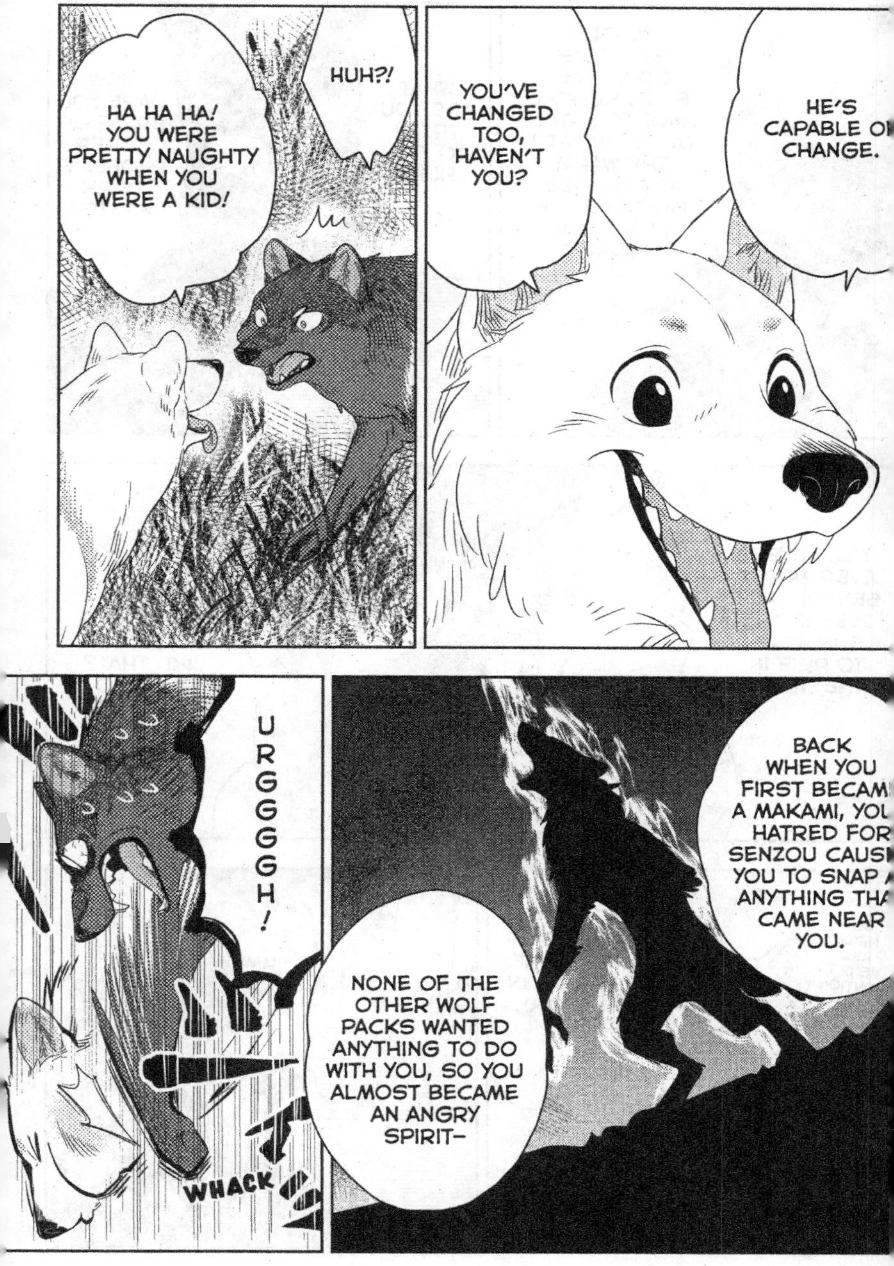
HE'S CAPABLE O CHANGE.
YOU'VE CHANGED TOO, HAVEN'T YOU?
HUH?!
HA HA HA! YOU WERE PRETTY NAUGHTY WHEN YOU WERE A KID!
BACK WHEN YOU FIRST BECAM A MAKAMI, YOU HATRED FOR SENZOU CAUS YOU TO SNAP ANYTHING THA CAME NEAR YOU.
NONE OF THE OTHER WOLF PACKS WANTED ANYTHING TO DO WITH YOU, SO YOU ALMOST BECAME AN ANGRY SPIRIT–
URGGGGH!
WHACK

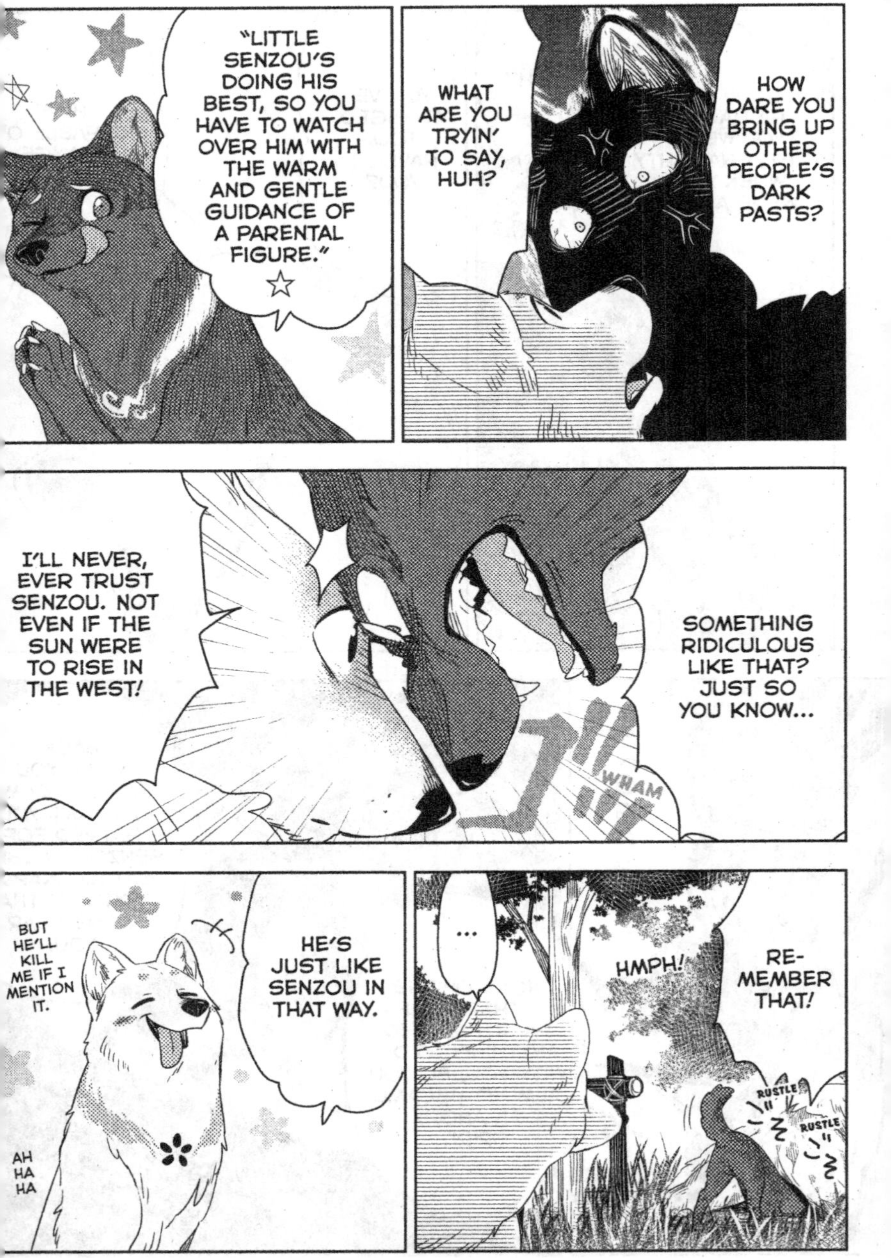
HOW DARE YOU BRING UP OTHER PEOPLE'S DARK PASTS?
WHAT ARE YOU TRYIN' TO SAY, HUH?
"LITTLE SENZOU'S DOING HIS BEST, SO YOU HAVE TO WATCH OVER HIM WITH THE WARM AND GENTLE GUIDANCE OF A PARENTAL FIGURE." ☆
SOMETHING RIDICULOUS LIKE THAT? JUST SO YOU KNOW...
I'LL NEVER, EVER TRUST SENZOU. NOT EVEN IF THE SUN WERE TO RISE IN THE WEST!
WHAM
RE-MEMBER THAT!
HMPH!
...
RUSTLE
RUSTLE
HE'S JUST LIKE SENZOU IN THAT WAY.
BUT HE'LL KILL ME IF I MENTION IT.
AH HA HA

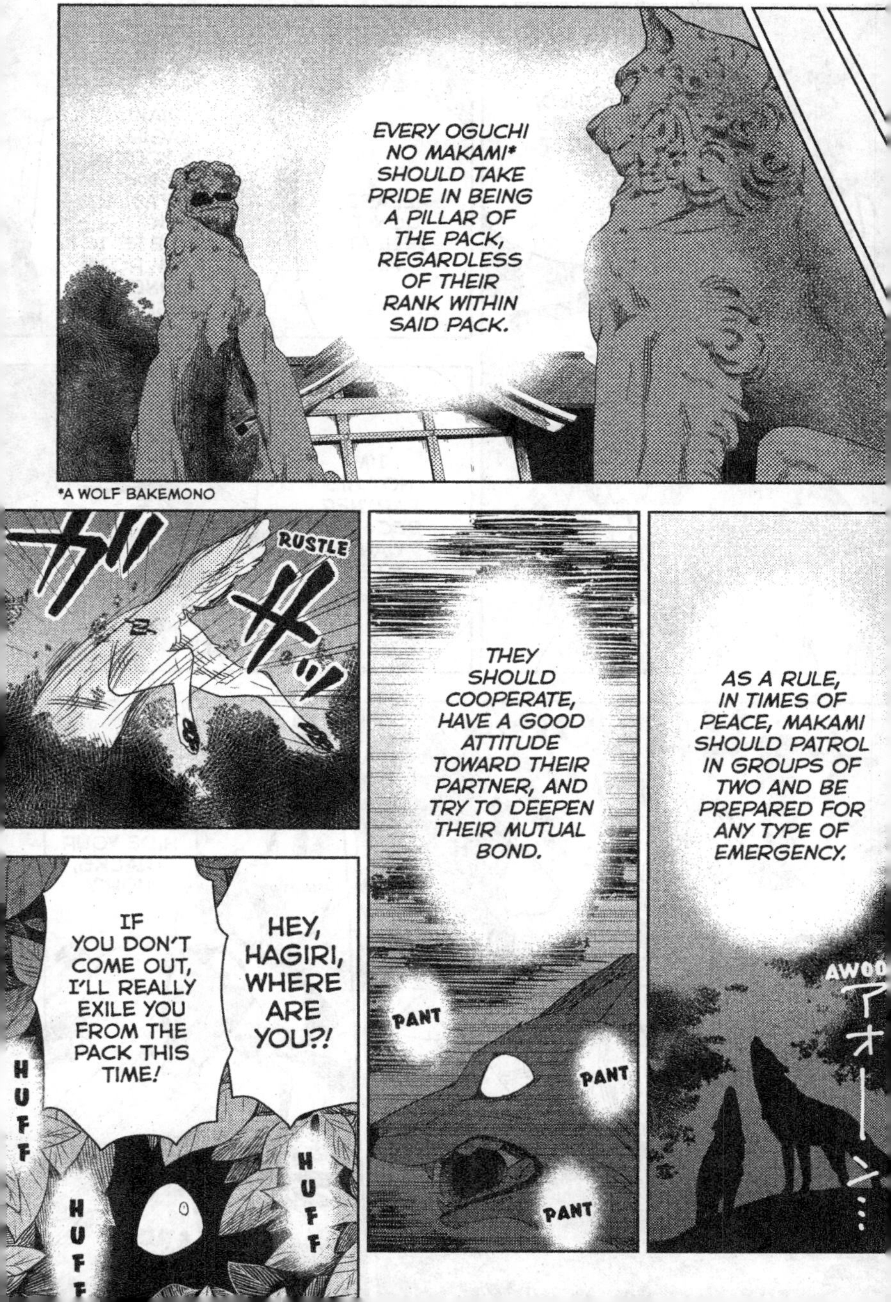
EVERY OGUCHI NO MAKAMI* SHOULD TAKE PRIDE IN BEING A PILLAR OF THE PACK, REGARDLESS OF THEIR RANK WITHIN SAID PACK.
AS A RULE, IN TIMES OF PEACE, MAKAMI SHOULD PATROL IN GROUPS OF TWO AND BE PREPARED FOR ANY TYPE OF EMERGENCY.
AWOO
アオーン…
THEY SHOULD COOPERATE, HAVE A GOOD ATTITUDE TOWARD THEIR PARTNER, AND TRY TO DEEPEN THEIR MUTUAL BOND.
PANT
PANT
PANT
RUSTLE
HEY, HAGIRI, WHERE ARE YOU?!
IF YOU DON'T COME OUT, I'LL REALLY EXILE YOU FROM THE PACK THIS TIME!
HUFF
HUFF
HUFF
HUFF

*A WOLF BAKEMONO

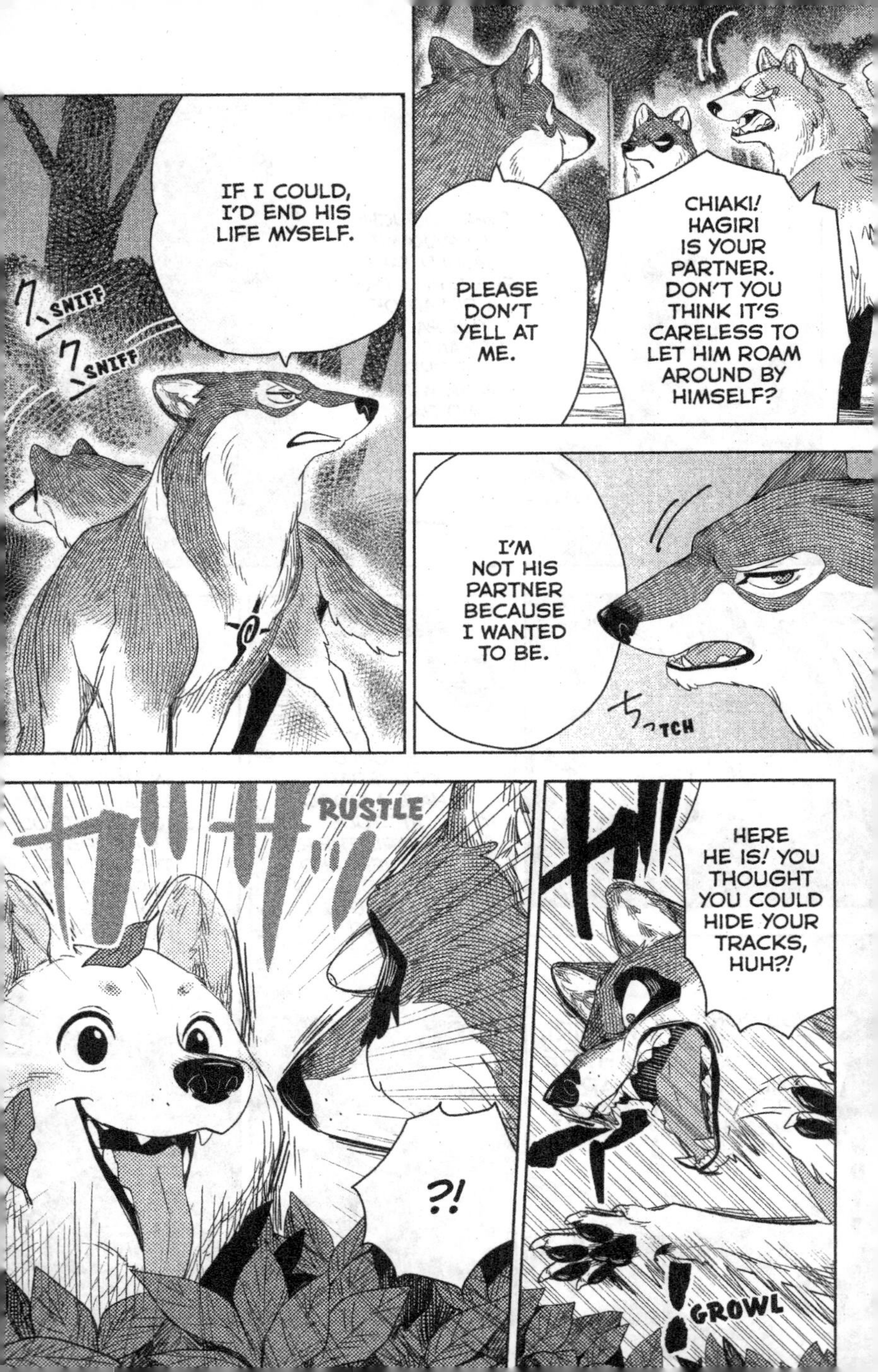
CHIAKI! HAGIRI IS YOUR PARTNER. DON'T YOU THINK IT'S CARELESS TO LET HIM ROAM AROUND BY HIMSELF?
PLEASE DON'T YELL AT ME.
I'M NOT HIS PARTNER BECAUSE I WANTED TO BE.
TCH
IF I COULD, I'D END HIS LIFE MYSELF.
SNIFF
SNIFF
HERE HE IS! YOU THOUGHT YOU COULD HIDE YOUR TRACKS, HUH?!
GROWL
RUSTLE
?!

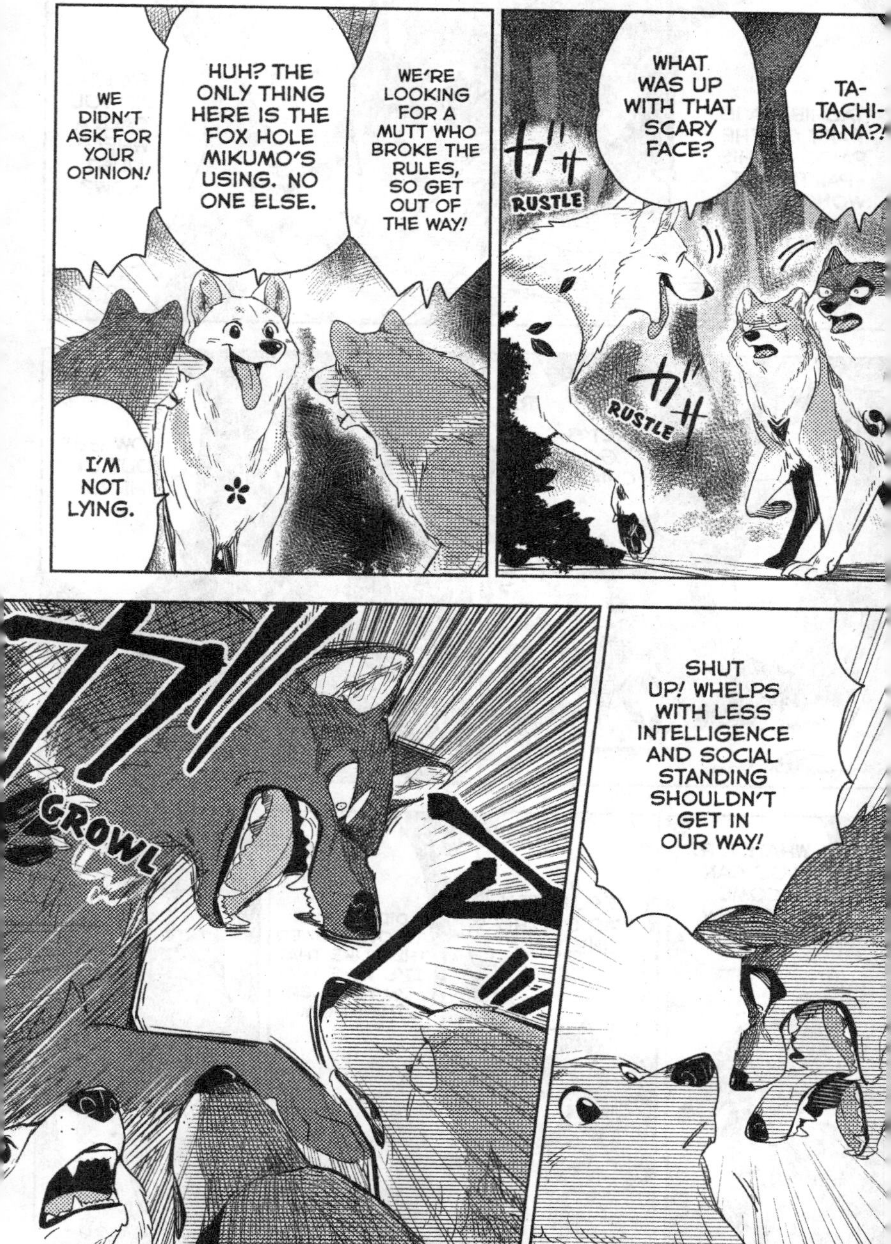
TA-TACHIBANA?!
WHAT WAS UP WITH THAT SCARY FACE?
RUSTLE
RUSTLE
WE'RE LOOKING FOR A MUTT WHO BROKE THE RULES, SO GET OUT OF THE WAY!
HUH? THE ONLY THING HERE IS THE FOX HOLE MIKUMO'S USING. NO ONE ELSE.
WE DIDN'T ASK FOR YOUR OPINION!
I'M NOT LYING.
SHUT UP! WHELPS WITH LESS INTELLIGENCE AND SOCIAL STANDING SHOULDN'T GET IN OUR WAY!
GROWL

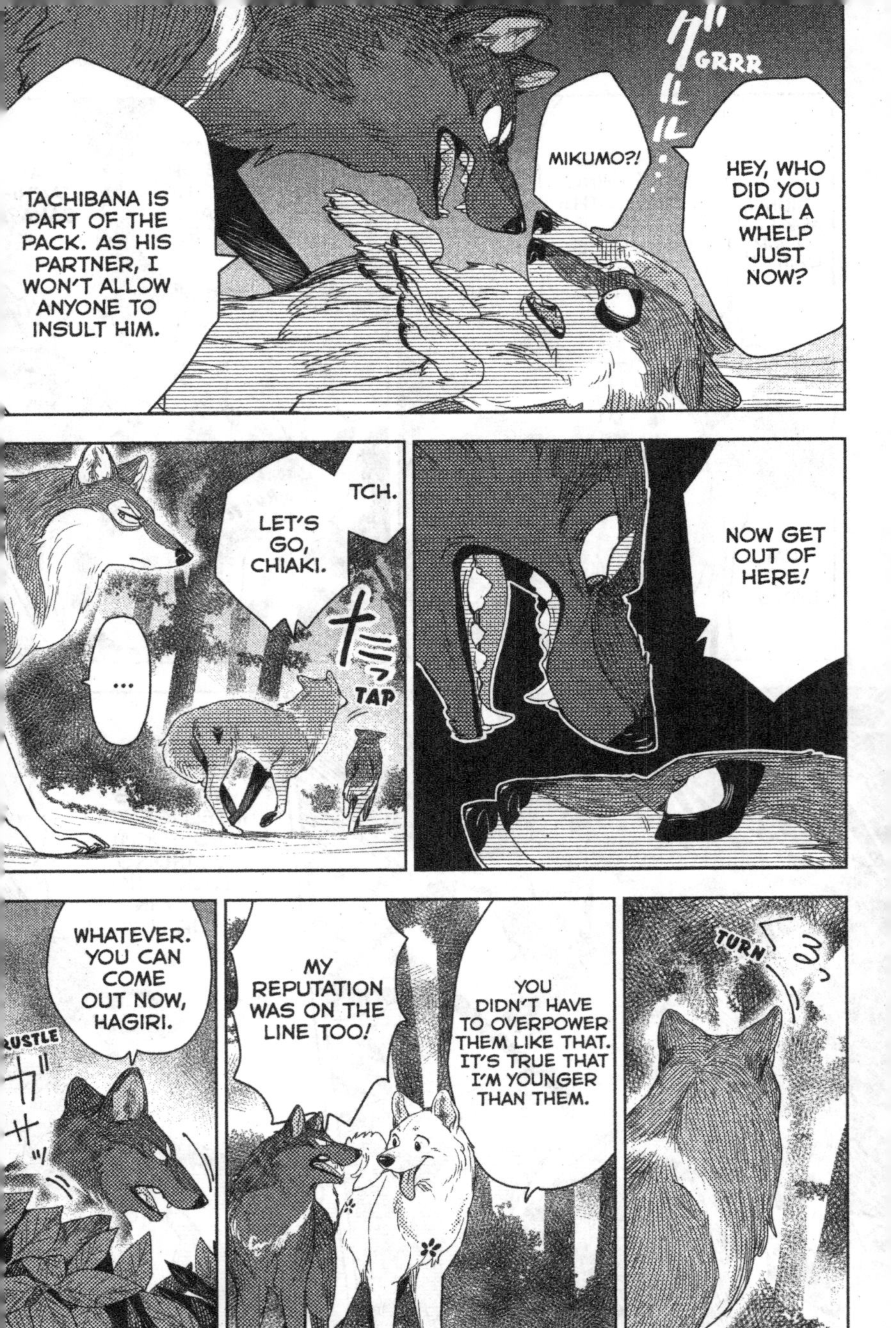
HEY, WHO DID YOU CALL A WHELP JUST NOW?
GRRR
MIKUMO?!
TACHIBANA IS PART OF THE PACK. AS HIS PARTNER, I WON'T ALLOW ANYONE TO INSULT HIM.
NOW GET OUT OF HERE!
TCH.
LET'S GO, CHIAKI.
TAP
...
TURN
YOU DIDN'T HAVE TO OVERPOWER THEM LIKE THAT. IT'S TRUE THAT I'M YOUNGER THAN THEM.
MY REPUTATION WAS ON THE LINE TOO!
WHATEVER. YOU CAN COME OUT NOW, HAGIRI.
RUSTLE

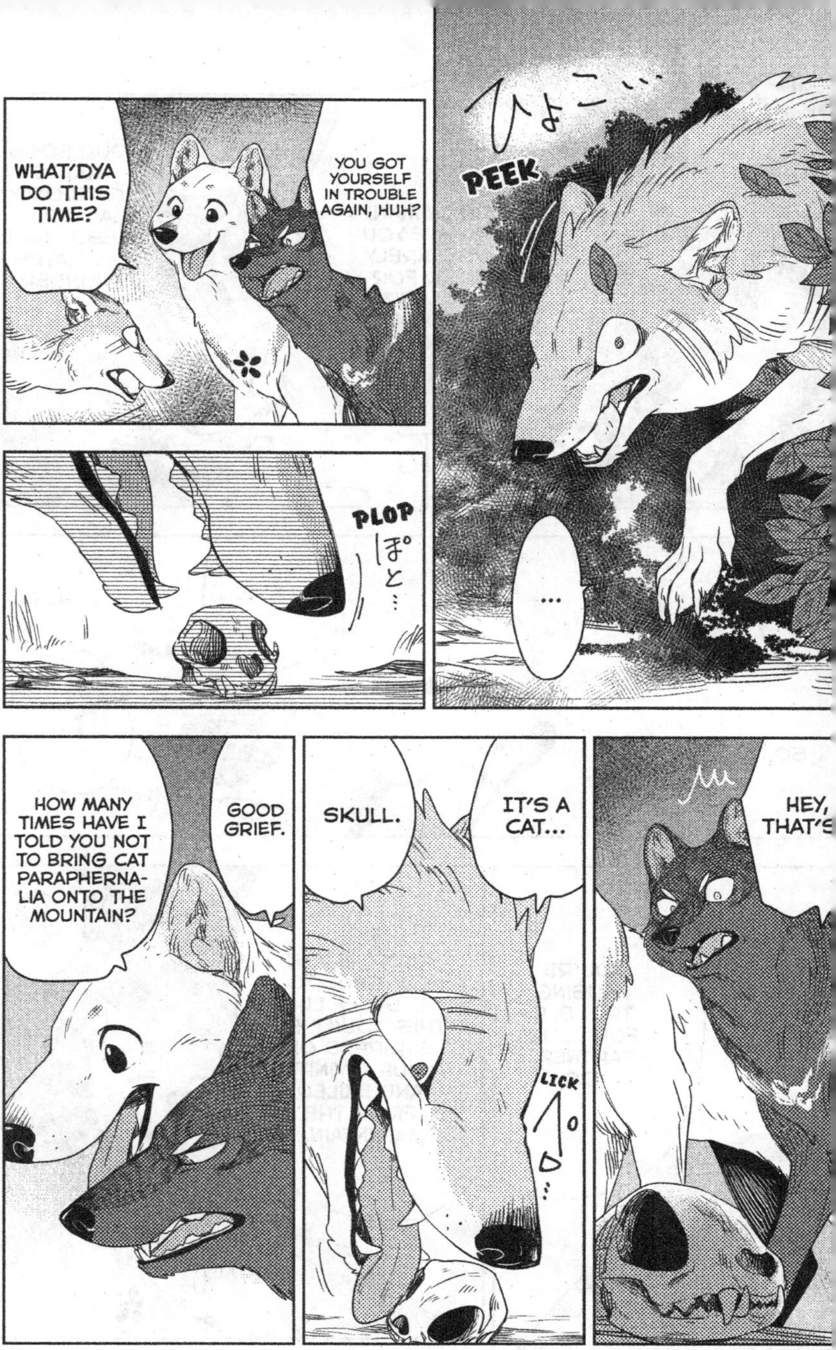
ひょこ
PEEK
...
YOU GOT YOURSELF IN TROUBLE AGAIN, HUH?
WHAT'DYA DO THIS TIME?
PLOP
ぽと…
HEY, THAT'S
IT'S A CAT...
SKULL.
LICK
GOOD GRIEF.
HOW MANY TIMES HAVE I TOLD YOU NOT TO BRING CAT PARAPHERNA-LIA ONTO THE MOUNTAIN?

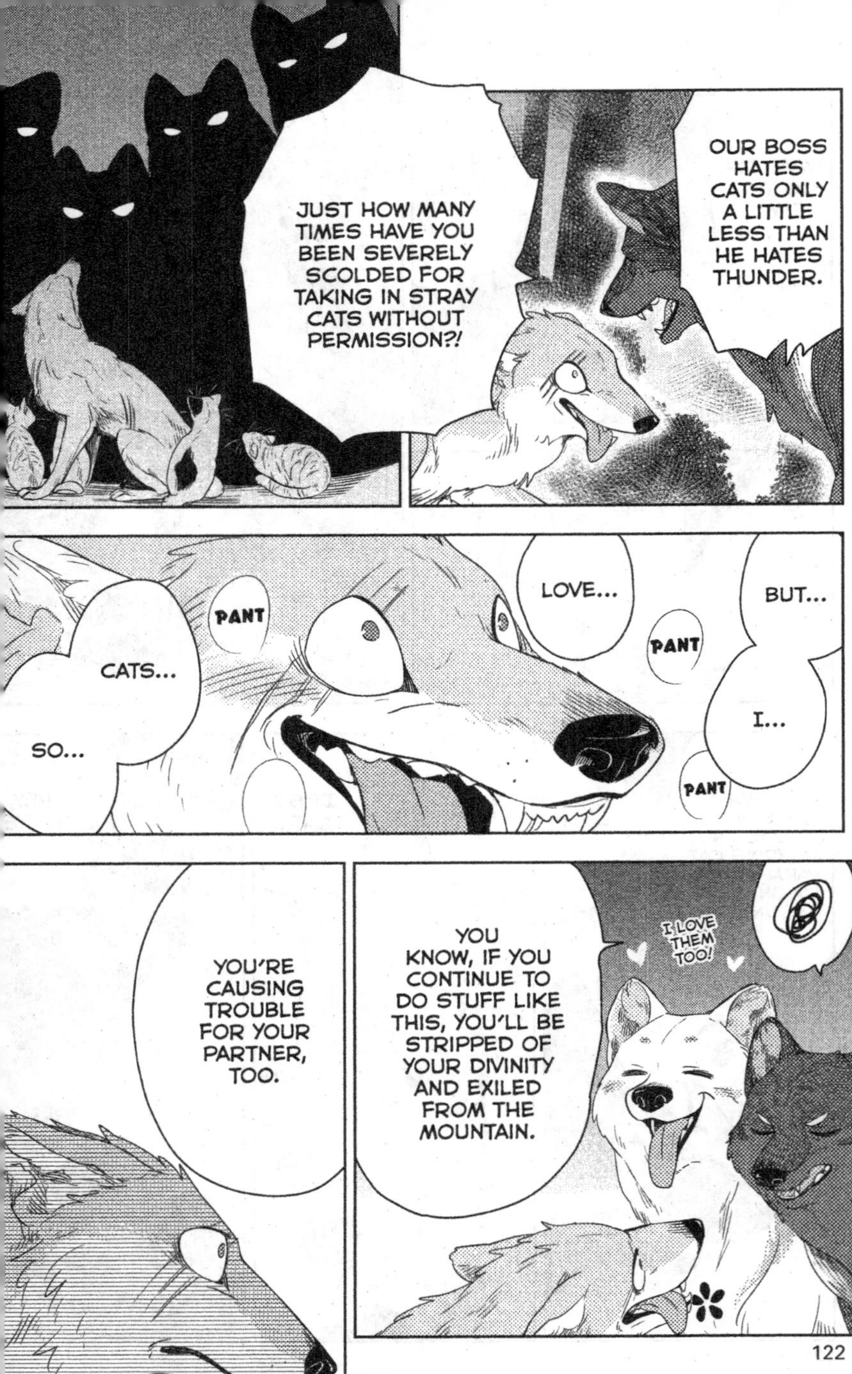
OUR BOSS HATES CATS ONLY A LITTLE LESS THAN HE HATES THUNDER.
JUST HOW MANY TIMES HAVE YOU BEEN SEVERELY SCOLDED FOR TAKING IN STRAY CATS WITHOUT PERMISSION?!
BUT...
I...
PANT
LOVE...
PANT
PANT
CATS...
SO...
I LOVE THEM TOO!
YOU KNOW, IF YOU CONTINUE TO DO STUFF LIKE THIS, YOU'LL BE STRIPPED OF YOUR DIVINITY AND EXILED FROM THE MOUNTAIN.
YOU'RE CAUSING TROUBLE FOR YOUR PARTNER, TOO.

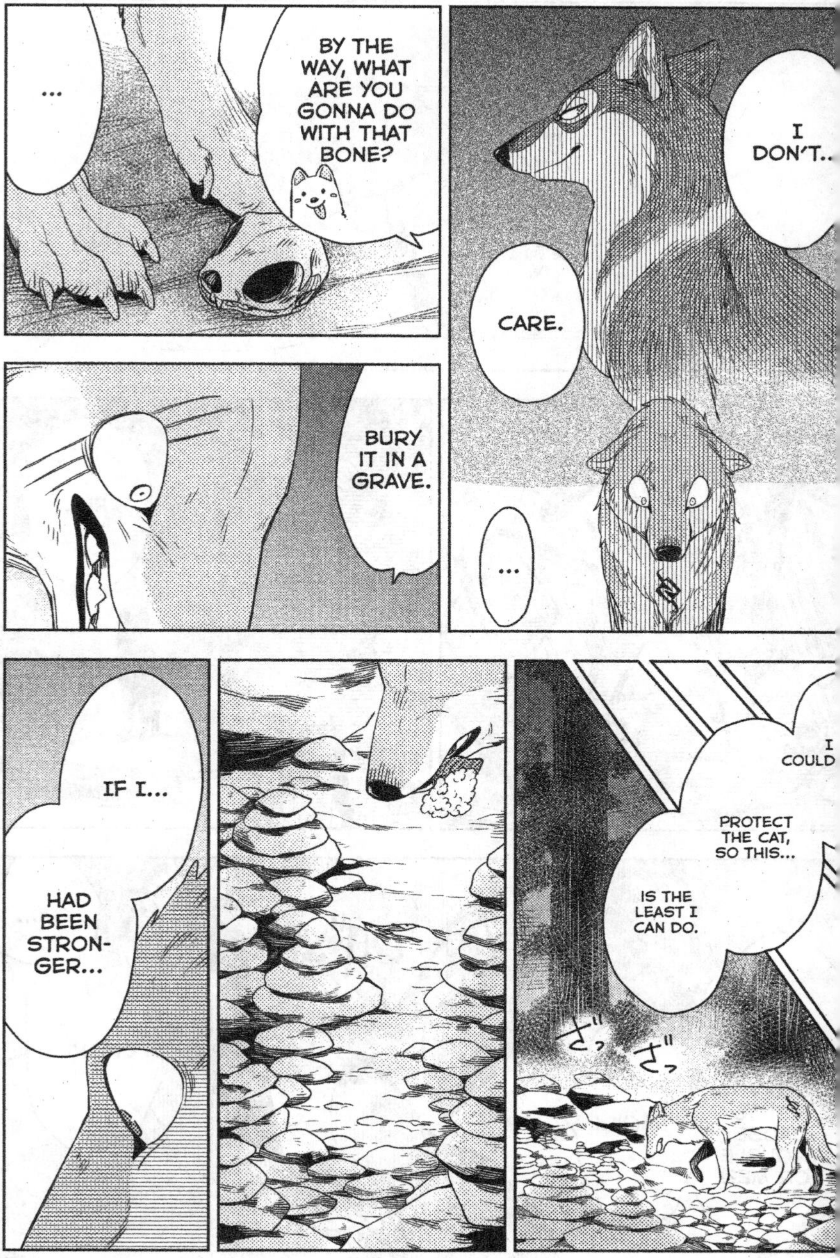
I DON'T...
CARE.
...
BY THE WAY, WHAT ARE YOU GONNA DO WITH THAT BONE?
...
BURY IT IN A GRAVE.
I COULD
PROTECT THE CAT, SO THIS...
IS THE LEAST I CAN DO.
ざっ
ざっ
IF I...
HAD BEEN STRONGER...

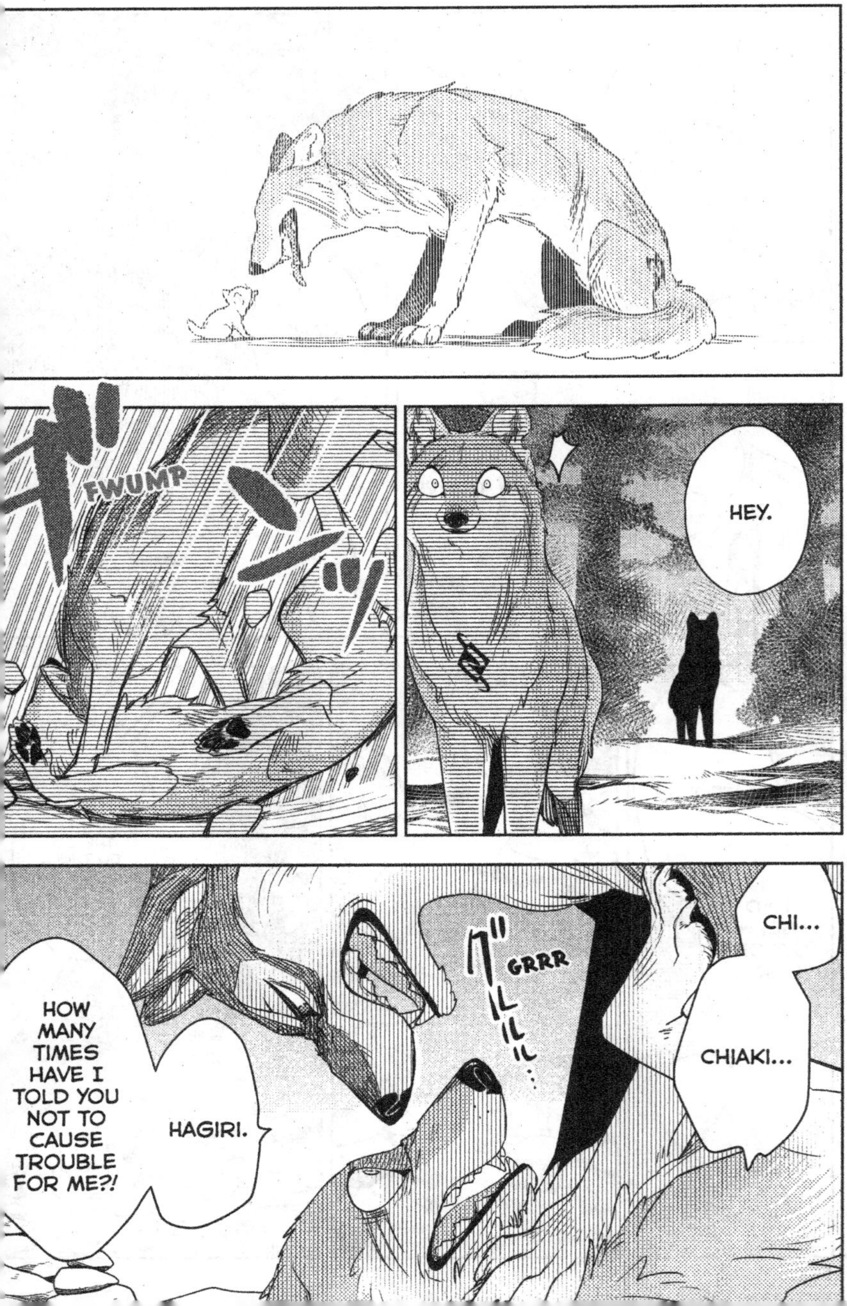
HEY.
FWUMP
CHI...
CHIAKI...
GRRR
HAGIRI.
HOW MANY TIMES HAVE I TOLD YOU NOT TO CAUSE TROUBLE FOR ME?!

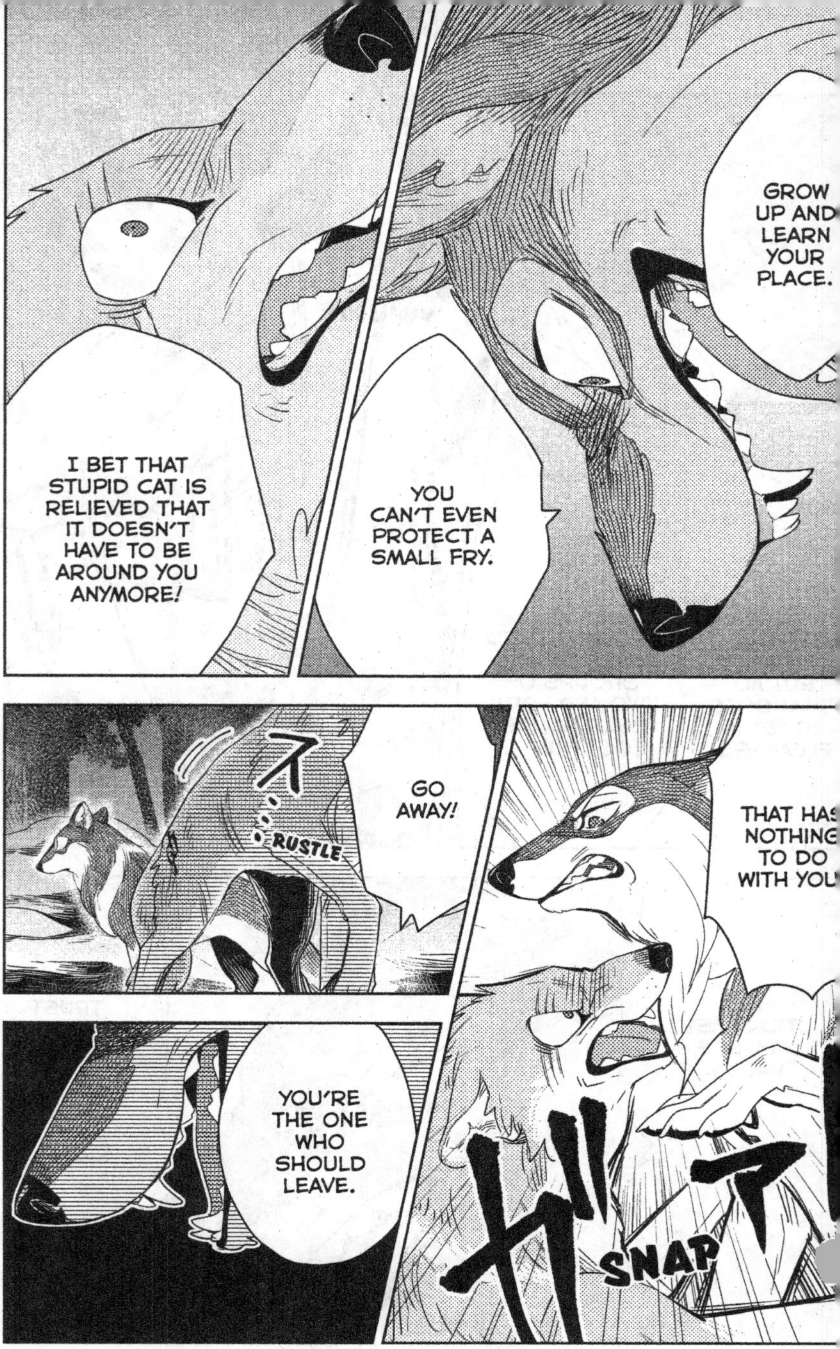
GROW UP AND LEARN YOUR PLACE.
YOU CAN'T EVEN PROTECT A SMALL FRY.
I BET THAT STUPID CAT IS RELIEVED THAT IT DOESN'T HAVE TO BE AROUND YOU ANYMORE!
THAT HAS NOTHING TO DO WITH YOU
SNAP
GO AWAY!
RUSTLE
YOU'RE THE ONE WHO SHOULD LEAVE.

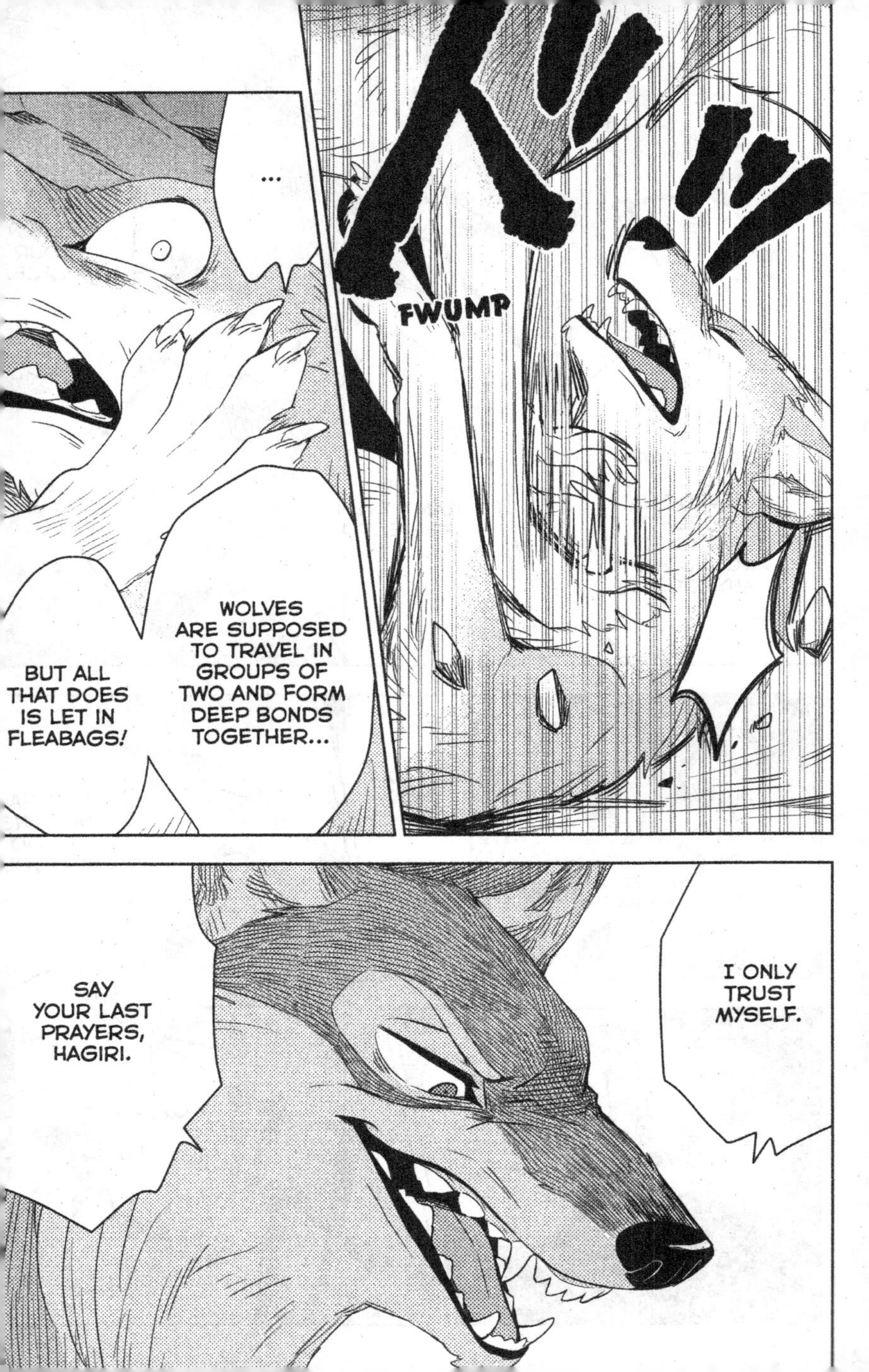
FWUMP
...
WOLVES ARE SUPPOSED TO TRAVEL IN GROUPS OF TWO AND FORM DEEP BONDS TOGETHER...
BUT ALL THAT DOES IS LET IN FLEABAGS!
I ONLY TRUST MYSELF.
SAY YOUR LAST PRAYERS, HAGIRI.

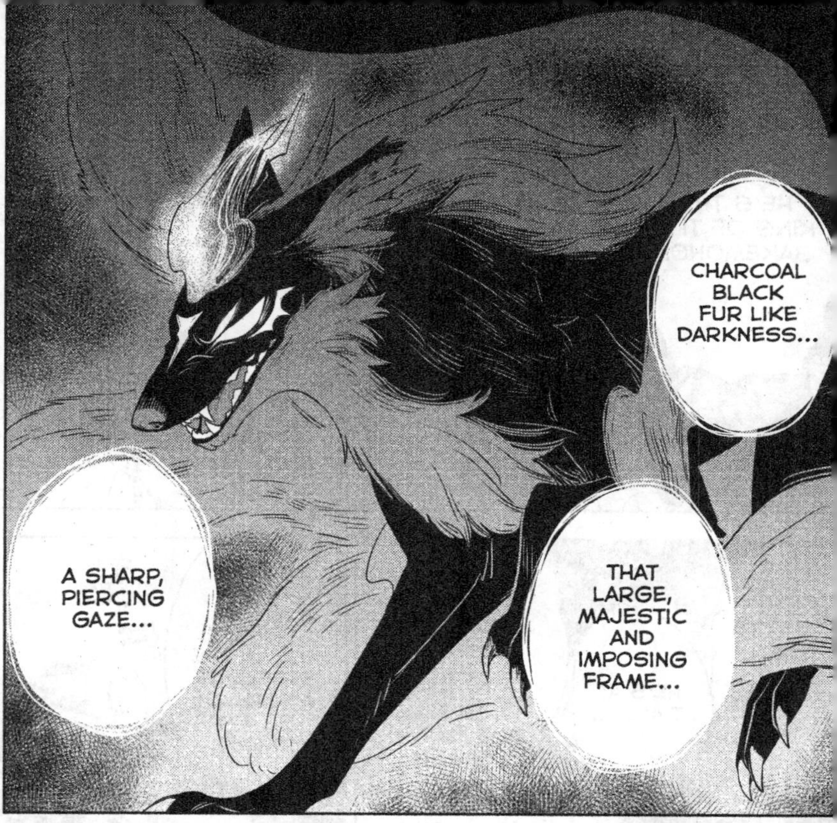
CHARCOAL BLACK FUR LIKE DARKNESS...
THAT LARGE, MAJESTIC AND IMPOSING FRAME...
A SHARP, PIERCING GAZE...

# Chapter 1

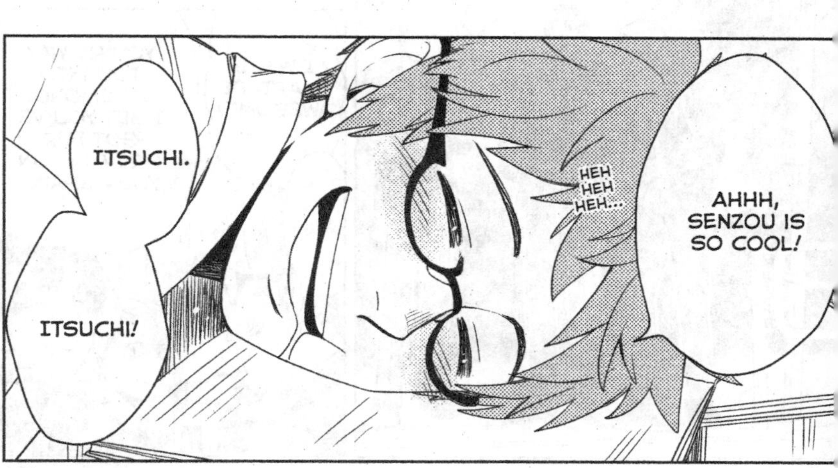
AHHH, SENZOU IS SO COOL!
HEH HEH HEH...
ITSUCHI.
ITSUCHI!

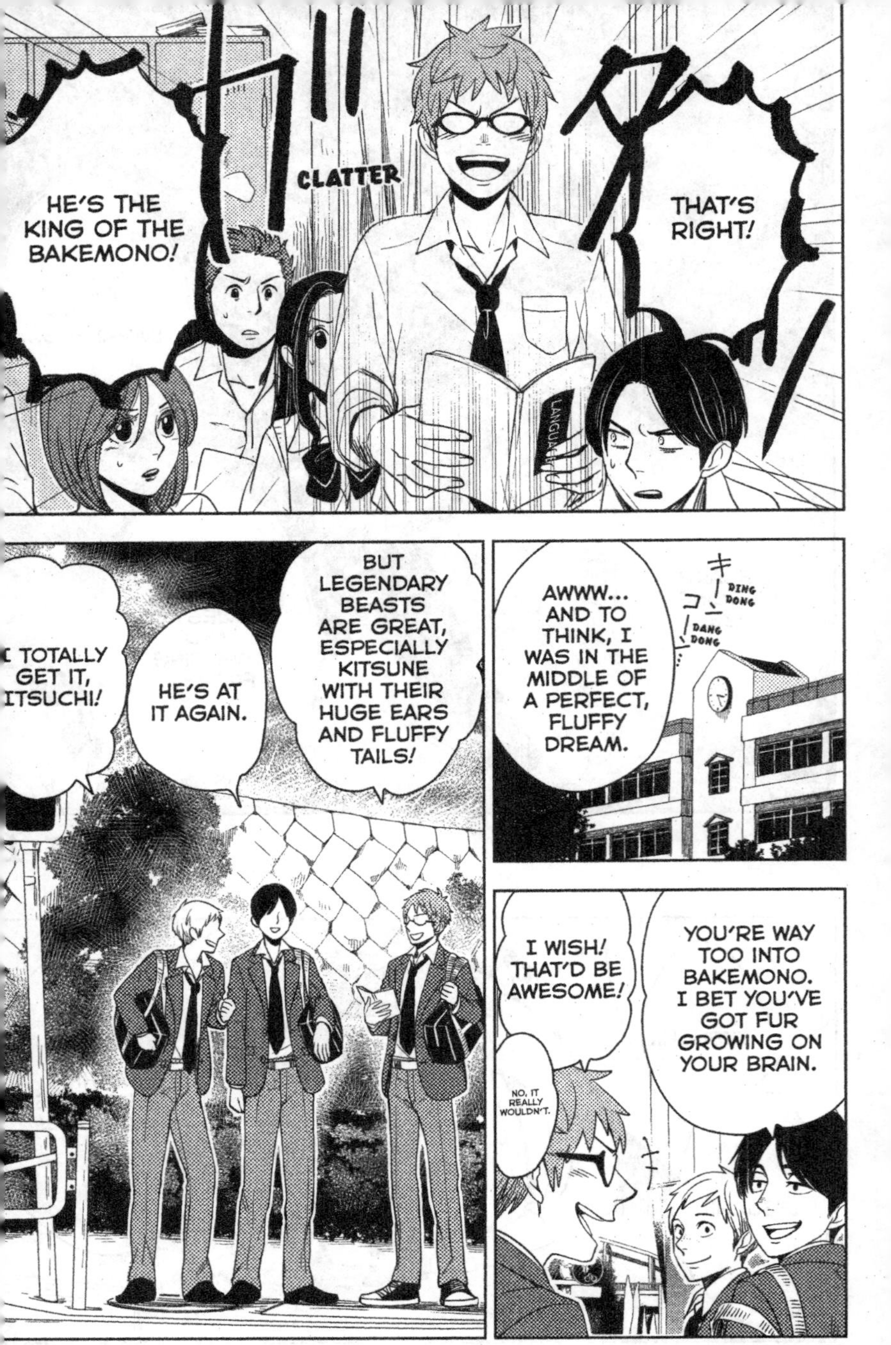
THAT'S RIGHT!
CLATTER
HE'S THE KING OF THE BAKEMONO!
AWWW... AND TO THINK, I WAS IN THE MIDDLE OF A PERFECT, FLUFFY DREAM.
DING DONG
DANG DONG
YOU'RE WAY TOO INTO BAKEMONO. I BET YOU'VE GOT FUR GROWING ON YOUR BRAIN.
I WISH! THAT'D BE AWESOME!
NO, IT REALLY WOULDN'T.
BUT LEGENDARY BEASTS ARE GREAT, ESPECIALLY KITSUNE WITH THEIR HUGE EARS AND FLUFFY TAILS!
HE'S AT IT AGAIN.
I TOTALLY GET IT, ITSUCHI!

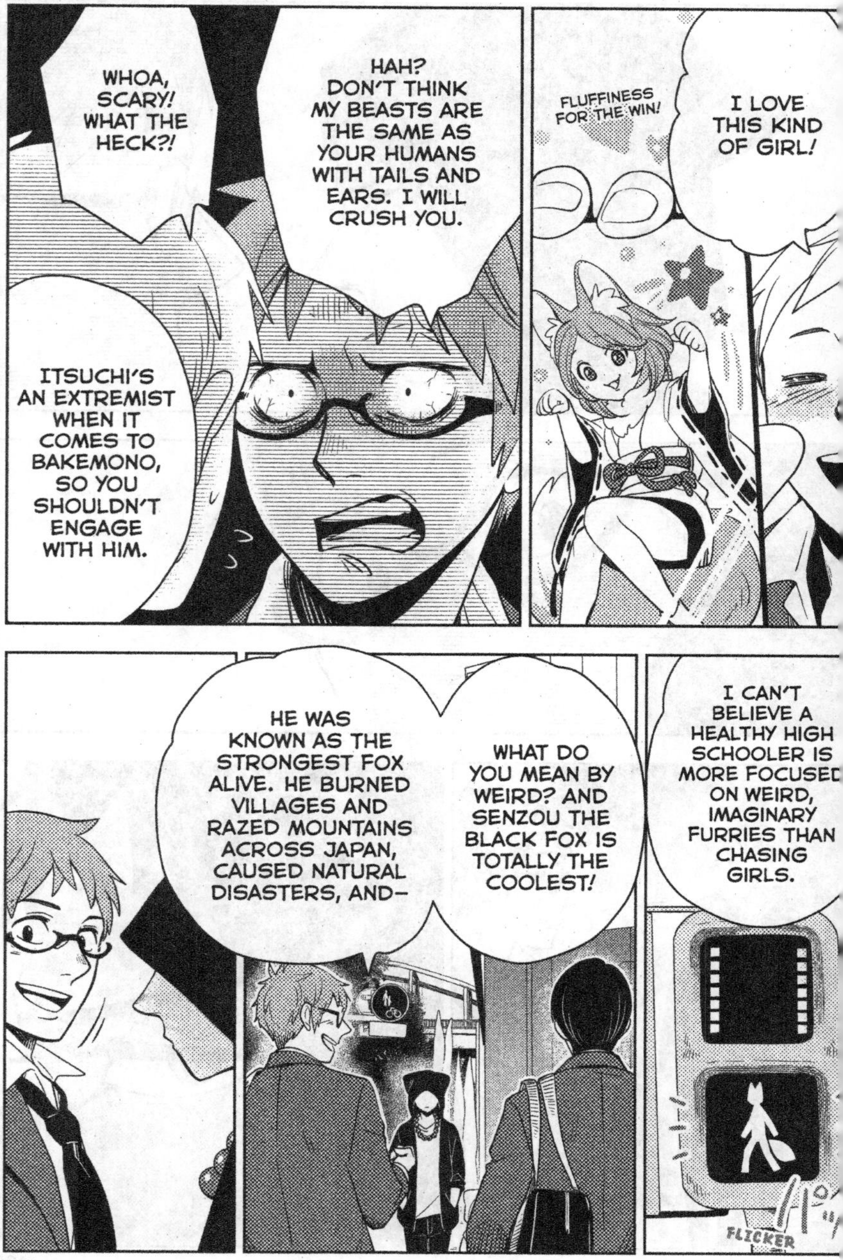
I LOVE THIS KIND OF GIRL!
FLUFFINESS FOR THE WIN!
HAH? DON'T THINK MY BEASTS ARE THE SAME AS YOUR HUMANS WITH TAILS AND EARS. I WILL CRUSH YOU.
WHOA, SCARY! WHAT THE HECK?!
ITSUCHI'S AN EXTREMIST WHEN IT COMES TO BAKEMONO, SO YOU SHOULDN'T ENGAGE WITH HIM.
I CAN'T BELIEVE A HEALTHY HIGH SCHOOLER IS MORE FOCUSED ON WEIRD, IMAGINARY FURRIES THAN CHASING GIRLS.
FLICKER
WHAT DO YOU MEAN BY WEIRD? AND SENZOU THE BLACK FOX IS TOTALLY THE COOLEST!
HE WAS KNOWN AS THE STRONGEST FOX ALIVE. HE BURNED VILLAGES AND RAZED MOUNTAINS ACROSS JAPAN, CAUSED NATURAL DISASTERS, AND—

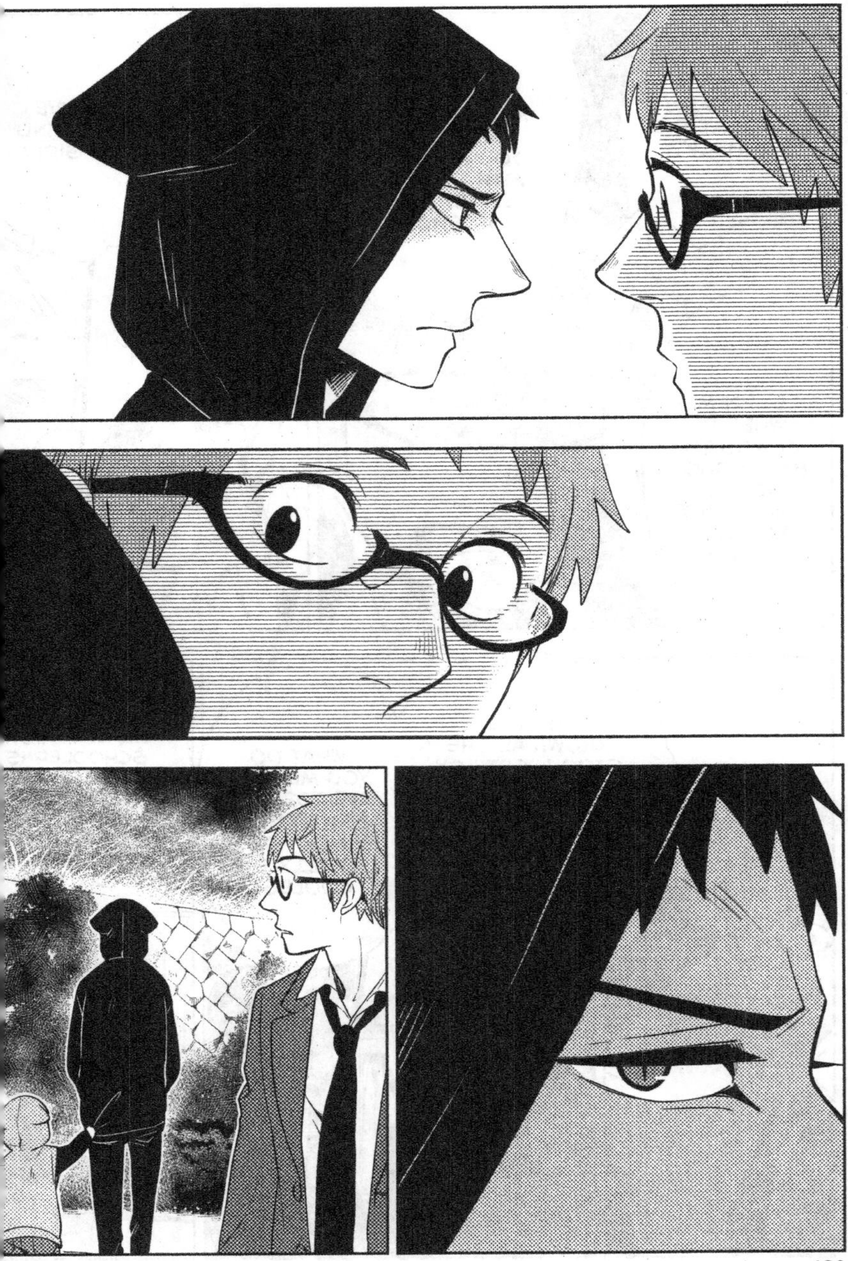

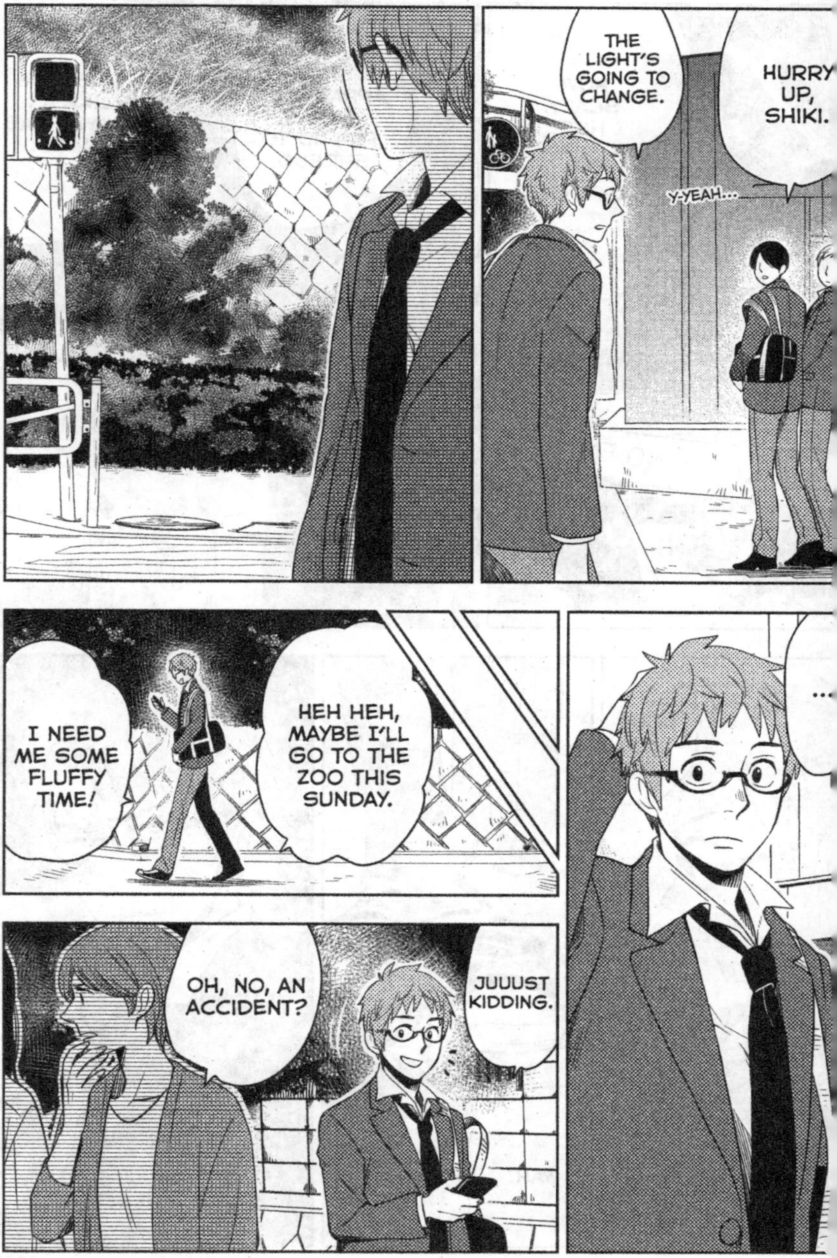
HURRY UP, SHIKI.
THE LIGHT'S GOING TO CHANGE.
Y-YEAH...
...
HEH HEH, MAYBE I'LL GO TO THE ZOO THIS SUNDAY.
I NEED ME SOME FLUFFY TIME!
JUUUST KIDDING.
OH, NO, AN ACCIDENT?

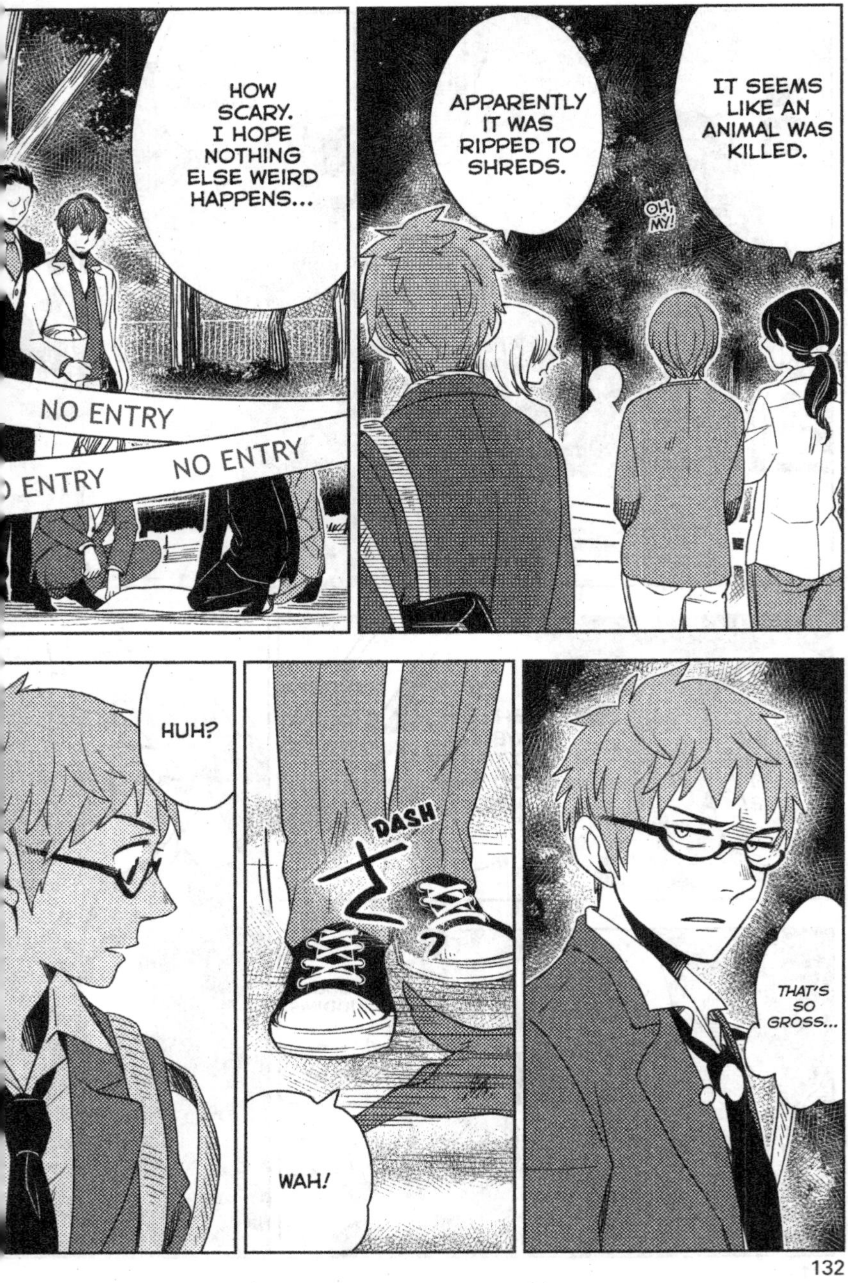
IT SEEMS LIKE AN ANIMAL WAS KILLED.
APPARENTLY IT WAS RIPPED TO SHREDS.
OH, MY!
HOW SCARY. I HOPE NOTHING ELSE WEIRD HAPPENS...
NO ENTRY
NO ENTRY
ENTRY
THAT'S SO GROSS...
DASH
WAH!
HUH?

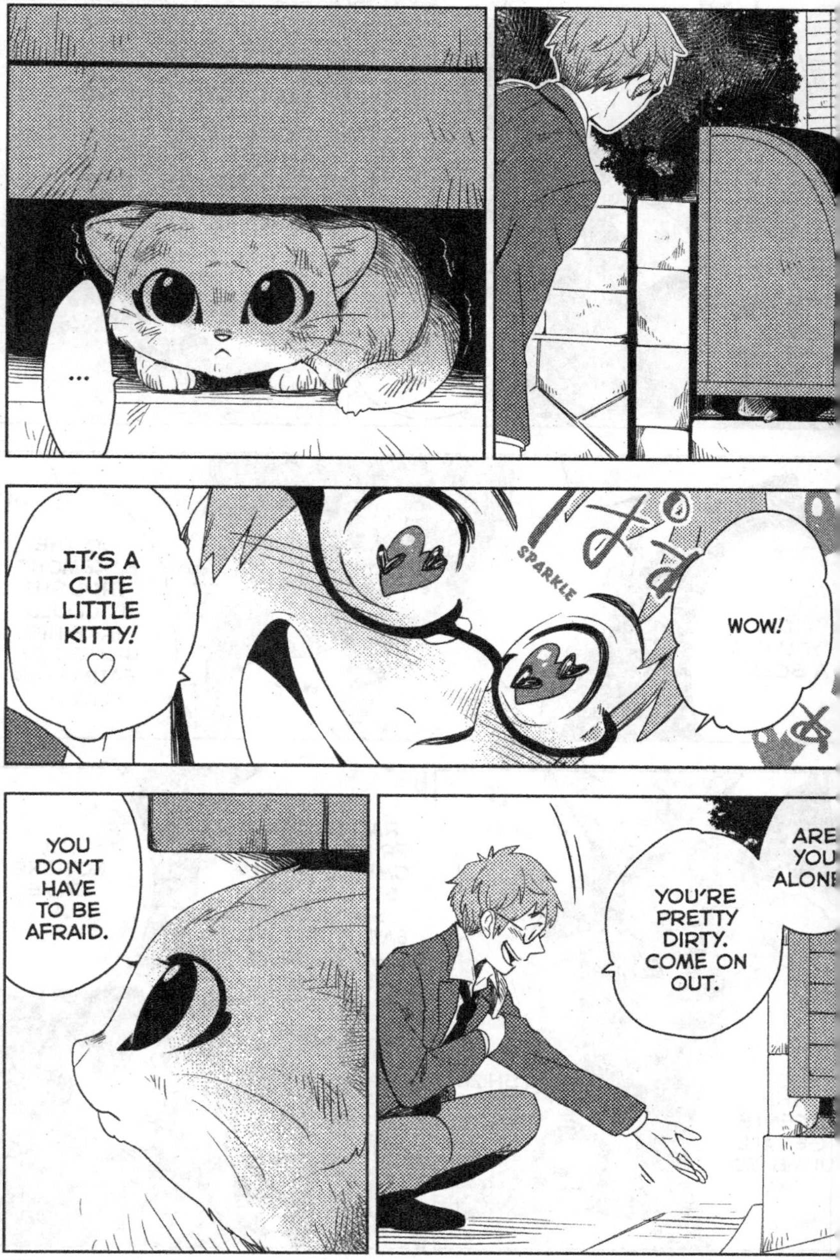
...
WOW!
SPARKLE
IT'S A CUTE LITTLE KITTY! ♡
ARE YOU ALONE
YOU'RE PRETTY DIRTY. COME ON OUT.
YOU DON'T HAVE TO BE AFRAID.

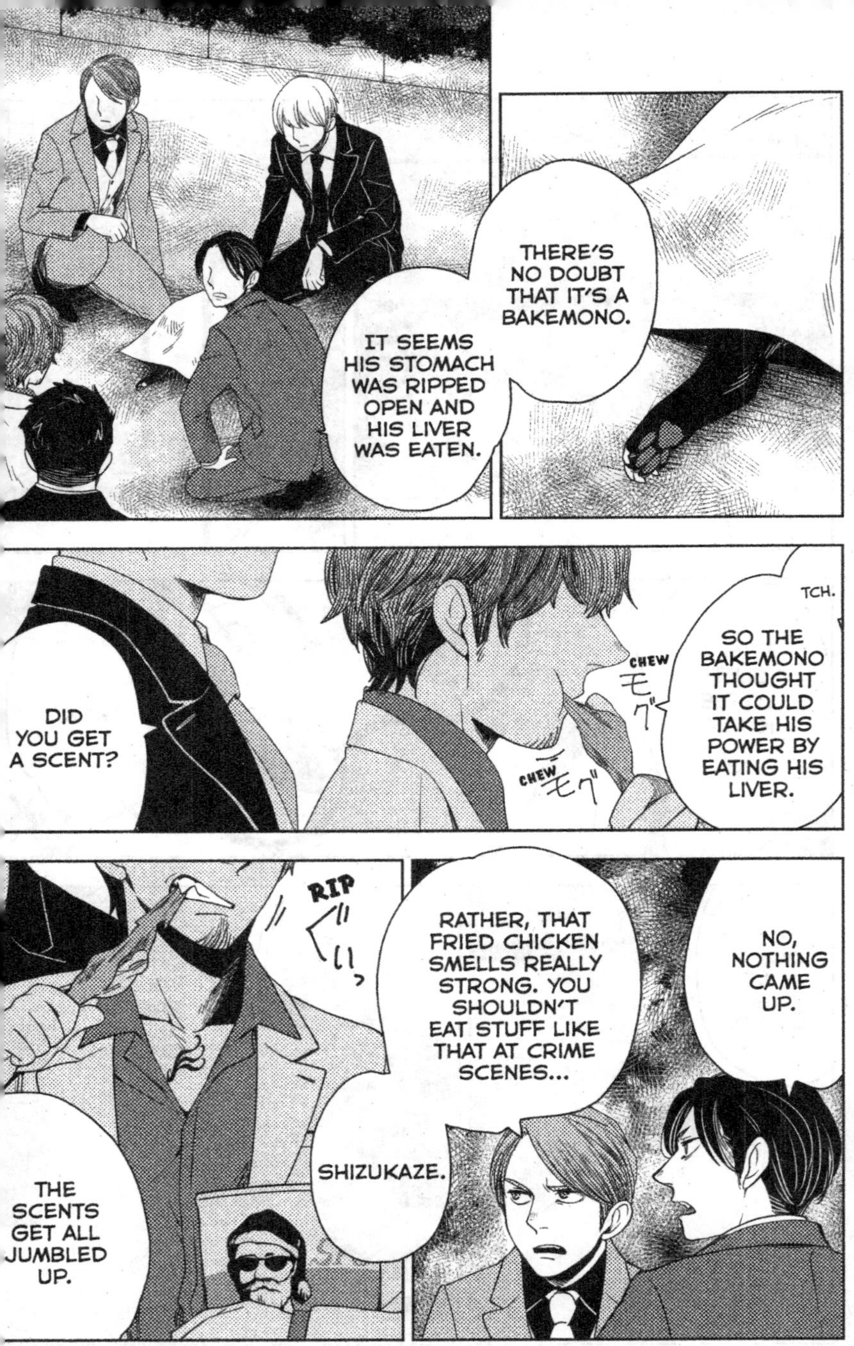
THERE'S NO DOUBT THAT IT'S A BAKEMONO.
IT SEEMS HIS STOMACH WAS RIPPED OPEN AND HIS LIVER WAS EATEN.
TCH.
SO THE BAKEMONO THOUGHT IT COULD TAKE HIS POWER BY EATING HIS LIVER.
CHEW モグ
CHEW モグ
DID YOU GET A SCENT?
NO, NOTHING CAME UP.
RATHER, THAT FRIED CHICKEN SMELLS REALLY STRONG. YOU SHOULDN'T EAT STUFF LIKE THAT AT CRIME SCENES...
SHIZUKAZE.
RIP
THE SCENTS GET ALL JUMBLED UP.

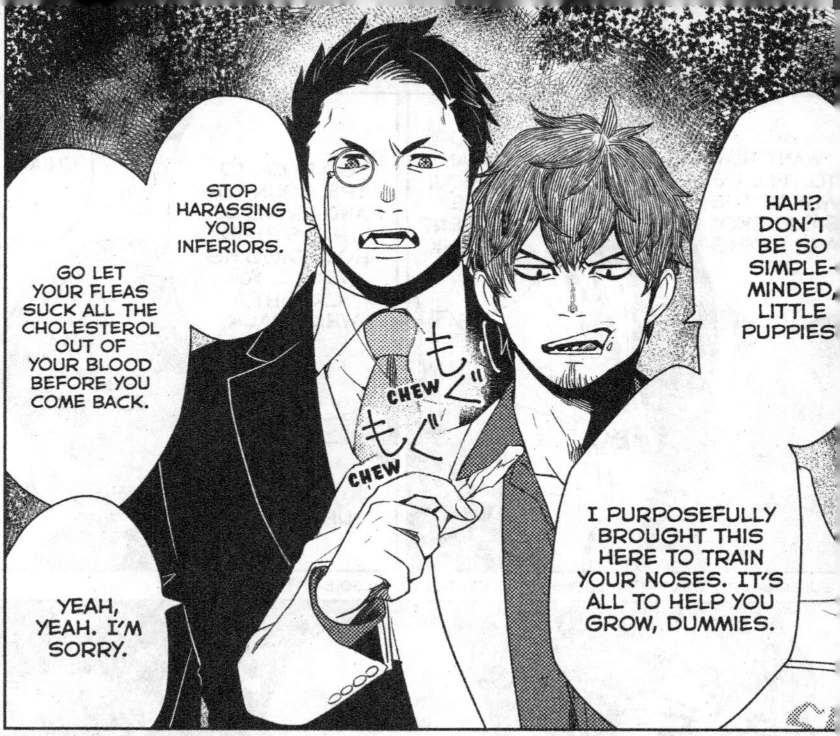
HAH? DON'T BE SO SIMPLE-MINDED, LITTLE PUPPIES
STOP HARASSING YOUR INFERIORS.
GO LET YOUR FLEAS SUCK ALL THE CHOLESTEROL OUT OF YOUR BLOOD BEFORE YOU COME BACK.
もぐ CHEW
もぐ CHEW
I PURPOSEFULLY BROUGHT THIS HERE TO TRAIN YOUR NOSES. IT'S ALL TO HELP YOU GROW, DUMMIES.
YEAH, YEAH. I'M SORRY.

*IN JAPANESE, "KAKUREMINO" LITERALLY MEANS "TO PROVIDE COVER" (INVISIBILITY), BUT IT'S ALSO THE NAME OF A SMALL EVERGREEN TREE.

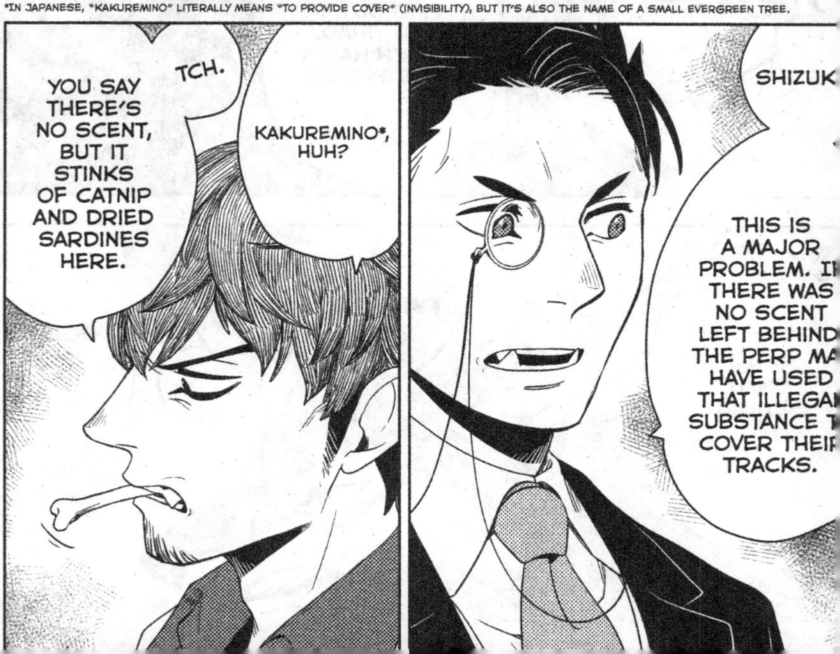
SHIZUK
THIS IS A MAJOR PROBLEM. I THERE WAS NO SCENT LEFT BEHIND THE PERP MA HAVE USED THAT ILLEGA SUBSTANCE T COVER THEI TRACKS.
TCH.
KAKUREMINO*, HUH?
YOU SAY THERE'S NO SCENT, BUT IT STINKS OF CATNIP AND DRIED SARDINES HERE.

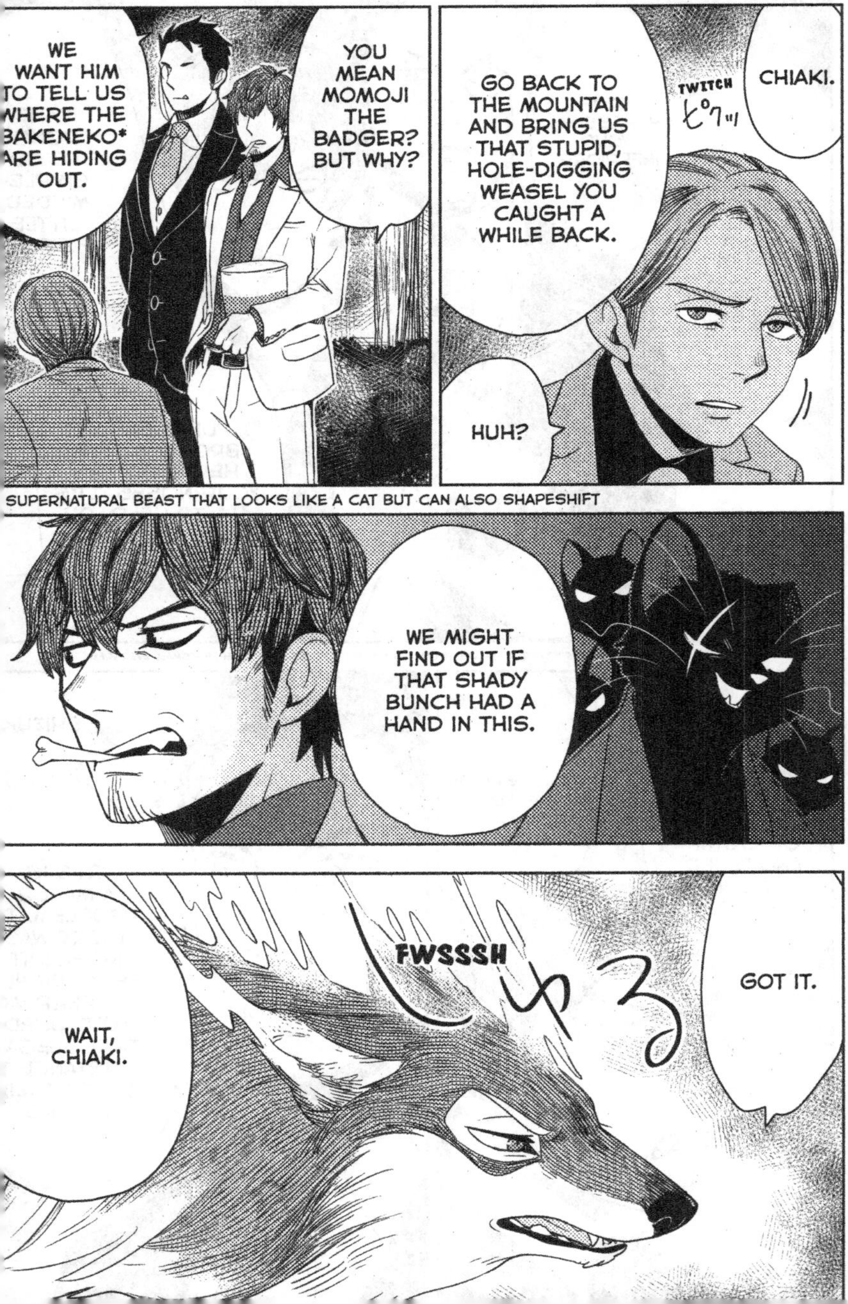
CHIAKI.
TWITCH
GO BACK TO THE MOUNTAIN AND BRING US THAT STUPID, HOLE-DIGGING WEASEL YOU CAUGHT A WHILE BACK.
HUH?
YOU MEAN MOMOJI THE BADGER? BUT WHY?
WE WANT HIM TO TELL US WHERE THE BAKENEKO* ARE HIDING OUT.
SUPERNATURAL BEAST THAT LOOKS LIKE A CAT BUT CAN ALSO SHAPESHIFT
WE MIGHT FIND OUT IF THAT SHADY BUNCH HAD A HAND IN THIS.
GOT IT.
FWSSSH
WAIT, CHIAKI.

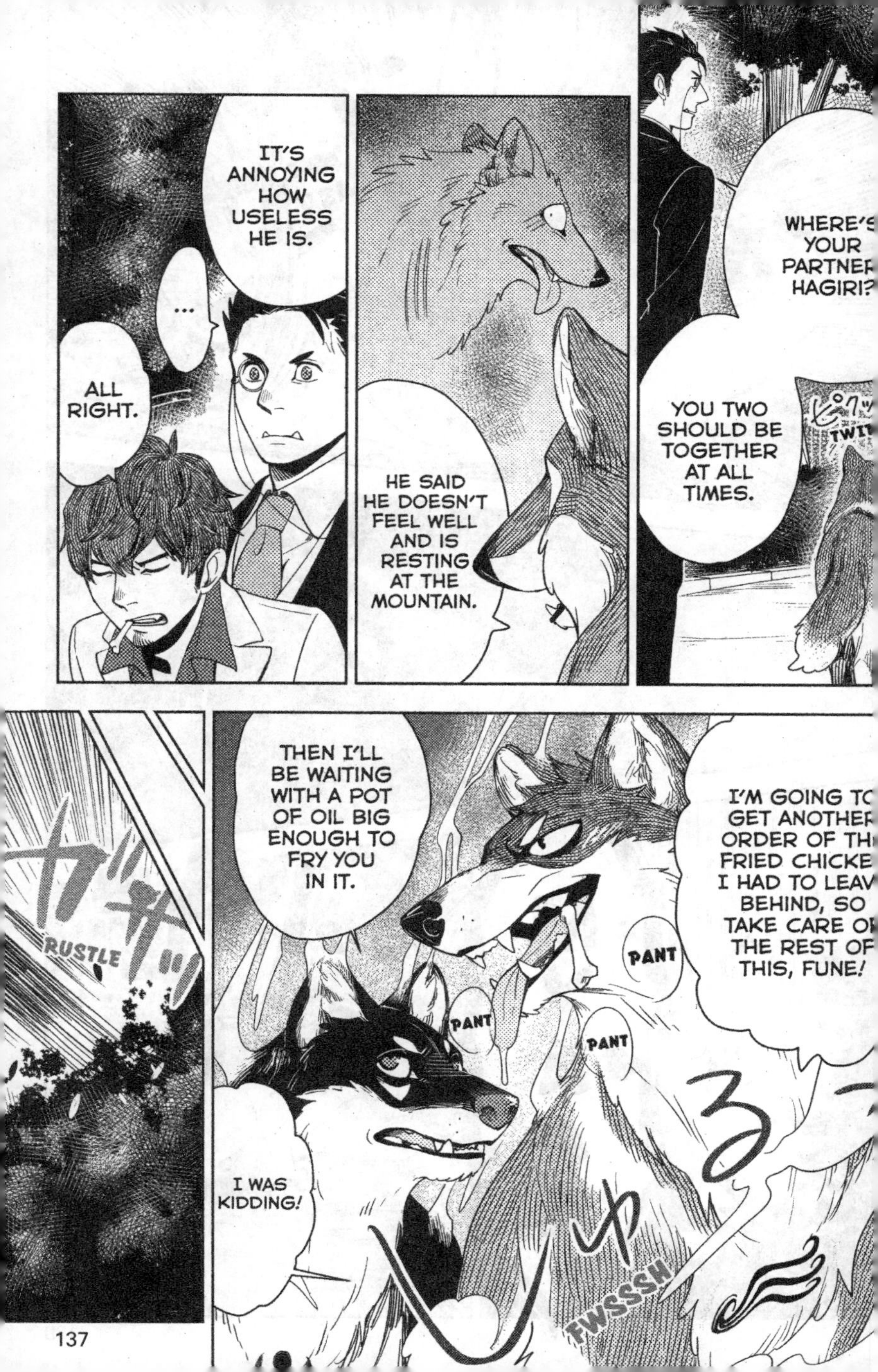
WHERE'S YOUR PARTNER HAGIRI?
YOU TWO SHOULD BE TOGETHER AT ALL TIMES.
TWIT
HE SAID HE DOESN'T FEEL WELL AND IS RESTING AT THE MOUNTAIN.
IT'S ANNOYING HOW USELESS HE IS.
...
ALL RIGHT.
I'M GOING TO GET ANOTHER ORDER OF TH FRIED CHICKE I HAD TO LEAV BEHIND, SO TAKE CARE OF THE REST OF THIS, FUNE!
PANT
PANT
PANT
THEN I'LL BE WAITING WITH A POT OF OIL BIG ENOUGH TO FRY YOU IN IT.
I WAS KIDDING!
FWSSSH
RUSTLE

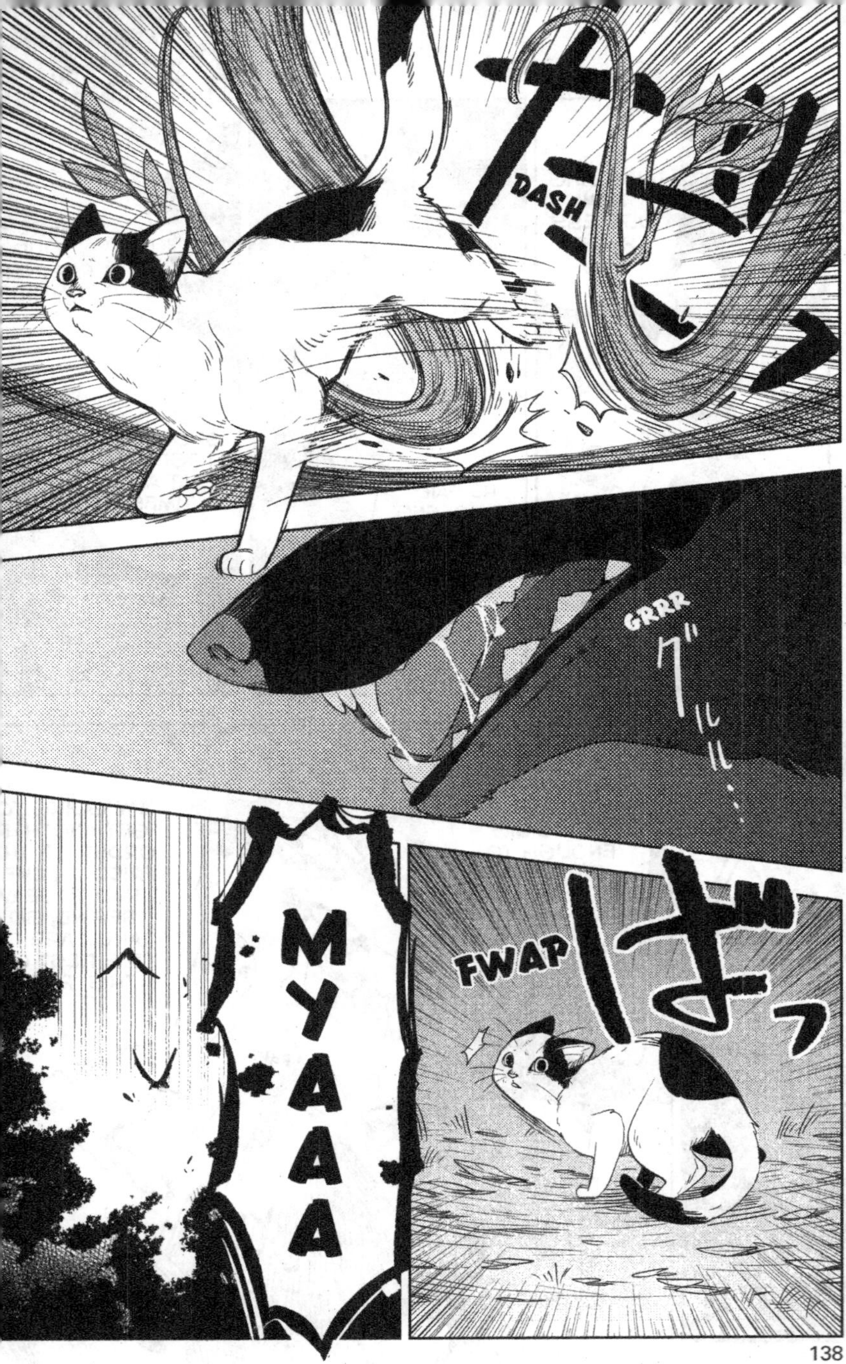
DASH
GRRR
グルル…
FWAP
MYAAA

# Chapter 13

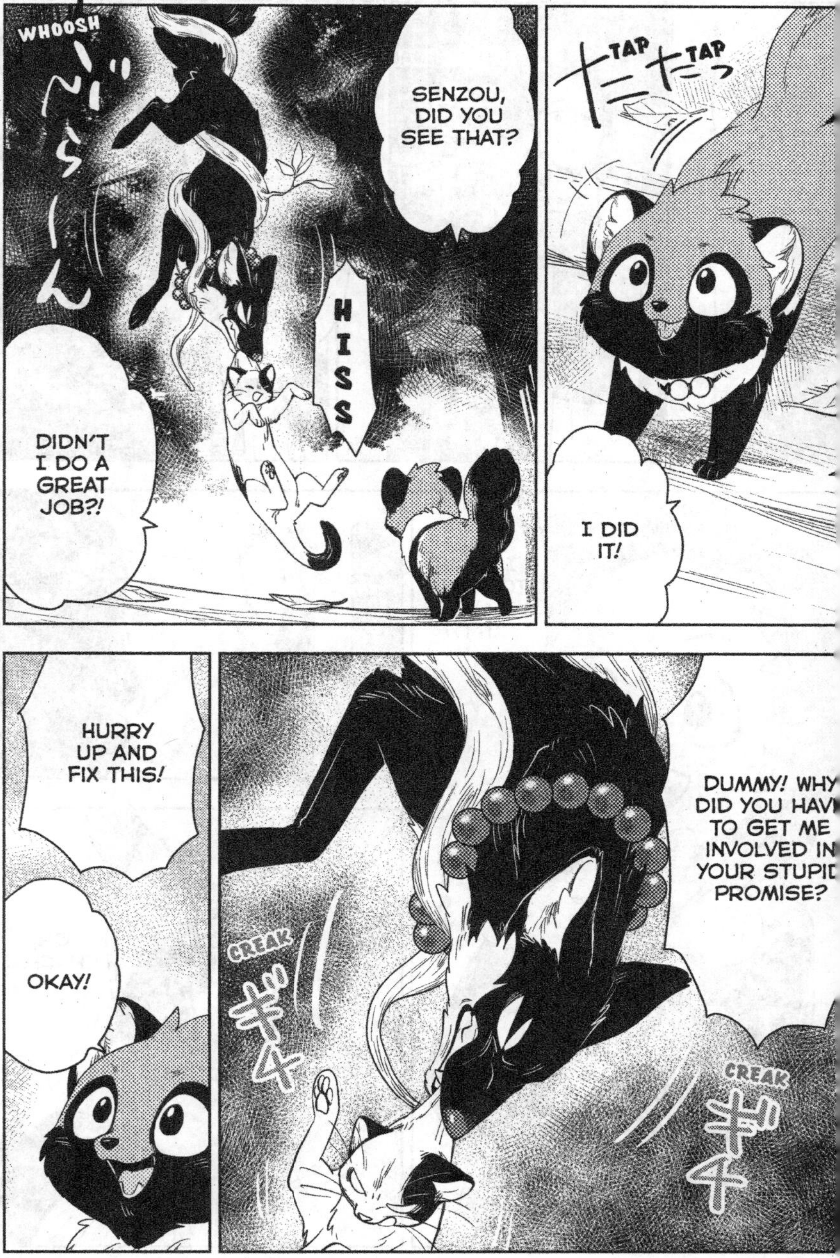

TAP TAP
I DID IT!
SENZOU, DID YOU SEE THAT?
WHOOSH
HISS
DIDN'T I DO A GREAT JOB?!
DUMMY! WHY DID YOU HAVE TO GET ME INVOLVED IN YOUR STUPID PROMISE?
CREAK
CREAK
HURRY UP AND FIX THIS!
OKAY!

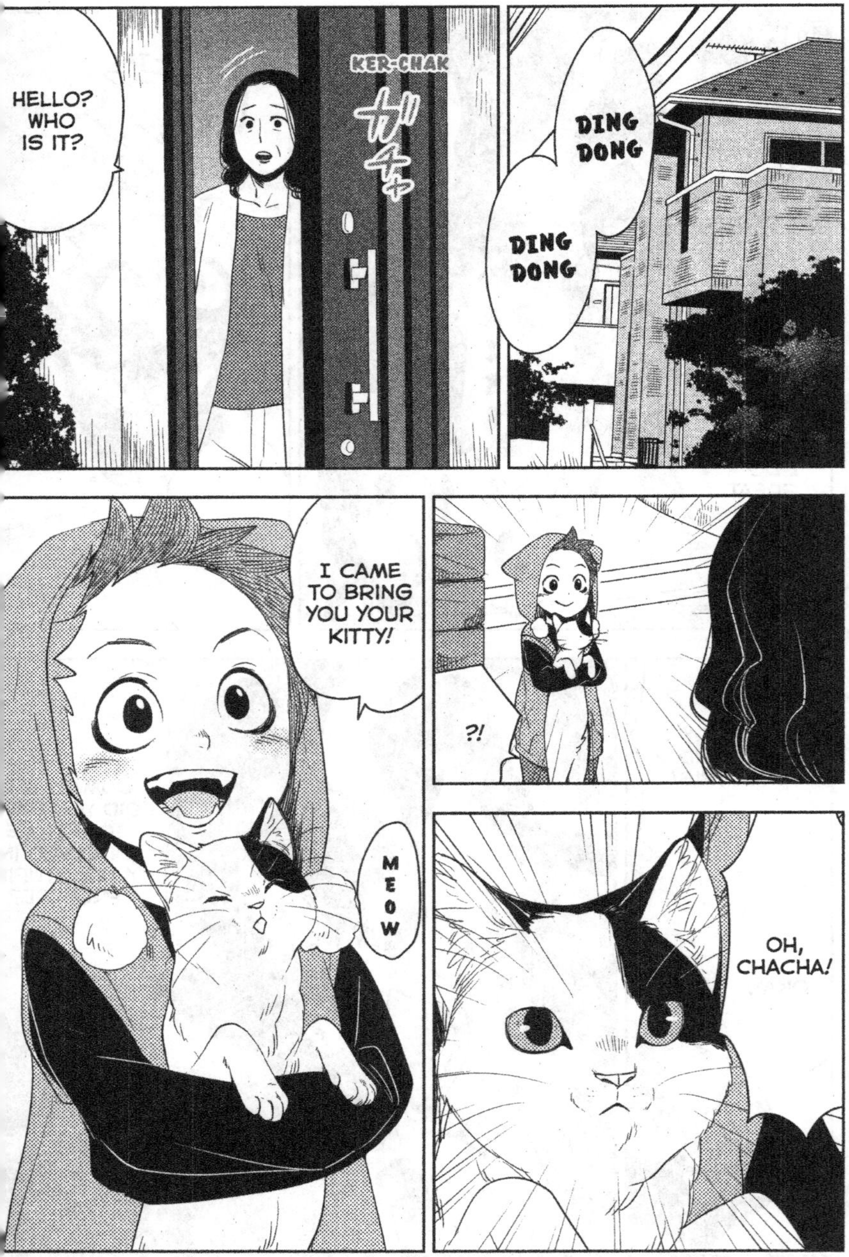
DING DONG
DING DONG
KER-CHAK
ガチャ
HELLO? WHO IS IT?
?!
OH, CHACHA!
I CAME TO BRING YOU YOUR KITTY!
MEOW

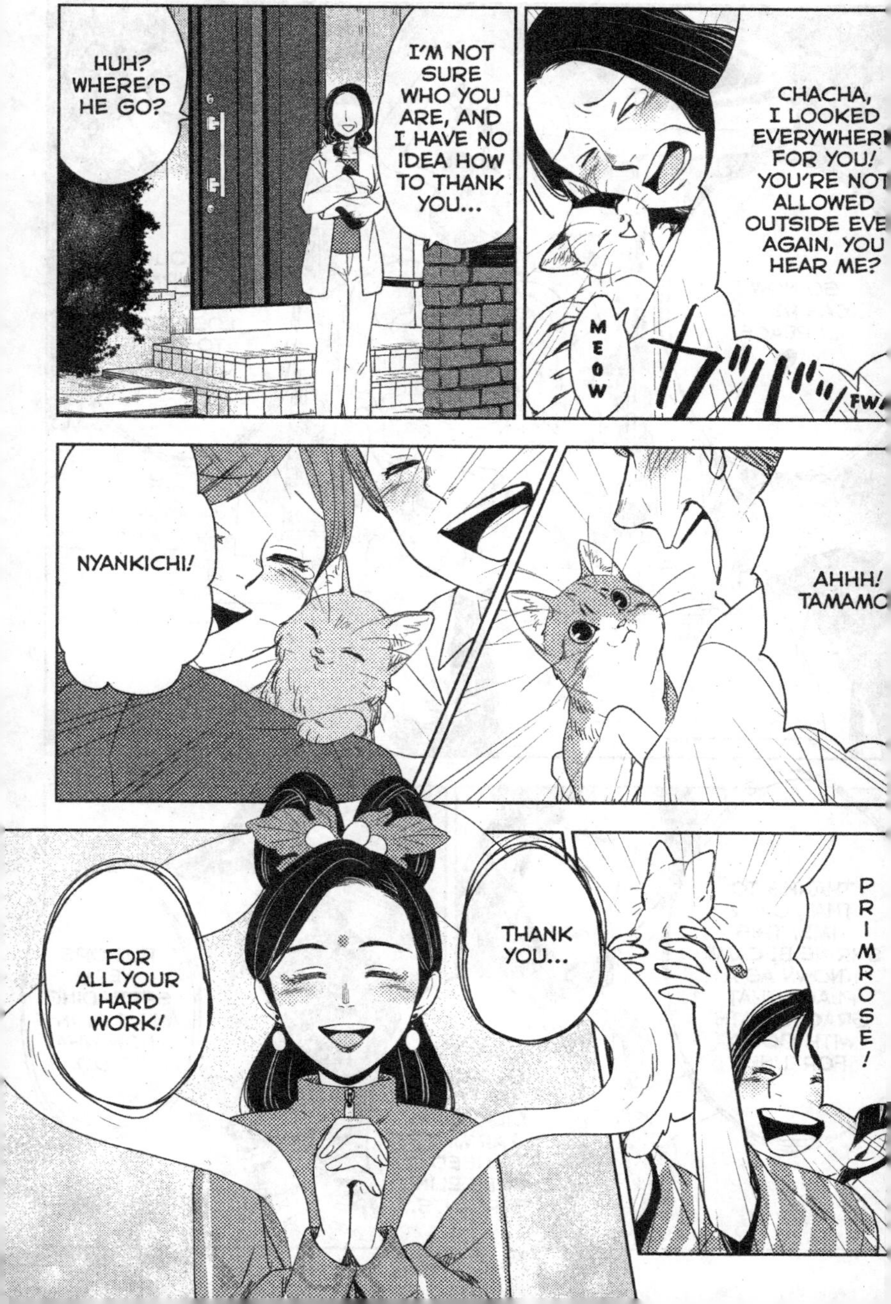

CHACHA, I LOOKED EVERYWHER FOR YOU! YOU'RE NOT ALLOWED OUTSIDE EVE AGAIN, YOU HEAR ME?
MEOW
FWA
I'M NOT SURE WHO YOU ARE, AND I HAVE NO IDEA HOW TO THANK YOU...
HUH? WHERE'D HE GO?
AHHH! TAMAMO
NYANKICHI!
PRIMROSE!
THANK YOU...
FOR ALL YOUR HARD WORK!

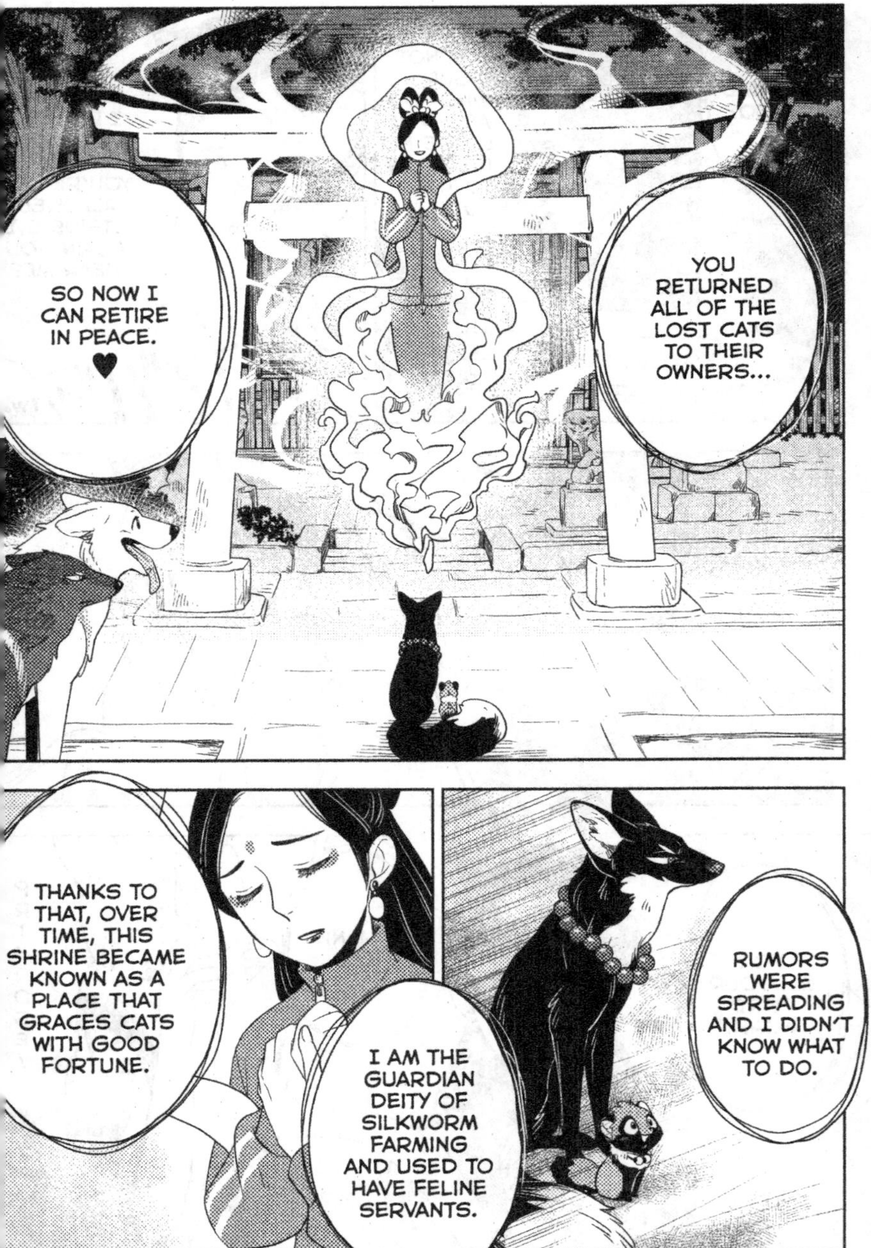
YOU RETURNED ALL OF THE LOST CATS TO THEIR OWNERS...
SO NOW I CAN RETIRE IN PEACE. ♥
RUMORS WERE SPREADING AND I DIDN'T KNOW WHAT TO DO.
I AM THE GUARDIAN DEITY OF SILKWORM FARMING AND USED TO HAVE FELINE SERVANTS.
THANKS TO THAT, OVER TIME, THIS SHRINE BECAME KNOWN AS A PLACE THAT GRACES CATS WITH GOOD FORTUNE.

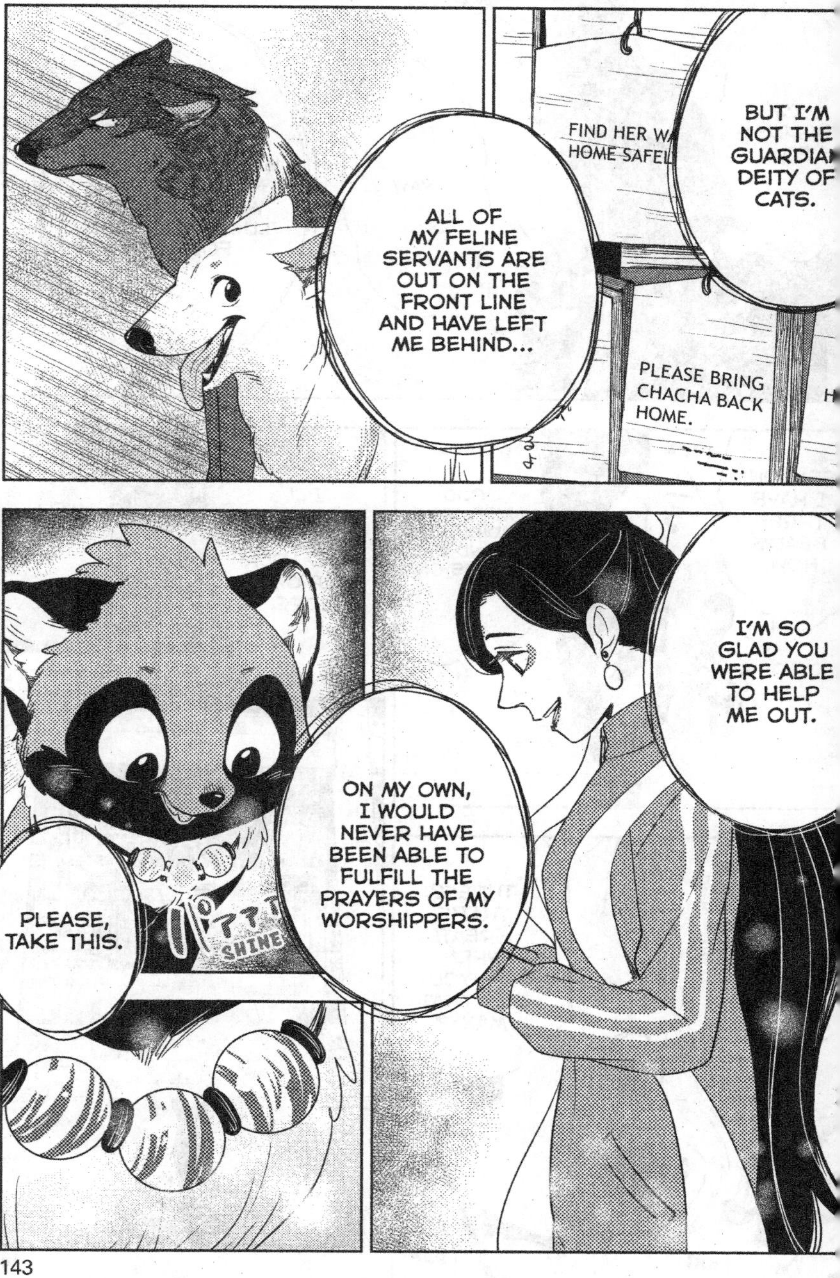
BUT I'M NOT THE GUARDIA DEITY OF CATS.
FIND HER WA HOME SAFEL
PLEASE BRING CHACHA BACK HOME.
ALL OF MY FELINE SERVANTS ARE OUT ON THE FRONT LINE AND HAVE LEFT ME BEHIND...
I'M SO GLAD YOU WERE ABLE TO HELP ME OUT.
ON MY OWN, I WOULD NEVER HAVE BEEN ABLE TO FULFILL THE PRAYERS OF MY WORSHIPPERS.
PLEASE, TAKE THIS.
SHINE

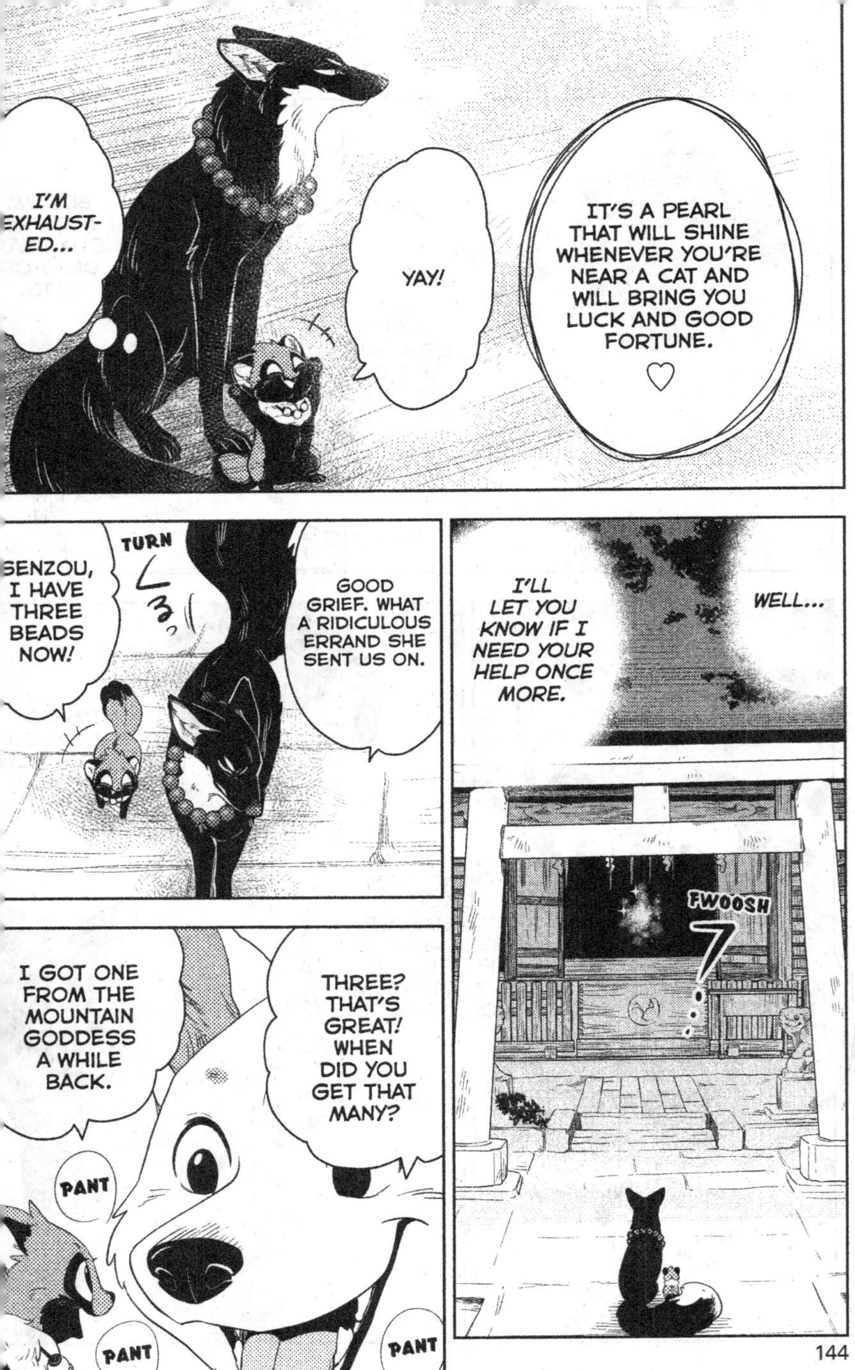
IT'S A PEARL THAT WILL SHINE WHENEVER YOU'RE NEAR A CAT AND WILL BRING YOU LUCK AND GOOD FORTUNE. ♡
YAY!
I'M EXHAUST-ED...
WELL...
I'LL LET YOU KNOW IF I NEED YOUR HELP ONCE MORE.
FWOOSH
GOOD GRIEF. WHAT A RIDICULOUS ERRAND SHE SENT US ON.
TURN
SENZOU, I HAVE THREE BEADS NOW!
THREE? THAT'S GREAT! WHEN DID YOU GET THAT MANY?
I GOT ONE FROM THE MOUNTAIN GODDESS A WHILE BACK.
PANT
PANT
PANT

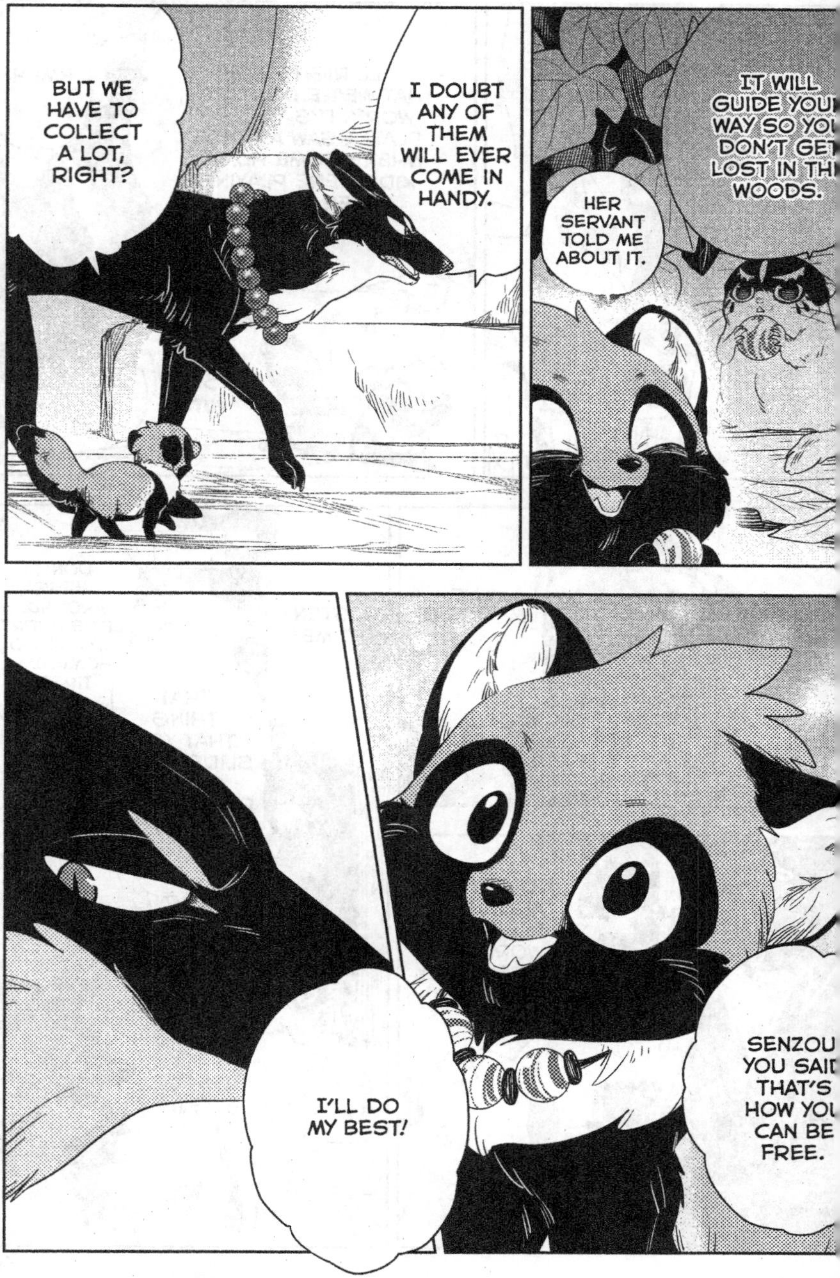
IT WILL GUIDE YOUR WAY SO YOU DON'T GET LOST IN THE WOODS.
HER SERVANT TOLD ME ABOUT IT.
I DOUBT ANY OF THEM WILL EVER COME IN HANDY.
BUT WE HAVE TO COLLECT A LOT, RIGHT?
SENZOU YOU SAID THAT'S HOW YOU CAN BE FREE.
I'LL DO MY BEST!

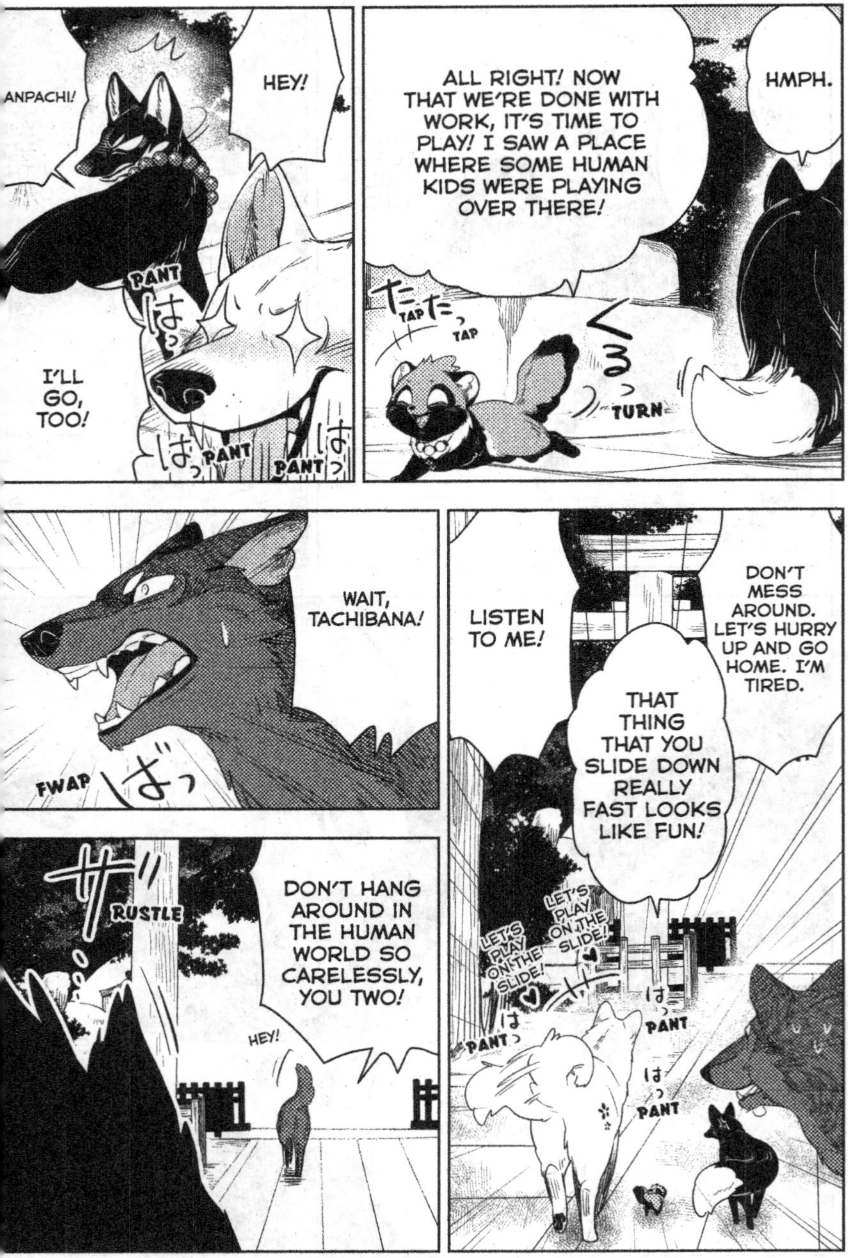
HMPH.
ALL RIGHT! NOW THAT WE'RE DONE WITH WORK, IT'S TIME TO PLAY! I SAW A PLACE WHERE SOME HUMAN KIDS WERE PLAYING OVER THERE!
TAP TAP
TURN
HEY!
ANPACHI!
PANT
I'LL GO, TOO!
PANT
PANT
DON'T MESS AROUND. LET'S HURRY UP AND GO HOME. I'M TIRED.
LISTEN TO ME!
THAT THING THAT YOU SLIDE DOWN REALLY FAST LOOKS LIKE FUN!
LET'S PLAY ON THE SLIDE!
LET'S PLAY ON THE SLIDE!
PANT
PANT
PANT
WAIT, TACHIBANA!
FWAP
DON'T HANG AROUND IN THE HUMAN WORLD SO CARELESSLY, YOU TWO!
RUSTLE
HEY!

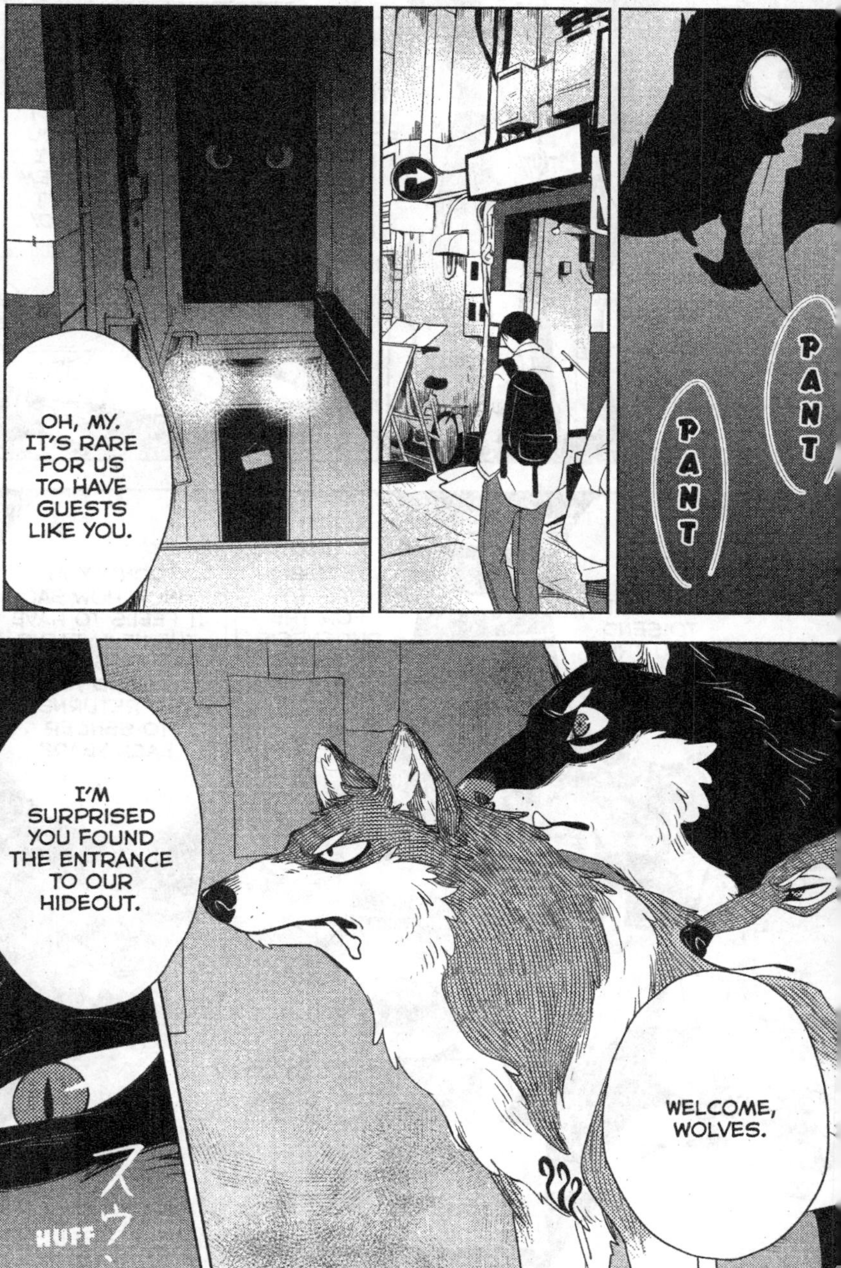
PANT
PANT
OH, MY. IT'S RARE FOR US TO HAVE GUESTS LIKE YOU.
I'M SURPRISED YOU FOUND THE ENTRANCE TO OUR HIDEOUT.
WELCOME, WOLVES.
HUFF
スウ…

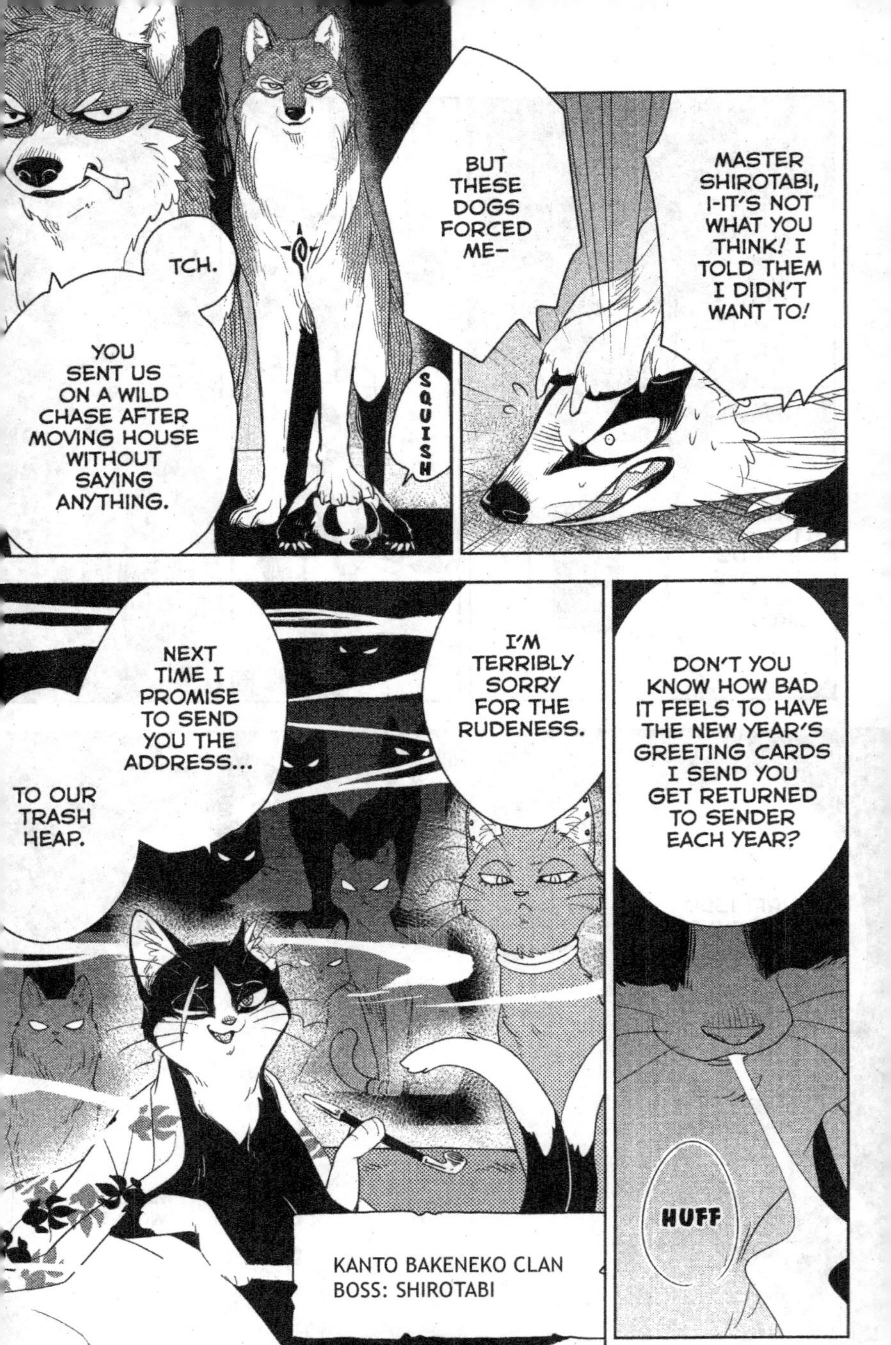
MASTER SHIROTABI, I-IT'S NOT WHAT YOU THINK! I TOLD THEM I DIDN'T WANT TO!
BUT THESE DOGS FORCED ME–
TCH.
SQUISH
YOU SENT US ON A WILD CHASE AFTER MOVING HOUSE WITHOUT SAYING ANYTHING.
DON'T YOU KNOW HOW BAD IT FEELS TO HAVE THE NEW YEAR'S GREETING CARDS I SEND YOU GET RETURNED TO SENDER EACH YEAR?
HUFF
I'M TERRIBLY SORRY FOR THE RUDENESS.
NEXT TIME I PROMISE TO SEND YOU THE ADDRESS...
TO OUR TRASH HEAP.
KANTO BAKENEKO CLAN BOSS: SHIROTABI

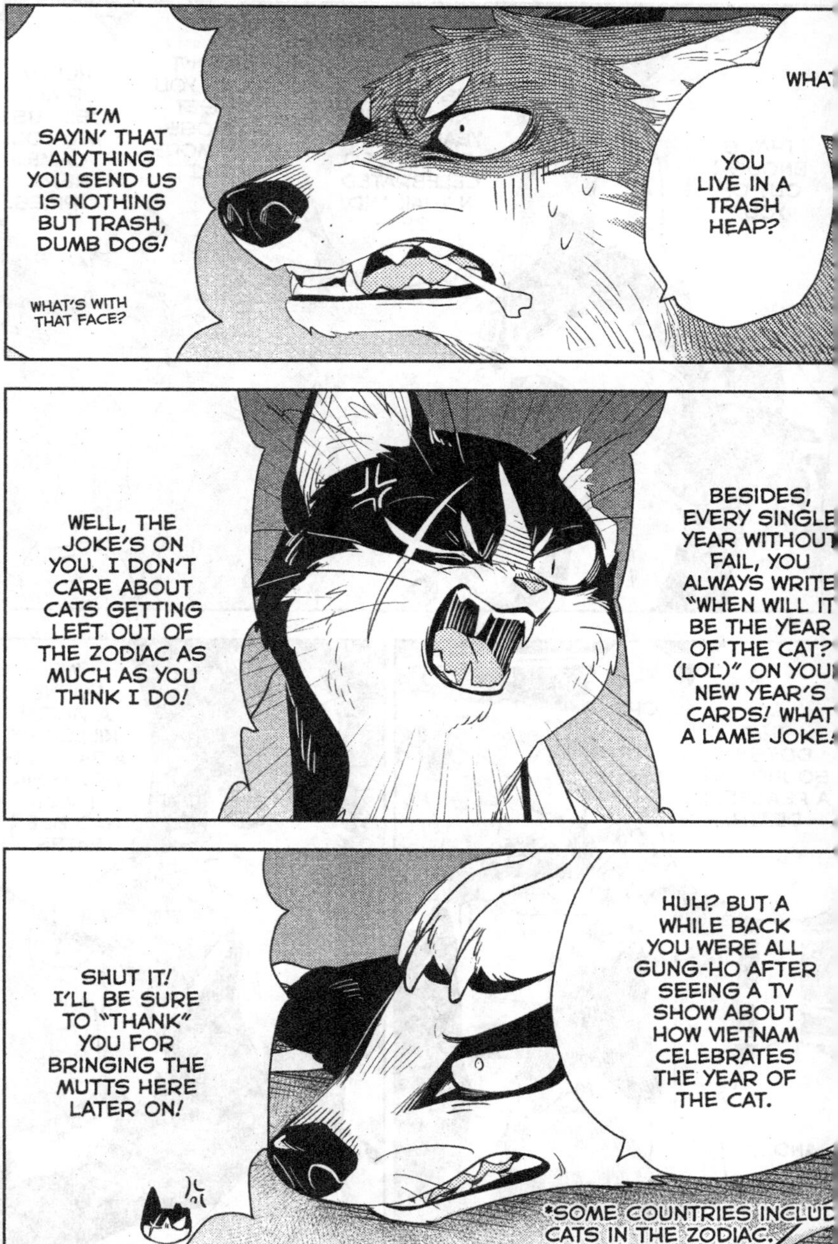
WHAT
YOU LIVE IN A TRASH HEAP?
I'M SAYIN' THAT ANYTHING YOU SEND US IS NOTHING BUT TRASH, DUMB DOG!
WHAT'S WITH THAT FACE?
BESIDES, EVERY SINGLE YEAR WITHOUT FAIL, YOU ALWAYS WRITE "WHEN WILL IT BE THE YEAR OF THE CAT? (LOL)" ON YOU NEW YEAR'S CARDS! WHAT A LAME JOKE.
WELL, THE JOKE'S ON YOU. I DON'T CARE ABOUT CATS GETTING LEFT OUT OF THE ZODIAC AS MUCH AS YOU THINK I DO!
HUH? BUT A WHILE BACK YOU WERE ALL GUNG-HO AFTER SEEING A TV SHOW ABOUT HOW VIETNAM CELEBRATES THE YEAR OF THE CAT.
*SOME COUNTRIES INCLUD CATS IN THE ZODIAC.
SHUT IT! I'LL BE SURE TO "THANK" YOU FOR BRINGING THE MUTTS HERE LATER ON!

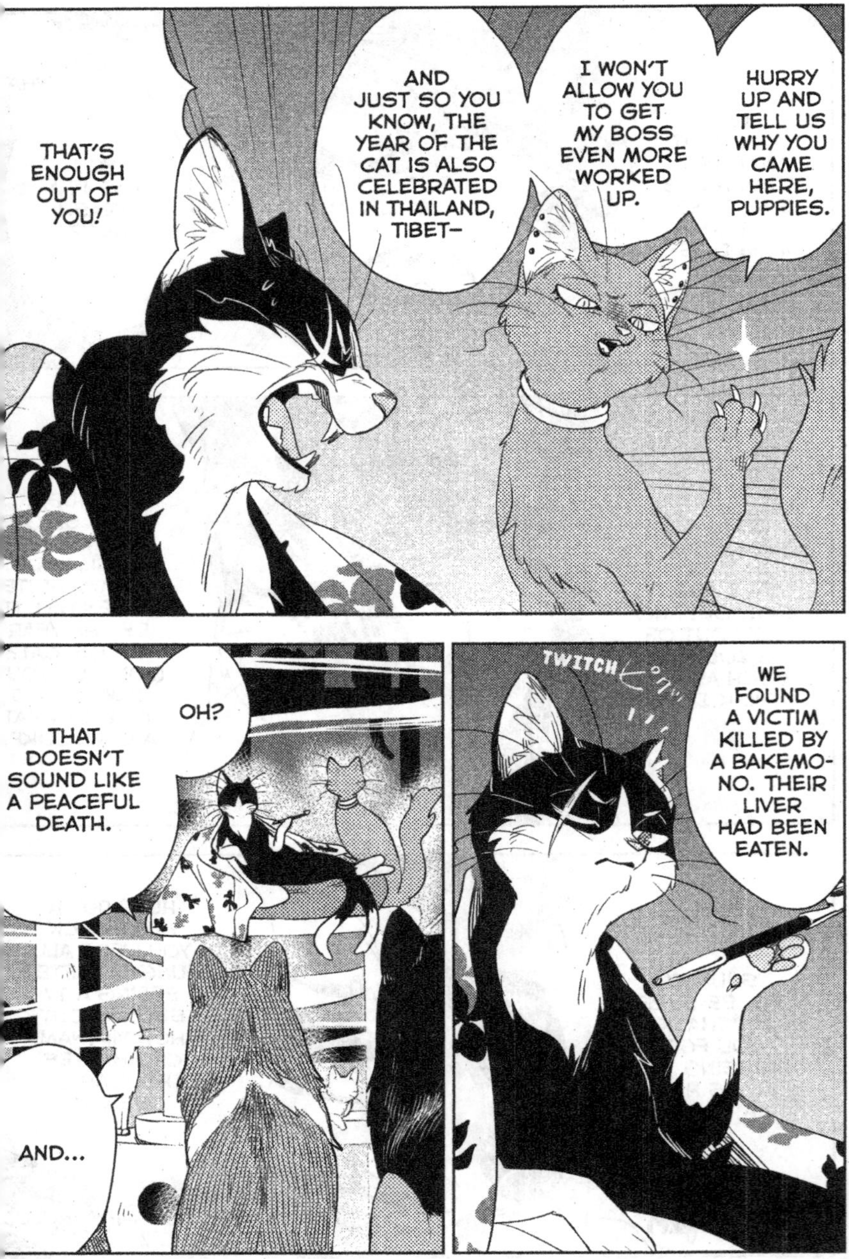
HURRY UP AND TELL US WHY YOU CAME HERE, PUPPIES.
I WON'T ALLOW YOU TO GET MY BOSS EVEN MORE WORKED UP.
AND JUST SO YOU KNOW, THE YEAR OF THE CAT IS ALSO CELEBRATED IN THAILAND, TIBET–
THAT'S ENOUGH OUT OF YOU!
TWITCH
WE FOUND A VICTIM KILLED BY A BAKEMO-NO. THEIR LIVER HAD BEEN EATEN.
OH?
THAT DOESN'T SOUND LIKE A PEACEFUL DEATH.
AND...

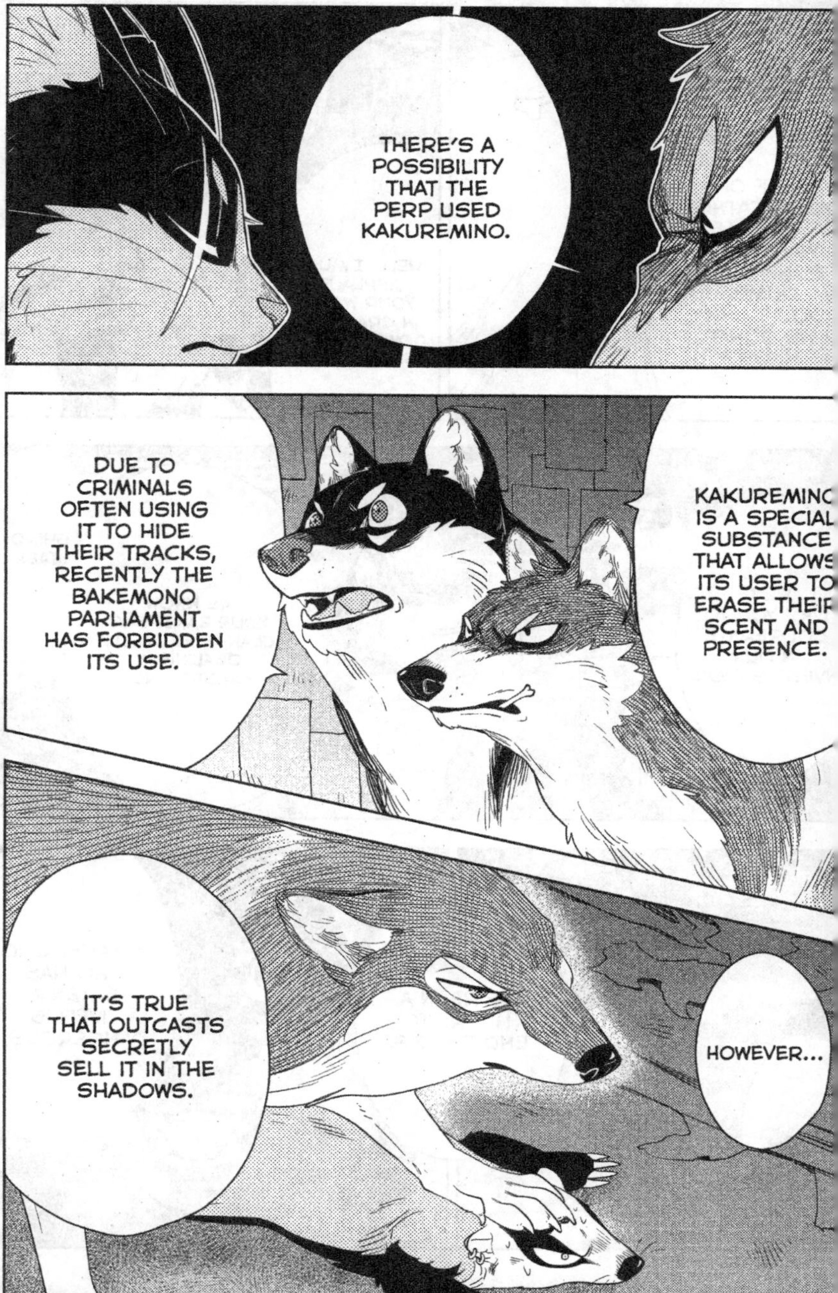
THERE'S A POSSIBILITY THAT THE PERP USED KAKUREMINO.
KAKUREMINC IS A SPECIAL SUBSTANCE THAT ALLOWS ITS USER TO ERASE THEIR SCENT AND PRESENCE.
DUE TO CRIMINALS OFTEN USING IT TO HIDE THEIR TRACKS, RECENTLY THE BAKEMONO PARLIAMENT HAS FORBIDDEN ITS USE.
IT'S TRUE THAT OUTCASTS SECRETLY SELL IT IN THE SHADOWS.
HOWEVER...

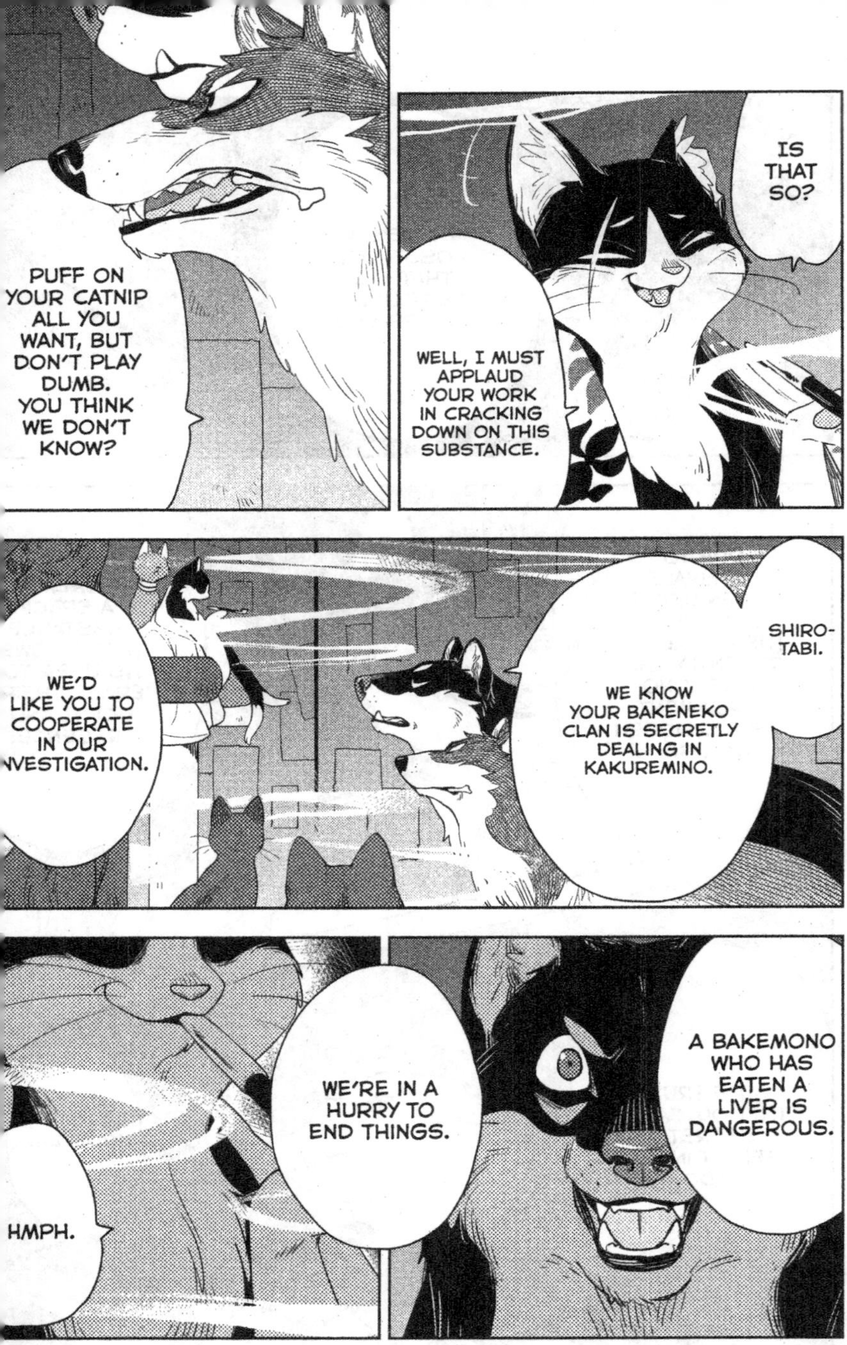
IS THAT SO?
WELL, I MUST APPLAUD YOUR WORK IN CRACKING DOWN ON THIS SUBSTANCE.
PUFF ON YOUR CATNIP ALL YOU WANT, BUT DON'T PLAY DUMB. YOU THINK WE DON'T KNOW?
SHIRO-TABI.
WE KNOW YOUR BAKENEKO CLAN IS SECRETLY DEALING IN KAKUREMINO.
WE'D LIKE YOU TO COOPERATE IN OUR INVESTIGATION.
A BAKEMONO WHO HAS EATEN A LIVER IS DANGEROUS.
WE'RE IN A HURRY TO END THINGS.
HMPH.

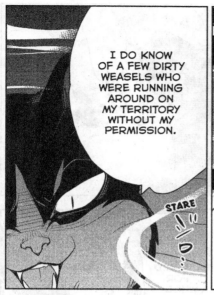

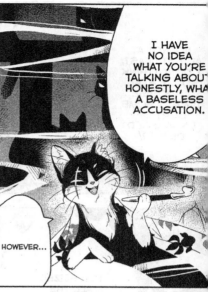

I HAVE NO IDEA WHAT YOU'RE TALKING ABOU
HONESTLY, WHA
A BASELESS ACCUSATION.
HOWEVER...
I DO KNOW OF A FEW DIRTY WEASELS WHO WERE RUNNING AROUND ON MY TERRITORY WITHOUT MY PERMISSION.
STARE
TRY ASKING THAT FILTH
CREATURE ROLLING AROUND UNDER YOUR PAW.
HUH?!
N-NO, WAIT! PLEASE GO EASY ON ME!
WHAT'S HE TALKING ABOUT, MOMOJI?
LOOM
WAH! UH, THAT'S...

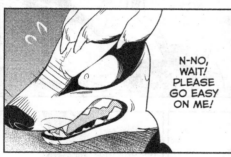

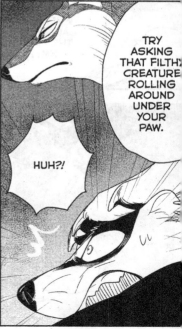

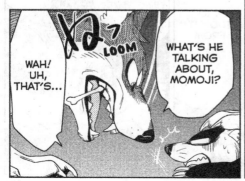

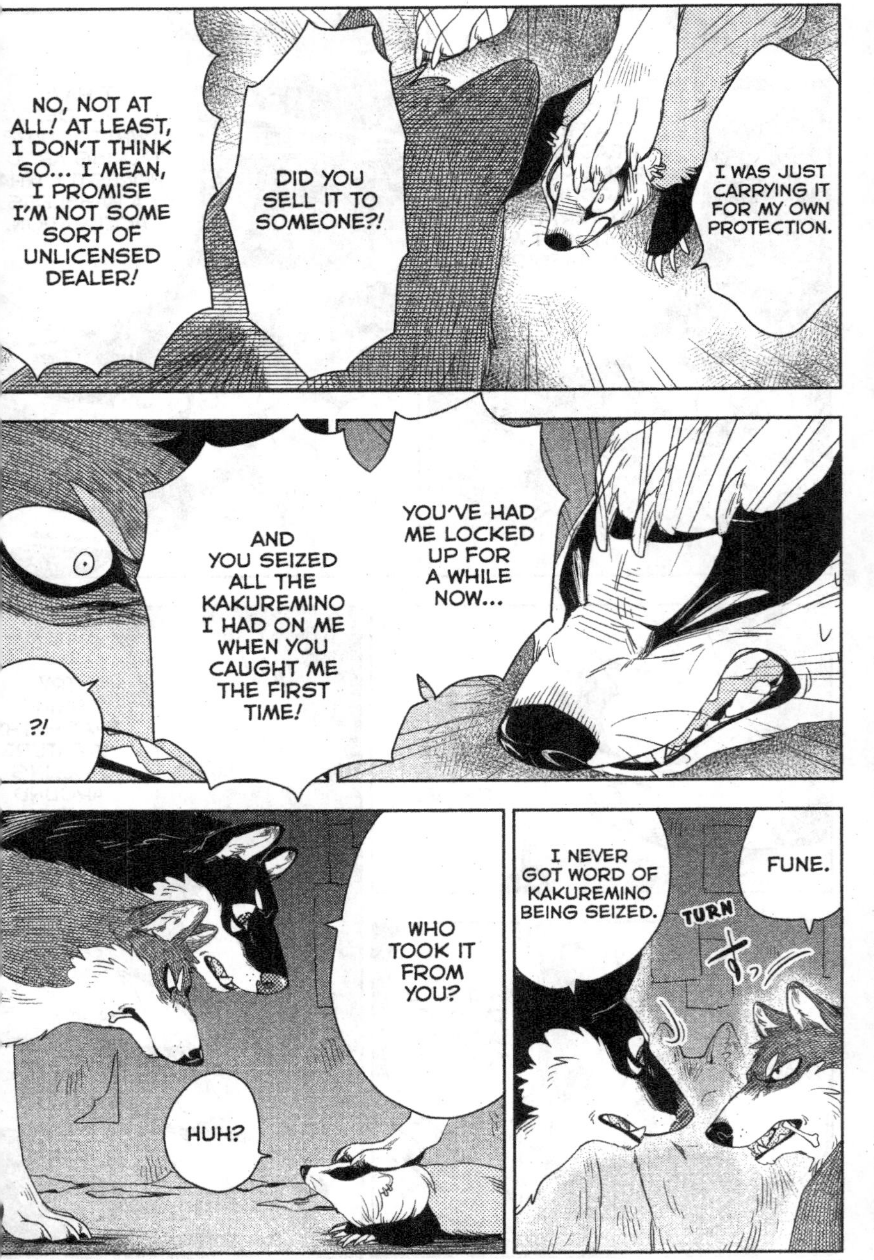
I WAS JUST CARRYING IT FOR MY OWN PROTECTION.
DID YOU SELL IT TO SOMEONE?!
NO, NOT AT ALL! AT LEAST, I DON'T THINK SO... I MEAN, I PROMISE I'M NOT SOME SORT OF UNLICENSED DEALER!
YOU'VE HAD ME LOCKED UP FOR A WHILE NOW...
AND YOU SEIZED ALL THE KAKUREMINO I HAD ON ME WHEN YOU CAUGHT ME THE FIRST TIME!
?!
FUNE.
TURN
I NEVER GOT WORD OF KAKUREMINO BEING SEIZED.
WHO TOOK IT FROM YOU?
HUH?

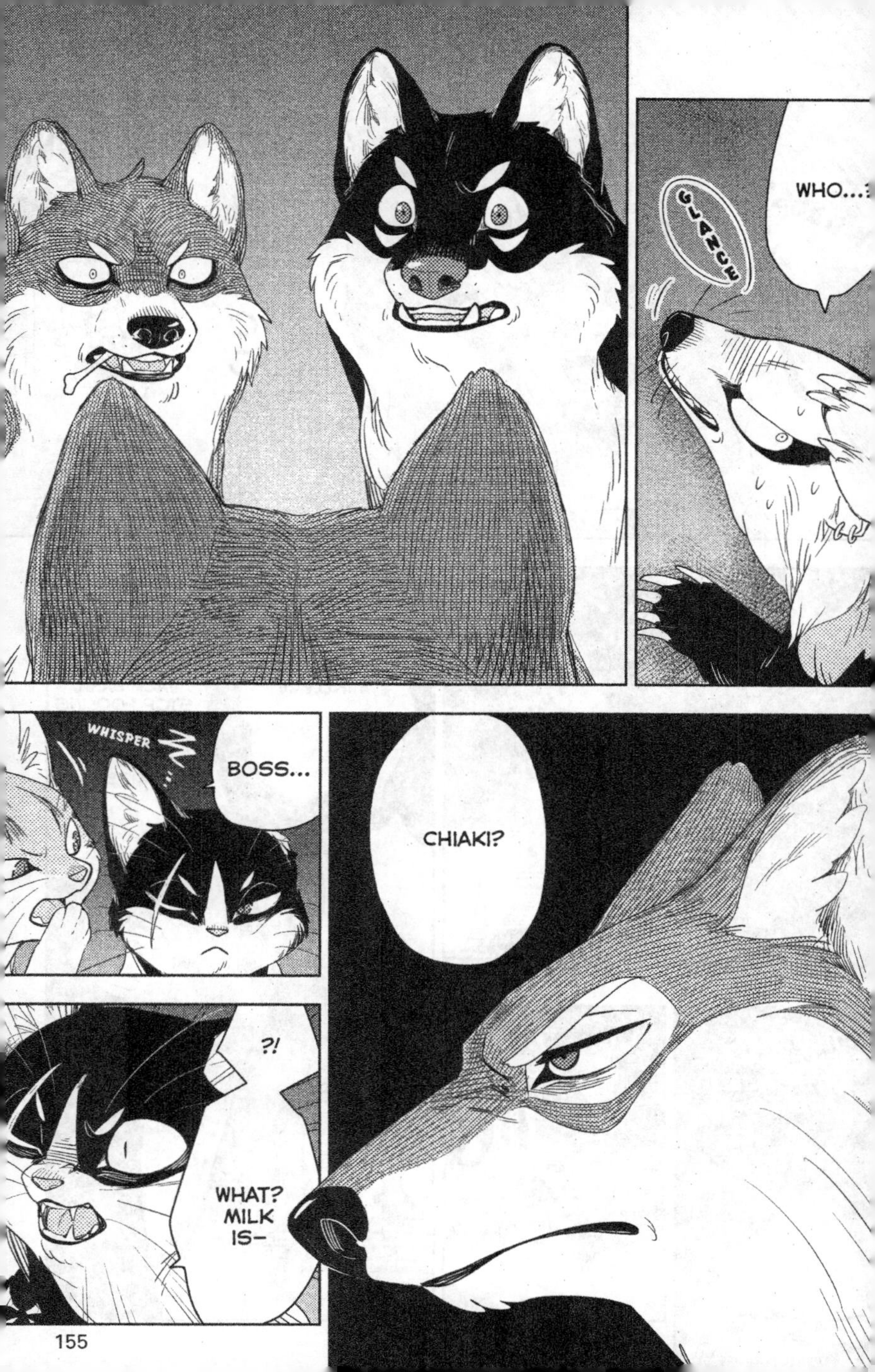
WHO...!?
GLANCE
CHIAKI?
WHISPER
BOSS...
?!
WHAT? MILK IS–

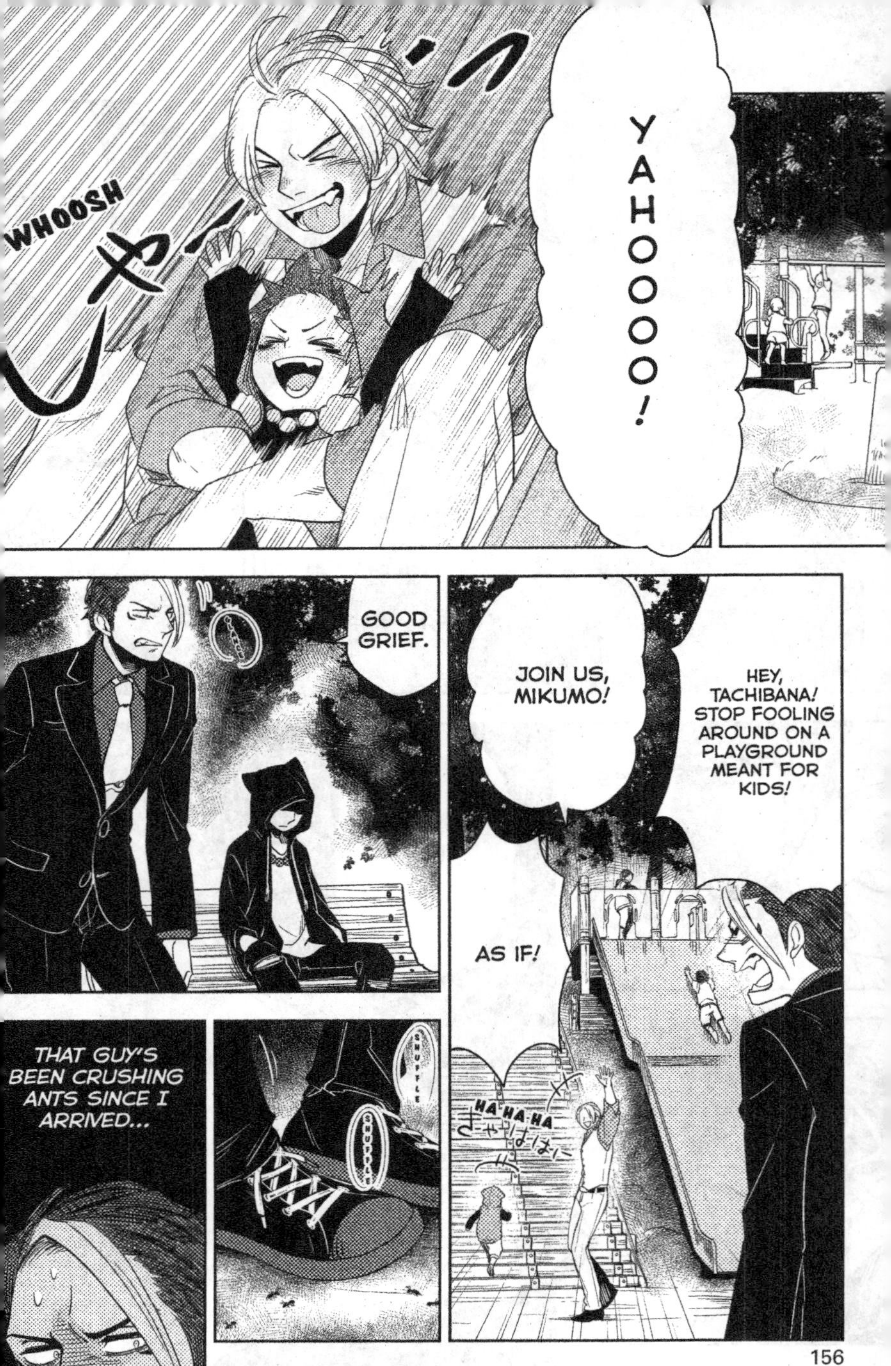
YAHOOOOO!
WHOOSH
HEY, TACHIBANA! STOP FOOLING AROUND ON A PLAYGROUND MEANT FOR KIDS!
JOIN US, MIKUMO!
AS IF!
HA HA HA
GOOD GRIEF.
SHUFFLE
SHUFFLE
THAT GUY'S BEEN CRUSHING ANTS SINCE I ARRIVED...

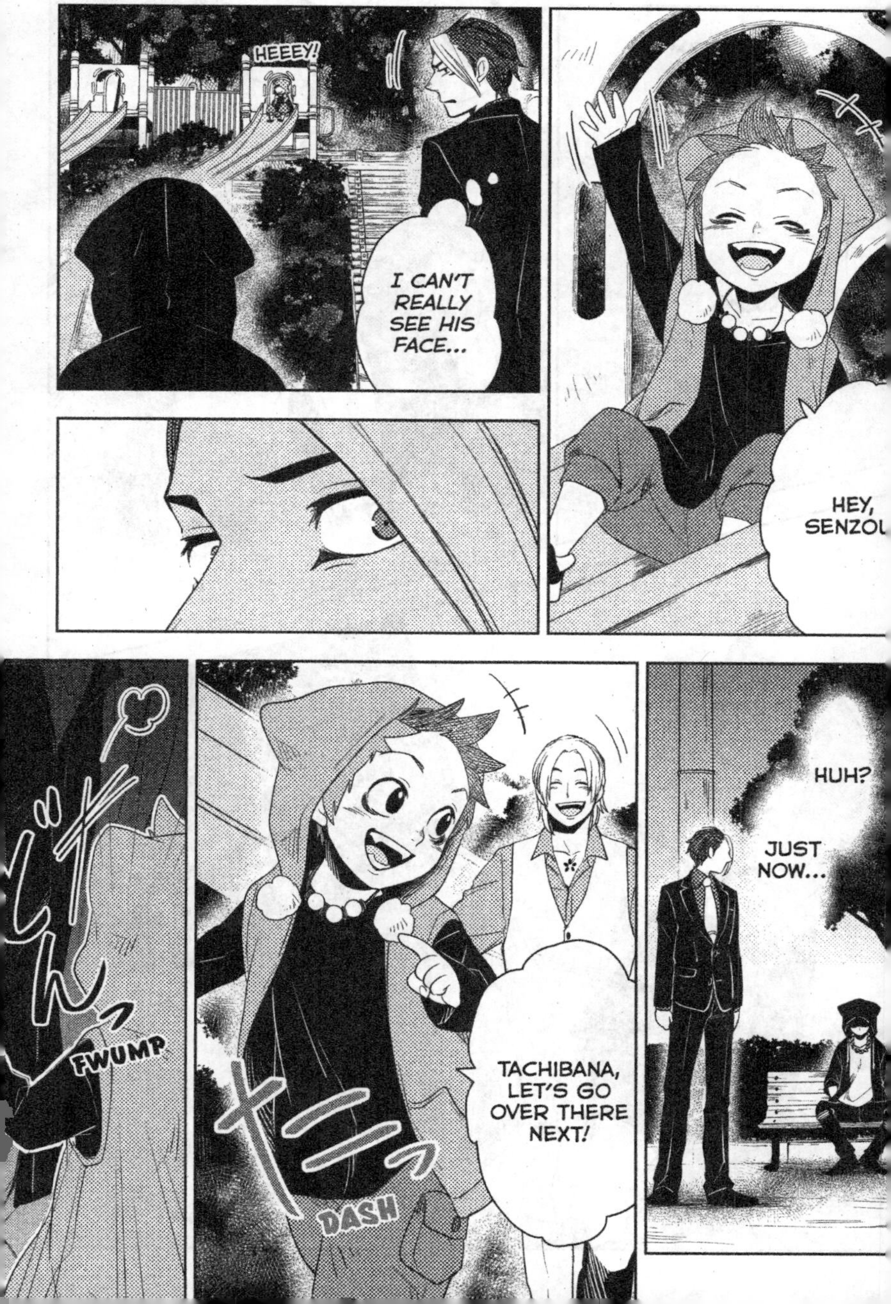
HEY, SENZO
HEEEY!
I CAN'T REALLY SEE HIS FACE...
HUH?
JUST NOW...
TACHIBANA, LET'S GO OVER THERE NEXT!
DASH
FWUMP

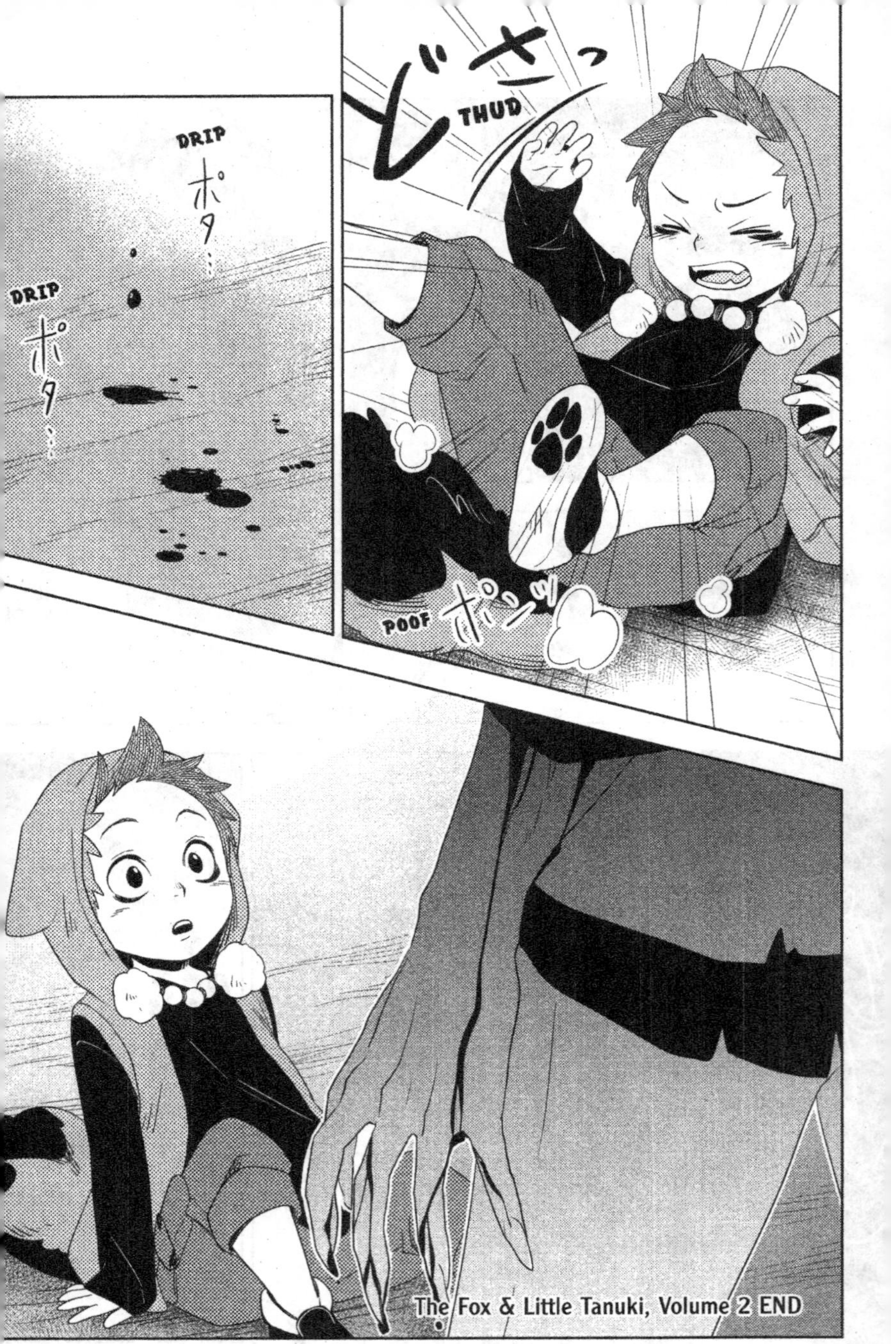
どさっ
THUD
POOF
ポンッ
DRIP
ポタ…
DRIP
ポタ…
The Fox & Little Tanuki, Volume 2 END

# A LITTLE BIT OF

# KORISENMAN

### A COLLECTION OF COMIC STRIPS
### THE AUTHOR UPLOADED TO SOCIAL MEDIA.

twitter.com/tagawa_mi    instagram.com/mi_tagawa

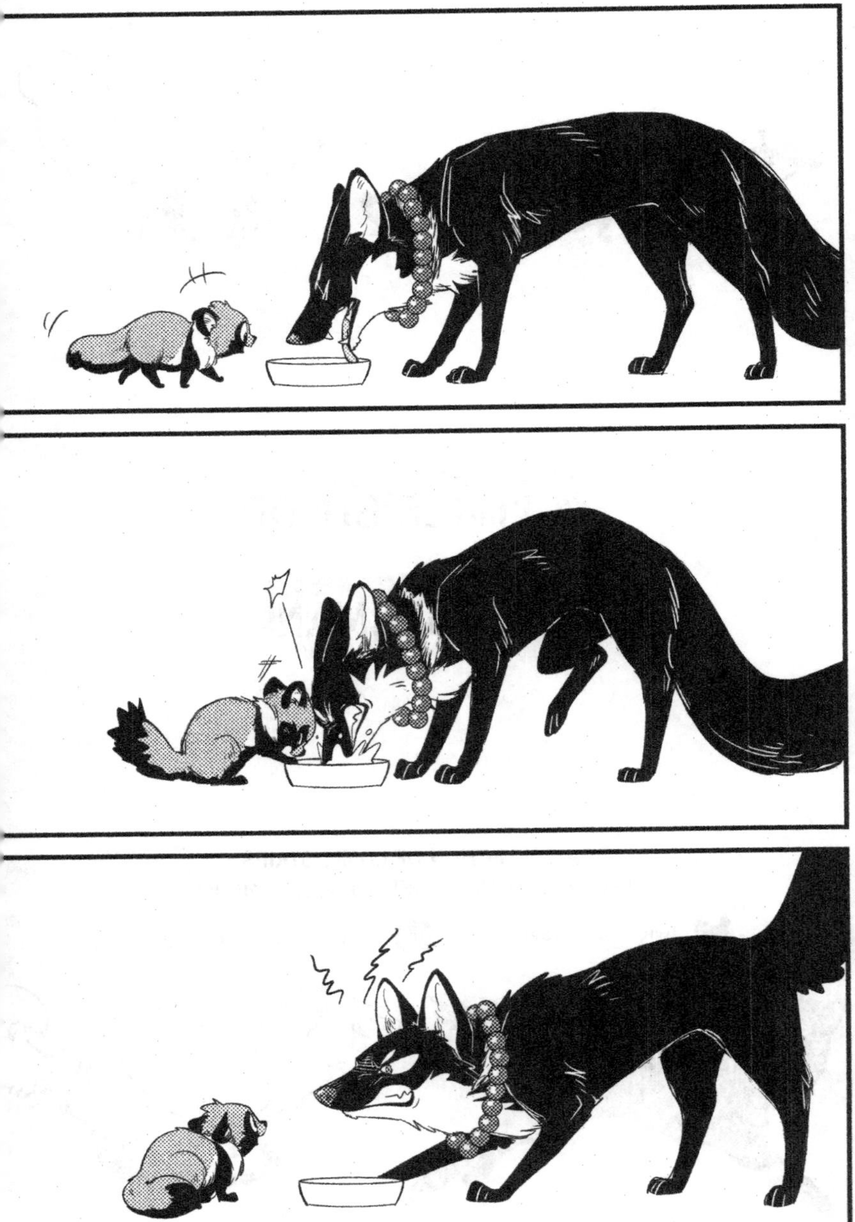

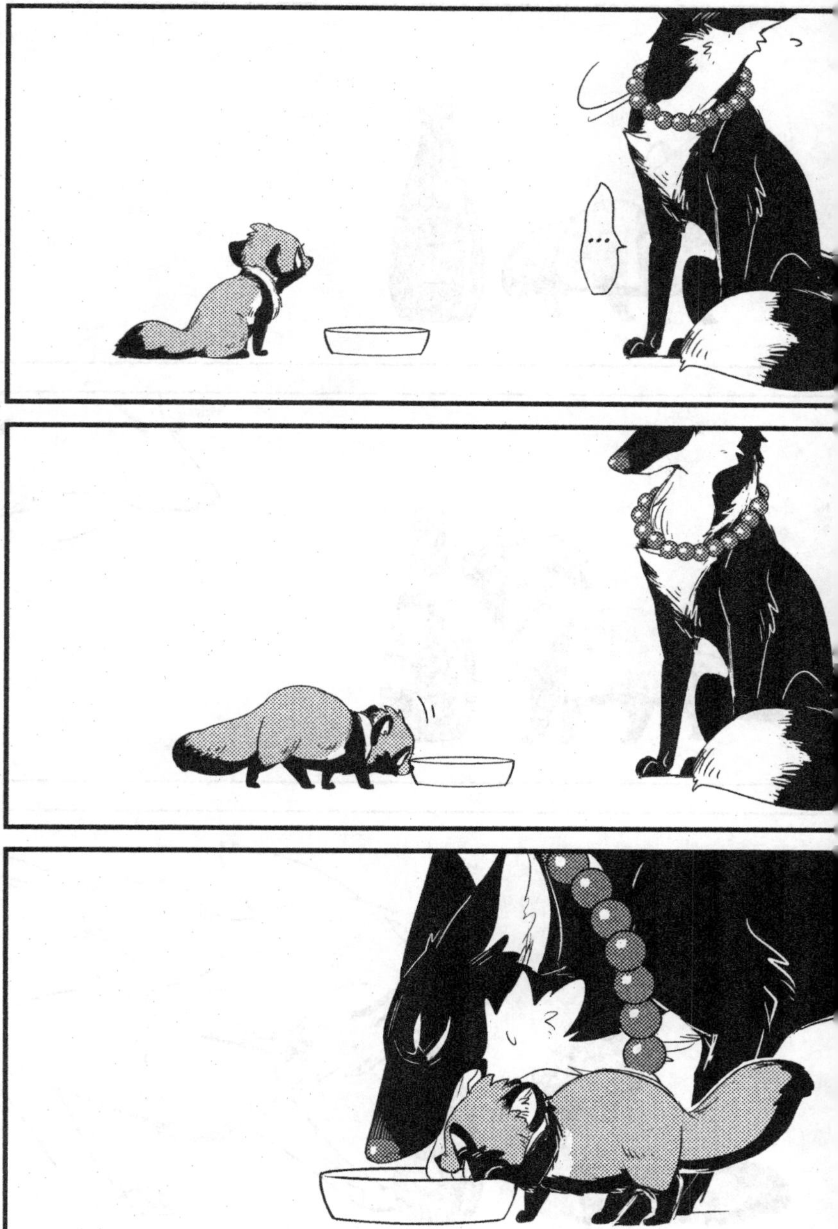
...

The End

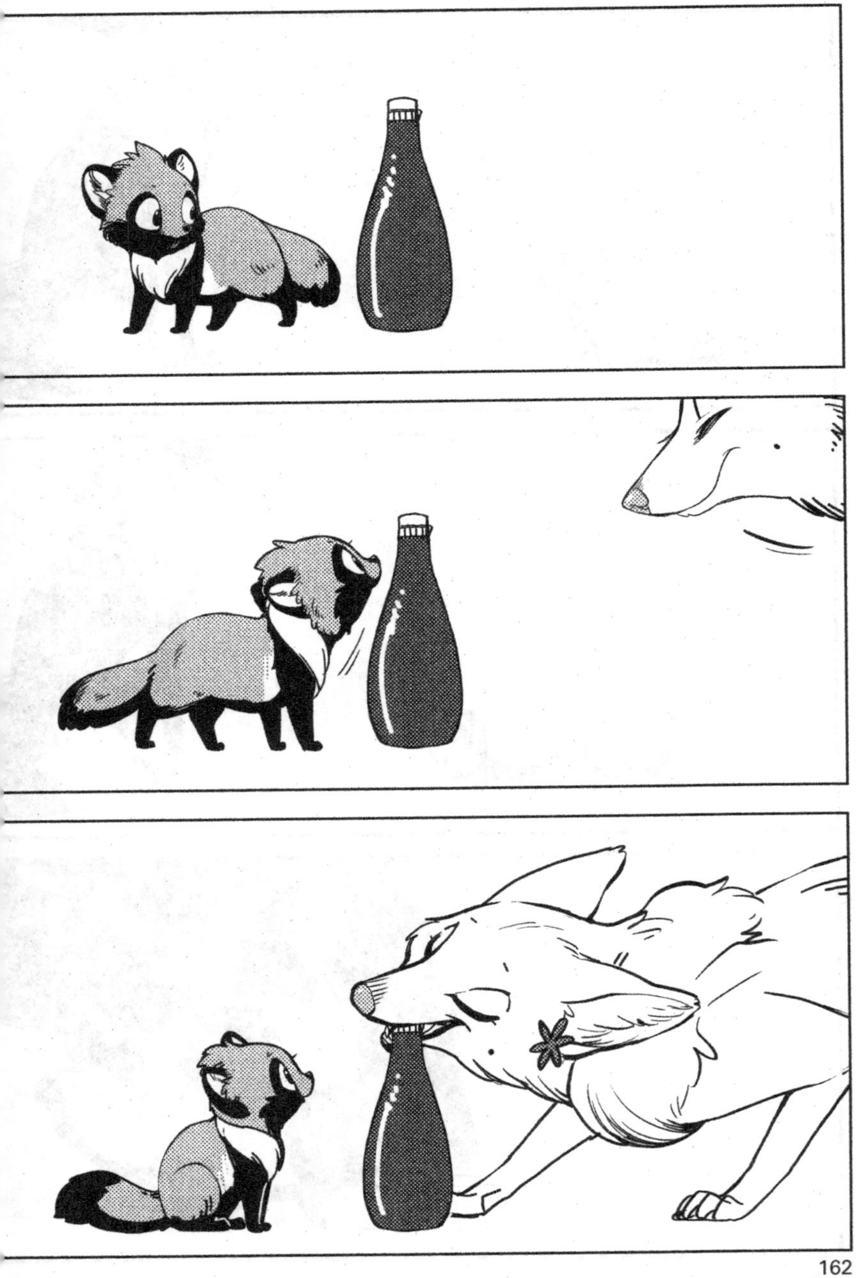

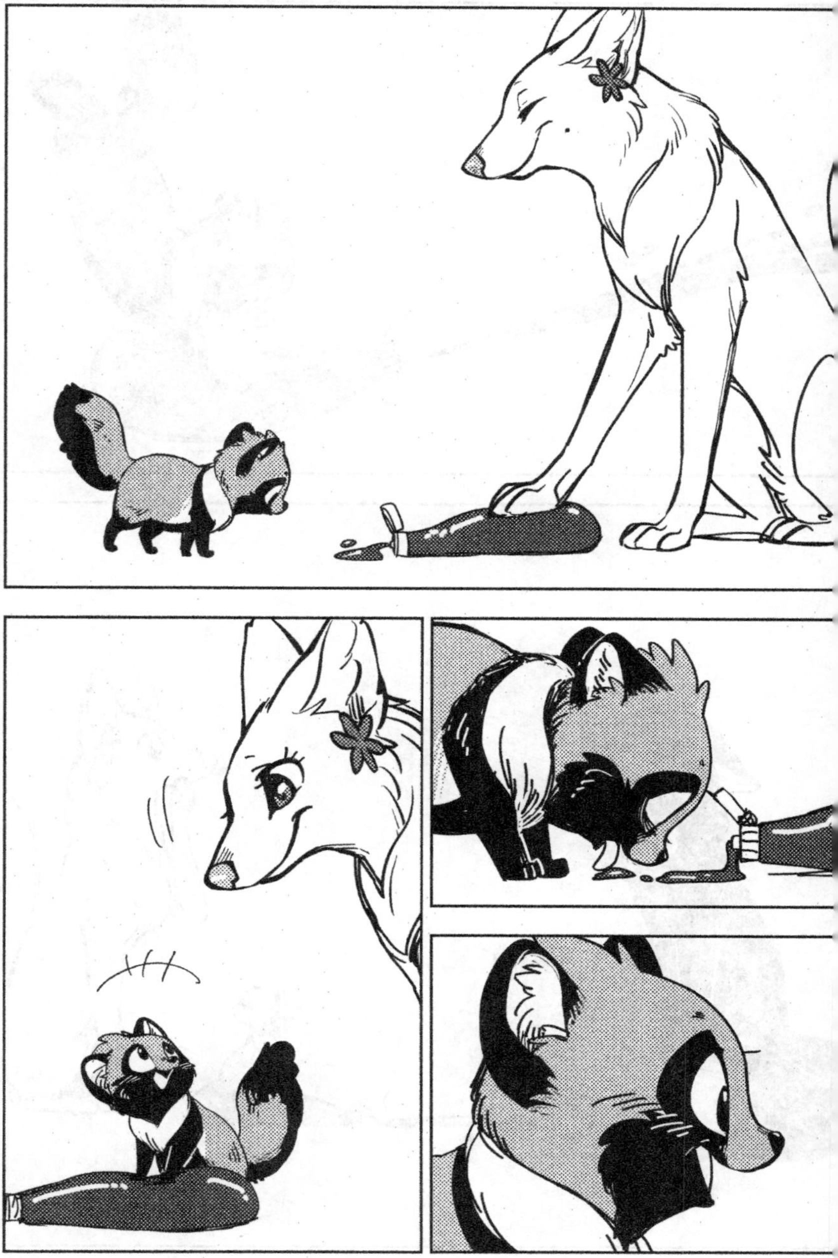

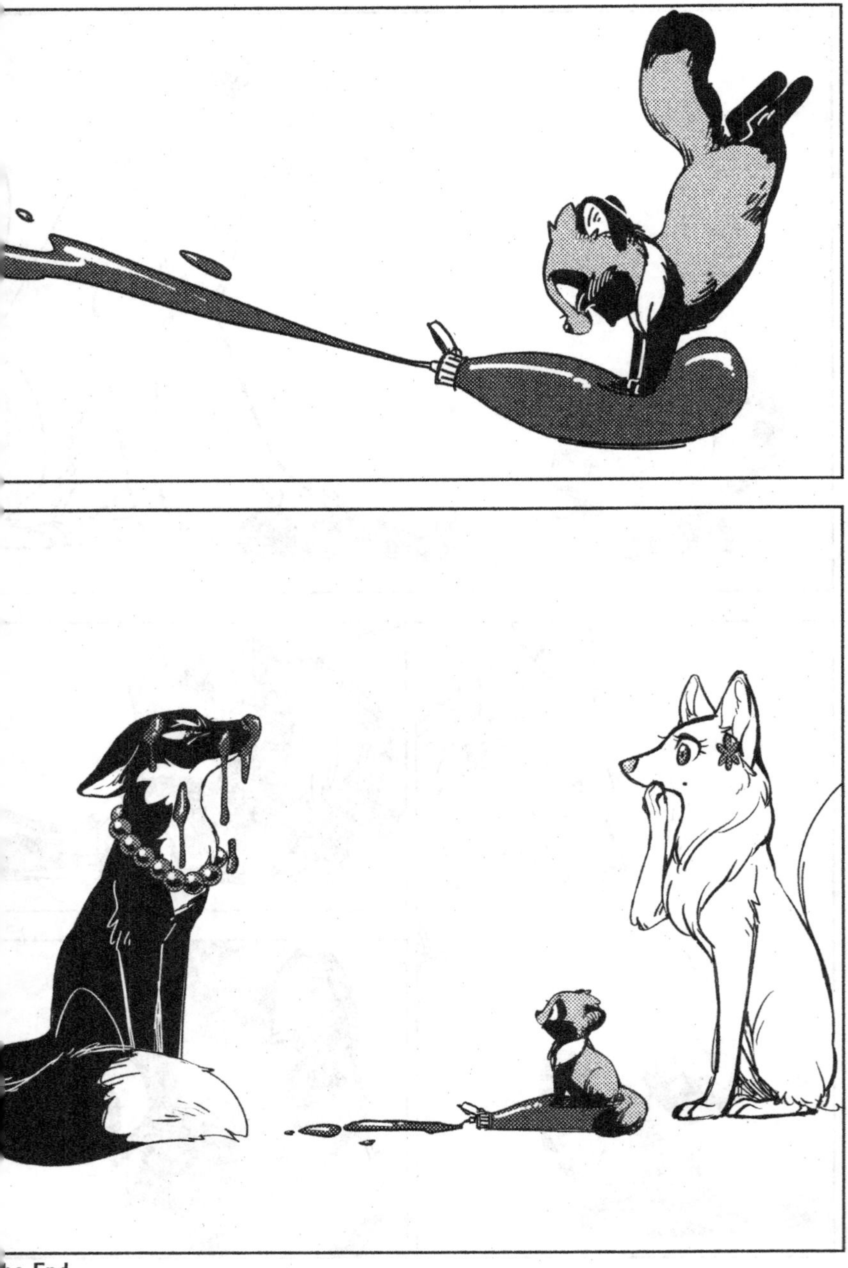

he End

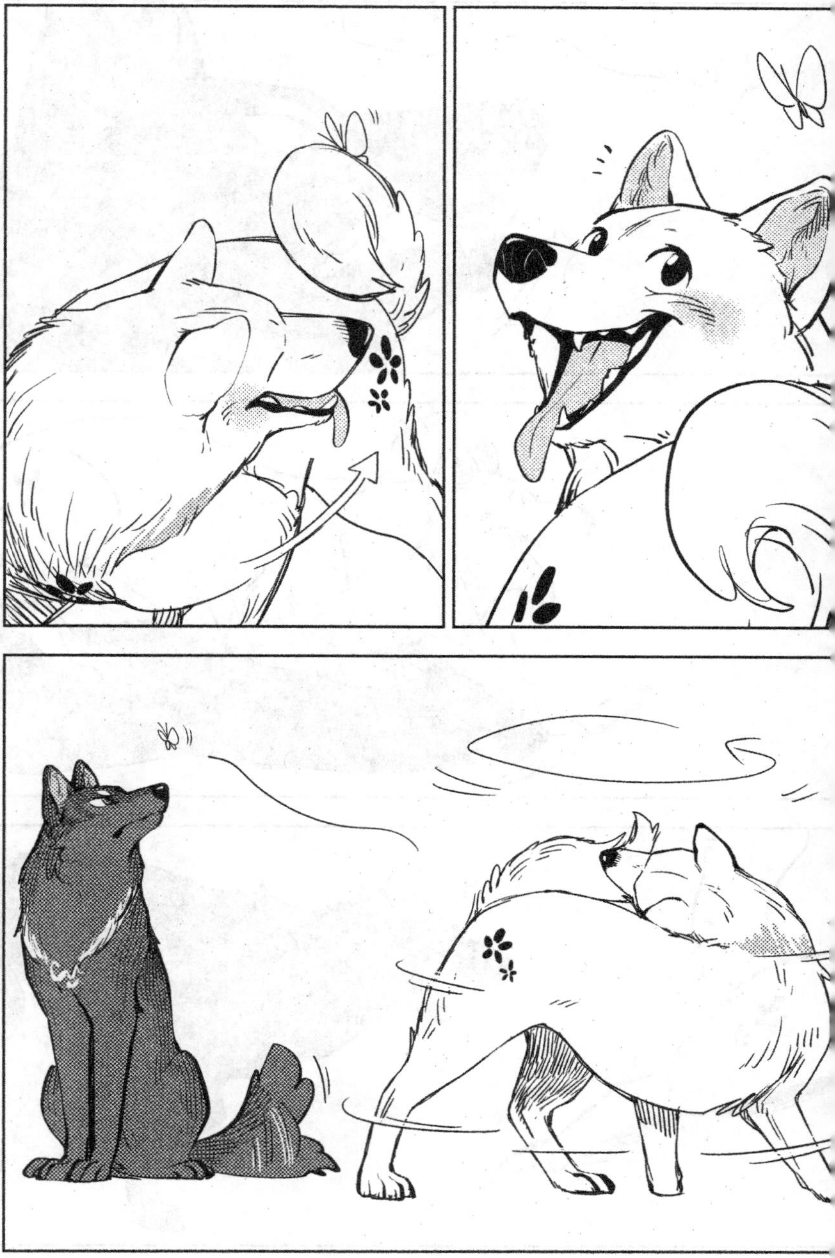

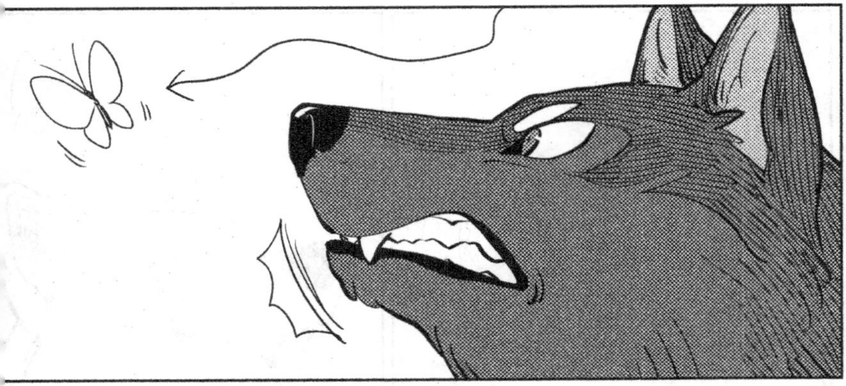

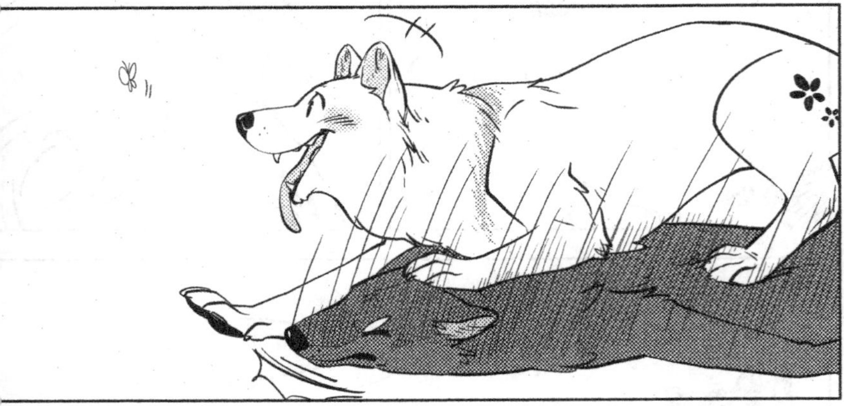

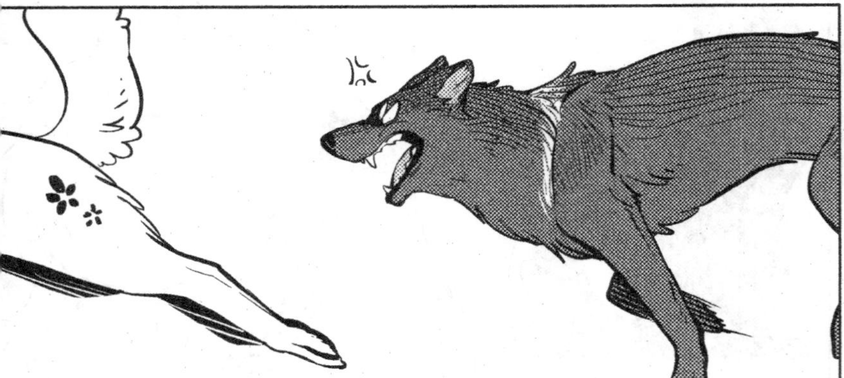

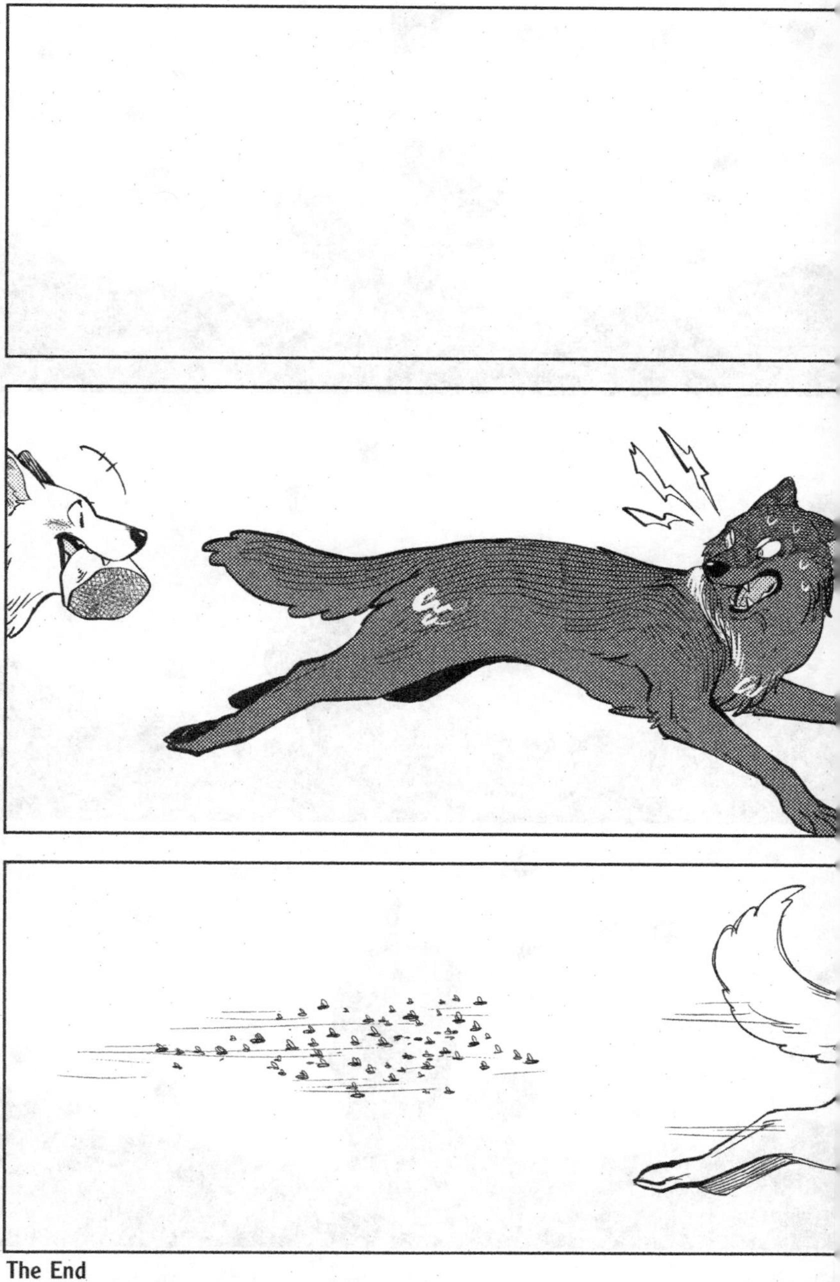

The End

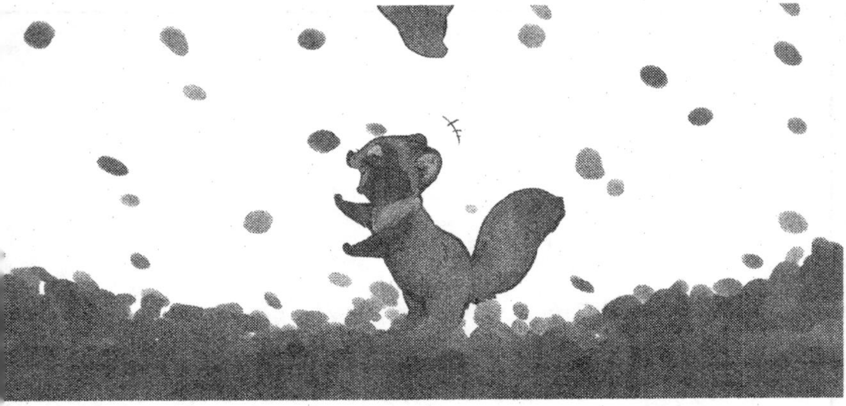
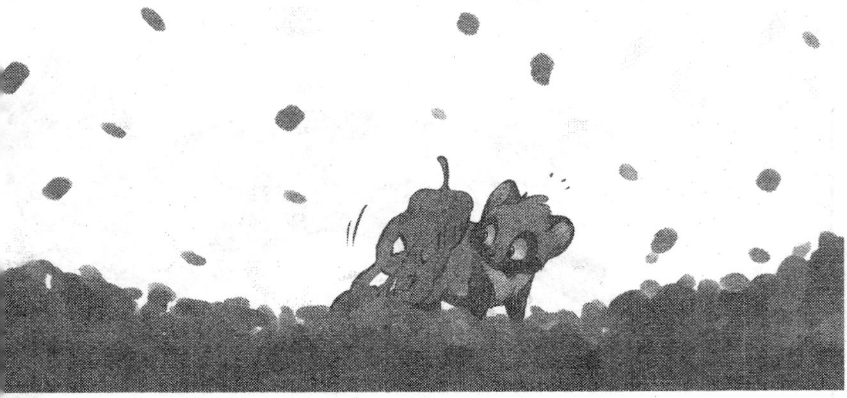
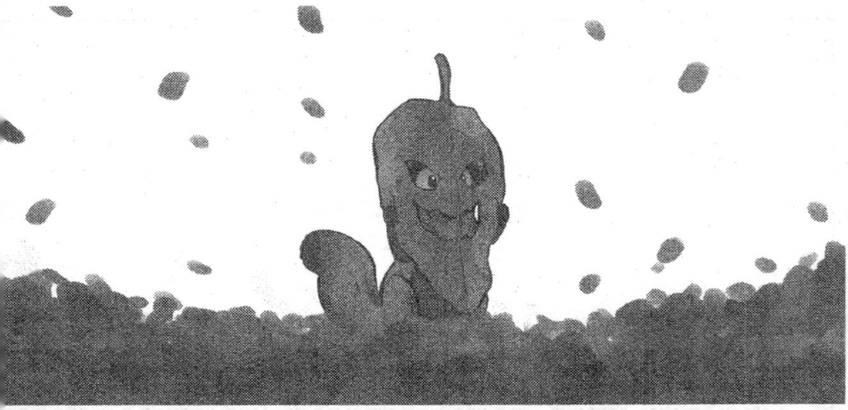

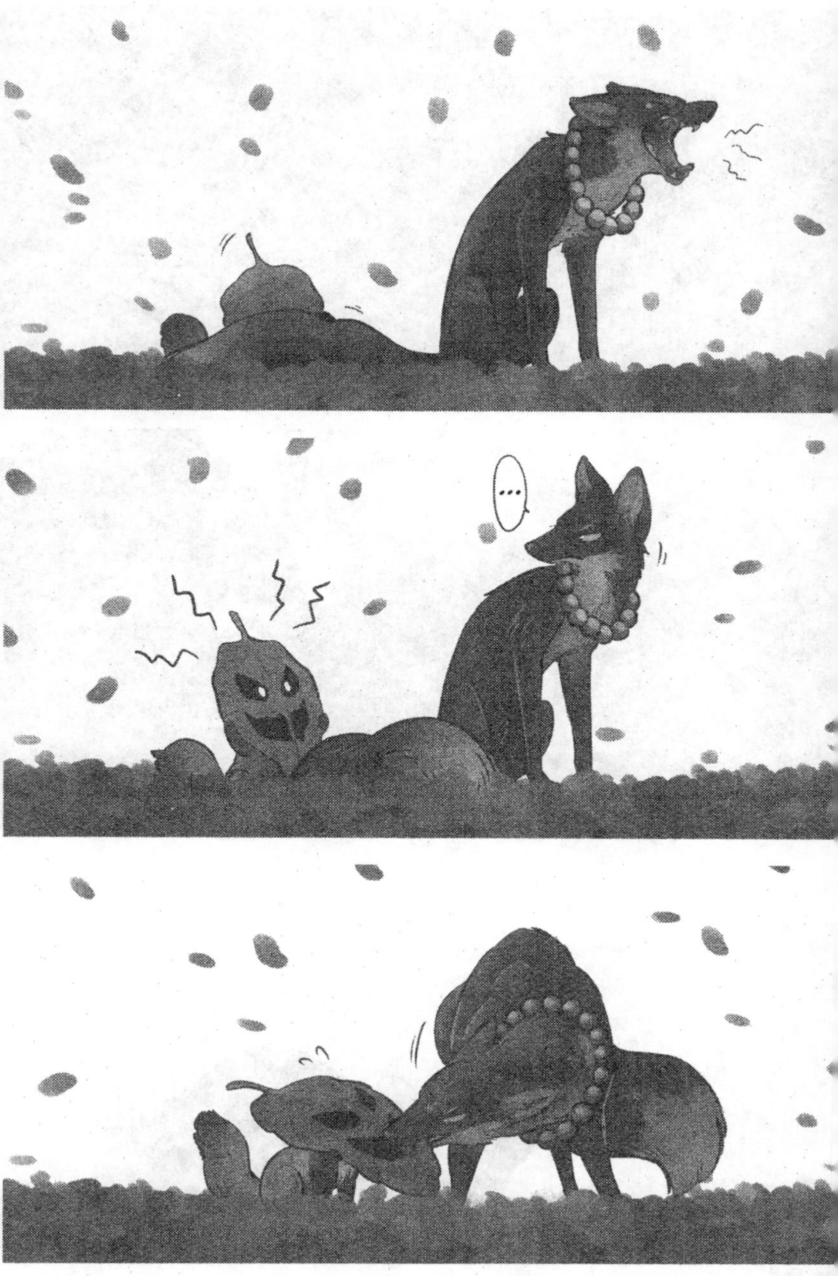
...

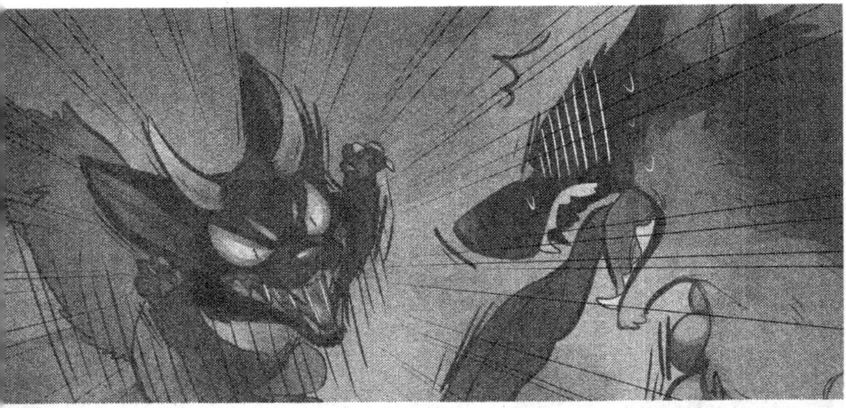
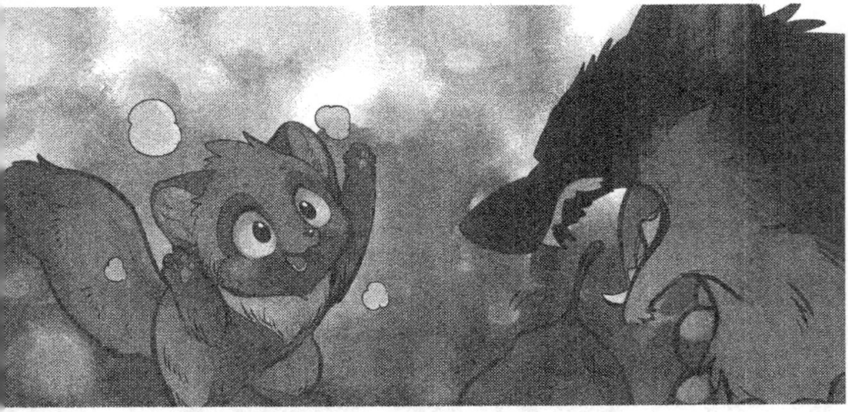
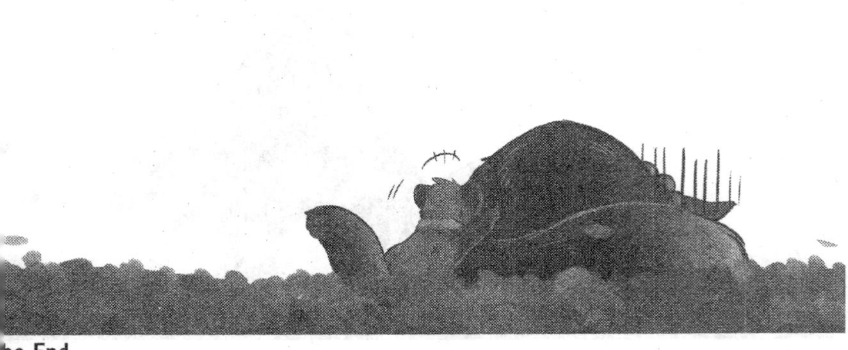
he End

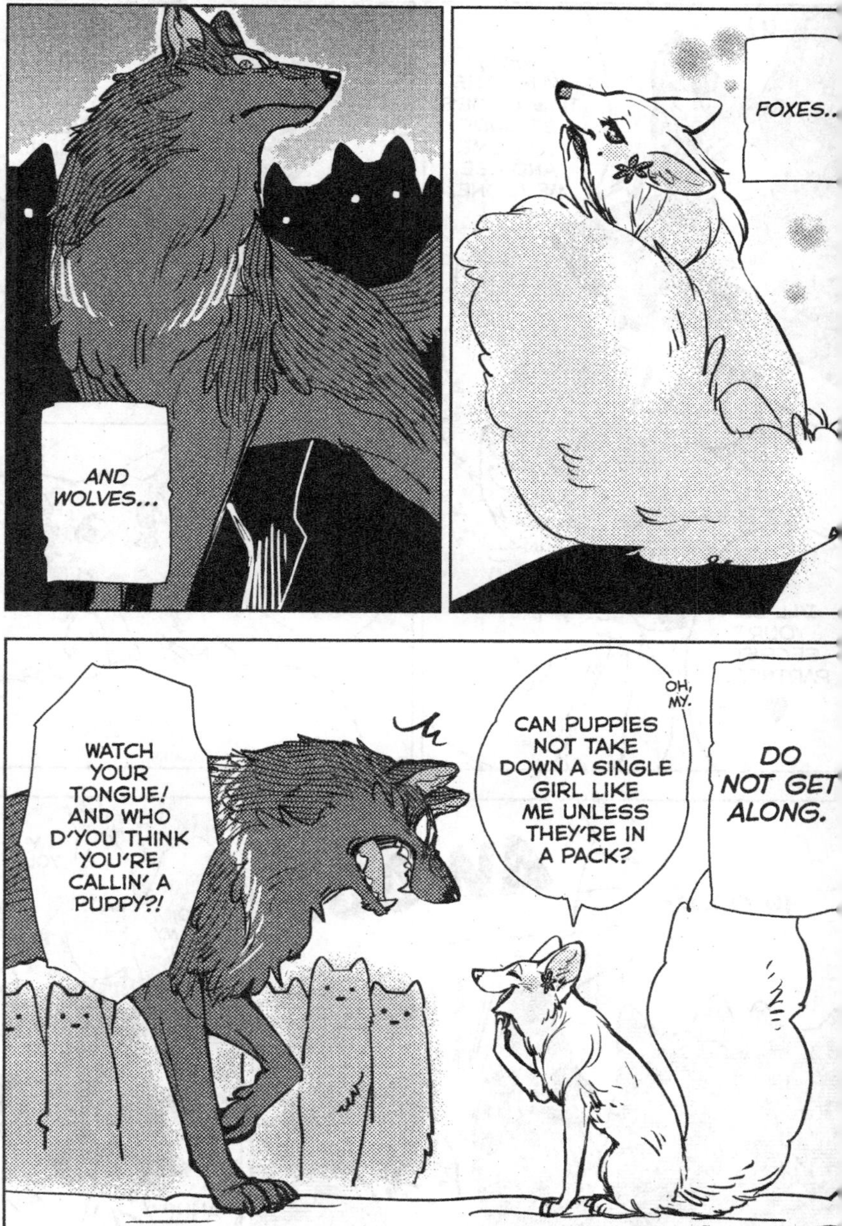
FOXES...
AND WOLVES...
DO NOT GET ALONG.
OH, MY.
CAN PUPPIES NOT TAKE DOWN A SINGLE GIRL LIKE ME UNLESS THEY'RE IN A PACK?
WATCH YOUR TONGUE! AND WHO D'YOU THINK YOU'RE CALLIN' A PUPPY?!

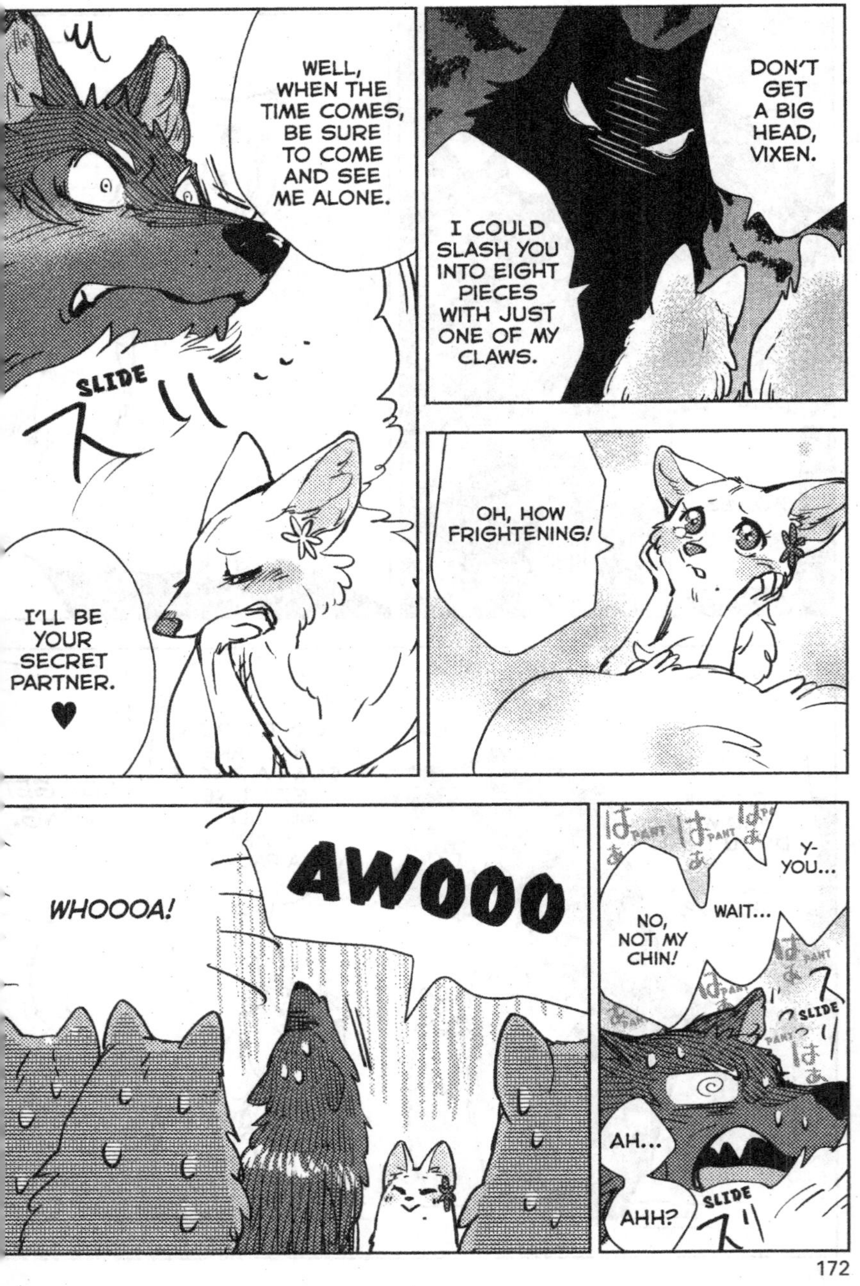
DON'T GET A BIG HEAD, VIXEN.
I COULD SLASH YOU INTO EIGHT PIECES WITH JUST ONE OF MY CLAWS.
OH, HOW FRIGHTENING!
WELL, WHEN THE TIME COMES, BE SURE TO COME AND SEE ME ALONE.
SLIDE
I'LL BE YOUR SECRET PARTNER. ♥
PANT PANT PANT
Y- YOU...
WAIT...
NO, NOT MY CHIN!
PANT PANT
SLIDE
PANT
AH...
AHH?
SLIDE
AWOOO
WHOOOA!

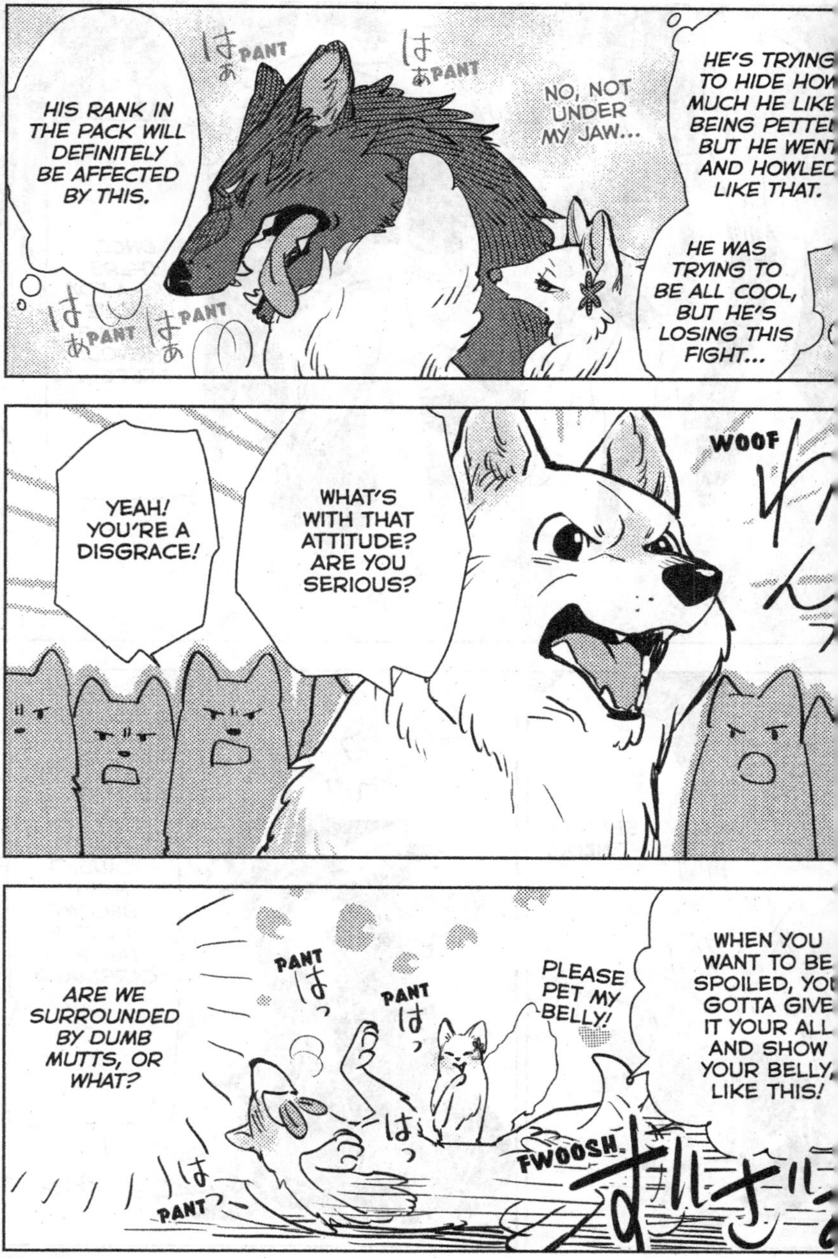
HE'S TRYING TO HIDE HOW MUCH HE LIKE BEING PETTE BUT HE WEN AND HOWLE LIKE THAT.
HE WAS TRYING TO BE ALL COOL, BUT HE'S LOSING THIS FIGHT...
NO, NOT UNDER MY JAW...
はあ PANT はあ PANT
HIS RANK IN THE PACK WILL DEFINITELY BE AFFECTED BY THIS.
はあ PANT はあ PANT
WOOF
WHAT'S WITH THAT ATTITUDE? ARE YOU SERIOUS?
YEAH! YOU'RE A DISGRACE!
WHEN YOU WANT TO BE SPOILED, YO GOTTA GIVE IT YOUR ALL AND SHOW YOUR BELLY LIKE THIS!
FWOOSH
PLEASE PET MY BELLY!
PANT はっ
PANT はっ
はっ
はっ PANT
ARE WE SURROUNDED BY DUMB MUTTS, OR WHAT?

The End

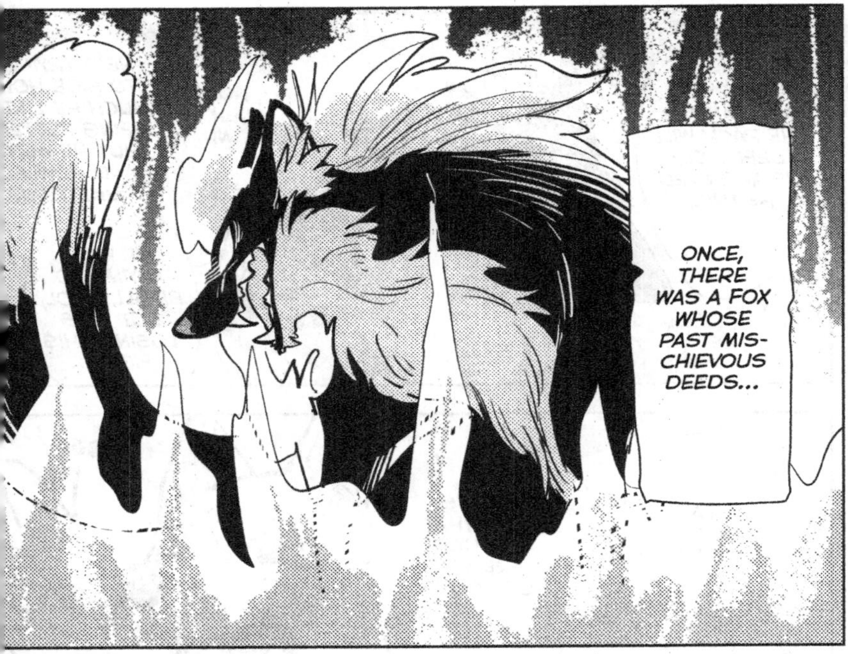
ONCE, THERE WAS A FOX WHOSE PAST MIS-CHIEVOUS DEEDS...

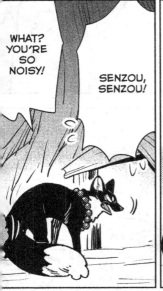

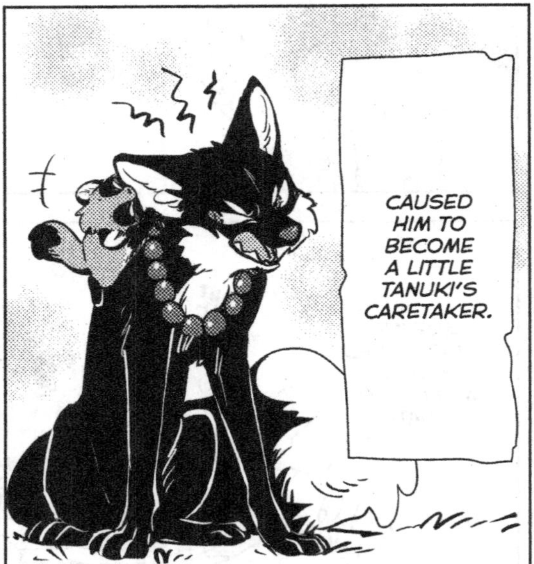
CAUSED HIM TO BECOME A LITTLE TANUKI'S CARETAKER.

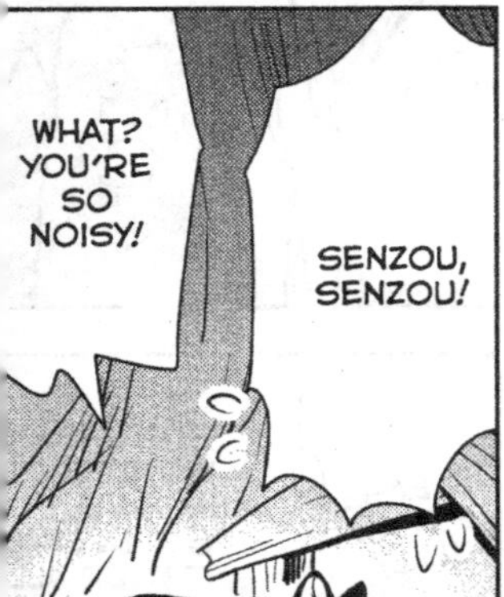
SENZOU, SENZOU!
WHAT? YOU'RE SO NOISY!

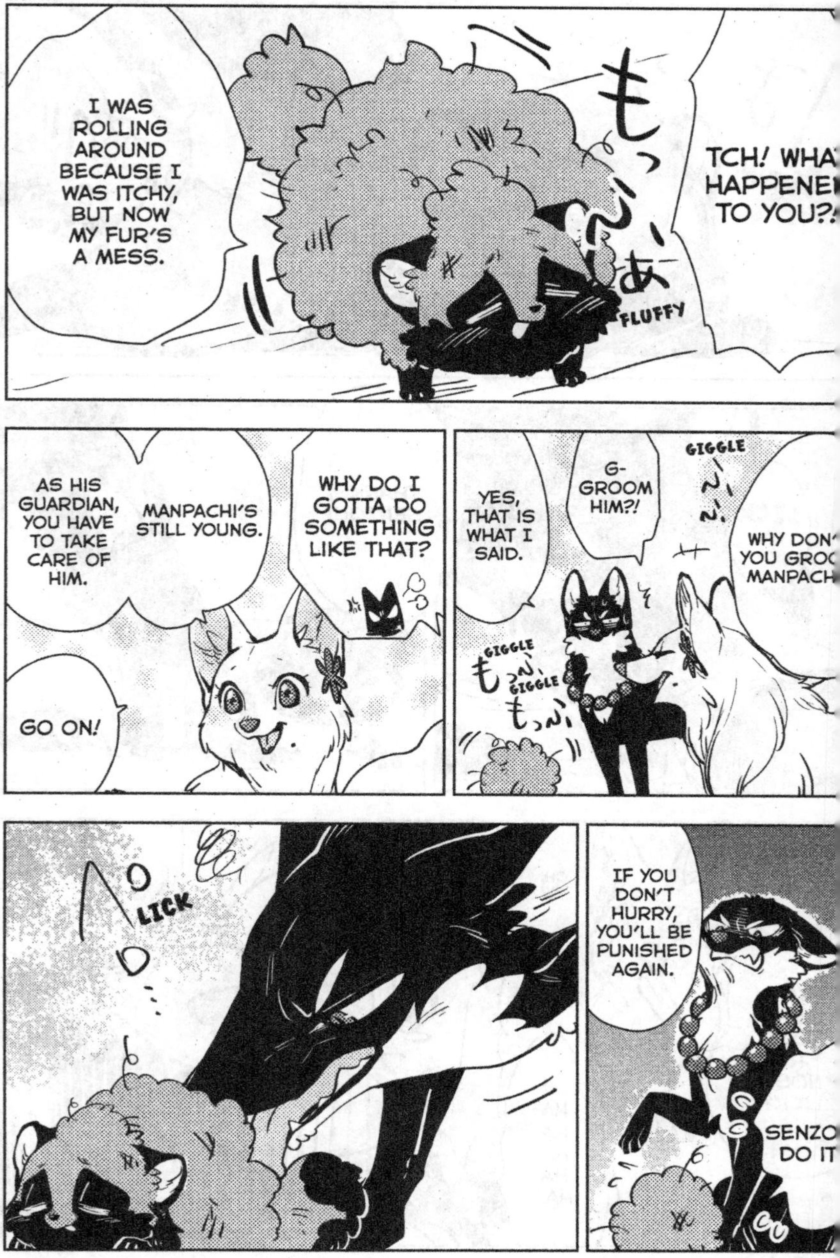
TCH! WHA
HAPPENE
TO YOU?!
FLUFFY
I WAS ROLLING AROUND BECAUSE I WAS ITCHY, BUT NOW MY FUR'S A MESS.
WHY DON'
YOU GROO
MANPACH
GIGGLE
G- GROOM HIM?!
YES, THAT IS WHAT I SAID.
GIGGLE
GIGGLE
WHY DO I GOTTA DO SOMETHING LIKE THAT?
MANPACHI'S STILL YOUNG.
AS HIS GUARDIAN, YOU HAVE TO TAKE CARE OF HIM.
GO ON!
SENZO
DO IT
IF YOU DON'T HURRY, YOU'LL BE PUNISHED AGAIN.
LICK

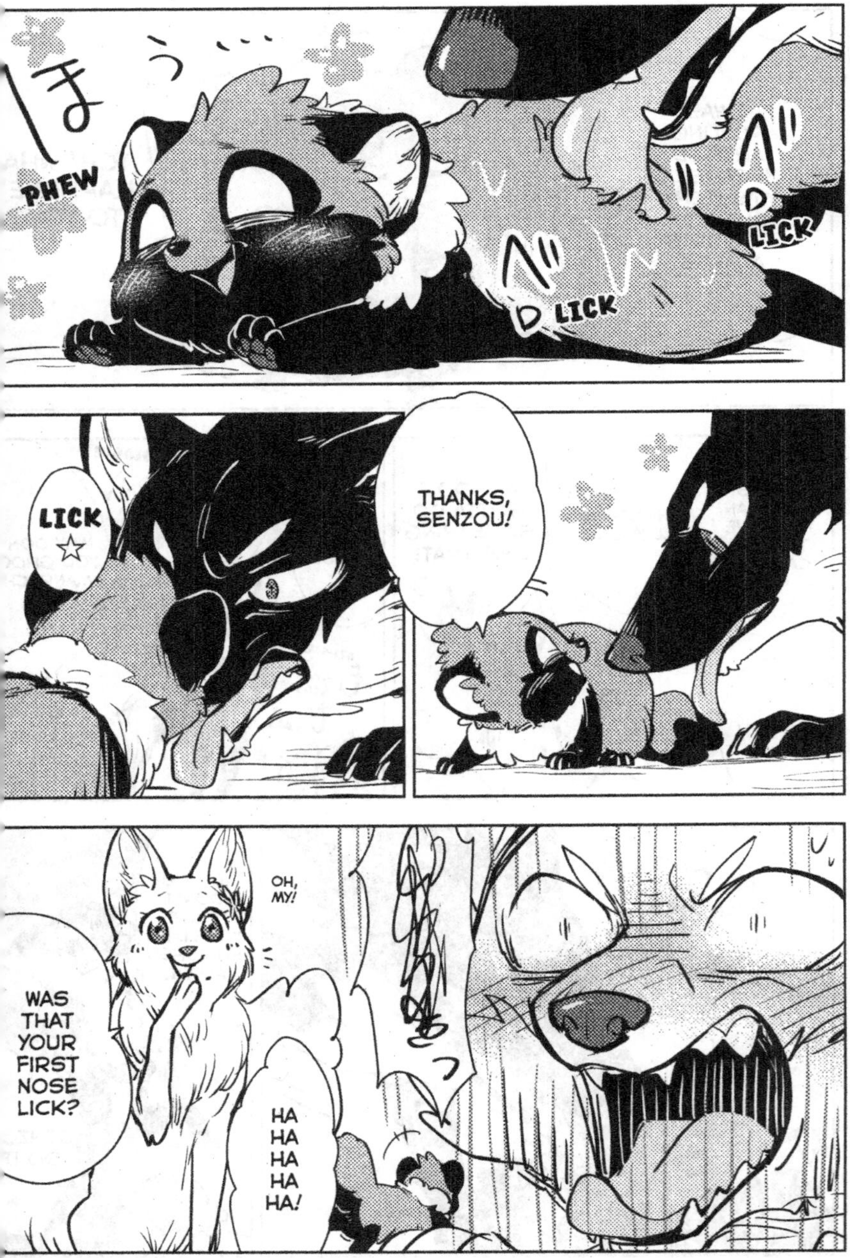
べロ
LICK
べロ
LICK
ほう…
PHEW
THANKS, SENZOU!
LICK ☆
OH, MY!
WAS THAT YOUR FIRST NOSE LICK?
HA HA HA HA HA!

he End

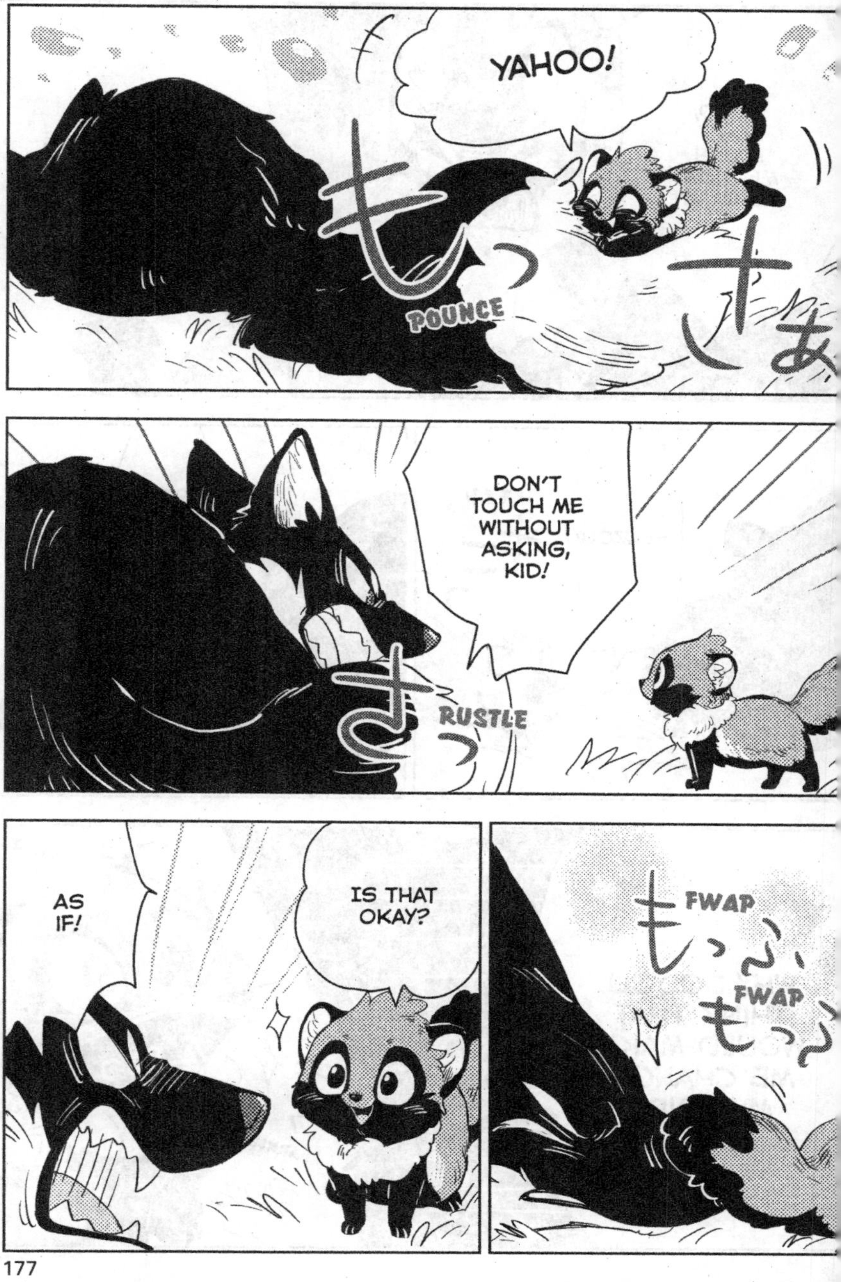
YAHOO!
もっ
POUNCE
さあ
DON'T TOUCH ME WITHOUT ASKING, KID!
さっ
RUSTLE
もっふ
FWAP
もっふ
FWAP
IS THAT OKAY?
AS IF!

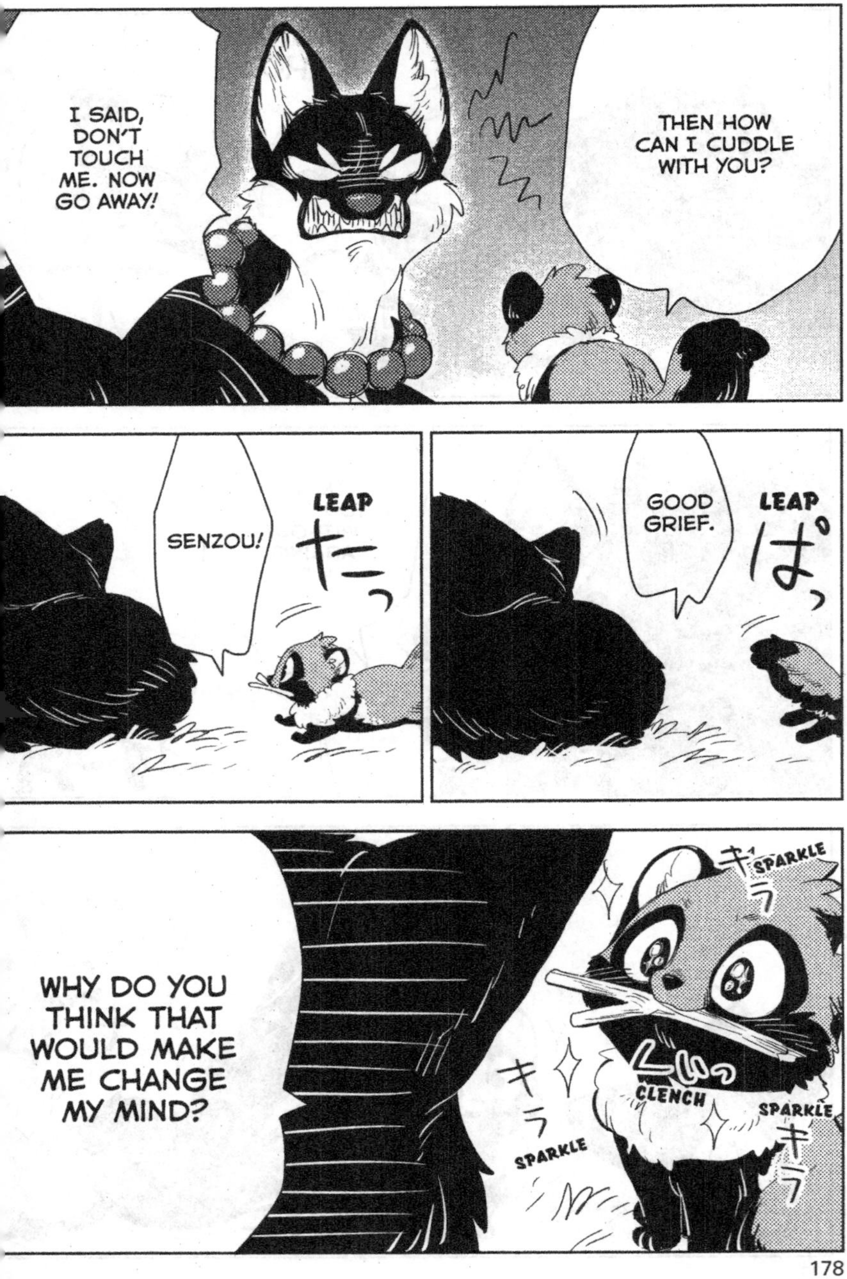
THEN HOW CAN I CUDDLE WITH YOU?
I SAID, DON'T TOUCH ME. NOW GO AWAY!
GOOD GRIEF.
LEAP
ぱっ
SENZOU!
LEAP
たっ
キラ
SPARKLE
くいっ
CLENCH
SPARKLE
キラ
キラ
SPARKLE
WHY DO YOU THINK THAT WOULD MAKE ME CHANGE MY MIND?

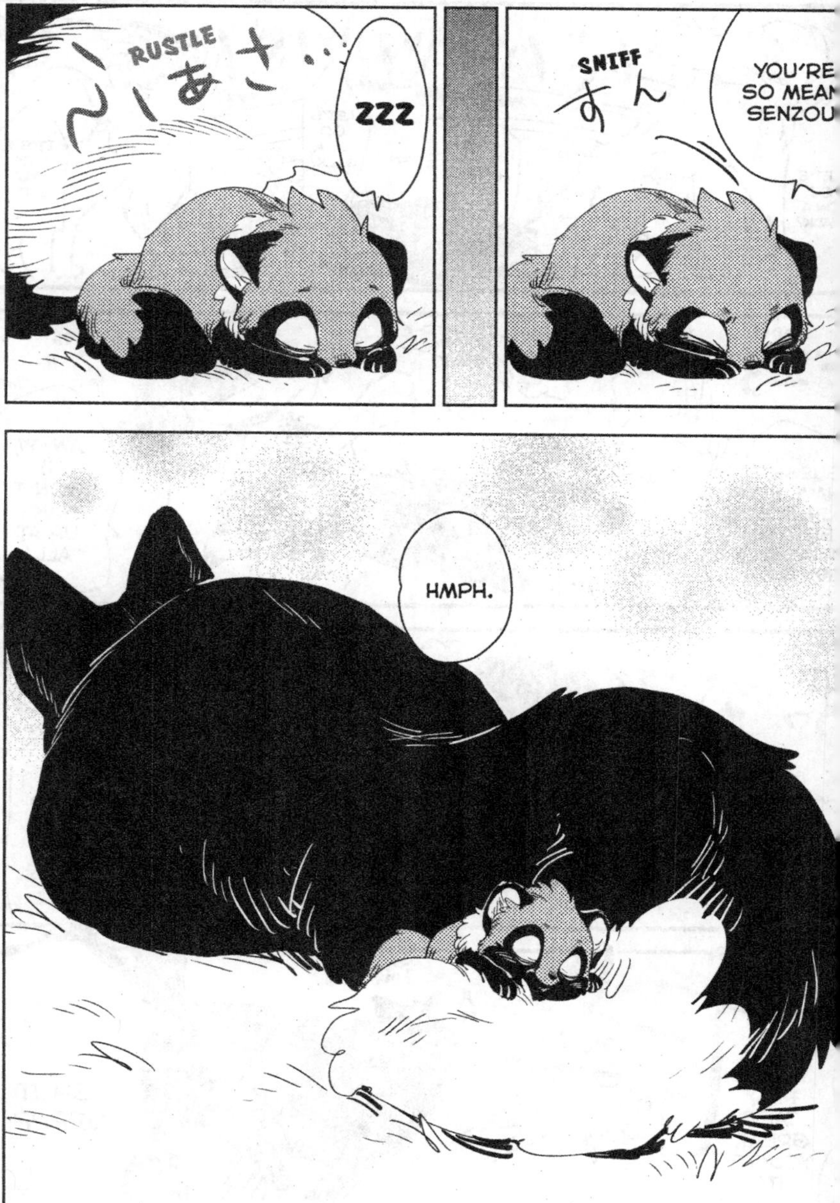
SNIFF
すん
YOU'RE SO MEAN SENZOU
RUSTLE
ふぁさ…
ZZZ
HMPH.

The End

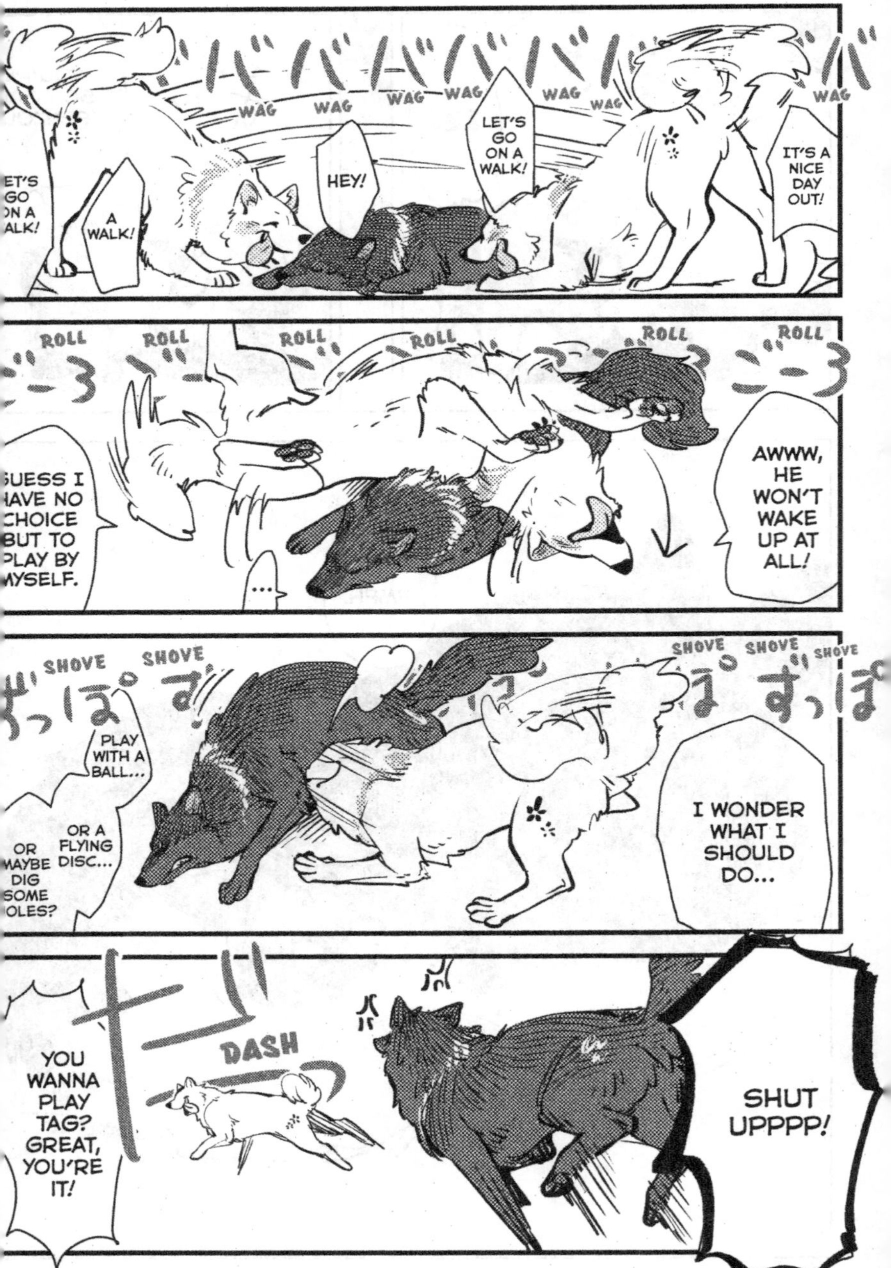
WAG
IT'S A NICE DAY OUT!
WAG
LET'S GO ON A WALK!
WAG WAG WAG WAG
HEY!
A WALK!
ET'S GO ON A ALK!
ROLL ROLL ROLL ROLL ROLL ROLL
AWWW, HE WON'T WAKE UP AT ALL!
...
UESS I HAVE NO CHOICE BUT TO PLAY BY MYSELF.
SHOVE SHOVE SHOVE SHOVE SHOVE
I WONDER WHAT I SHOULD DO...
PLAY WITH A BALL...
OR A FLYING DISC...
OR AYBE DIG SOME OLES?
SHUT UPPPP!
DASH
YOU WANNA PLAY TAG? GREAT, YOU'RE IT!

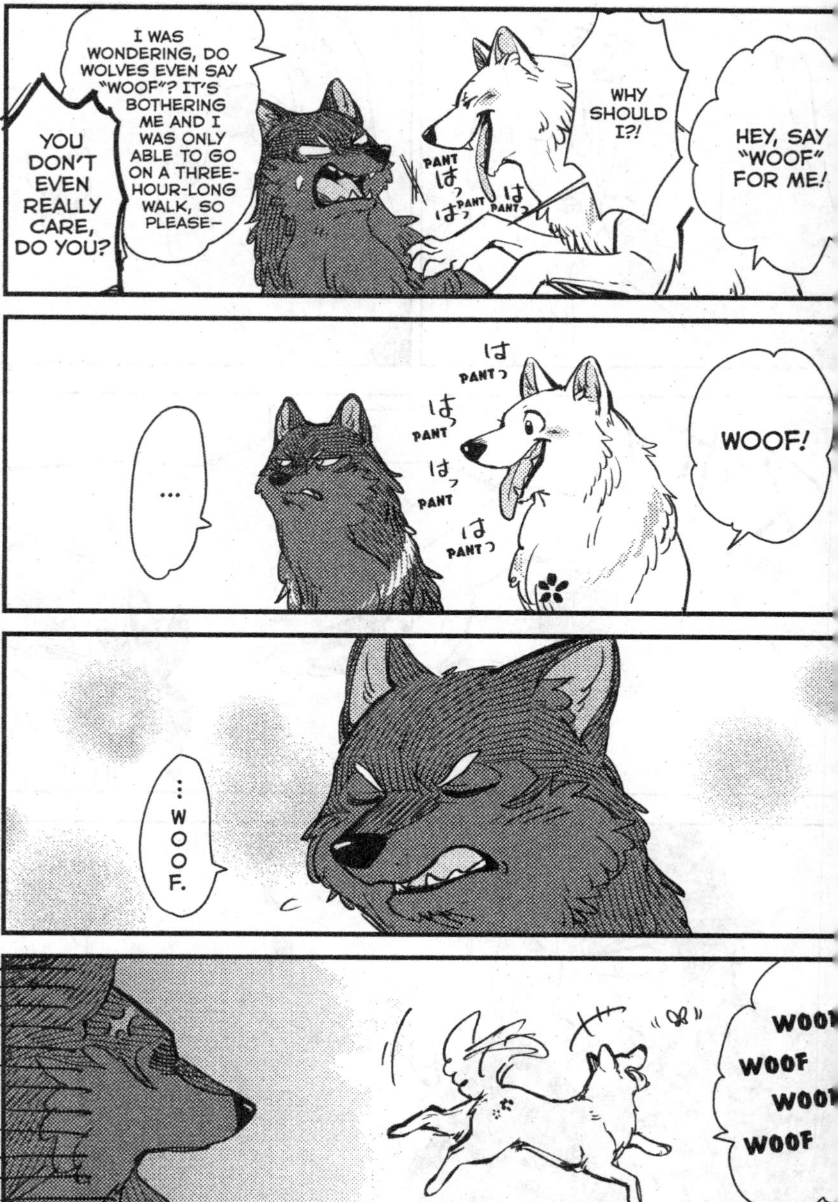
HEY, SAY "WOOF" FOR ME!
WHY SHOULD I?!
は PANT
はっ PANT
はっ PANT
PANT はっ
I WAS WONDERING, DO WOLVES EVEN SAY "WOOF"? IT'S BOTHERING ME AND I WAS ONLY ABLE TO GO ON A THREE-HOUR-LONG WALK, SO PLEASE–
YOU DON'T EVEN REALLY CARE, DO YOU?
WOOF!
は PANTっ
はっ PANT
はっ PANT
は PANTっ
...
...WOOF.
WOO
WOOF
WOO
WOOF

The End

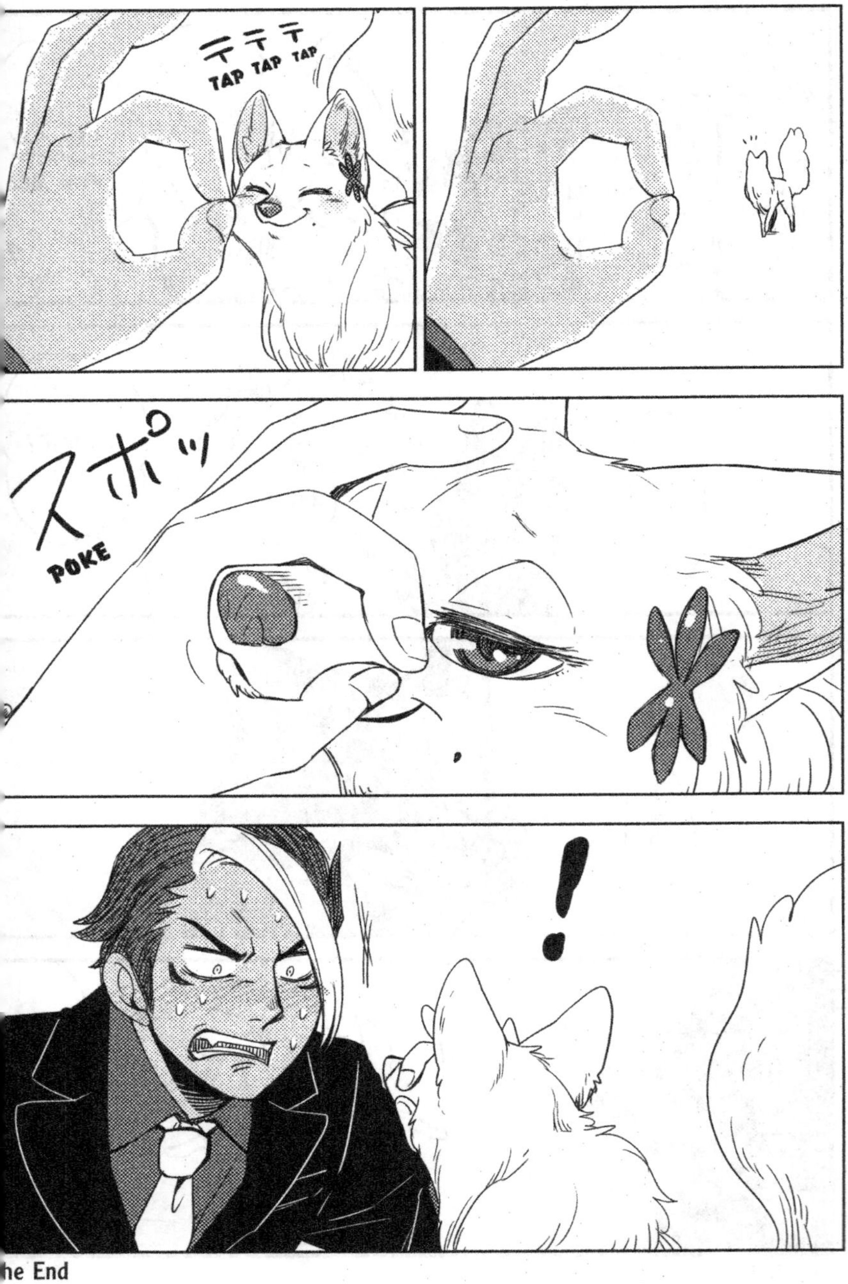
テテテ
TAP TAP TAP
スポッ
POKE
!
he End

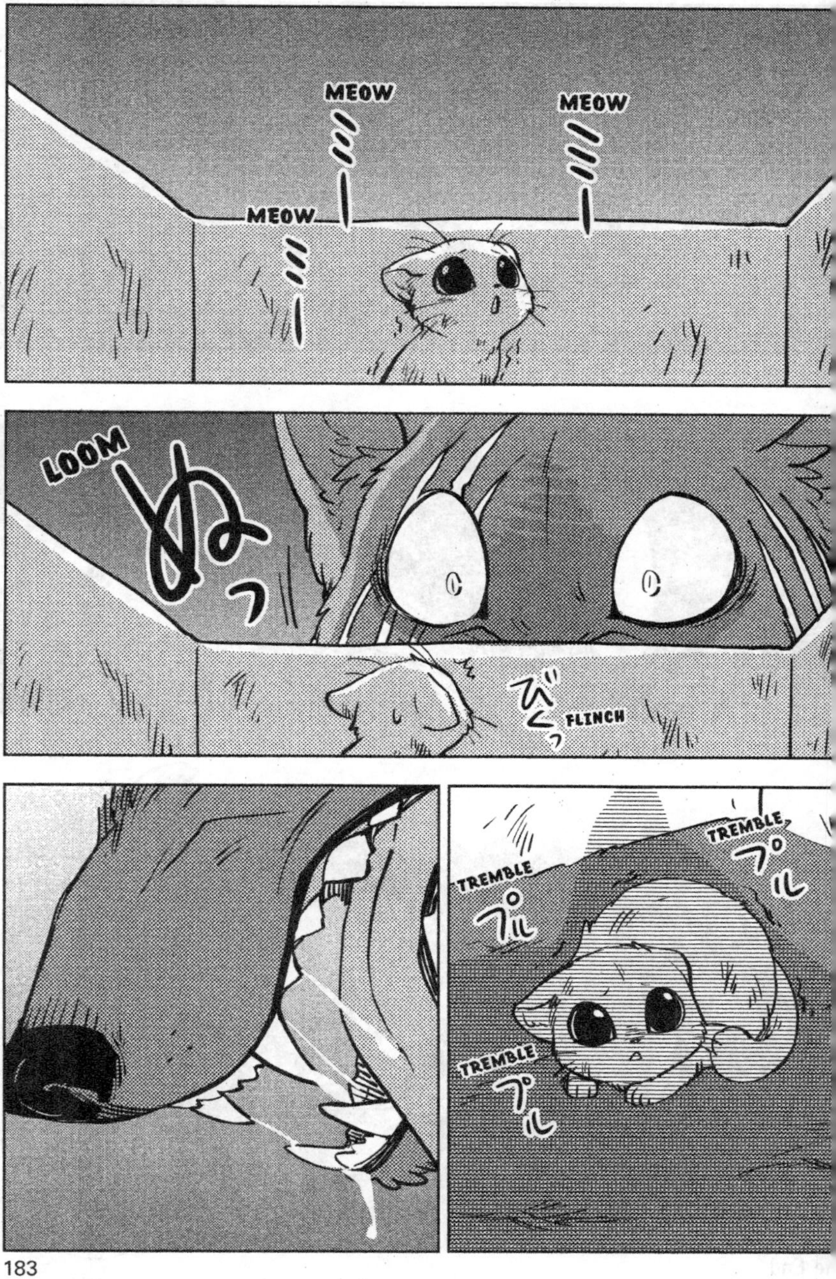
MEOW
ミー
MEOW
ミー
MEOW
ミー
LOOM
ぬっ
びくっ
FLINCH
TREMBLE
プル
TREMBLE
プル
TREMBLE
プル

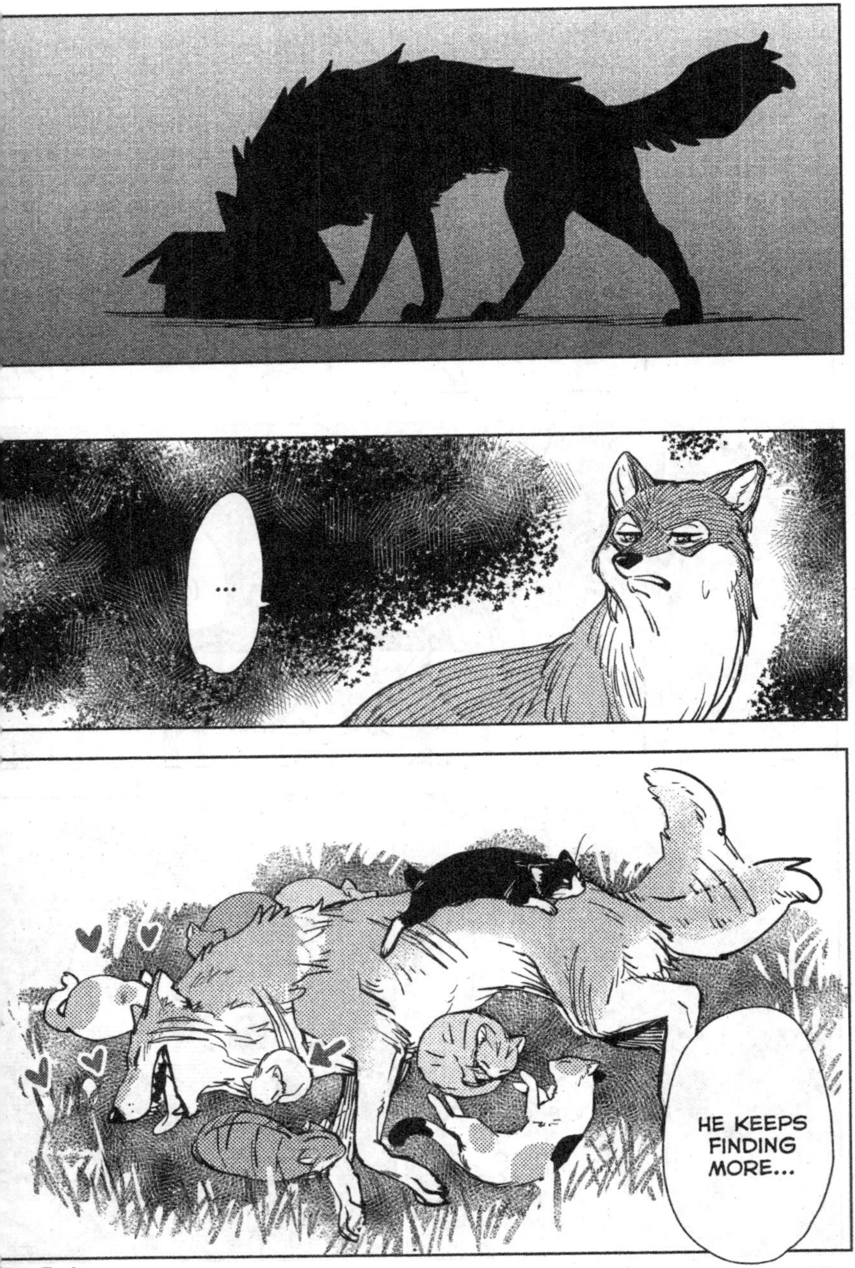
...
HE KEEPS FINDING MORE...

The End

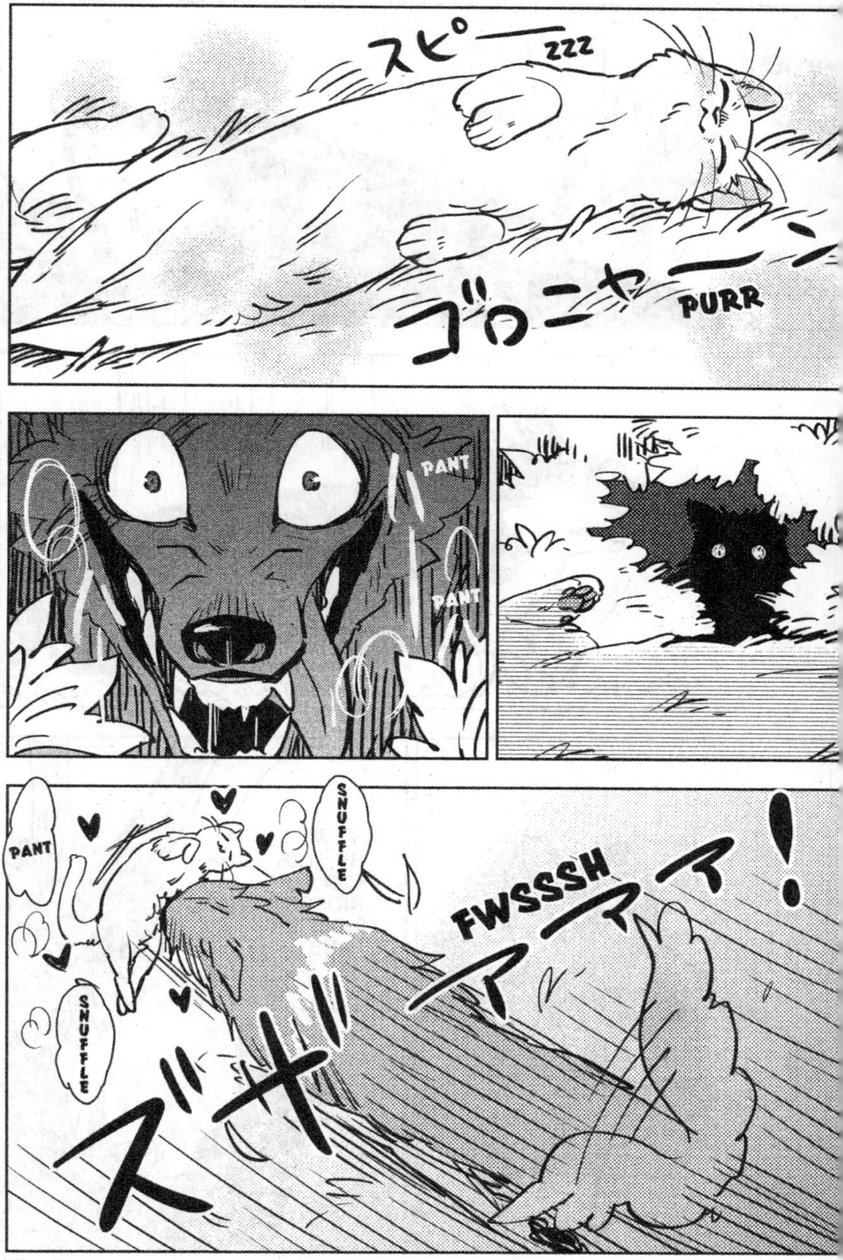
スピー
ZZZ
ゴロニャー
PURR
PANT
PANT
ズザアーア！
FWSSSH
SNUFFLE
PANT
SNUFFLE

The End

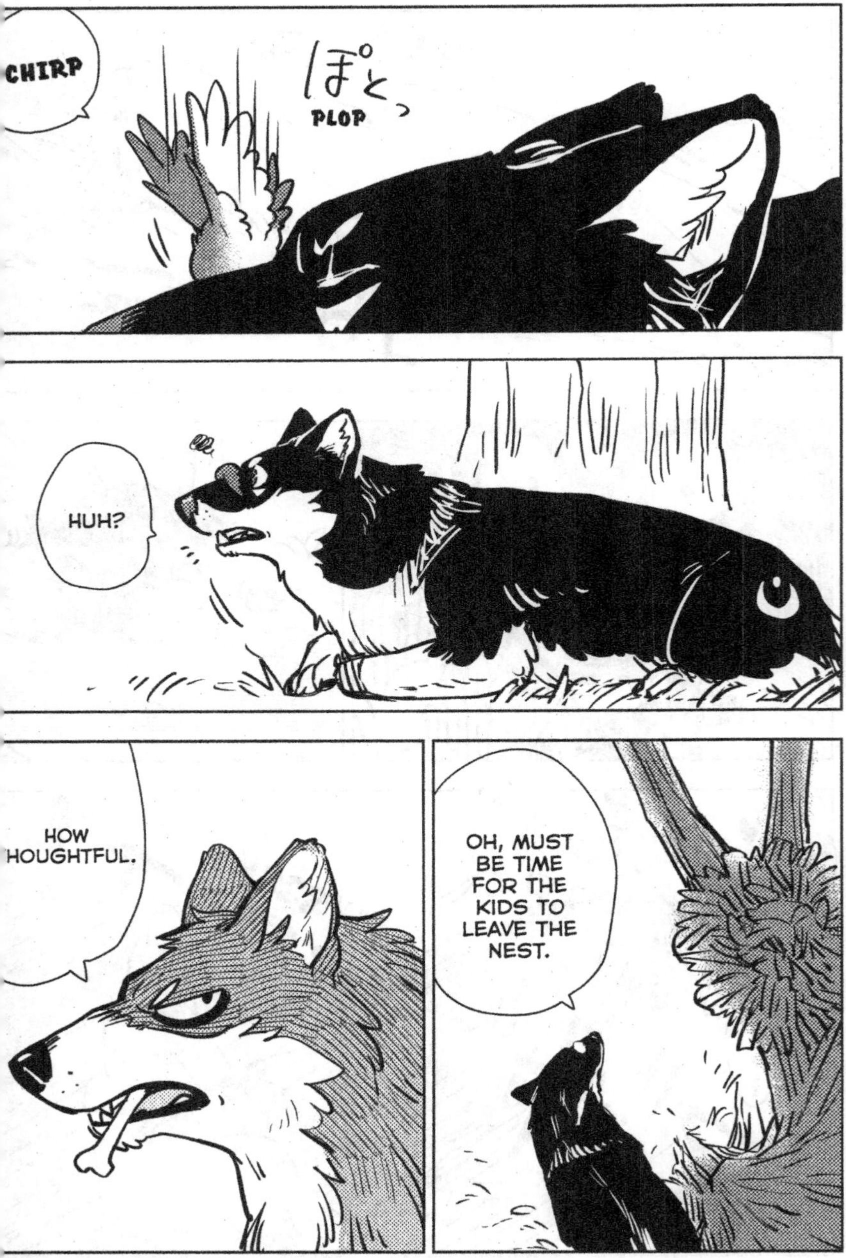
ぽとっ
PLOP
CHIRP
HUH?
OH, MUST BE TIME FOR THE KIDS TO LEAVE THE NEST.
HOW HOUGHTFUL.

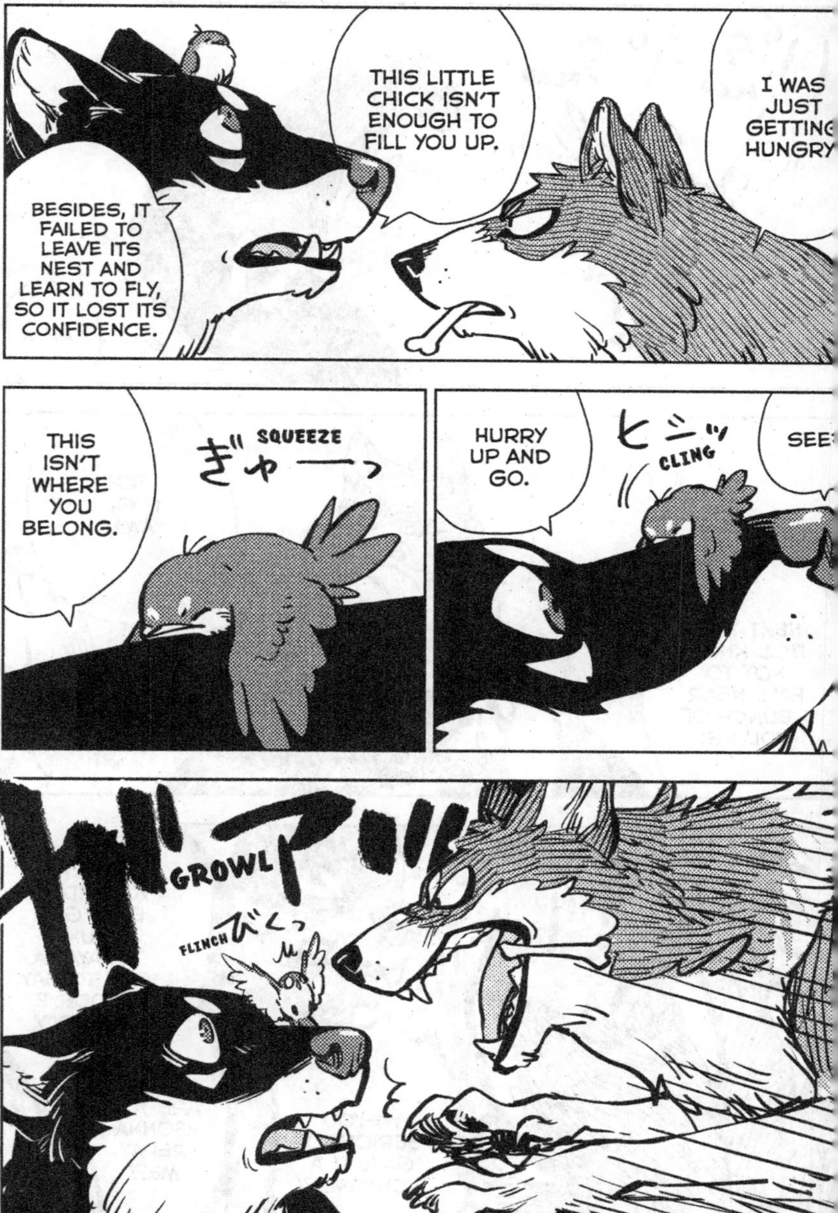
I WAS JUST GETTING HUNGRY
THIS LITTLE CHICK ISN'T ENOUGH TO FILL YOU UP.
BESIDES, IT FAILED TO LEAVE ITS NEST AND LEARN TO FLY, SO IT LOST ITS CONFIDENCE.
SEE
ヒシッ
CLING
HURRY UP AND GO.
ぎゅーっ
SQUEEZE
THIS ISN'T WHERE YOU BELONG.
ガアッ!!
GROWL
びくっ
FLINCH

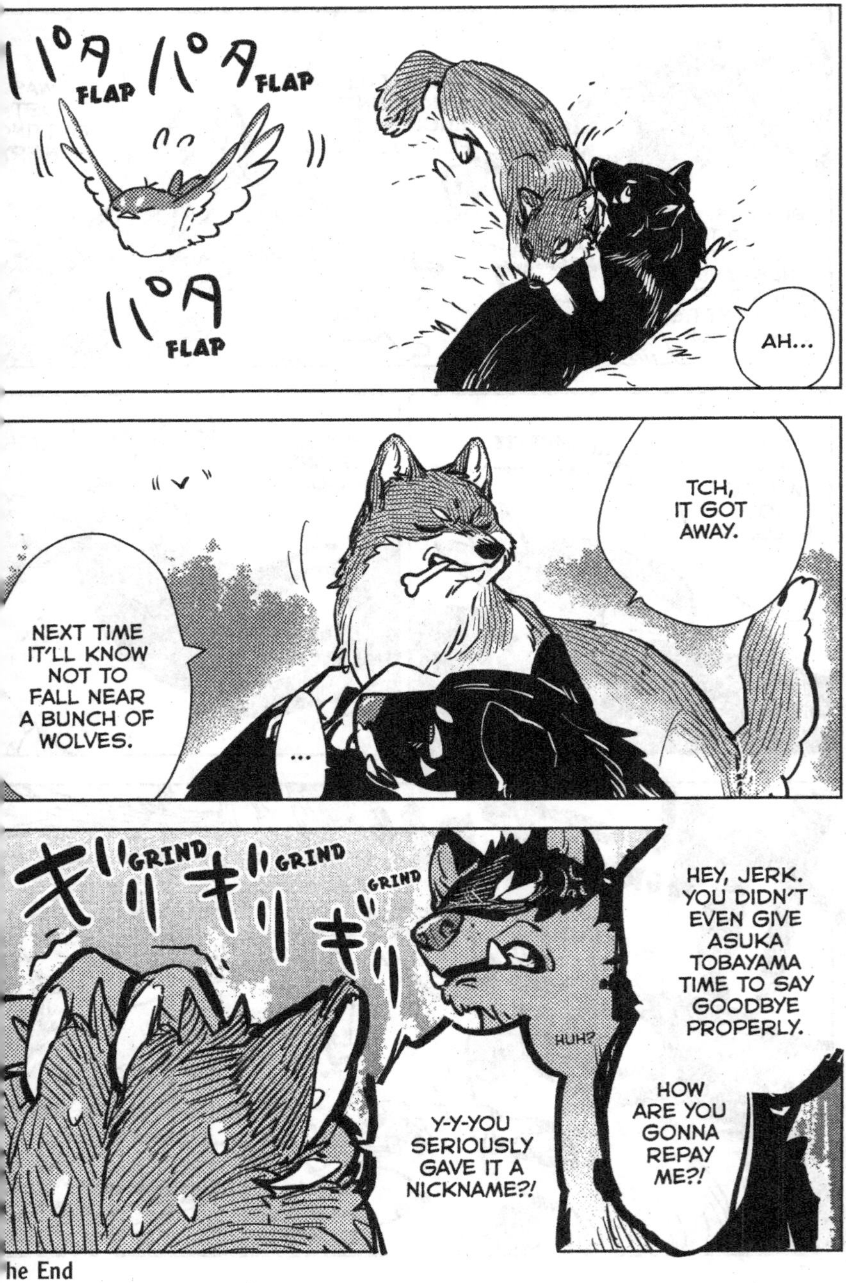
AH...
パタ FLAP
パタ FLAP
パタ FLAP
TCH, IT GOT AWAY.
...
NEXT TIME IT'LL KNOW NOT TO FALL NEAR A BUNCH OF WOLVES.
HEY, JERK. YOU DIDN'T EVEN GIVE ASUKA TOBAYAMA TIME TO SAY GOODBYE PROPERLY.
HUH?
HOW ARE YOU GONNA REPAY ME?!
Y-Y-YOU SERIOUSLY GAVE IT A NICKNAME?!
ギリ GRIND
ギリ GRIND
ギリ GRIND

he End

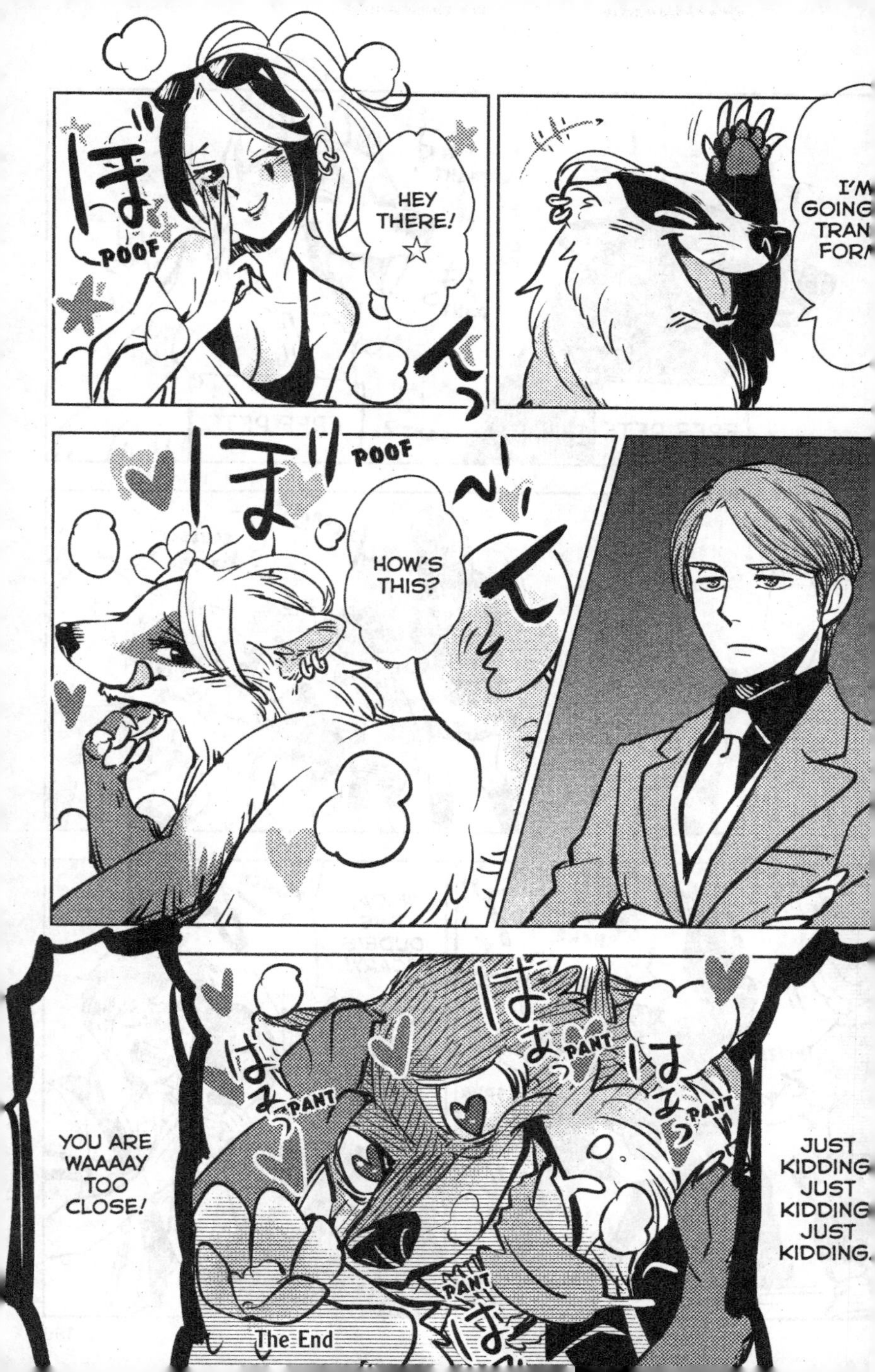
I'M GOING TRAN FORM
POOF
HEY THERE! ☆
POOF
HOW'S THIS?
JUST KIDDING JUST KIDDING JUST KIDDING.
PANT
PANT
PANT
YOU ARE WAAAAY TOO CLOSE!
PANT
The End

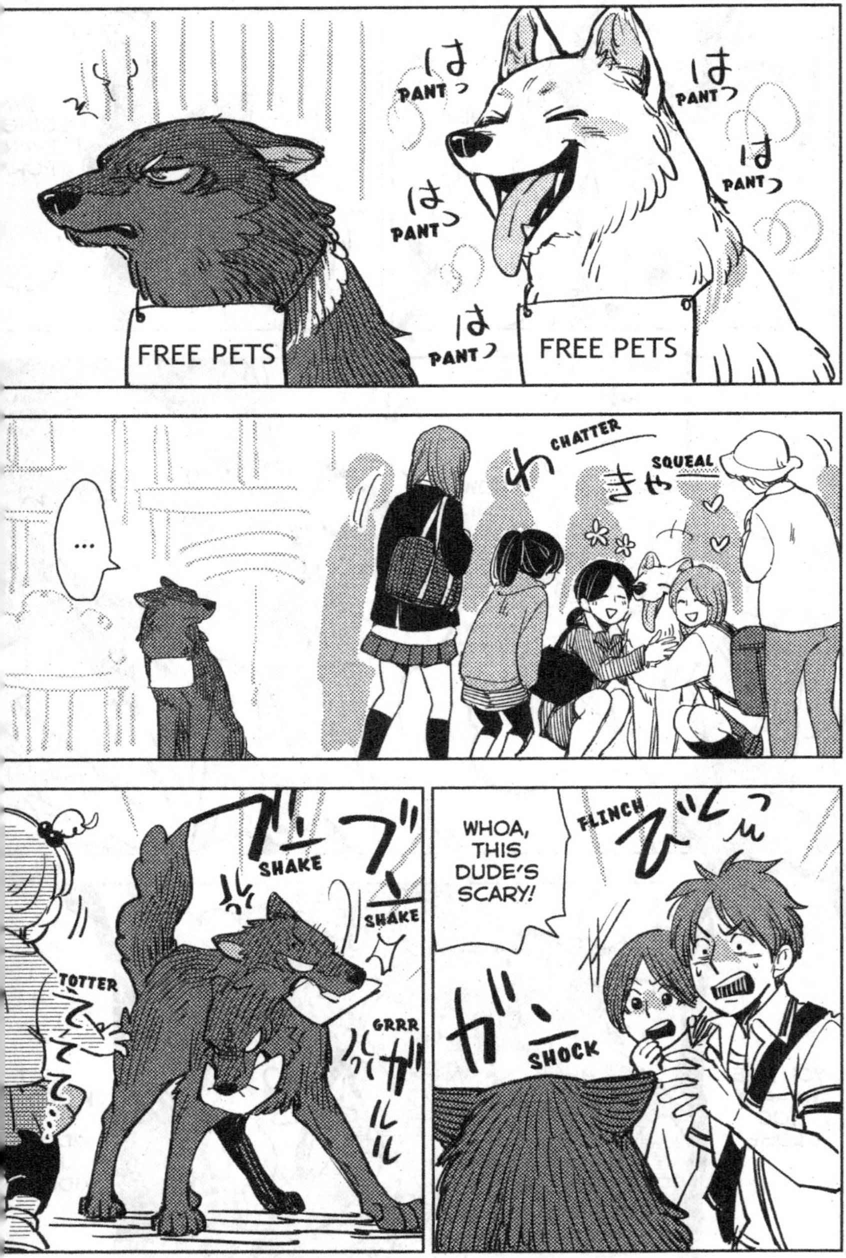

はっ
PANT
はっ
PANT
はっ
PANT
FREE PETS
はっ
PANT
はっ
PANT
FREE PETS
めっ
CHATTER
きゃ
SQUEAL
...
WHOA, THIS DUDE'S SCARY!
びくっ
FLINCH
ガーン
SHOCK
ブン
SHAKE
ブン
SHAKE
TOTTER
GRRR
ガルルル

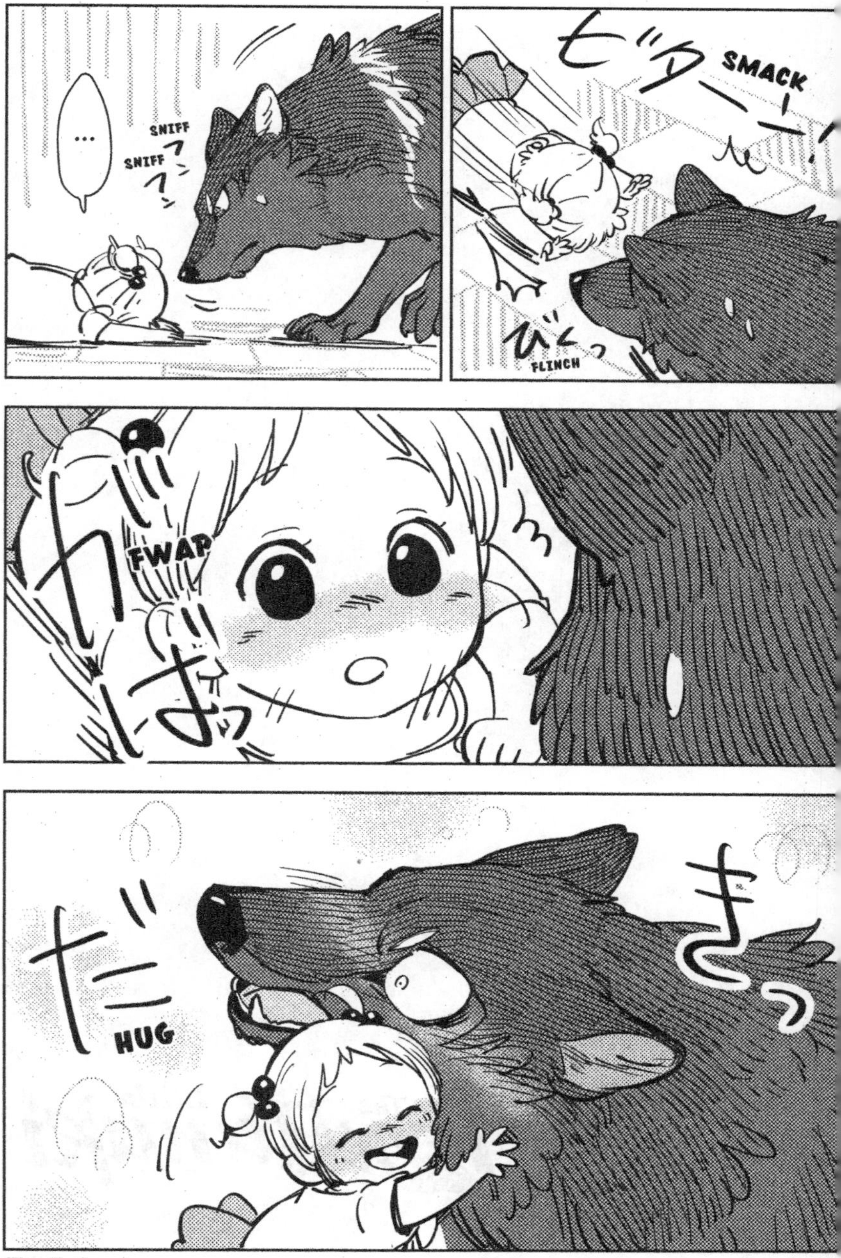
SMACK
FLINCH
...
SNIFF
SNIFF
FWAP
HUG

The End

The Little Fox & Tanuki

KORISENMAN

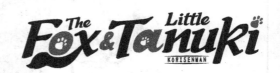

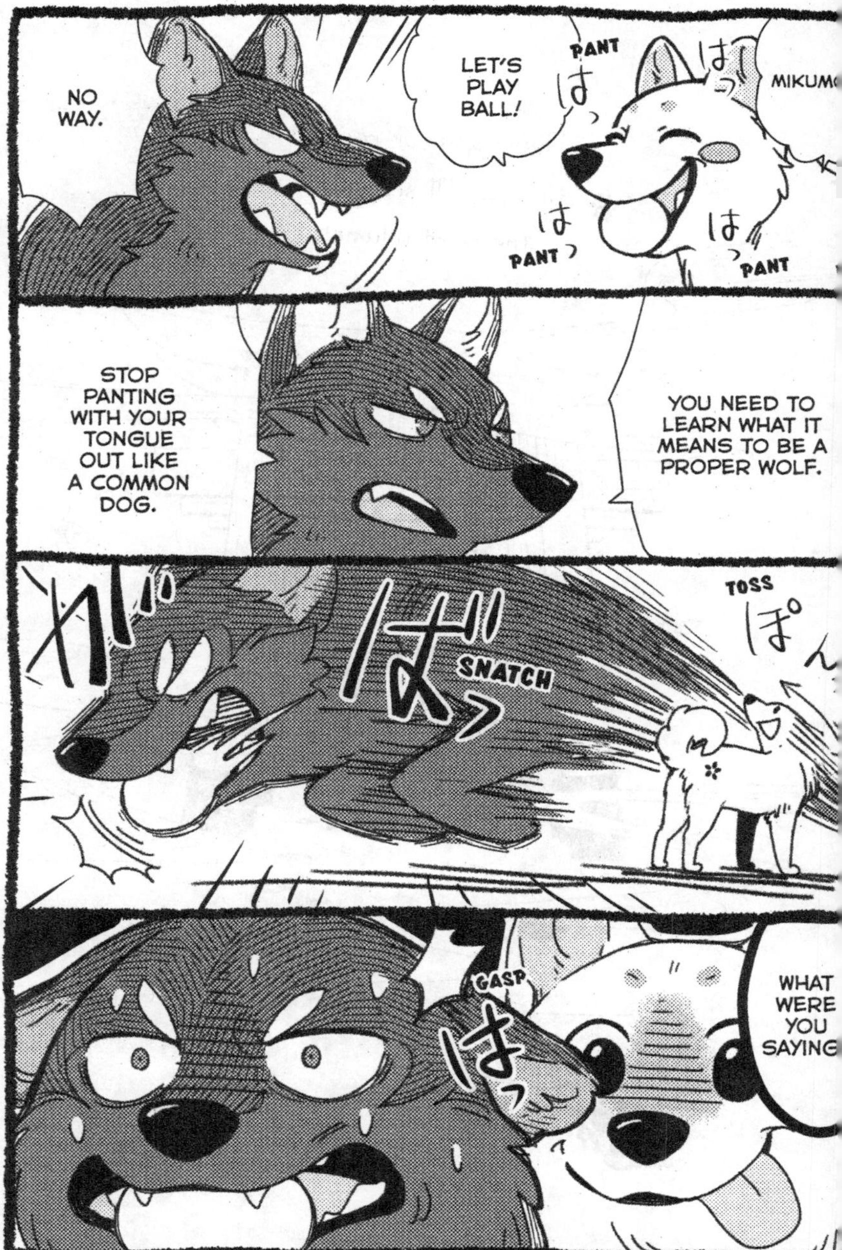
MIKUM
はっ
PANT
LET'S PLAY BALL!
はっ
PANT
はっ
PANT
NO WAY.
YOU NEED TO LEARN WHAT IT MEANS TO BE A PROPER WOLF.
STOP PANTING WITH YOUR TONGUE OUT LIKE A COMMON DOG.
TOSS
ぽん
SNATCH
ばっ
ガバ
WHAT WERE YOU SAYING
GASP
はっ

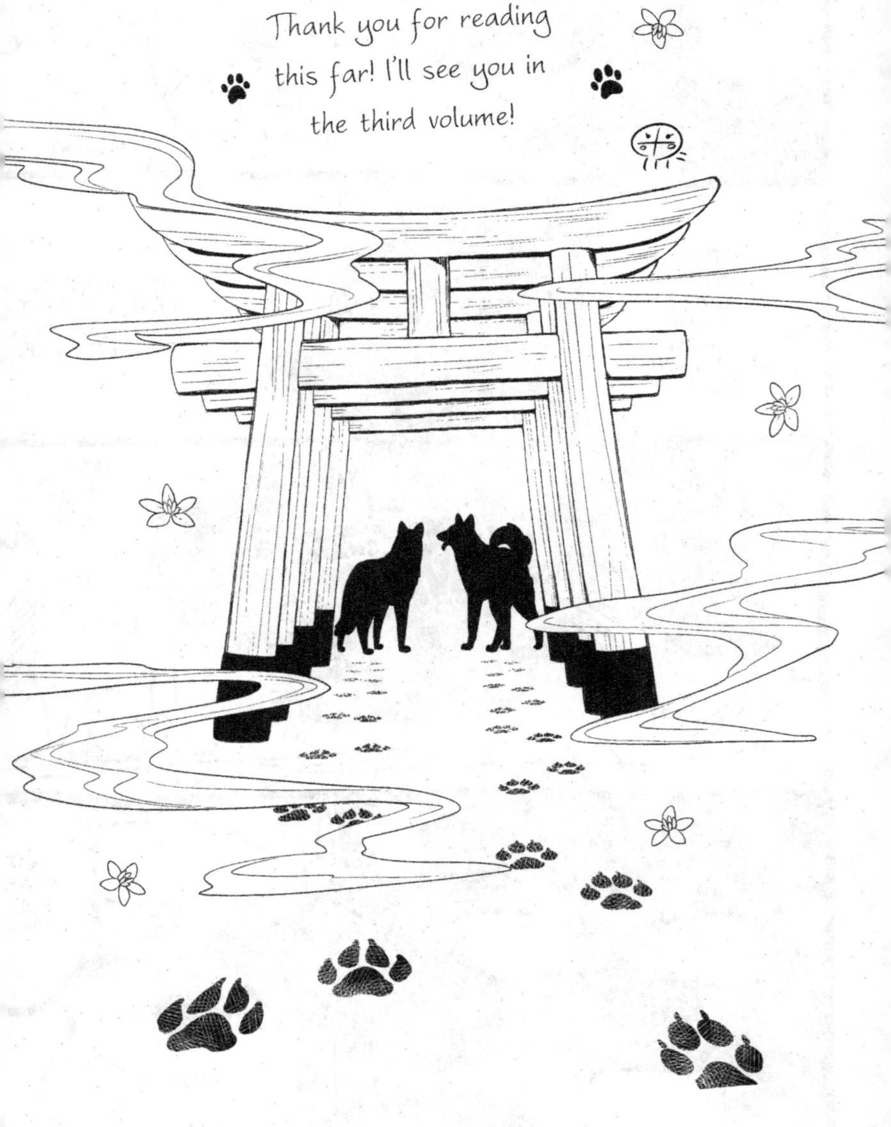
Thank you for reading this far! I'll see you in the third volume!

The Little Fox & Tanuki

KORISENMAN

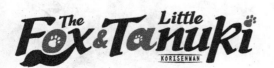

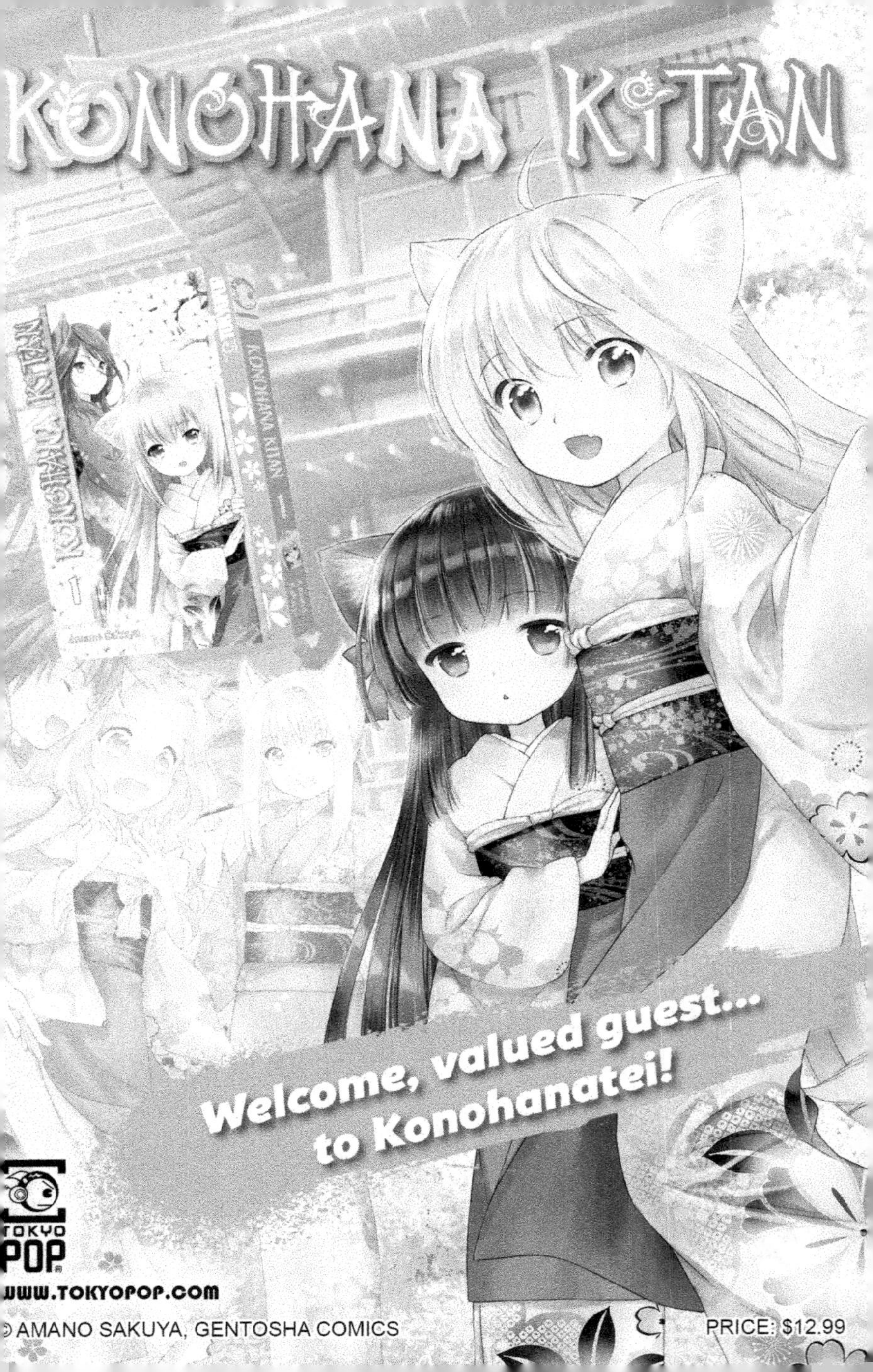

KONOHANA KITAN
Welcome, valued guest...
to Konohanatei!
TOKYO POP
WWW.TOKYOPOP.COM
© AMANO SAKUYA, GENTOSHA COMICS
PRICE: $12.99

# GRIMMS manga Tales

The Grimm's Tales reimagined in manga!

Beautiful art by the talented Kei Ishiyama!

Stories from Little Red Riding Hood to Hansel and Gretel!

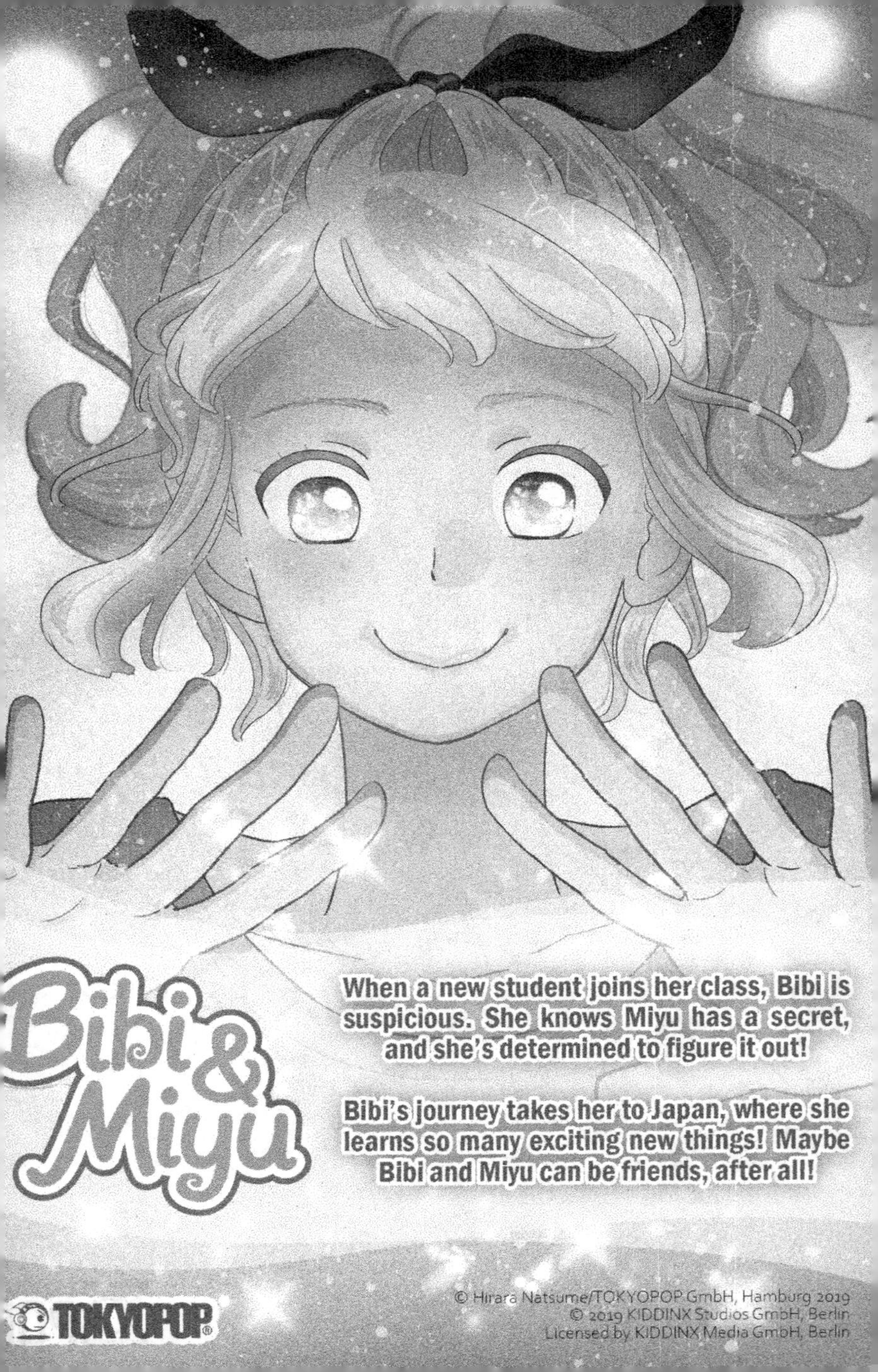
Bibi & Miyu
When a new student joins her class, Bibi is suspicious. She knows Miyu has a secret, and she's determined to figure it out!
Bibi's journey takes her to Japan, where she learns so many exciting new things! Maybe Bibi and Miyu can be friends, after all!
TOKYOPOP®
© Hirara Natsume/TOKYOPOP GmbH, Hamburg 2019
© 2019 KIDDINX Studios GmbH, Berlin
Licensed by KIDDINX Media GmbH, Berlin

# Disney *Marie* — MIRIYA & MARIE

☆ **Inspired by the characters from Disney's The Aristocats**

☆ **Learn facts about Paris and Japan!**

☆ **Adorable original shojo story**

☆ **Full color manga**

Even though the wealthy young girl Miriya has almost everything she cou ever need, what she really wants is the one thing money can't buy: her missi parents. But this year, she gets an extra special birthday gift when Marie, magical white kitten, appears and whisks her away to Paris! Learning the a of magic is one thing, but getting to eat th tastiest French pastries and wear the mo beautiful fashion takes Miriya and Marie journey to a whole new level!

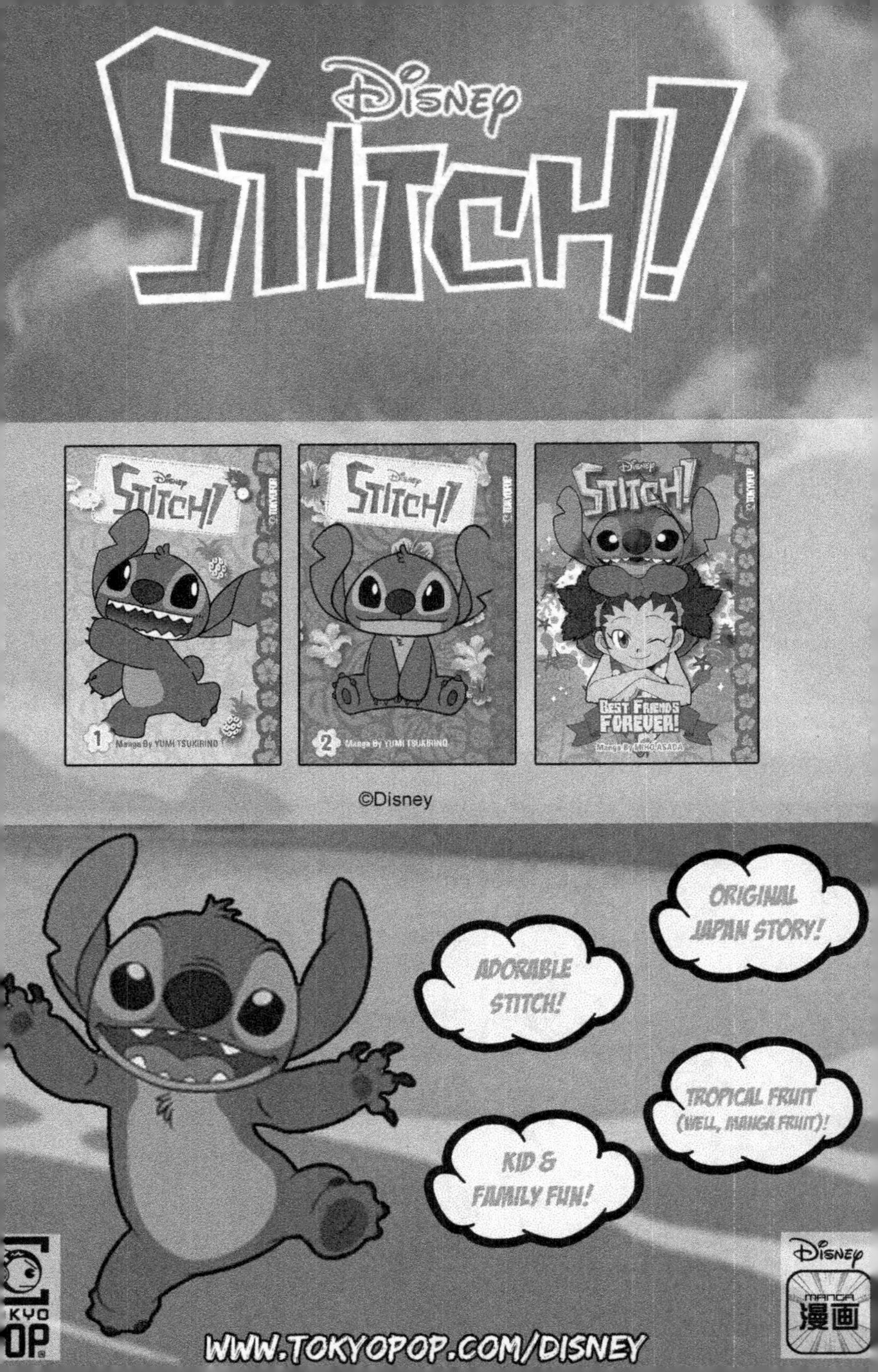
DISNEY
STITCH!
1 Manga By YUMI TSUKIRINO
2 Manga By YUMI TSUKIRINO
BEST FRIENDS FOREVER!
Manga By MIHO ASADA
©Disney
ORIGINAL JAPAN STORY!
ADORABLE STITCH!
TROPICAL FRUIT (WELL, MANGA FRUIT)!
KID & FAMILY FUN!
WWW.TOKYOPOP.COM/DISNEY

THE NEWEST DESCENDANTS MANGA WITH BRAND-NEW VILLAIN KIDS!

The original Villain Kids have worked hard to prove they deserve to stay in Auradon, and now it's time some of their friends from the Isle of the Lost get that chance too! When Dizzy receives a special invitation from King Ben to join the other VKs at Auradon Prep, at first she's thrilled! But doubt soon creeps in, and she begins to question whether she can truly fit in outside the scrappy world of the Isle.

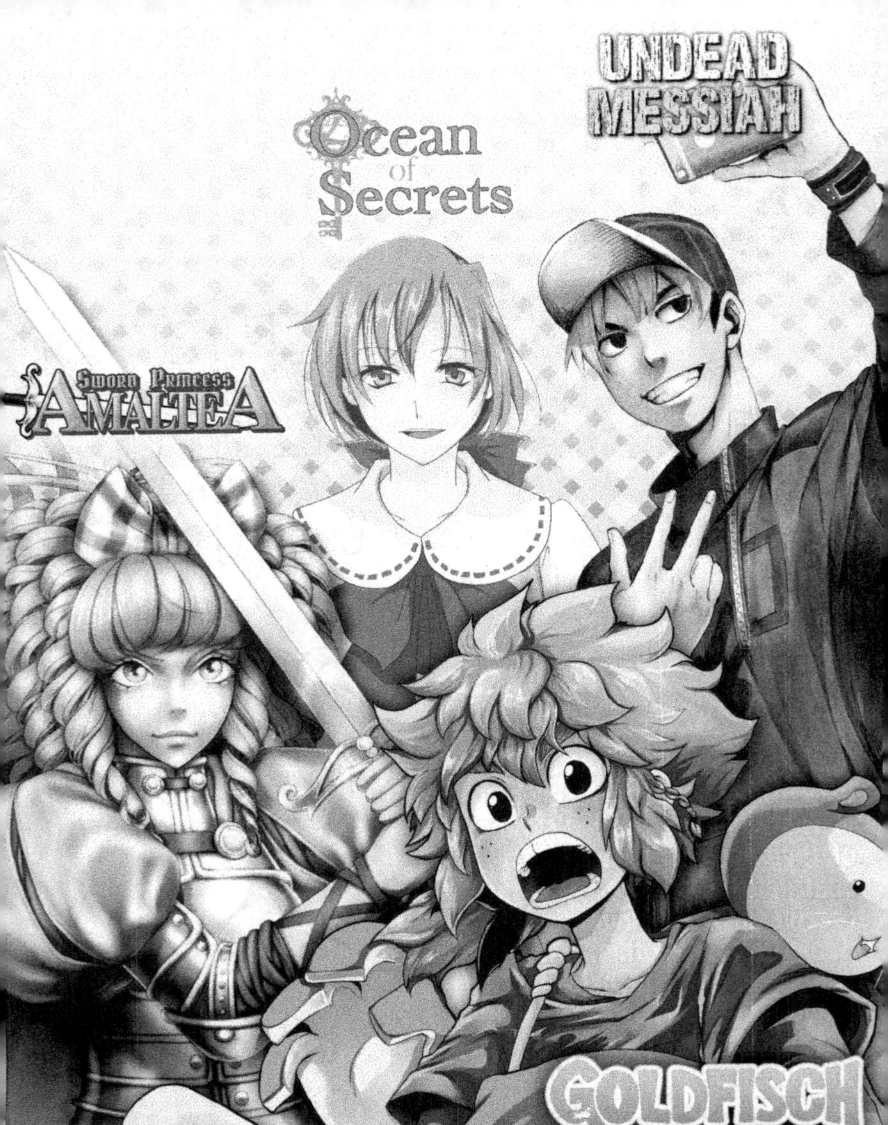
UNDEAD MESSIAH
Ocean of Secrets
SWORD PRINCESS AMALTEA
GOLDFISCH

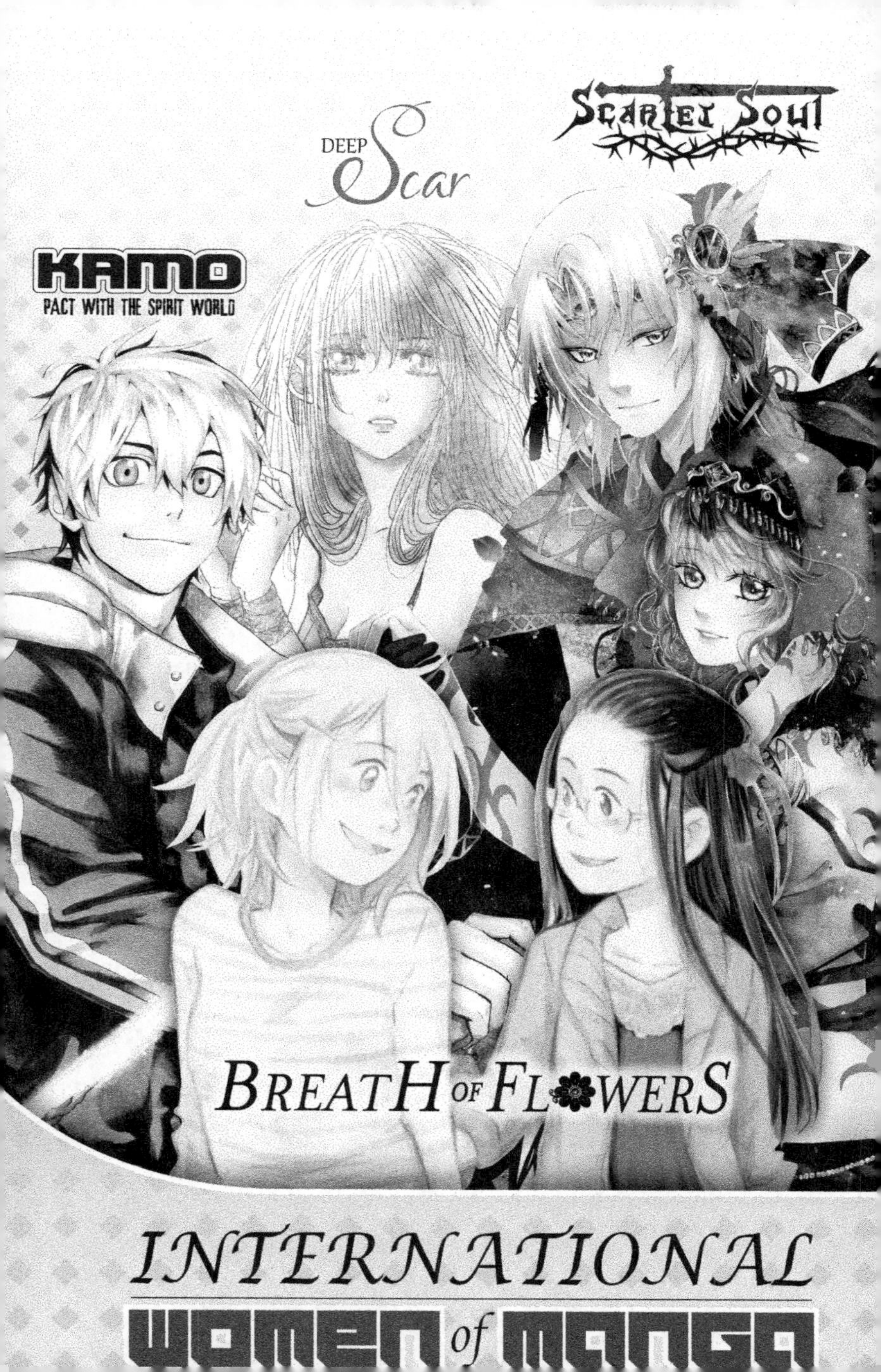
SCARLET SOUL
DEEP Scar
KAMO
PACT WITH THE SPIRIT WORLD
BREATH OF FLOWERS
INTERNATIONAL
WOMEN of MANGA

## *The Fox & Little Tanuki 2*
## Manga by Mi Tagawa

---

Editor - Lena Atanassova
Marketing Associate - Kae Winters
Translator - Katie Kimura
Copy Editor - Massiel Gutierrez
QC - Akiko Furuta
Licensing Specialist - Arika Yanaka
Cover Design - Soodam Elesti Lee
Retouching and Lettering - Vibrraant Publishing Studio
Editor-in-Chief & Publisher - Stu Levy

A  Manga

TOKYOPOP Inc.
5200 W. Century Blvd. Suite 705
Los Angeles, 90045

E-mail: info@TOKYOPOP.com
Come visit us online at www.TOKYOPOP.com

www.facebook.com/TOKYOPOP
www.twitter.com/TOKYOPOP
www.pinterest.com/TOKYOPOP
www.instagram.com/TOKYOPOP

ISBN: 978-1-4278-6405-5
First TOKYOPOP Printing: August 2020
10 9 8 7 6 5 4 3 2 1
Printed in CANADA

# STOP

## THIS IS THE BACK OF THE BOOK!

How do you read manga-style? It's simple! To learn, just start in the top right panel and follow the numbers:

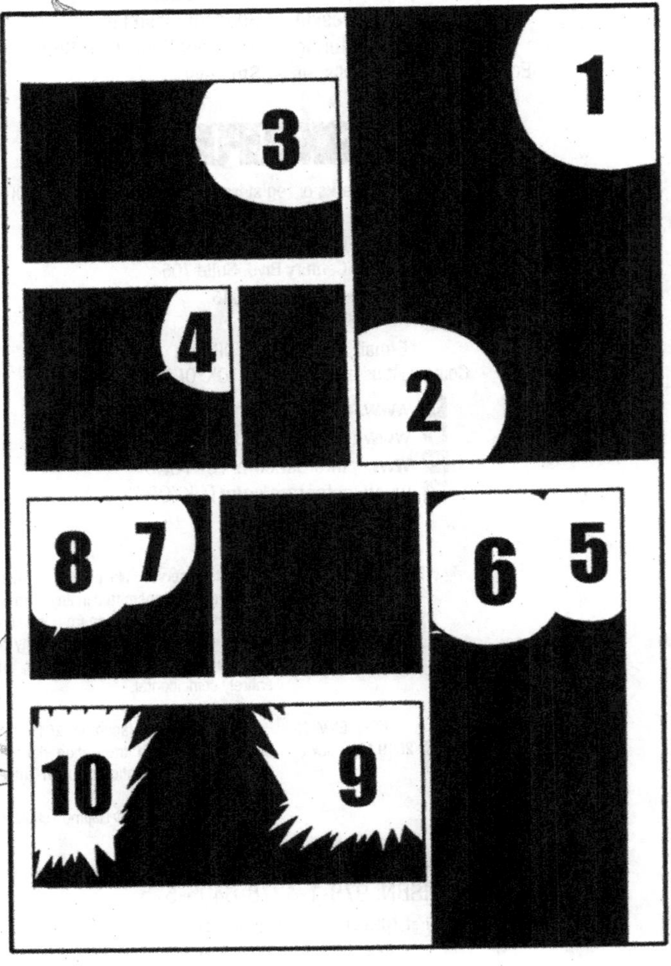
1
2
3
4
5
6
7
8
9
10